WHISPERS

A NOVEL

WHISPERS

Cover design by: Getcovers

Marginal Impact Publishing LLC

ISBN-13: 979-8-9898848-4-1

Ebook ISBN-13: 979-8-9898848-5-8

First Edition: April 2026

Printed in the United States of America

WHISPERS

A NOVEL

PIPER ANDERSON

MARGINAL IMPACT PUBLISHING

Author's note

Whispers is a labor of love to me for many reasons. I have a vast education in psychology, and another reason is that it's deeply personal. My mental health has been quite a journey for me for as long as I can remember. If you read Dearly Beloved by Wilt Rhys (my alternate pseudonym), then you know a little about those issues. While I took several creative liberties because it's fiction, every flashback and the main character's struggles with anxiety are very much nonfiction. I won't tell the stories of those near and dear to me who have schizophrenia because their stories are not mine to share. I based Serene Meadows on a particular time in my life when I was placed in a similar situation under false pretenses, and I met some of the most amazing people. Mental health didn't control them. Yes, mental health was and is an ongoing struggle for them, but it didn't define them. It didn't make them a person to be feared or someone less than. The people I met were not only the most amazing but also some of the funniest. They are responsible for my life motto: Weird is different, and different is good. Mental health struggles don't make someone a good or bad person. We all have our individual struggles. You don't make it through childhood, adolescence, and adulthood without some breaks, scrapes, and bruises. For some, those injuries are external, and for others, they are internal. As a published author since I was ten, I have received a tremendous amount of advice, whether solicited or not. I'm sure every author can relate to being told, "Write what you know." I don't know what "cozy," "soft," and "normal" mean. I know the grittier parts of life. The parts no one likes to talk about for fear of being "othered." To all of those who struggle with their mental health and those who are close to others who struggle with mental health, you are not "other," and you are not alone. I wrote Whispers to give voice to and humanize those who've ever felt they had to hide the spicier sides of their personalities, and to help those who have loved ones with struggles they don't understand. There is nothing trivial about mental health, different types of assault, neglect, and abuse. And I take none of these topics lightly. Your mental health is very important, if not to you, then to me. Put yourself first because there are many triggering topics discussed in this novel. If you aren't in a place where you can read certain topics, don't feel pressured. I've listed triggers to watch out for at the back of the book. The back of the book also lists resources for those experiencing depression, suicidal thoughts, or suicidal ideation. If you've experienced intimate partner violence, I have also listed those resources. If I can leave you with a bit of wisdom, according to me, you are not alone, and there are blessings in the storm. And sometimes you are the storm, and that's okay too.

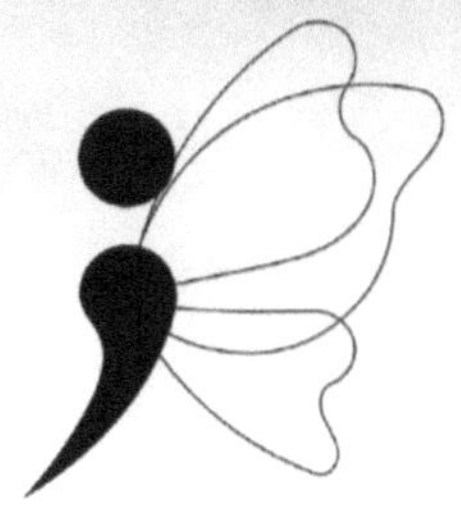

<u>Dedication</u>

For anyone who has ever been made to feel "other'd" because of a different outlook on the world. Remember, weird is different and different is good. Let's go crazy!

WHISPERS

A NOVEL

BEFORE

Chapter One

*A*mina Raichand

"Deez viwet lights end."

From the mouths of babes. Am I right? My eyes shutter, and I make a concerted effort to press my lips into a firm line to keep from laughing. My eyes water, and my nose stings. Unfortunately, my smile can't be wrangled into such submission.

"These violent delights have violent ends," I correct in a hushed tone.

Giggles so pure that if I were the emotional sort, tears would've pricked my eyes, intruding on the precious silence. I gaze down into brown doe eyes. The sweetest, cherubic caramel-skinned face leans back from its previous position, lying in my lap, permitting innocent scrutiny of my expression. Small arms hug my waist. It's a tight fit for both of us atop the toddler bed. I managed to squish my—not at all big—behind onto it, but smashed as it is between the guardrail and the little girl tucked under the brightly colored Disney princess blankets, you'd think I had a *badonkadonk*. I steal a glance sideways at the identical toddler bed across the room and at the peaceful expression on the lighter-skinned sleeping boy lying atop it.

"Shh…" I whisper. "You're supposed to be asleep, little girl."

Another too-loud giggle escapes adorable, plump lips. Bright, open brown eyes continue to gaze at me. So open…Innocence might as well be a living, breathing thing. From that laugh to the flush of youth in those chubby cheeks, it's almost tangible. Everything about this little person screams **I'M NEW HERE!** The open heart. Wonder. Hope. All things meant to mislead someone to believe this brave child came from a supportive, loving, and caring home and not the world of neglect, abuse, and trauma she's already endured in her mere four years on Earth. This small child, who has experienced the ugliest sides of humanity, possesses an indomitable spirit. She's resilient and has the instinct to dream and believe in her dreams.

Not. Like. Me.

I couldn't.

Wouldn't.

I can't fathom opening my heart or life in such a way as to allow someone else, or anything else, the power to hurt me or disappoint me, not anymore. I am the master of my fate and the captain of my soul. Yet Kaylee snuggles into my lap without reservation, giving love she'd never received freely. And I love her, her younger brother, and the baby sleeping in the other room as much as I can. Possibly more than I'm allowed.

"They wuv each other," Kaylee said in her high-pitched voice, as if we were the only two people on the planet, or in the room.

I snicker, shaking my head—this little girl and her ten-second memory.

That, amongst many other things, is the reason I love children so much. Yes, children can lie. When they get caught doing something they were warned against, children instinctively lie. Even caught with their hands in a literal cookie jar, they'll lie right to your face. But those are surface lies, so to speak. Ultimately, they're honest. And easy. They accept you for everything you are and everything you aren't. Quirks and all. Bad habits and imperfections. You could be silly, smart, or as dumb as ever. Wake up with bedhead, morning breath, and drool dried to your face, and they accept you. Their love defines the word unconditional. No matter how inconvenient you make their lives, they love you. It baffles me how anyone could not love a child. Adults, my peers, were never that cool, making it incredibly easy not to love them and prefer solitude. For me, loving and protecting a child are foregone conclusions. That thought breaks through my rough exterior, and tears prick my eyes as I study Kaylee's round face. Unfortunately, not all adults, guardians, and caregivers feel the same way I do about children.

I blink rapidly to erase the moisture from my eyes. No need to Debbie Downer this bedtime ritual.

"Shh...you're gonna wake your brother up."

I need that like a hole in the head. There is still a butt ton of charting to do. I turn my left wrist. The face of my Samsung Galaxy smartwatch lights up.

7:00 p.m.

Dagnabbit!

"I'm right. I'm right," Kaylee chants in a sing-song voice. "Ooh, baby. I'm right."

Laughter bubbles from in my belly. My stomach quivers from the force required to subdue it. Because of her little-kid accent, oddly similar to an exaggerated Boston accent, it sounds like Kaylee said, "I'm white. I'm white!" Although both toddlers are biracial, mixed with Black and Caucasian, the inadvertent joke shifts my dour mood. I fight to keep my composure and win.

"Yes," I whisper. I gently ease Kaylee's head from my lap and extricate myself from her tight hold. Placing her head to rest on her pillow, I heft myself from the miniature bed. Popping and cracking sounds rend the air. That would be embarrassing if my audience wasn't a four-year-old who found the entire thing amusing. Kaylee grins as if in on an enormous secret. "You're sort of right," I answer, trying to explain her observation of Romeo & Juliet. "It's a complicated situation."

"Comp-lie-cated?" Thin dark brows scrunch together.

Decisions. Decisions.

In hindsight, maybe picking *Romeo and Juliet* as a bedtime story wasn't the best choice. As one of my favorite Shakespearean tragedies, I thought it'd be cute to stream the movie Gnomeo & Juliet as sort of an introduction to one of the classics. While we watched it one evening, I mentioned that it was a play based on the actual tragedy by William Shakespeare. I didn't think the kids had even listened to my spiel, let alone remembered my throwaway, half-hearted promise to read them the story. But they did, of course. And they badgered me about it for weeks until I couldn't take it anymore. So, here we are...

Me trying to explain a plot and the intricacies of star-crossed relationships way over this little one's pay grade. Not my brightest decision, but I'd read somewhere that introducing children to big words, terms, and intelligent ideas helps shape young minds and raises their IQ. Who knows when these kids will be removed from here by the state and placed somewhere else? They might never have another opportunity to encounter this form of literature. Not one to ignore a teachable moment, I capitulated and brought in my large, gold-rimmed book of classics.

Kaylee still watches me. Expectation alight in her wide eyes. I don't have it in me to explain why the story isn't the romance she thought it was. Neither of us deserved to have our dreams of life, love, and romance crushed.

"Don't worry about it. They love each other so much. Now, close those eyes."

"Like you're in wuv," Kaylee hedges, smiling as if she were sharing some juicy *chisme.*

"I'd rather take a hammer to the dome," I grumble before I catch myself and consider my audience. "Maybe one day," I tack on evasively. "Now, it's time to go *mimis*."

"I'm not too tired yet."

"You don't have to be. Don't you want to get big?"

"And find wuv and have long hair?" Kaylee asks in a wistful voice.

"Um, yeah. We're gonna work on your life ambitions another night. Set your sights a tad higher, sweets. Now sleep."

"How?"

"Close your eyes really tight." I demonstrate. "And think about all the special things you want to happen when you're a big girl."

"Like more stories."

"Just like that." I place a quick kiss on her forehead, then turn and repeat the action on Kaylee's brother, Nate, and then shut off the lights. Sensing the darkness, the night light casts a soft glow on the room. One last glance shows Kaylee has followed the instructions. Her eyes are closed. Leaving the bedroom, I pull the door shut behind me.

Two more bedrooms are at the end of the dark, short hall. The door on the right stands slightly ajar. Pushing it open, I gaze across the dim room at the ornate white wooden crib.

A fuzzy pink blanket covers what appears to be a small lump in the center of the mattress. Like a turtle popping its head out of its shell, a head of blonde curls pops out from under the blanket. Large, rosy, squishy cheeks, set in a smooth alabaster face, go in and out sucking on a pink silicone Soothie pacifier. Hazel-green eyes find me before I can tiptoe out of the room.

"You're supposed to be asleep too, baby girl. What's up with you monsters tonight?" I ask with a laugh.

At the sound of my voice, Stephanie sits up fully. The fluffy blanket slides down the baby's tiny back, revealing a small, stout body clad in a yellow onesie with white ducks dotted all over it. The binky her little lips pucker around sails out of her mouth. Dimpled hands wrap around the crib bars, a prisoner begging for release. Stephanie pulls herself to stand. Bouncy, blonde curls stick up in every direction. This wasn't the look of a baby intending to go back to sleep soon.

I flip my left wrist over.

7:20 p.m.

"Ma. Ma," Stephanie babbles, bouncing on the mattress. "Ma. Ma."

Short, chubby arms that dimple at the elbow reach for me. Hands grab at the air in excitement for me to pick her up. Rolling my eyes, I shake my head and smile. Cuteness overload at its finest. Resistance is futile. Plus, even though it's wrong on many levels, my heart squeezes at that sweet baby voice calling me mama. That isn't in my future, no matter how much I want it. I thought I'd accepted it, because there'd be no one to impregnate me, but each time Stephanie says the words, it feels like my heart is in some compression device set to torture.

Unable to ignore the eighteen-month-old's siren's call, I lift her too-small frame into my arms. Rubbing her back, I hug her tight.

"No. A-mi-na. Amina," I say, breaking my name into syllables for her. Nuzzling her neck, I breathe in her delicious, baby-powder-fresh scent.

"Ma. Ma," Stephanie repeats, emphasizing her adamant rejection of the correction. "Ma. Ma."

One more tight hug, then I lay her back inside her crib. I cover her with the blanket and stick her pacifier between her lips. Gazing into her eyes provides Stephanie with the connection she missed before being placed here, which is part of the reason for her stunted growth. With the pad of my thumb, I stroke between her fair eyebrows. It's the baby shut-off switch. At least, that's what I call it. Throughout my time working with kids, I discovered this trick worked on children ages birth to five. If rubbed with just the right amount of pressure, it lulls a baby to sleep, just as it does now, after only three minutes.

Stephanie's mouth forms an "O" as she yawns around the pink silicone. By some balancing miracle, the pacifier doesn't fall. It teeters on the edge of her bottom lip until the yawn ends. Hazel eyes drift closed and then reopen. Once. Twice. Three times before they shut for good.

Thank God!

"Night, night, precious," I murmur.

Chapter Two

I survey the living room. It's immaculate. Toys are all tucked away inside blue totes pushed under the cherry-stained oak end tables on each side of the long grey couch. On top of the end table on the farthest end of the couch were two remotes—one for the Blu-ray player and the other for the Roku television. Lemon Pledge polished every wooden surface, leaving the entire front room smelling fresh and clean. Pre-moistened electronics wipes removed any dust or fingerprints from the 50-inch flat-screen TV hanging on the far wall. The vacuum cleaner imprints straight lines onto the carpet. Not even a stray piece of lint dares to mar the carpet's perfection. I vacuumed the couch and loveseat cushions, too. I don't have to see the kitchen to know it is just as spotless.

Please, last twelve hours.

Satisfied that everything is nice and tidy, I head to the designated office area in the back of the living room on the opposite side of the wall leading to the hallway with the bedrooms. Drilled into the wall above the desk is a long, horizontal, smoky-taupe metal cabinet. All important papers, binders, and anything not meant for child fingers or prying eyes live in that cabinet. A desktop computer monitor sits in the farthest corner of the desk, where the desk meets the wall. Next to the computer monitor is a cordless phone in its base. The desktop is well-organized by me. A tall, three-drawer filing cabinet stands beside the desk. I sink into the rolling chair in front of the desk.

Time to make the donuts.

I smirk at my corny joke. Rubbing my hands against my black yoga pants, I swing my feet and let my sneakers' soles scrape against the plastic runner beneath the chair. I twirl twice in my chair, letting my eyes scan my immediate surroundings. Left. Right. Deep breath in. Loud breath out. Anxiety has me in a chokehold, and when I'm anxious, motivation is hard to find. My stomach tightens. I take another deep breath to calm myself. Nervous energy won't allow me to focus, even though that's exactly what I need to do.

What time is it? I shake the wireless mouse on the mouse pad. The computer screen glows to life. My gaze immediately skitters to the far-right bottom corner of the screen.

7:35 p.m.

Seven-fricking-thirty-five!

They are torturing me. Purposefully. They must be.

Do they want me to snap? Go off like some stereotypical mad black woman? In my head, I see myself doing it, picture myself sweeping everything off the desk with my forearms, overturning the chair, and the filing cabinet. The vision is so clear that my breathing becomes labored, and my heartbeat races. I take a deep, cleansing breath through my nose, blowing it out through my mouth. Violence won't solve anything, but how many times does this have to happen before I'm within my rights to get mad? What is a good excuse to go off without people holding it against me? My entire life, I've never been able to find an answer to that question. This isn't the first time I've wondered about this. Is there such a thing as justifiable rage? Passionate crimes of rage? Does that exist? Is it possible to speak assertively without judgment? Is it irrational to think that others should consider my wishes and needs?

Every day, I clean the crap out of this house. Make sure everything for the morning is ready before I leave, to lighten the others' load. Do I get the one thing I request? The only thing I've needed in three years.

Nope.

Must. Sidetrack. Myself. Before I throw a thirty-two-year-old-sized, toddler-esque tantrum! Taking another deep breath and releasing it loudly, I straighten my ponytail. Smooth my edges, then stand and reach into the cabinet above the desk. I retrieve the only white binder amongst a sea of black binders and set it on the desk. An insert in the front plastic pocket on the binder reads in big, bold black letters: **INNOCENT TREASURES SHELTER WHERE EVERY CHILD IS SAFE. COMMUNICATION LOG.** The children's shelter, which houses children aged 0-6 removed from their family homes by DCFS (The Department of Children and Family Services) and temporarily places them here until suitable foster homes, group homes, family re-unification, or other arrangements can be made, features a picture of a Jack-in-the-box and a well-loved brown teddy bear under its name.

Opening the cover, I thumb through the daily log pages. Multi-colored tab dividers separate the logs specific to each child in residence. They require us, the staff, to keep this antiquated logging style rather than allow the more efficient option of computer logs. Since we have so many responsibilities, especially because Innocent Treasures is one of the very few state-run children's shelters in the small town of Precious, Indiana, typing logs would be faster. Between cleaning, cooking, feed-ing—sometimes, depending on the age of the child—diaper changing, answering business calls from social workers, scheduling appointments, taking children to appointments, etcetera, etcetera documenting, in writing, each child's mood, behavior, intake of nourishment, what they watched on television, time, quality and length of each nap, when they woke up in the morning, and when they went to sleep at night, how many times they used the restroom, the type of movement they had in the restroom...

It's a lot.

These daily logs are extensive and aren't the easiest thing to do for each hour of a twelve-hour shift, if you're an employee concerned with doing your job correctly. *My* 7 a.m. to 7 p.m. shift is, of course, meticulously documented. Flipping through the logs for several days confirms it. Starting from 7 p.m. to 7 a.m. on most days... It's a mystery what happens. If the state audited our logs, a social worker popped up for a surprise check or they needed records for a court date for any child, we would be screwed.

Innocent Treasures can legally house up to 8 infants or toddlers at any time. In my three years of employment, the house hasn't ever been at capacity. Thank God! Six children are the closest we've ever been to full. Right now, there are only three children, which is rare. And also means we're due to have at least two intakes at any time. After scanning the logs to ensure I didn't miss anything, I put the log binder away. Without a shadow of a doubt, I know the kitchen is clean, but I push back and rise from my rolling chair to check anyway.

The much-abused triangular-patterned white-and-grey linoleum floor is as clean as it's going to get without replacing it. White-tiled countertops shine to perfection. Even the blond oak cabinets' faces are free of the children's handprints left daily. The two JustForKids plastic picnic tables require a lot of elbow grease, but I got yellow tops, red benches, and blue frames looking good as new. Stephanie's highchair is just as spotless. And so are the white flat surface stove and microwave. I flip the light switch off and return to the office area with a deep sigh.

I can't put it off any longer. Aggravation electrifies my insides. The house phone hasn't rung once since 5 p.m. But maybe... I reach down, pull open the bottom drawer of the desk, and grab the newest Samsung

Galaxy cell phone I recently upgraded out of my purse. Why I needed an upgrade, I don't know. Nobody calls me, and I don't have anyone to call, but I like to have the latest devices. For aesthetic reasons, I guess. A finger swipe over the black screen brings it glowing to life. Unlocking it isn't necessary again, since no one calls me and I don't call anyone. Anyone who steals my phone, hoping for valuable information, will only be practicing, as I don't keep personal information on it. Noticing the time, irritation stabs at my left temple.

7:45 p.m.

Seven-flipping-forty-five!

No missed calls. No voicemail. No text messages. My molars grind involuntarily. Deep breaths are harder to take. Going through my embarrassingly short list of contacts isn't necessary. My visible recent calls list displays the number I need twice every night for the past week, eliminating the need to scroll. If I continue swiping, I know the display will show twenty more instances of the number being called every night I work. A tap of my left thumb on the name brings up the option to call. I press the icon so hard that I almost drop my phone. Placing the phone to my ear, I wait.

And wait.

"Hello?" answers a husky female voice after several rings.

"Hey, Deonna. It's Amina," I say with a forced lightness I don't feel.

"Hey, *chica*! What's up?"

What's up? My outrage at her casual, nonchalant tone is untameable. My skin heats. If I were a dragon, I'd be breathing fire. My boss, ladies and gentlemen. The world's most clueless or insensitive person ever. The nerve!

"Good," I say after an audible sigh, fighting to remain calm. "How are you?"

"Fine, sweetie, what's up?"

"Um... do you know what time it is, by any chance?"

A brief pause. "Seven forty...seven. Why?"

God, give me strength. My eyes bulge at Deonna's (the house manager, the person who makes the schedule, and is in charge of the adherence to said schedule) light-hearted response. *Why? Why?!* I think my heart is going to explode.

"Remember my class," I respond in an even tone, belying the very real rage boiling in my blood, "Tuesday and Thursday at eight? It's Tuesday. Quentin's not here...again."

"Oh!" Deonna laughs.

I hold my phone a few inches from my ear. Shake my head to make sure I'm hearing correctly. Is she laughing? Laughing! At my expense. I chuckle too, mine is without humor. And place the phone back to my ear.

"Sorry, *chica*," Deonna apologizes, sounding anything but sincere. "I forgot. He called earlier. He's running a little late. I told him it was fine as long as he's there by eight."

Eight?

I've only been taking classes for the last year and a half, specifically scheduling those classes for 8 p.m., so that I have plenty of time to get across town, or more accurately, to get to another city, since Precious is so small it doesn't have a community college. My shift ends at 7 p.m. I've been here since 6:50 a.m. because I believe in being on time and respecting that the person, aka Quentin, has been on for 12 sleepless hours.

Can my time ever be respected? Am I not allowed to voice my frustration? Again, when is it okay to go off on someone? Is there a correct way to go all the way off on your employer without getting fired?

"Deonna, I can't keep being late," I say, "keep" being the operative word there.

"Sorry. He'll be there soon," she apologizes, again, without an ounce of sympathy, then...

Silence.

I pull my phone away from my ear. Inspect the screen through narrowed eyes. The home screen greets me. *Oh, no, she didn't!* She hung up without waiting to hear my feelings on the situation.

She hung up!

Guess that since it isn't her life, she doesn't give a crap about the impact her complete disregard has on the only other thing, besides the children here, that's good in my life.

This isn't the first time in the last twenty-odd years that I've found myself in a situation similar to this. No one accepts no. The circumstances might change, but the outcome is always the same. People don't respect my boundaries. Not that I'm the best at setting them. It's the principle. My forehead might as well have "doormat" tattooed on it. I get angry like everyone else. But those lessons, I assume, people learn during infancy or childhood. Conflict resolution or whatnot? I never learned. Conflict makes me uncomfortable. Nervous.

Why can't I state my wishes in a level-headed, rational way and have others respect them? Is being abrasive the only way to assert oneself? Could I have said more to make my feelings known? Possibly. Deonna wouldn't have listened, though. No one listens when I try to stand up for myself.

This isn't my first rodeo. As dumb as it sounds, I dream of being a woman who exudes confidence, of walking around, speaking my truth loud and proud. There's this old song by Katy Perry called "Roar". One day, while listening to random, shuffled music, something about it resonated with me. From then on, I'd belt it out in the shower or in the car, envisioning people metaphorically hearing me roar and taking my thoughts and opinions seriously. However, whenever a situation arises, like tonight with Deonna, or any other time I need to advocate for myself, I don't meow, let alone roar. And if, by chance, it sounds like I'm asserting myself, the situation reverses, and I'm portrayed as the villain.

Whenever even a whiff of confrontation is on the horizon, my stomach cramps. My heart clenches as if in a Vice Grip and is about to explode all at the same time. I get a stabbing headache. Breathing becomes a shallow venture. All the things I should say to stick up for myself well up, but never break through the surface. That makes advocating for myself harder. My physiological response doesn't stem from a lack of knowledge about setting boundaries, but from a history of those boundaries being continually trampled. Breathing techniques are coping mechanisms I employ to ease anxiety, but when is it okay to abandon said coping strategies and lose it?

Answers forever elude me. Maybe if my formative years hadn't beaten politeness, decorum, and an only speak-when-you're-spoken-to mentality into me, I'd know.

I want to call Deonna back. Demand respect. Tell her I'm over the flagrant disregard for me as a valuable employee and fellow human being. Maybe yell, or at least speak in a stern voice that brooks no argument. Maybe quit my job. Of course, none of that will happen. Just thinking about it twists my intestines into knots. Plus, I'm not independently wealthy. I have rent to pay for an apartment I don't spend any time at since I'm always working. And I can't leave the kids. They're more than a job. Working with them in this capacity is a cause near and dear to my heart. I don't suffer from delusions of grandeur. Helping them all is impossible. I might not help or have a positive influence on more than one. But that one makes the irritation and stress worthwhile.

On a small scale, I understand. Deonna manages Innocent Treasures, Soothing Hearts, and Little Angels. Each shelter caters to children who are wards of the court, spanning a range of ages. Staff with individual priorities work at every home. Managers are required to be available all hours of the day and night to facilitate emergency intakes, social workers needing immediate placement for kids, and other duties outside my comprehension. With responsibility for a dozen staff, overlooking one employee's specific scheduling needs probably isn't intentional. I sympathize with her position and can't imagine having such responsibilities. However, there is a thin line between having sympathy and being a doormat.

Keys jangle in the front door. I twist my wrist. 8:10 p.m. Great! Bending over, I yank open the bottom drawer, exerting more force than necessary, drop my cell into my purse, then jerk the bag out by its straps.

The door slams shut as if sleeping children aren't right down the hall. Heavy footsteps come from behind me. My stomach cramps, of course. I sling my purse strap over my shoulder. Turn. Slowly.

"What it do, shawty?"

Quentin Kelly. Where stereotypes go to die.

If my eyes could roll any further, I'd be staring at the back of my head...from the inside. The sight of him irritates my soul, and not just because he's an hour and ten minutes late. He's what happens when a small-town, privileged, white kid has nothing more adventurous to do but watch *8 Mile*. Apparently, in his mind, oppression is absorbable through too many viewings of *Roots*, *Amistad*, and *Don't Be a Menace*.

Cropped-close dirty-blond hair with a fresh lineup and fade. Expertly groomed mustache and goatee. Pale green eyes. Ridiculous thick gold chains. Nike's match the neon green in his flat-billed hat. Crisp white T-shirt. Fashionable skinny jeans sag off his behind. He's like the five-foot-ten love child of Scottie P from the movie *We're the Millers*—I'm convinced somewhere on his body is a misspelled tattoo—and Post Malone.

"Baby girl, work with me," Quentin says in an appropriated accent that even I don't have a right to use, and I'm black! "I fucks wit you heavy, but yoga pants, off-the-shoulder sweatshirt, no makeup...? Everyday? You don't even want a nigg—"

"Don't. Even. Think. About. It," I say, unsure why I have to. People say my golden-honey eyes are expressive, which is why I often cast them down. Wonder what my glare is expressing now? "No one should use that word, no matter how much pigment they have. Or don't have."

I brush past him. Wisely, he steps aside.

"Where are you going? You need to brief me," Quentin demands.

Screw you! Of course, I don't say that. "Read the communication log." I rush out the door, slamming it in my wake.

Stephanie's earsplitting wail filters through the door. Pressing the unlock button on my key fob opens the driver's door of my silver Hyundai Elantra. An unbidden smirk curls my lips.

Chapter Three

My chest heaves. Sweat from my scalp provides enough humidity to revert my hair's edges. If I could see myself now, I'd say I probably resemble a little girl who'd tossed and turned all night on a cotton pillow without her bonnet. Thank goodness, my brunette hair is slicked into a ponytail; otherwise, I'd be a frizzy, nappy mess. On each inhale and exhale, breath scrapes my windpipe. It's hard to control my breathing.

Tugging open the lecture hall door, cool air whooshes out to smack my overheated face. I stop the door from opening too wide and outing my tardiness. The last thing I need is the entire class, although not a huge class, turning to gawk at my arrival. So, I peek through the small crack into the classroom.

"...And millions of people are being put to death. Similar to Rwanda," Professor Phillip McCravy said. His strong, resonant voice bounces through the room and off the tall walls and high ceilings.

Brown hair is generously interspersed with grey strands. Circular wire-frame glasses adorn a slightly weathered tan face. Professor Mc-Cravy appears somewhere between his late fifties and early sixties, but his regular casual attire of worn blue jeans, an untucked gunmetal button-down shirt, and six-foot frame leaning against his wooden desk shoves "relatable" down your throat. If this were a movie, he'd be one of those teachers who takes a job with disadvantaged youth, but he struggles to reach them, so he appropriates their culture and adopts their slang to gain acceptance and make a difference. Only in this scenario are his students mostly adults who, like me, suffered extenuating circumstances that kept them from pursuing a college education earlier in life. Despite his act of nonchalance, I doubt he's composed enough to overlook my dark complexion standing out amidst a sea of lighter skin long after the lesson began.

Written on a whiteboard hanging behind him is Sociology 101 GENOCIDE IN DARFUR

Tiers of stadium-style seating loom before me. Most seats are empty, which isn't abnormal for night classes. Professor McCravy turns towards his desk, and it's time for action.

Adrenaline spikes my heart rate. I open the door further and slip inside. Holding the doorknob slows the door's closing and keeps my entrance soundless. No way am I sitting anywhere near the front. Bountiful, wavy, black hair cascades down the back of a Latina woman seated at a desk towards the middle of the classroom. Even sitting, I can tell she's taller than my five-foot-two, so I take an inconspicuous seat behind her chosen desk to use her as a shield. I place my merlot-colored backpack on my desk.

Professor McCravy returns his attention to the class. Denim eyes made larger by the lenses of his glasses skate past the woman in front of me, but don't notice my sudden appearance.

My bag provides an extra layer of protection from discovery. But now, even though seated, my breathing remains erratic. I attempt to draw in a deep breath to no avail. Breath scratches my lungs and burns my throat. Calm eludes me. Like a rock climber searching for a handhold with sweaty palms, my breath slips from my grasp. Panic clouds my mind. I have asthma, and a track star I am not.

Wanting to show my face in class if only for five or six minutes, I swung into a parking spot and then sprinted across Hillard Brand Community College's parking lot as soon as my feet met the asphalt. Now I'm paying for it. I need my inhaler. Grabbing the gold accent chain attached to the zipper of my backpack, I drag it slowly. It sticks before eating two teeth. I yank once. Twice. And my bag falls with a loud *thud*. Eleven pairs of eyes fling in my direction.

"Miss Raichand," Professor McCravy calls, "nice of you to grace us with your presence tonight."

Dropping my keys in the patchwork pattern ceramic bowl on the stand near my front door, I flip on the light switch, close the door, and toe out of my high-top Chuck Taylor All-Star Classics. Familiar silence welcomes me, embracing me in its suffocating arms. Soft fibers of Gothic-style rose gold and black Berber carpet tickle my feet through my socks. The lines I vacuumed into it last Thursday are still visible. Good thing I'm wearing my hoodie. Crisp Autumn days and nights leave a chill in the air that speaks of my prolonged absence.

Backpack and purse in hand, I flop into my comfy maroon recliner in the living room with a huff. Both items slip onto the floor. I fight the elastic band from my hair, releasing my ponytail. Lifeless—like me—brunette strands tumble to the middle of my back. Running my fingers through the fine mass disperses the inevitable hump that forms in the center from wearing it up all day. My head sinks into the cushy headrest. I'm hungry. I should eat. But after the exhausting and frustrating day I've had, I don't have the motivation to do anything other than sit, stare, and blink. If breathing weren't involuntary, I wouldn't do it either.

Ah... Home. I sigh. My gaze wanders around my spacious one-bedroom apartment. Of course, I can't see the bedroom from here. However, I know that from the perspective of anyone who's ever spent a second around me, the decor of my entire apartment, especially my room, is the antithesis to my wallflower modus operandi. For Pete's sake, I wear yoga pants, and on the off chance I'm feeling risqué, leggings, and a nondescript shirt or hoodie every day, depending on the weather. Don't get me started on makeup. Outside of tweezing my eyebrows, washing my face, making sure I'm not growing a mustache, and lip gloss, I don't bother. This comes from a lifetime of experiences that prove that attention, in any form, leads to devastating consequences. Attention from people equals drama. But, here, at my apartment...

Attention is good. No one sees my apartment. I barely ever see my apartment. Decorated in varying shades of red, pink, and white with black accents, my place may seem to have an overt obsession with Valentine's Day to unsophisticated eyes. In actuality, it's my take on Gothic Romanticism with the sturdy, burgundy, velvet Chesterfield tufted sofa, armchair, and loveseat living room set. A queen-sized, stained-black, wooden, four-poster Gothic masterpiece of a bed with a beautiful, ornate hand-carved head and footboard is the focal point of my bedroom and not in a medieval castle where it belongs. When I lie on the black and maroon velvet damask sheets and a satin pillowcase, I feel like royalty.

Hanging in antique 8x10 inch brass frames on the walls are my favorite quotes, some from movies, others by notable figures, written in flowing, elegant script:

"There is always some madness in love. But there is also always some reason in madness." **~Friedrich Nietzsche**

"Nothing is impossible. The word itself says, 'I'm possible!' **~Audrey Hepburn**

"Parting is such sweet sorrow, that I shall say goodnight till it be morrow." **~Romeo and Juliet, William Shakespeare** hangs over my bed, the quote.

No expense was spared in creating my sanctuary. There are all the familiar trappings of a home, like warmth and comfort, but it's far from it. It's a cage, a gilded cage, but a cage, nevertheless. It's a prison of my own making, but instead of confinement, it's meant to keep others out. I don't lack self-awareness. I acknowledge that this way of thinking is unhealthy. I don't want the solitude I cleave to, but whenever I try to add people to my life, it ends badly. If past experience is the best predictor of future experience, then, whether I prefer it or not, being alone, is the key to my happiness, even if the thought causes an immensely painful fissure to crack my heart and tears to pool in my eyes. That is why I try not to dwell in this mood often. Plus, there are the kids. They may rotate, but they fill a void and provide a certain type of love that's eluded me my entire life. It isn't the exact love I crave, but it's pure and enduring. Everything isn't meant for everybody. Lots of people with my background aren't lucky enough to get half of what I have. So, I count my bless—

What the...?

Vibration against my leg startles me. Leaning down, I reach into my long-forgotten purse on the floor beside the recliner and retrieve my cell phone. No one calls me unless it's work. If this is Quentin asking me to come in early, I will yeet this phone out the nearest window.

Looking at the screen, I sit up and check the caller ID. The name Boulanger, R., stares back at me. Answering numbers that aren't pre-programmed into my phone isn't something I do. But a sudden chill of awareness runs through me. I swipe the on-screen icon to answer the call.

"Hello?"

"Hey, Gabby," says the deepest voice I've ever heard.

"Nope. Wrong number."

"Who's this?"

"Umm... You called me. Who's this?"

"I'm Batman." Rumbling laughter caresses my ear and does strange things to my insides. "Guess."

I chuckle without humor. "You're serious?"

"Is it still alright if I stay for a while?"

Sheesh! What a conundrum. The man's voice is made for audiobooks and erotic fantasies. If I were a bolder woman... Scratch that. I know firsthand how deceptive voices can be. Take radio personalities, for example. Some of the best voices come attached to faces only mothers can love.

"Sorry. I'm not who you're looking for."

"Don't sell yourself short," my mystery caller says, tone full of suggestion. "I think you're exactly who I'm looking for."

Hmm... That opens all sorts of doors in my mind that it shouldn't. I don't know this man. People bad. Solitude good. Anyway, stranger danger. My stomach growls, reminding me that I still haven't eaten.

"Well, Batman, gotta go."

"Wait! Beautiful."

I press end and heave myself up from my recliner. Time to eat.

Chapter Four

S hards of light stab my eyelids. I battle to keep my upper and lower lashes interlaced so they don't lift. Oh, my goodness! Attempting to moisten my mouth, I smack my lips. Ugh! I feel like I swallowed a Brillo pad. Or a toilet brush. My mouth is so dry. Something hard presses against my cheek. Turning my head causes pain. A pinch between the crook of my neck and shoulder blade reminds me of something Genie from my favorite movie, *Aladdin*, said.

"Ten thousand years will give you such a crick in the neck!"

Noise. Loud noise. Ringing. No. Blaring. A siren.

My alarm. Where's my phone?

One minute, I'm eating a leftover cheesy bean and rice burrito from Taco Bell, and the next, dim light peeks through my kitchen blinds. Of course, I'd fall asleep at the pub-style kitchen table. Nice big fancy schmancy bed in my beautiful bedroom, and I sleep at the kitchen table most nights. Gazing at myself, I discover I'm still wearing yesterday's clothes. I didn't even take a shower. Great! Why did I leave the living room? My recliner would've been more comfortable. And the noise...

Where's my cell phone?

With great reluctance, sinking the entirety of my body weight into my midsection and without lifting my head, I push away from the table. Slowly, I raise my head and swipe the back of my hand across chapped, crusted lips. Nothing like a little drool on the kitchen table to put your life in perspective.

Twelve-hour shifts with only one day off a week, in-person classes twice a week, and daily online classes. I'm burning the wick at both ends. My initial goal was to occupy so much of my time that loneliness wouldn't find even a crevice to seep through, no way to coax me into some false sense of extroversion that might have me doing something stupid like downloading a dating app.

Some minimal-effort loser with just the right bait—pictures with his nieces or nephews, or him next to a douchey truck with a cute puppy, gazing at a still lake at sunrise, or across an open field—would lure me in, entice me to strike with a pithy bio that says something like, "I'm not built for dating in this generation. I don't have a roster. I take commitment seriously. I can't do one more 'talking' stage or 'situationship'. No, I don't want to be your 'sneaky link'. I want one person to plan trips with. One person to laugh with. One person to come home to. One person to make a lifetime of memories with." He'd waste my time, break my heart, and throw bad penis at me as a consolation prize for swiping right. Gross! Been there, done that. Not impressed. At the ripe old age of thirty-two, I expect more. Deserve more. But when that demon of loneliness creeps in, I find myself accepting things I'd never accept if I weren't wallowing in lovelorn self-pity. And let's not speak of friends.

My penchant for revisiting largely one-sided friendships knows no bounds. I get absorbed in other people's problems and lives, get drawn into being there for them, to my great detriment, to the point that I neglect my own needs and obligations. And while I know this is who I am, what I'm prone to do, I'm loath to stop it when the loneliness spirals out of control. This is why I know I need to combat those negative feelings in any way that I can, but this schedule... *Sheesh!* It's whooping my tail. I don't have time for anything. Decent sleep is the most important thing. And... Siren. Again.

Where's my phone?

Finally, I stand on unsteady feet. The wobble in my legs further underscores that I'm not sleeping enough. Grabbing my cell phone off the cherry oak coffee table in the living room, I dismiss the alarm and check the time.

6:09 a.m.

And I still need to shower.

Ugh!

Time to make the donuts...

My jaw drops. The involuntary stillness in my chest is evidence that I'm not breathing. Breath is lodged in my throat. How the heck does this happen? The doorknob slips from my grasp, and the door shuts harder than intended. Why I don't slam it, I don't know. There's every reason to slam it.

This place looks like a bomb went off. Quentin sits at the desk in the makeshift office area. Under his weight, the hard plastic bows in a way that would leave a bigger man sprawled on the floor. He chomps on a charred piece of toast while scrolling through his phone, oblivious to my arrival. Makes perfect sense, given how loud the television is. I'm sure the neighbors down the street can hear it.

As far as the eye can see, there are toys strewn everywhere. Toys I had organized before I left—might I add—late last night. The kids don't even get up until about 6:45 a.m. My shift starts at seven. Raising my left arm and twisting my wrist illuminates my smartwatch's screen. It also draws my attention to the kitchen. What appears to be orange juice is suspended mid-run, dried to the refrigerator door and cabinets. There's also an orange juice streaked with—milk?—puddle on the countertop. Multiple large Legos are arranged in obstacle-course style from the living room to the kitchen. Shaking my head, I return to my watch.

6:50 a.m.

The kids were awake for five minutes. My shift starts in ten minutes, and it's already off to a bang. I'm not surprised. A majority of Quentin's shift is spent in silence. Yes, from time to time, one of the kids will wake up from a bad dream. Stephanie might whine. Once in a great while, there are emergency intakes, but Deonna comes for those. Ultimately, he has twelve hours of solitude. Given the sensitive nature of our job, we aren't permitted to sleep. Scanning the living area, I notice globs of strawberry jam smashed into the carpet. Strawberry jam, hand, and fingerprints litter the once-clean filing cabinet, walls, and couch cushions. And...

I sniff the air.

What is that smell?

"Miss Mina!" Squeals a high-pitched voice. Seconds later, the pitter-patter of little bare feet on carpet sounds.

"Ay, yo, chill!" Quentin gripes, not sparing a glance in the direction of the noise or me.

"Miss Mina!" Another excited screech joins the first.

The owners of the two voices race around the corner and into the living room. Neither stops until two short sets of light brown arms wrap around my legs. Teetering to keep my balance, I return the two exuberant toddlers' hugs as best as I can without kneeling.

"I missed you," Kaylee whines adorably.

"No, me miss her," Kaylee's younger brother, Nate, adds as if it's a competition.

They aren't mine. God, I wish they were. I wish I were at a place in life where I could take them home. Someone so young and precious shouldn't have to deal with so much. Yet, they gaze up at me with longing and love. Open. Unconditional love. Trust and adoration shine through their round doe eyes.

"You saw me before you went *mimis* last night, sillies," I remind them, injecting a lightness to my tone that I in no way feel given the state of the house. "I missed you both, too, though."

"Nu-uh!" Nate denies shaking his head. "Dat was thrwee days ago."

Chuckling, I ruffle his dark head of silky curls. To Nate, everything was three days ago. Time is an unfathomable concept to his three-year-old mind.

In another life, I'd be married to a good man who cherishes me. One who looks at me like I hang the stars and the moon, and vice versa. A provider. A man who does honey-do lists and pumps gas. Someone who fusses about my online shopping habit. I would nag about his dirty clothes, which never make it into the laundry hamper. We'd have a stable home of our own, big enough for biological and adopted children. Maybe we'd have pets and a spare room for in-laws and visiting friends.

In that alternate universe, I'd give these kids a home, one filled with support, love, and happiness. Something I, and they, never had. To top it off, it seems the kids jumped out of the frying pan and into the fire, I muse, taking in their grubby faces. For the umpteenth time, I wonder why Quentin works here. It's clear to anyone with eyes that he doesn't give a flying flip about kids. Five minutes is not enough time to get this grubby. He had to have fallen asleep. If the level of disaster hadn't given it away, then his extra wrinkly, baggy shirt did. Those weren't typical wrinkles. Anyone who made it to adulthood knows what sleeping in clothes looks like.

"No matter how many days it is, I always miss all of you. Why don't you," I coach my order as a suggestion, "sit over there on the floor and watch cartoons?" Patting their backs gets them moving.

"Okay," both toddlers acquiesce in concert, skipping to the indicated spot and sitting.

Quentin claps. "Right on time."

I jump. How in the world? "I've been here for"—glancing at my watch— "five minutes."

"Well, damn, shawty! Make noise."

My heartbeat gallops, thumping so strong it may burst through my chest. Irritation is a lit match to the kindling of what is my nervous system. Sweat dampens my forehead. There's so much I want to say, but something lodges it in my throat as usual, keeping me from expressing my anger meaningfully. Hands jittery, I stare deadpan.

He looks me up and down. Quentin's lip curls, exposing a diamond embedded in his eyetooth.

"Don't you ever dress up? Let a nigg—"

"What did I tell you about that word?" I intone.

"Chill, I was 'bout to say brotha."

Right! Rolling my eyes, I shake my head, then glance down at my outfit. Black-and-white camouflage, relaxed-fit cargo joggers with an off-the-shoulder maroon peasant top. My hair's twisted up with a black claw hair clip. What more did I need to do?

"Let a brotha see somethin'," Quentin amends his statement.

"Unless you mean a brother in Christ, I don't see a brotha."

I'm not overtly religious, but Quentin's cultural appropriation irks my pickle. Caucasian people, or any people, can come from a culture where they present this way. His skin color has nothing to do with my annoyance. Black people do not corner the market on hip-hop, hood behavior, ignorance, improper speech, or anything else. However, he left his second phone unlocked here once, and I may or may not have participated in some light espionage, looking to see who the owner was, of course. There were tons of family pictures that reminded me of those old black-and-white television shows I stream. *Leave It To Beaver. The Partridge Family.* This particular man was raised in the suburbs.

"Most girls wear dresses. Skirts. Show off your shape a little," he advises in disgust as if he's witnessing a faux pas of grand proportions. "Give a man something to look forward to."

Who made him the fashion police?

"I'm not here to impress anybody," I inform him.

"But, I'm saying, yo! Like, what you wear on your day off?" Quentin asks, sitting forward as if genuinely curious.

Perhaps he is. No way in the world do I intend to explain my mental health to him. That most days I'm so despondent it's a wonder I get dressed at all. Sniffing my disdain causes another rancid whiff of air to assail my nostrils. Where's that coming from?

"I hungry, Miss Mina," Nate says.

"Me too," Kaylee echoes her brother's sentiment.

I laugh without humor. Nate's bare chest bears remnants of God knows what. No telling where his matching nightshirt is to his navy shorts. Kaylee has the same mystery food in her fine, shoulder-length, brown curls. Her frilly pink nightgown is also worn out.

Quentin stands and stretches. "Y'all don't need nothin' else."

Sure, they don't. His cooking abilities are right up there with his work ethic.

"We'll get you something to eat in two minutes."

"One. Two," Nate says, counting on his fingers. Pride glows in his grin.

"That's right! Good job." I laugh. "But, how about I let you know when two minutes is? Watch your show."

"I'm out," Quentin proclaims, returning my attention to him.

The balls on this guy.

Sheesh!

"You're supposed to debrief me. That's why it's a good idea to get here before your start time. And clean before the end of your shift, in case you missed the memo."

A hand waves away my reminder. "That's woman's work."

My molars grind in anger. Stomach muscles clench.

Shoving his phone in his back pocket, Quentin shrugs. He pulls his keys from a front pocket. "Run and tell Deonna." His dirty blond brow arches. "'Q's not doing his job,'" he says, mimicking a woman's voice.

Everything in me stills. Pain lances my temple.

Breaking out of my statue impersonation, I rub the side of my head. "Just go. Leave."

"Yeah. Leave," Kaylee chimes in with a giggle.

"Don't have to ask me twice." Quentin strides past me.

This sucks!

My face is hot. My body is hot. It may be a cool fall day outside, but I'm experiencing my own personal heat wave.

"Wait!"

He turns towards me.

I want to lose it. The situation warrants it. Right? It feels like a firm "tell-off" moment. Movies always have a stand-your-ground scene. Where the timid main character finds their voice, but this isn't a film. An assertive backbone is equal parts nature and nurture. It manifests with proper guidance from decent role models in childhood and is reinforced by positive experiences. I never stood a chance. Cinema is all I have to rely on for examples of morals, standards, and appropriate interpersonal relationship reactions. Saying I get it wrong from time to time is an understatement. Social cues in these circumstances elude me.

"Where's Stephanie?" I ask instead of addressing the flagrant disrespect.

Quentin smirks. "She's waiting for you in her crib. Peace."

As he leaves, my brows pull together. Suspicion propels me to the nursery.

"Ma. Ma," Stephanie squeals in delight. Hands gripping wooden bars, elation stretches her lips.

The reason my heart squeezes this time is twofold. Stomach rolling, shock roots me to the spot in the doorway. My eyes bulge.

Brown fecal matter coats once blonde curls. Poop is smeared all over the crib bars and mattress. It crusts on chunky pale thighs and knees. It's running up the backside of the cute yellow ducky spotted onesie I'd put her to bed in. Her rosy cheeks are almost invisible due to the diarrhea mask painting her tiny face. Somehow, little David Copperfield got her soiled diaper off and thrown into the middle of the room without unsnapping her onesie. The putrid smell that permeates the entire house is stronger here.

And he knew!

Left her this way for God knows how long.

Sonofabiscuiteatingbulldog!

Chapter Five

"They all lived happily ever after."

• • •   Once again, Nate lies asleep in his toddler bed, oblivious not only to the end of the story but to the beginning, too. I sit cross-legged on the floor between his and his sister's beds. He only complains about getting a bedtime story because his sister demands one. Ever the competitor, he goes over the top, even cries, yet once his small head hits the pillow. That's all she wrote. While reading, I rub his back in a circular motion. Make no more than three revolutions, and he's out.

"I wanna be a pwincess and marwy a pwince," Kaylee declares louder than necessary since I'm sitting right beside her.

"Shh!" Nate stirs. Tosses back and forth and resettles. Smiling to soften my rebuke, I nod. "Me too," I agree in a whisper. "Lucky for you, you're already a princess."

Her face lights up. "I are?" she asks in awe and wonder.

Shocking how such small things bring happiness. Guilt makes my smile falter a bit. Part of me doesn't want to give her a false idea of reality. Truth is, no matter how good a woman you are, you might never get the guy, or a prince, like in this fantasy. Look at me. Thirty-two and still single. Not even a prospect of a man on the horizon. A relationship isn't the pinnacle of happiness. It doesn't erase or cure the past, nor does it guarantee a bright future. There's more to life than a relationship. Loneliness is still possible within the confines of a relationship.

However, humans crave closeness. We aren't solitary creatures by nature. The more one is denied love and displays of affection, the more those things are craved. Not dissimilar to myself, Kaylee and her brother suffer attachment issues. Corny as it might be, desiring a loving partnership is, for some, the goal of life when they've never experienced it. Yes, there's more to life, but discouraging that ambition or shaming someone for wanting such a basic, fundamental, human need isn't within me, especially when I'm familiar with the feeling. When not in my jaded mood, I sometimes wish someone had given me encouragement at Kaylee's age.

I place the book on the floor beside me. Kneeling beside Kaylee's bed, I tuck the sheet tight around her. "Yes, you are," I vow, gazing into her dark eyes. I tap the tip of her adorable nose. "And one day you're going to meet a prince, get married, and have pretty babies."

Beaming, Kaylee giggles. "Like you? I wanna be pwetty when I get big just like you."

Choosing to understand "big" as height, not weight, my smile returns. My mind, on the other hand, refuses to disassociate big from large. Hefty. Fat. So, the smile is of the gee-thanks-for-this-company-pen-bonus-even-though-I've-worked-here-for-twenty-years variety. Indulgent. I'm not ugly, but princess beautiful, I am not. Supermodel beautiful is a far reach, considering I'm 5'2". I snort.

"You're already pretty. You'll be way prettier than I am when you grow up."

"Next stowy," Kaylee demands with a grin.

I chuckle without sound, rolling my eyes. The things I do for these kids. I wouldn't trade my job or the time I'm privileged to spend with them for the world, but sometimes I curse myself for giving into their every whim. They deserve it, though. Reading multiple books doesn't cost me anything. Movies and books are my jam. And this gives them everything they need in terms of education and psychological care.

Two other books lay on the ground beside me. Tonight, we're taking a break from the heaviness of *Romeo and Juliet*. All the choices are more child-friendly. *Get In A Fight* by Stan & Jan Berenstain. I bristle at that title. *The* Berenstein *Bears* were a large part of my childhood, a security blanket in the unpredictable storm that was my life. I don't care what the Mandela Effect says. The name of the book series is now, and in my mind, forever will be *The Berenstein Bears* and not the allegedly correct *The Berenstain Bears*. My heart rate accelerates at the audacity of anyone buying into that insanity. Reading the title of the next book calms me, *Where the Sidewalk Ends* by Shel Silverstein.

I hold both books up to Kaylee, waiting for her decision. Several heartbeats pass. An adorable crease forms between Kaylee's eyebrows. She's taking this decision very seriously.

"Umm... That one," she says, again too loud, pointing to the much-abused white cover book on the left: *Where the Sidewalk Ends.*

This girl is good. She picks it because it's thick. Little does she know it's not one story. It's full of individual poems.

"You sure?" I ask, knowing darn well she won't change her mind.

Kaylee nods. "Yep."

I open to one of my favorite poems first. Kaylee snuggles into her bed, preparing for fun. She loves how I use different inflections and facial features while reading. I'm all about providing a dramatic reading. It's not just reading. It's an experience.

"'I cannot go to school today says little Peggy—'"

A mass in my peripheral catches my attention. I turn. My eyes must bulge out of my head. Because they're dry and I'm not blinking, this must be a dream or a hallucination at least.

"What?"

Shaking my head, I say, "Are you dying?"

"What? No. Why?"

I check my watch, rub my eyes, and blink. Focusing my gaze on the display again, I resume gawking at Quentin.

"It's 6:46? You're here. Are you lost?"

He chuckles. "Girl, you silly! A brotha can take a hint sometimes. I heard you this morning."

Other than narrowing my eyes, I let the comment slide. This occasion is momentous. Kaylee, ever talkative, for once is silent. Her little mind must be having as hard a time as mine is processing the sight before us—this Quentin mirage. With as often as he's late, I figured he was incapable of taking corporeal form before 8 p.m. And what does that say about me? Being a ghost, with some metaphysical inability to show up on time, made it easier for me to rationalize his constant tardiness rather than call him on his BS. My aversion to confrontation, apparently, knows no bounds. I need to get out more and stop watching so many movies.

"Speaking of being early."

"Miss Mina, you gotta finish. Go away, Qentin! It's stowy time."

Quentin smirks and shrugs. Dismissal from a four-year-old is not bothering him.

"Be nice," I reprimand.

Laughter simmers, close to boiling over. Kaylee's gumption inspires me. Her spirit might get her into trouble as a child; however, it'll benefit her in adulthood. She won't take crap from anyone. I don't want to snuff it out, more like redirect it. Teach her tact. Time and place. That sort of thing. Laughing, no matter how hilarious her indignation, is counterproductive.

"We're almost done," I inform Quentin.

This is shocking. I might actually make it home to do laundry or homework. I could stare at the wall without worrying I'm forgetting something for the first time in I don't know how long. I might veg out, watch some TV without rushing to go to bed. Really, I wish this were a school night. I'd be early to class for once. Beggars can't be choosers, I guess. He heard me this morning. That's a start. Maybe on Thursday, he'll make it here on time or close to it.

"Aye, I'mma go to the store for an Icee real quick."

I scowl.

"Real quick," he rushes to assure me. "It's around the corner. You want somethin'? I'll get you somethin' on me."

Skeptical doesn't begin to describe the look I level at him. It's not like he's ever done anything to earn my trust. But he's here early, and the store is no more than 3.5 minutes away. If I let him get me munchies, I won't have to get them for my unexpected free night, and I won't have to spend any money. Win-win.

"Hmm... Okay. You have to come right back. Don't be late. Sour Patch Kids, Flamin' Hot Cheetos with Limón—they have to have Limón—and the jalapeño Fritos Cheddar Cheese dip."

"I want candy, too," Kaylee whines.

Dang-it! Downside to having kids around. "He'll get you something, too," I say. Quentin grimaces and gives an infinitesimal shake of his head, which Kaylee doesn't notice. At her gleeful smile, I have to make an amendment, or this could get volatile. "But you can't have it until after breakfast in the morning."

"But—" Kaylee begins to rebut.

"Or you don't have to get any candy," I remind her.

Her argument dies a quick death, and I feel like garbage. I hope that caveat will allow her toddler's brain to forget the candy. Quentin, while offering to get me something, doesn't intend to get the kids anything. Jerk! The issue is mine, though. Why did I mention candy? I know better than to do that with little ears present. This isn't my first rodeo. It is, however, my first experience with Quentin showing up early. My lack of restraint can be blamed on this new territory I'm treading tonight. I'll be home about three hours earlier than normal. This never happens. An entire movie's length of extra time. Ooh! There are a few movies I've been dying to stream. Anticipation gives me the shivers.

"Fo' sho'," Quentin agrees, interrupting my mental celebration. "Be back in a couple minutes."

As soon as he's gone, I continue reading. Reading. Reading.

And read some more.

Forty-five pages.

Sixty pages.

Kaylee's eyelids droop. I trail off as if the poem has ended. It hasn't, but what will she know? She's four and can't read. Plus, my hands are shaking in rage. My stomach growls, not from hunger, but in solidarity with my nervous system. It's furious too.

Grabbing the books off the floor, I straighten from my crouch. Every joint capable of cracking does as I stand, which calls forth a fit of quiet giggles from Kaylee. That girl never misses a moment to appreciate humor, no matter how tired she is. Beyond finding humor in anything right now, I check my watch.

7:35 p.m.

Everything in me wants to breathe fire. Yell. Lob these frickin' books as hard as possible across the freakin' room. I grip them tighter in an effort to keep my dreams from becoming reality. These kids don't deserve to witness such unrestrained violence. It's not their fault I work with an inconsiderate prick. I should never have let him leave. I should've taken off like the Road Runner the moment he appeared in the doorway. Who cares if it was fourteen minutes early? It's not like I haven't accumulated way more than 40 hours per week for years. Fourteen minutes is nothing.

"Close those eyes, sweetie pie. Go mimis," I say, pulling my crap together enough to give this precious angel the gentle send-off to dreamland she deserves.

For once, Kaylee doesn't fight. Her doe eyes are alert. Too aware. She understands the way only children from abusive homes can that emotions are high, and I hate this for her. Hate that she feels my hidden ire because being attuned to turbulent situations is a fundamental part of her being. I leave before she can intuit any more of my anger. It's not directed at her, and I'm empathetic enough to know she'll misunderstand if I don't escape this room. Turning off the light, I pull the door shut as the nightlight casts the room in a soft glow.

Sliding Doors. The Jacket. Nobody realizes their brilliance. These are the movies I watch on my day off. Laundry should have been on the agenda, but after the week I had, I couldn't do it. Couldn't bring myself to do anything that would require haste or demand more focus than lifting my head to shovel Cheetos dipped in cheddar cheese into my mouth.

Unhealthy? Maybe. But I couldn't care less.

It's embarrassing to admit, but even washing my behind holds no appeal for me. The last movie to round out my day of peace is *Romeo + Juliet.* It's been on my mind since I read it to the kids last week. Most people prefer the 1968 Zeffirelli version. It's a closer adaptation of the play. Not me. I adore the 1996 Baz Luhrmann adaptation. It affects me on a profound level, no matter how often I watch it.

"See? Right there," I shout at the television. "He loves her so much. They just met! Where's my Romeo? Sheesh! At this rate, I'll take a George like Queen Charlotte. Problems and all."

Emotional. It makes me long for things better left unsaid. Worse, I think I might be a tad toxic. What woman in their right mind wants to be love-bombed like Romeo does Juliet? Different times, I guess. Look what George was willing to endure for Charlotte and vice versa. Sheesh! That's definitely *Love & Other Drugs* sort of devotion. Often, it's like I'm from a different era, flung into a world that I don't belong in. My morals and values are all from days of yore.

One major difference between me and others nowadays is, I think, ceasing reminiscing about my day off, that... I glance at my smart-watch.

8:15 p.m.

I respect people's time.

I need to quit this job.

I. Need. To. Quit. This. Job.

Self-centered isn't a descriptor I use for myself. More than any-thing, I attempt to sympathize with others, to recognize their struggles, and appreciate that our struggles are different. Being full of myself doesn't gel with my whole self-deprecating shtick. This place, however, wouldn't function without me. I believe that wholeheartedly. Who else would accept doormat-style treatment while having their boundaries stomped all over?

One day is not enough of a reprieve. Outside of the children, this place is driving me insane. Or at least to drink. I need a drink. Ooh! Vodka. Sadly, I can't have a drink because I have class, a class I should have been in fifteen minutes ago, not including drive time. As sus-pected, Quentin's fourteen-minute hiccup was a onetime occurrence. After that, he returned to his previously scheduled routine of arriving late every day for seven days.

Here we are back on Tuesday, and he's going for the gold in unpunctuality.

Keys jangle in the front door, snatching my attention from the black computer monitor I've been staring at since completing the com-munication logs. The door eases open. Keys knock against the wood.

Swiveling away from the desk towards the entrance, I wait. What nonsense is Quentin about to spew tonight? His imagination never ceases to amaze—

"*Lo siento, chica,*" Deonna says, squeezing her buxom frame through the doorway and yanking her keys from the lock. "Sorry. Sorry. So sorry."

Her wry smile appears repentant. Looks are deceiving, though, and I know too well she doesn't give a flying flip about my time. Casual top, capri pants, brown leather strappy sandals don't scream I-made-it-a-priority-to-get-here. Black, wavy hair thrown into a haphazard bun does nothing to convince me my conjecture is wrong.

Contrition etches into each feature of the Latina's expressive, round face, which confounds me.

"Where's Quentin?" I ask.

Deonna tosses her brown satchel purse onto the couch. "He called in." Her unkempt eyebrows scrunch in mock concern. If it were real, she would've made more of an effort with scheduling. I'm over an hour and twenty minutes past my shift. "You need to go, I know. I'm sorry."

She's right. If I book it, I might make it to class for the last five minutes. Provided I don't hit every red light, which seems to be the luck I'm working with these days. I remain seated. Suspicion immobilizes me. I have to know one last thing.

"When did he call?" I ask, leg bouncing in agitation.

Brown eyes search the living room, the tidy office area, even the kitchen through the open doorway to the right. She observes each spic and span square inch. Quentin is usually here when she drops in. Her shock at how clean I keep the house is warranted. Surprise doesn't explain her hesitance in answering my question, though. With each passing second of loaded silence, what could account for her reticence crystallizes in my mind.

My fingers tap the desk, joining the rapid leg bounce, to provide a soundtrack for this awkward moment. Of course, my gut tightens.

Perspiration dampens my underarms. Great, just what I need. To go to class musty. Secret better do its job. I'm testing its purported 24-hour deodorant protection capabilities tonight.

"Umm... This evening. I believe." Deonna finally answers.

Hope my smirk is as sardonic as it feels. "Oh, okay."

I want to say more, a lot more, but a lump forms in my throat, preventing whatever defense I may mount for myself. Gripping the armrests of the chair, I clench my teeth just as hard, then push to my feet.

"Tomorrow you won't—"

Yanking open the bottom drawer of the filing cabinet, I retrieve my purse. "Like you said, I have to go," I interrupt whatever bull crap she's about to spout. Leaving without sparing her another glance is as close as I come to confronting her.

Chapter Six

Per usual, Professor McCravy is sitting on top of his desk. Legs swing back and forth like an antsy child. Given his height, his desk must be pretty high to pull off such a task. Although it's more like a table than a desk, so...I'm stalling.

"...and they think they have the right to do it," he finishes saying.

Pulling the door open, I exert minimal force to keep it from making a sound. I slip through the slight opening to avoid notice.

"Miss Raichand, we've gotta stop meeting like this," Professor Mc-Cravy says, interrupting his lecture.

All eyes swing towards me and my silent approach to an unoccupied desk at the back of the lecture hall. Awesome! Add this to the craptastic night I'm already having. With a nod of my head and a tight-lipped smile, I drop into my seat and allow my backpack to flop onto the floor.

"Do me a favor. Stop by my desk after class? That is...as long as you can fit it into your busy schedule."

Ah! Sarcasm. I know thee well.

"Umm... Sure," I say noncommittally. Do I really have a choice? No. But with everyone staring at me, it's hard to muster an ounce of confidence. Death by firing squad is more appealing to me than being the center of attention, especially, since I'm 100% in the wrong, and he's still gazing in expectation at me. What does he expect? My solemn vow in blood? "Absolutely. I'll be there, Professor McCravy," I tack on, hoping this is the answer that'll release me from his and the entire class's scrutiny.

Professor McCravy hops off the desk.

It works.

For the eleven remaining minutes of class.

Wonderful.

Students pass me and file out of the classroom. When the last student, a lanky, dorky-looking guy younger than most of the night students, and nosy given his lollygagging, moseys out, I trudge down the carpeted short steps and approach Professor McCravy's desk.

Deodorant, please don't fail me now. I'm sweating to the point I'm sure wet spots are forming on my shirt. Boobs and armpits. Fantastic!

This is it. I know it. I've evaded being dropped by some miracle all this time, but I'm not stupid enough to think I can outrun fate any longer. Why couldn't I have more considerate coworkers? Why?

Sea-green eyes, magnified by lenses embedded in trendy wire-rim glasses, bore into my soul. They track my progression until I'm standing before Professor McCravy, seated behind his table-desk. In his dark blue-and-green plaid flannel button-down and worn skinny jeans, he resembles a younger man using an old-age filter on social media. If ever there was a personification of try-hard, he'd be it. He leans back in his seat, hands clasped behind his head, gaze laser-focused on me. Pushing back in his rolling chair, he plops long legs and Dr. Martens loafers on the desk with a thud.

Oh, good! He's super comfy while preparing to bring the ax down on my fate.

"Ah! Amina. A-mi-na," he drawls, breaking my name into syllables.

He's torturing me. I gird myself against the upcoming emotional gut punch.

"Does it mean anything?" he asks.

"What?" I adjust my backpack and purse. Nerves cause me to inspect my shoes as well. "My name?"

He nods.

I shrug. "I don't know. It might."

"Hmm... You never asked your parents?"

Yep. Definitely torture. A cat playing with a mouse before it eats it. "Didn't have any parents to ask," I answer, sure he doesn't give a flying flip about the meaning of my name or my sad life story. "I'm not even sure my parents were the ones who named me."

He grimaces. Bet he wasn't expecting that answer. Hefting his legs from the tabletop, he scoots up to his desk and glances at the open notebook that I didn't realize was lying in front of him until now. Discomfort is written all over the tightness in his expression and the crease between his bushy brows.

Maybe sympathy can change his mind. One can only hope. Being dropped from this class will push back my entire life goal. At this rate, I might as well abandon the dream.

He scans whatever he's written. "I wanted to discuss your grades."

A boulder lands with a thud in my gut. "My grades are fine."

Professor McCravy snorts at that. "When you're here to turn things in. Participation is half your grade. Can't participate if you're not here," he points out in a bright, condescending tone. "Tonight you were here for a whole fifteen minutes."

Impressive. He must have started counting when I was peeking through the door. How generous.

"I know you're here on scholarship," he continues. "That's one of many reasons I've tried to look the other way. Plus, when you have turned in assignments and contributed, you've brought a lot to the discussion, and that's rare. Even among the older students like yourself."

Thanks. Offense taken.

"It's evident in how you carry yourself," he assures, noticing my wince. "You don't look older than the eighteen and nineteen-year-olds who take my earlier classes. Regardless, I know you're intelligent. That's why I've looked the other way at your absences. Unfortunately, when you're here, you're also tardy."

"I know. I'm sorry," I rush to explain in my defense. "I work and my boss—"

Professor McCravy holds up his hand, effectively, silencing me.

"The syllabus I distributed at the beginning of the semester clearly states that after the third absence, I can drop you."

"I'll lose my scholarship," I say, voice quavering with emotion. It's not his responsibility. The blame is on my shoulders. I don't know how I could've rectified the situation other than quitting my job, which I absolutely can't do unless I've decided to forgo my apartment in favor of a cardboard box. "I've been—"

Again, he raises his hand, interrupting the creation of the on-the-spot excuse I'd been crafting.

"I know. That's the—"

"My grades are good," I interject, fight-or-flight nerves taking over.

"Like I was saying," Professor McCravy says through tight lips. "That's the reason I'm willing to offer you a deal. I have fewer dedicated students who are only passing solely because they're here. It doesn't sit right with me to drop you when I know you're making the effort to get here, even if it's for five minutes."

For the first time tonight, my heart rate slows. This is good. No matter what the deal is, I'm taking it. I have to. "Okay."

"There's another student in a similar position. I want the two of you to present a PowerPoint on the genocides in Darfur."

A tidal wave of relief washes over me. My vision spins. Swooning from happiness seems a very real possibility. "I can do that. I'll do the entire thing if necessary."

For the first time, he smiles, a true smile that crinkles his eyes at the corners. "That won't be necessary. This is his Hail Mary as much as yours. If both of you put in the work, I'll pass you. You have roughly 2.5 weeks until the next class. I'd prefer that you not miss any more class," he hedges, and I get the meaning.

He'd prefer it, but he's giving me some wiggle room if I can find a way to work with this other student.

"Tardy's one thing. Absent is harder to gloss over. This assignment will cover your missing participation points. You'll still need to pass the final as well."

I release a much-needed breath. I can do this. "Who's the other student?—If you don't mind me asking."

Not that I'd know whoever it is, since I'm late too often for it to matter, but I don't recall bumping into anyone else during my mad dashes to class. Since I linger after class out of misguided guilt, I know for a fact my car is the only car in the lot when I leave.

Professor McCravy glances at his notebook. "Justin Beale. He's in the class right before this one. Actually, he's supposed to be meeting me here," he says, pausing to look at his smartwatch, "soon. He has a class across campus at the same time as this one and needs to double back afterward. I'll introduce you next Tuesday. Provided you're able to stay a little late again."

Can't argue even if I want to. With a nod, I turn and head out. My steps are a thousand pounds lighter exiting than on entry.

"Oh! Amina," Professor McCravy calls before I make it out the door.

I turn.

"Class starts at eight—FYI," he says, smiling.

On another nod and a weak smile, I turn and resume my escape. The last thing I want is to give him more time to think of anything else to say. He might notice my other educational deficits. There's a paper I'm pretty sure I'm missing.

Just as I enter the hall, I'm struck.

Not literally, but the person in front of me stops me just as sure as a smack to the face. I'm not great at guessing people's ages, but the man has to be either around my age or a couple of years older. And gorgeous. Our gazes collide. A charismatic grin upturns sensual lips.

Sensual lips? Sheesh!

I've never thought in such flowery terms before, but that's the only way to describe them. He has flawless alabaster skin, and his golden-blonde hair is cut into a stylish undercut. Light brown eyes seem liquid in the way they reflect light. There's nothing overtly sexy about his navy blue crewneck sweater, pulled over a light blue collared shirt and jeans. Still, the way it fits his six-foot frame, narrow shoulders, and visible, even through his clothes, lean, muscular chest does things to me that no man's voice has, except when it comes to my mystery caller, in years. Decades? It's been that long. This man is more than attractive. It should be a crime against humanity to walk around looking this delicious. He should be locked away...

In my bedroom.

"Excuse me," he says in a raspy baritone. "Is Phillip still in there?"

"Phillip?"

A dark brow quirks. His grin becomes impossibly sexier.

Good Lord!

He shakes his head. "Professor McCravy."

Duh! "Yeah. Sorry," I stammer. "I. He. Are you Justin?"

"Last time I checked," he quips, tousling strands of his hair with large hands and long fingers.

"Awesome. He said he's waiting for someone named Justin. That's why I asked. I'm not stalking you."

Shut up. Shut up right now. Why am I still talking? I mentally scold myself.

He chuckles. A deep, throaty sound that, for some reason, has me wishing I wore something a lot more flattering than black yoga pants and a ribbed, black cotton tank top under a Heather Grey pullover, crop top hoodie tonight. On any given day, I don't care how I'm dressed, but compared to his soft-looking designer sweater, I feel dumpy, like I should have put a better foot forward, although I have no idea why I'm suddenly self-conscious. My MO is understated. Who cares what anyone thinks of me? I'm not here to impress anyone, but a niggling in my mind tells me I wouldn't mind impressing him. A little.

"I better go," Justin says when the awkward silence stretches between us. "Can't afford to keep him waiting. Nice to meet you..."

His weighted pause reminds me of my manners. "Amina."

"Nice to meet you, Amina."

"You too." Oh, my goodness. Was that the appropriate response? I grip the shoulder straps on my backpack for something to do with my hands. I've never not known what to do with my hands before. Where is this coming from? The way he grins at my response isn't confidence inspiring.

He maneuvers around me while I do my best impression of a speed bump.

This night has my emotions yo-yoing all over the place. Interaction with Deonna. Down. Getting to school faster than usual. Up. Professor McCravy catching me. Down. Being offered the chance of a lifetime when I expected to be dropped from class. Up. Meeting ridiculously handsome Justin Beale, whom I'm supposed to be working with—alone—for two and a half weeks, while looking like who did it and why. Hmm...that's sort of a mixed-emotional response. Let's say the string got a knot in it halfway down. Right about the time I started rambling about stalking.

Shucks. I continue down the hall and out of the building before I do something dumb like glance back at him over my shoulder longingly like some rom-com character. This isn't our meet-cute.

Chapter Seven

This. Was. A. Mistake. Propping my elbows on the oak table with a soft thud, my eyes drift closed. A much-needed break from reality. Just for a minute. My head makes a slow descent into my upraised hands. Crap! Unused to wearing a full face of makeup—false eyelashes included—my fingers detour in the nick of time. I run them through long, center-parted bangs framing each side of my forehead. Pressing my face into my palms would ruin an hour and a half's worth of makeup artistry.

It took entirely too long to follow the online "everyday" makeup tutorial. To think, some women do this every single day. No way does it take them this long to look as if they woke up like this. Although I guess that's not what they're going for. The idea of makeup is to enhance what is already there. By the time I finished evening out what I thought was my already even skin tone with foundation, lining my eyes and lips, plucking my eyebrows to create a "natural" arch, pinkening my cheeks with blush, and highlighting, I was unrecognizable.

When Quentin saw my oversized deep-V-neck heather grey sweater with split hemlines that revealed my hips, black pleather leggings, large gold hoop earrings, and five-inch black pumps, his jaw dropped. It could've been because I look like the clown I feel like while wearing makeup, but from what I gathered, it was shock and maybe appreciation. I've never been good at reading men's reactions well, especially when it comes to me. For the first time, part of my hair was up in a high ponytail, and the other half hung in beach waves reaching just below my breasts. Now, I understand how Tai felt in *Clueless* after Dionne and Cher made her over, except I did it to myself. Attention feels...a little good, I'm not gonna lie, but also awkward like I'm wearing a costume.

Speaking of awkward...

Opening my eyes, I rest my chin lightly on my palm so as not to erase my new face and gaze around Hillard Brand Community College's library. Although I've attended classes here for the last year and a half, I'd never been inside the library until tonight. If I'm being honest, since I'm under huge time constraints when I'm here on any given night, I didn't know there was a library until Justin suggested last night that we meet here tonight after our formal introduction by Professor McCravy.

The library is a large, spacious one story building with an open floor plan. Shelves of books stretch almost the entire length of the perimeter inside. The staff has a help desk near the entrance. A cluster of testing cubicles or privacy desks is near the middle of the room. There are multiple tables with desktop computers for students to use. Oak tables with matching oak chairs are scattered throughout, so people can study or work together in groups. Golden lamps adorn each table. Since it's so late—9:30 p.m., according to my cellphone—only one other table, besides the one I'm sitting at near the back window, has a golden lamp on. A few students mill around, but I don't see Justin yet.

Where did he go?

Of course, with his classic handsomeness, he looks scrumptious. He's wearing a beige crewneck sweater and jeans. Whatever he does for a living allows him to afford some snazzy clothes. I'm no fashion guru or anything, but tonight's sweater has to be another designer one. I wouldn't dare touch it. I'd combust from embarrassment to ask, but it looks super soft. Cashmere maybe? His cologne smells intense. Spicy. Fresh. Woodsy. Expensive. Ten minutes ago, he stepped away to take a phone call, and I haven't seen him since.

Not that we've gotten much done in the way of studying or putting together a plan, I hope he didn't leave. The self-deprecating part of myself thinks I must have said something stupid, and he decided I was too stupid to live, so he took off. As judgmental as I am, I'm not this bad on the regular. Intrusive thoughts are one thing, but this self-doubt isn't there. I don't like it. Overthinking. He's just a guy, yet here I am dressed to impress. Impressing people is the last thing I want—usually. Attention makes my skin crawl, but I want and crave his attention.

I've met the man a total of twice in my life. *What is wrong with me?*

"Hey! Sorry about that," Justin says, appearing from nowhere in front of me. Reclaiming his spot, the oak chair across from me, he sits down. "Forgive me?"

The arresting smile he bestows upon me reveals almost the entire top and bottom row of his even, straight, white teeth. His upper lip curls at each end, displaying a hint of mischievousness, and takes my breath. It scatters whatever thoughts were whirling around my mind. I don't know why I didn't notice his thin, well-groomed, Dread Pirate Roberts à la *The Princess Bride*-style mustache before, but this unadulterated smile pulls it into focus. His entire face lights up, making me wonder, not for the first time, what his skincare routine is. The way his skin glows with vitality says it puts mine to shame. Unfair. Justin is the perfect blend of pretty and handsome with his sharp jawline.

"You forgive me?" he asks once more, making me aware I'm gawking.

"There's nothing to forgive. Phone calls happen," I say, excusing his absence. "Is everything okay? Do you need to go?"

Please, say yes.

Say no.

Ugh! Part of me wants him to leave because my anxiety is at an all-time high. I'm making natural pauses in conversation uncomfortable, and I don't feel like myself. Makeup isn't totally to blame. The clothes aren't either. This is an outfit I already own. I didn't buy it for the occasion. As amazing as it is, occupying the same space as someone so attractive feels off. It's me. I know it. I want him to stay and be captivated by my intelligence and beauty; however, I also want him to go.

Release me. My nervous system is suffering from his proximity. Dry mouth. Cold sweat. Palpitations. Hot flashes. Chills. I'm freaking out. I couldn't be further from my comfort zone. Should anyone find so much comfort in being alone? Is there any hope of finding anyone I can tolerate in my space if I can't stomach this benign outing? Deep inside, I long for a partner, yet I'm so used to keeping my head down, I forget that sometimes it's okay to look up, to smell the flowers and enjoy the company of others.

"Nope. I'm good," Justin's baritone answering my forgotten question interrupts my internal dilemma. "Do you need to go?" he asks with an arched brow. "Sitting at the end of your seat and white-knuckling the chair like that looks like you're ready to sprint out the door."

I loosen my death grip on the chair. He's too observant for his own good. Or maybe my own good as it turns out. Something between a laugh and a croak of embarrassment leaves my mouth.

"I'm good," I squeak, stealing his phrase. "Lucky for you, I don't have a curfew."

Chuckling, he leans back in his chair, relaxing more now that I don't look as though I'm about to take flight to get away. "It was my grandmother's caregiver. It's Gucci, though."

I have no idea what that means. My forte is television, movies, and obscure movie quotes. A polite smile lifts my lips. Bobbing my head up and down helps the illusion of understanding. Hopefully.

"I hear you're on scholarship too." Justin drums his fingers on the tabletop. "You 'in danger' of losing yours too?"

Conscious of our location, my gaze roams the area surrounding us. His fingers must be a lot beefier than I thought. The tune he's tap-tapping out is loud. It might as well be drumsticks hitting the wood instead of flesh and bone. Thank God there aren't a ton of people here tonight to distract.

"Umm... Yeah. You hear right," I stammer—so articulate—glancing at him again. "It's a catch twenty-two. The short story is, I got my scholarship 'cuz of my stupid job, and I'm super close to losing it because of my stupid job."

Justin snickers. "That sucks. Sounds like you really love your 'stupid' job," he says, mimicking me.

Averting my gaze, I fight to suppress what would undoubtedly be an unladylike laugh-snort combo. It's a sinus-stinging moment before I return my gaze to him.

"Believe it or not, I actually love my job. It's my coworkers I could do without. The stupid cr—" I interrupt myself and think of a daintier word than shit. Men prefer soft women. "The stupid, disrespectful things they do irritate my soul."

His smirk says my self-edit didn't fool him. "Your soul? Whoa! That's pretty irritating." Justin laughs. "Well, I've met one, two, or...ten stupid people before. I get your frustration. What do you do?—If it's cool to ask."

Drawing the left corner of my bottom lip into my mouth, I chew it, contemplating his request. We're here to study genocide in Darfur, not get to know each other. A serious, worthwhile topic that's responsible for half of our grade.

You want to know him, though. Dang intrusive thoughts.

I do. With a deep breath, I release my lip and grin. Decision made. "I work with abused, neglected, or orphaned children in the foster care system. It's near and dear to my heart. I love kids. Especially, the babies and toddlers I work with. They're at the coolest stage they're ever going to be at that age. They're little sponges. Or seeds. No. Not seeds. Replanted plants. However, I'm not sure that's a good analogy. I don't have a green thumb. I've killed everything I've tried to grow," I ramble.

Justin does what's fast becoming his signature smirk.

Heat rushes up my neck and suffuses my cheeks. If my skin were lighter, he'd see the beet-red blush through my matte makeup.

Urban Decay All Nighter setting spray, do your job. Keep my makeup in place because even though I'm sweating like a whore in church, I can't stop talking.

"I haven't killed any children, though.—Thankfully. I mean, I'm pro-choice. You know if you have to. More like pro-life for myself, t hough.—To each their own, I guess."—*Shut up! Shut up. Shut up!*— "Anyway..." I sigh, wishing a pit would open beneath my chair and suck me in, "kids are really accepting. You don't need to be rich. Don't have to be pretty. You don't need to impress them. Doesn't matter how smart or dumb you are. All they want is attention. Love. Do that, and they'll adore you. Adults are never that cool. A child's love is the best example of unconditional love. The kids I work with experience the worst life has to offer and are inflicted with emotional wounds whose infections can take years to spread. I'm privileged enough to meet them at a time when my influence might heal some of those wounds. At the very least, I try to provide them a positive experience they can hold on to and take with them throughout the rest of their lives."

Straightening in his seat, Justin regards me with thoughtful yet direct light-brown eyes. He nods. "Deep. You said working with them is near and dear to your heart?" His brow quirks. "May I ask why?"

Gulping, my gaze drops to my lap. He's cute. But... "Maybe once we know each other a little better, I'll tell you all about it. There's still two and a half weeks for me to depress you," I say with a sheepish shrug, attempting to inject some levity into the conversation. "Patience is a virtue."

Humor sparks in his light eyes. "I can respect that. Actually, you impressed me, Babe. That's not easy to do. Is that why you take night classes? Your job?"

My heart stutters. Did he call me babe? I don't know how to take that. A man hasn't used a term of endearment when referring to me in so long. Isn't it a bit soon for nicknames, or is this how people do it nowadays? Dating hasn't been part of my life for a long time. This isn't a date, though, so maybe he's one of those people who throws names around without meaning. My eyes lift heavenward. Or, I'm reading way too much into an innocent slip of the tongue.

"Yeah," I answer after a brief pause, collecting my runaway thoughts. "Absolutely. I work from seven in the morning until seven at night. Six days a week. Nights are all I have."

Justin's eyes bulge. "Damn! When do you have time for a social life?"

"I don't," I respond with a shake of my head.

It's the sad truth. This "study" date is the closest I've had to a social life in years, and I tried to bail on this in my head several times.

Frowning, Justin scans the library, turning his head this way and that. He stretches his arms high above his head. Following his gaze, I notice staff pushing in chairs at unoccupied tables and tidying the deserted library.

"It's looking pretty dead in here," Justin observes aloud. We make direct eye contact, loaded eye contact. The vibe between us isn't giving off study-partner vibes. Even with my limited experience with male-female relations, I sense the obvious mood shift. Unsure of what to do, I shift in my seat.

Breaking our stare-off, I snatch my tablet off the tabletop and put it into my backpack. I brought it to avoid using public computers to search for information. For some reason, I'd thought the library would be full and wasn't sure a desktop computer would be available. Little did I know, we wouldn't get more than a cursory search done, and that was done by me alone while he was on his call.

"You wanna go get something to eat?" he asks, jerking his head towards the exit.

"Umm..." Decisions. Decisions. Yes, I want to spend more time with him. No, it isn't necessary for the project. Also, I don't work again until Tuesday morning. This is the most time I've spent out of the house in years, and I'm "peopled out"—for lack of a better word.

To eat or not to eat. That is the question.

Justin puts on his best puppy-dog pout. The ice around my heart and resolve cracks. Would going to eat be a date? He sort of asked, right? "Yes" is on the tip of my tongue.

Chapter Eight

It's three days before I agree to see Justin again. I wanted to say yes when he asked me to go eat. However, a knot formed in the pit of my stomach. A heaviness built, leaving unshakable unease behind. So, I made an excuse to dip. Not really an excuse. Needing to wake early for work means my bedtime can't be much after ten o'clock, maybe even before it if I intend to get anywhere close to eight hours of sleep. Justin utilized each of those days to make sure out of sight wasn't out of mind. He texted me each morning and each night. None of the text messages were about Genocide, Darfur, or our PowerPoint.

Morning One Text:

> Morning! Hope your day is as beautiful as you!

So unused to getting notifications on my phone, let alone good-morning texts from anyone, I assumed it was a message from my phone carrier advertising a new phone plan or something. I didn't check until the afternoon, once the kids were down for a nap.

> Good afternoon. Sorry for the late response. Didn't see your text.

He responded so fast I wondered if he'd been holding his phone all day. Then I remembered most people were so attached to their phones that they might as well be an extra appendage. I'm the only weirdo without dating apps, social media, or friends. The only reason I have a cellphone is... For emergencies, I guess. For an alarm. On-demand news.

> It's cool, Babe. You said you get up at the butt crack of dawn. Wanted to catch you before your day started.

Aww... It'd been a long time since anyone cared about my day. Once in a while, when biological urges strike, I call an old trusty FWB. He doesn't answer, but then at twelve in the morning I'll get a casual: U up? Text. It's usually on my day off, and we both understand what the deal is. Past normal pleasantries, we don't do much talking, and he never cares how my day is going or how it went. Rinse and repeat that for a few weeks, then we're back to being virtual strangers until the next time one of us has a proverbial itch.

Unsure how to respond, I sent a smiley face and went about my day. Then, later that night, once I got home, late per usual, my text notification dinged. Reclining in my comfy maroon recliner, I dug my phone out of my purse, unlocked my device using my thumb for biometric identification, and opened the text app.

> Hey, gorgeous. When you gonna let me take you out again?

I smiled at the screen.

> Again? When was the first time?

> Thought about you today.

> Me: Really! Why?

Can't a man think about a beautiful woman?

My interpersonal skills were rusty. I didn't know the proper response. Was he flirting? Just being nice? Was I reading more into it than he meant? Erring on the side of caution, I moved the conversation to more familiar topics.

We have a lot to do for the PowerPoint. It has to be five minutes.

That's easy. We should try to get as much done as possible as soon as possible. Want me to come over there?

Laughing, I responded.

Do you even know where "there" is?

Once you give me your address, I will.

Let's meet at the library tomorrow night. It's late. I'm hopping in the shower then going to bed.

OK. Sleep tight. Dream of me, baby.

Morning Two Texts:

Morning, lovely study buddy! Excited to see you tonight. Maybe we can get a drink after the library.

Considering the first day was a fluke, I didn't check my phone until even later that afternoon. It wasn't intentional, sort of. Justin is more attractive than any man has a right to be. On the off chance I do date, I don't go for guys I don't find attractive. They're just not as attractive as Justin. He's...

Wow!

Without ever having seen his abdomen, I know it's solid. Everything about him looks sculpted. His jawline. Straight nose. Neck muscles. Rectangular, lean torso. Even through his shirt, his chest looks knock-on-able. Lickable. Low self-esteem isn't something I suffer from. Not that I have particularly high self-esteem either. I'm attractive to some and unattractive to others. That's reality. Leagues are in the eye of the beholder, but the way he speaks to me... It doesn't add up. He should be married, yet context clues say he's single. Or, I'm reading him wrong. That's possible. I don't have much experience with man-woman relationships beyond passing encounters and movies. Textual relations are worse.

> Just saw your text. How's your day going?

> Look who it is. Thought you were ignoring me. LOL.

> Me: Nope. Just super busy.

> Justin: Oh, I see. Too busy for me. LOL.

So confusing. Everything he says seems like a trap. There's no safe answer, and for some reason, I can't decide if I like the attention or not. Whenever I want to answer with something flirtatious, my stomach muscles twist.

> So... When do you want to study?

Know what I just realized?

Me: What?

It's Friday.

The library's open, right?

The sooner we get started and make real progress on our assignment, the sooner we'll be done. Considering we're in two different classes, his being before mine, I don't know how we're expected to turn in a PowerPoint together. I'll have to confer with Professor McCravy.

Might be. We should get a drink before we study.

At his suggestion, my stomach knotted again. I read the text over and over, unsure how to respond without coming off as a prude. I'm a grown-ass woman. Grown-ass women drink. I drink. A glass of wine at home on occasion. Shots at a bar with some acquaintances in my twenties. I drink. With men I have a hard time forming coherent sentences around? Not so much. Plus, Justin is a lot. Even his texts are overwhelming. Our first meeting was nerve-racking. When Professor McCravy officially introduced us, I almost tripped over my own shoe while standing stationary, shifting my weight from one foot to another. At the library, I over-shared. No settings with Justin were relaxed. What the heck would happen at a bar?

Hey, I have to make dinner for the kiddos. Text you in a couple of minutes.

And that was how our text exchange on the second day ended. The coward's way. Oh, he texted me that night. Especially when at nine, I still hadn't made it to the library, but I didn't reply. To increase the odds of not giving in to something I wasn't sure of, I shut off my phone.

I'm not a shut-my-phone-off person. There's never been any reason to. Phone calls were so irregular for me that I entertained a wrong number a few weeks ago, but yesterday, DND wouldn't do. Guilt would make me check the screen, see Justin's text, and end up at a bar with him. I want to know him. I do. But I don't want to get to know him in a bar. Yet. They're yucky and loud with sloppy drunk people trying to get into each other's pants. However, today, Day Three... Defenses are low. He wears me down.

Chapter Nine

Fluffy blueberry waffles. A square of artistically sculpted butter. Maple syrup. Put that together with the best coffee in the world at Petty's and you have my kryptonite. Of course, the all-American boy, man, would love the local diner that serves all the most delicious, classic all-American comfort food. They're also the one place that serves breakfast all day. Don't know how he did it, but Justin somehow managed to play the absolute right hand. He found my weakness to get me to agree to meet him here on a Sunday night.

Guilt hadn't helped either. After intentionally, by accident, not receiving his text messages Friday night and part of Saturday, it didn't sit right with me. I felt bad and worried he gave up on me. Dang! My fickle heart got scared. Not just because he might tattle to Professor McCravy that I didn't cooperate and therefore get me dropped, but some part of me fears he might not like me anymore. So dumb! First, I think he's a bit extra now…? It's not like he declared undying love for me or anything. He could be Southern. Or one of those people who uses pet names with no emotional attachment whatsoever. Those conflicting thoughts led me to turn my phone back on. And shock of all shocks, Justin texted not eight seconds after my phone finished starting up. That was enough of a sign for me. I would've agreed to meet anywhere. His mentioning that Petty's had the best pancakes only sweetened the offer.

Petty's is retro, 50s-inspired with black-and-white checkered floors, and red vinyl booths with white center pleats. Silver chrome barstools with red vinyl seats surround the large counter, which features a turquoise-speckled Formica laminate countertop. There's a jukebox too. It's such a throwback. I half expect Danny Zuko, Sandy, Rizzo, and Kenickie to stroll in as I gaze around, avoiding eye contact with Mr. Tall, Blond, and Yummy.

"I take care of my grandmother," Justin says, continuing the conversation we were having before the waitress placed his plain buttermilk pancakes in front of him and my waffles in front of me. "She suffered a stroke a year ago. Then we found out she's suffering from a rapidly progressing form of dementia."

I'd picked up my fork but dropped it at that news. "Oh, my gosh! I'm so sorry. That's gotta be so hard. Is it just you? Do your parents help at all? Your siblings?"

Justin shrugs and shakes his head. A frown so forlorn, I want to reach over and grab his hand, bows his sumptuous lips. I don't. "It's just her and me. She raised me. There's a caregiver who comes on nights I have class or need a break. Breaks are few and far between."

I nod. Able to empathize with needing breaks and sympathize with the rest. "I'm sorry. I blew you off when you probably really needed a break. Then I go and ask invasive questions. Batting a thousand here, huh?" I chuckle without humor.

His smirk is heart-stopping. "No, it's cool. I believe everything happens for a reason. Like meeting you." He winks. "Plus, she's lived a long life. She was all I had, and now I'm all she has."

Not quite knowing how to respond to any of that, I lift my fork and dig into my waffles. He does the same with his pancakes. Bland pancakes if you ask me. Between bites and chewing, I gaze at his plate through my lashes. His table manners are impeccable. I'm not a slob, but the way he eats shows true breeding. Most of the men I've eaten with shovel food in as if their plates are going to be taken away at any moment. Who comes to Petty's for plain pancakes? Can you even call yourself a pancake connoisseur if you don't add bananas, chocolate chips, blueberries, strawberries...something?

"Sounds like you're really close to your grandma," I comment once half of my waffles are gone. Eloquent he might eat, he still demolished those pancakes. His plate is clean. That isn't too surprising considering he didn't use syrup. *No syrup! Who does that?* "Working with little kids all the time, I can totally relate to needing breaks. Not that it's anything like caring for a sick relative, but I get the idea of needing to branch out. Sometimes I feel like I'm gonna lose my mind if I don't talk to someone with more of an extensive vocabulary than 'potty' or 'no-no'." Nervous laughter bubbles out of me as heat warms my cheeks.

He laughs. Whether with me or at me, I'm unsure. Verbal diarrhea seems to be a symptom of hanging out with him.

It's another cool autumn night. I'm wearing a maroon sweatshirt dress, black tights, and thigh-high boots. Petty's may as well think it's summer outside with as cold as they keep it. I was freezing when we first got inside, and now I regret dressing for the weather. With all these social faux pas I'm making, it's hot like fire. Meanwhile, Justin sits across from me in another designer two-tone, cream-colored sweater and jeans that look like they were painted on. Blond locks are side-parted and gelled to perfection. Not too stiff, not too wild.

So annoying! Especially, when my makeup looks like some online beauty guru got a hold of me and said, "Glam? Challenge accepted."

"You're funny, you know that?" Justin says with a chuckle. He poses it as a question, but I take it as rhetorical. "I'm really happy you finally decided to come out with me. Sorry if I made you uncomfortable. I assume that's why you ghosted me." He quirks a well-groomed brow.

Busted. "No," I lie. "Remember, I work a lot. I get people'd out easily. It's not your fault at all. I should've said something. So, *I'm* sorry."

Great! Could I *be* a bigger butthole?!

"You'd think the college would be more understanding considering your situation," I say instead of lingering too long on my jerky behavior. "Isn't there some kind of bereavement time you should get?"

His answering smirk is quizzical. "You'd think. But that's not really how that works. At least Phillip's giving me this opportunity. I can't afford to lose my scholarship."

"Me either. I totally understand. If I lose mine, that's it for me."

Relating so much to his plight, I don't notice the waitress until a long, invoice-looking piece of paper slides onto the table between us.

Justin glances up.

The waitress, who appears in her late fifties—give or take—blushes from the tips of her sneaker'd feet to the top of her curly red hair. She adjusts her glasses. "No rush." She grins back at Justin. He puts his hand over hers, still holding our check. "I can split this for you," she offers.

My teeth clench. I knew it! I'm not jealous. She's old enough to be both of our mothers' ages. If they were young when they had us, possibly, but still. Something felt off to me about his attention. And she sees it too. Of course, she doesn't assume that we're together. Why would we be?

"We're together," Justin says, stunning me. "It's only right I pay for our first date. I asked her. I'm a gentleman."

I snicker. The waitress's mouth is open wide enough that a fist could fit inside it.

It takes her a second to recover before she responds. "Oh. Oh!" Curls smack her face how I want to when she clears her mind with a shake. "Absolutely. Just come to the counter when you're ready. I'll take care of you."

Yeah, I bet.

Jennifer, per her name tag, slinks away. More swing in her hips than necessary, in my opinion.

Justin chuckles. I roll my eyes.

"Hey," he says, drawing my attention away from the ostentatious waitress. "I'm gonna run to the restroom real quick." He snatches the receipt from the table. "And pay this. Be back."

"I can pay for mine." His offer was sweet. It went a long way towards helping me feel more comfortable with him. More than any nicknames would.

"Amina," the way he says my name is heavy. Weighted. A wealth of meaning behind it, but uppermost condemnation. "I got it. My Grammy would tan my hide if I didn't act like the gentleman she raised. Plus, I meant what I said. This is our first date. I'm trying to impress you by paying this,"—he steals a glance at the receipt— "thirty-five eighty-three. Let it happen," he stage whispers. "There's more to come."

I giggle. Freaking, giggle. Middle school girl-style. Justin winks then saunters towards the bathrooms.

"So... Umm... I had a really good time. Even though we didn't do any work. We're gonna need to buckle down from now on." My tone is part humor and part reprimand. "No more delaying the inevitable, Mister."

We laugh when I wag my finger at him.

"Monday, right?" Justin verifies.

"Correct," I confirm.

We linger outside Petty's in the parking lot. Dry, discolored leaves litter the asphalt and crunch beneath our shoes as we stroll towards our vehicles. Neither of us seems in a hurry to end our acquaintance. The restaurant is a lighthouse; its exterior lights draw potential customers. Its luminescence makes it impossible not to see each other. Justin halts, standing tall and unflappable. Two steps place me in front of him. Nerves and a wealth of embarrassment keep me warm inside. The night's more than crisp. My nose is cold. We watch each other. I want to yank the hood of my sweatshirt dress over my head. Since that would ruin the waterfall effect I'm going for with my high ponytail, I resist. I'm freezing, but don't want to go. Don't want to break eye contact first.

Funny how our earlier discomfort—No, I'm projecting. Justin wasn't uncomfortable in the slightest. I, however, was so hot from nervousness that spontaneous combustion felt like a real threat. It felt like I was on fire. As our linner "lunch + dinner" progressed, though, I loosened up. I only got a tad anxious that he might dine and dash on me when his run to the restroom turned into an epic journey. If not for the fact that he wasn't wet when he returned to our table, I would have thought he fell in with how long it took him.

"Well," Justin's smooth baritone breaks the silence first. "Better get goin'. Don't want you to freeze that cute butt off out here."

"I'm fine." I interlace my fingers, joining my hands sleeve to sleeve, end to end, so it looks like my hands are in one of those muff things.

Justin quirks a brow at my gesture. "Sure, you're not." He rolls his eyes and laughs.

He reaches out. Long, strong fingers do a little tap-tap on my hip. His touch sets me on fire. At least it feels that way. That was through the clothes. Sheesh! I'm hot for an entirely different reason now.

"I should go," I echo his suggestion, reverting to my classic avoidant style. "It's late."

"Alright, beautiful. Get home safe." He smirks, turns, and walks away.

I stare after him. The spot he touched tingles, and I continue to feel that slight, brief pressure. I ponder the resulting swarm of butterflies fluttering through my tummy as he crosses the lot to his metallic-tinted, candy-apple-red Ford Ranger. When we arrived, anxiety kept me from noticing the paper plates affixed to his back window. For a guy on scholarship, he must have come into some money because his truck is brand new. I'm not a truck aficionado, but I swear I saw a commercial for that truck, and it's next year's model.

Justin hops in his large truck. For reasons unclear to me, I still watch and wait. Our time together hadn't been as awkward as I worried it'd be. At least, it hadn't ended that way. Other than one moment of oversharing, I held it together enough to witness his personality. We have more commonalities than I first thought. Once he slips into his truck and out of my field of vision, I press my key fob to unlock my car door.

Hmm... There's no accompanying electrical click. I inspect my key fob, turning the small black box this way and that in my hand, inspecting it. What am I doing? I don't know anything about electronics. Good thing my key is inside it. I pull the key out of its hidey-hole in the side of the device. Then unlock the door. Getting in, I close the door behind me.

Tossing my purse to the passenger seat, I situate myself. Justin's truck begins backing out of its spot. It's taking him longer than I suspect it normally would for him to drive away. Maybe that touch left an impression on his mind, too. It'll star in my dreams and be the precursor for more adult activities. Activities we can explore together in real time as we get to know each other better. That touch is the most action I've gotten in a couple of years.

Suddenly, bright, piercing white lights illuminate my car's interior. I lower my eyes to evade the glow. None of the dashboard lights is lit.

Weird. Foot on the brake, I press the button to start the car. Nothing. Could be a user error. I repeat the process and push the button again. Still nothing. My gaze snaps up in time to see Justin's boxy truck bed pull to the mouth of the lot.

Crap!

I shove the door open and break into a dead run, ignoring the shock of icy cold wind lashing my cheeks. Racing to the driver's side window of Justin's truck, I knock on the glass. His brown eyes widen before the window slides down. Bass from some rap song vibrates up my fingers as I curl around them around the open window frame. Lil Wayne, I think, since I'm not a big music fan unless it comes from a movie, repeats over and over again about how he's got a sweet tooth. The music lowers.

"Hey, do you know anything about cars?" I ask, steamrolling whatever Justin is about to say.

He frowns. His startled expression shows he wasn't expecting that. "A little, why?"

"Mine won't start. I pressed the button thingy. The lights didn't even come on."

"Let me take a look. Back up, Babe. I don't want to run over your toes." He shoos me away with a hand.

I use the excuse to jog back to my car and use the minute to assess my reaction to being called babe. There was almost no physical response. Almost. At least I wasn't as averse to it this time. No red flags popped out. My stomach didn't clench as tightly.

I reach my Hyundai's driver's side door at the same time Justin backs into the spot beside my car. Leaving his headlights on, he hops out of his truck and goes around to the hood of my car.

"Pop the hood."

Since I left the doors unlocked, it's nothing to open the door, reach in, and pull the hood release lever. He lifts the hood faster than I ever have, finds the hood strut without incident, and the hood stays open. His blond head disappears under the open hood.

I'm a bit impressed. He didn't hesitate. In his designer clothes and new truck, he didn't strike me as the type of guy to jump at the chance to get covered in grease. That's if it's greasy under there. Whenever I get the oil changed or tires rotated, those guys always get greasy. Grease must cover everything under there.

"Hmm…"

That doesn't sound good. "What's wrong?" I ask. Dread replaces butterflies.

He crooks a finger at me. And if the situation were different, I'd let some of the instant dirty thoughts that pop into my head at that gesture grow roots. Instead, I join him at the front of the car.

"You see that?" Justin points at a box at the top towards the right.

"Yep."

"See anything different?"

By the inflection of his tone, I guess there's something obvious I'm supposed to see. He might as well be showing me…A car engine. And he is, which is why I have no idea what's different.

Looking askance at him, I lift my eyebrows and shoulders.

"I'm no mechanic. But I think—and this is just a wild guess—there's supposed to be cables here," pointing to the square box to the top right, "and here. Negative and positive connection cables." He pauses, looking towards me. His pointed stare clues me in that I'm once again missing something. Off my blank expression, his eyes bulge in clear astonishment. "There's supposed to be cables that connect your battery to the engine. No way to get power to anything if you don't have those."

Oh! "Oh my gosh!" I lean in for a closer inspection as if that's going to make the cables magically appear. "What the heck? How does that happen?"

Justin removes the hood strut from its hood attachment and returns it to its rightful place. He slams the hood shut. "Do you stash an extra key somewhere?"

"I have one of those little magnetic boxes inside the wheel well." Reluctance stills my answer.

The censure in his light brown gaze is why I hesitated. If losing keys were an Olympic sport, I'd be a gold medalist. No, keeping a spare key isn't the smartest, but when you don't have anyone to help in emergencies, you do what you have to do.

Turning, Justin leans back against the hood. He crosses his arms over his chest. "Well, looks like somebody borrowed your cables. You have AAA?"

"Nope." I pout. "Wouldn't it have been easier to take the whole car? Why just the cables? Don't you need tools to get those out?"

"I do. I'd use mine, but it only works if I'm driving your car or riding in your car." Justin pulls his cell phone from his back pocket and checks it. "I'd say I'd take you to the auto parts store, but it's closed. I'll take you home if you want. I have a quick stop to make first."

Pushing my sleeve up, I check my smartwatch. I don't know why. I don't have anyone to call. My gut tightens. But there's nothing else to do. I sigh. "Okay."

Chapter Ten

Lush green blades of overgrown grass snake up galvanized steel tube legs. Ankle height. If not for my over-the-knee boots keeping grass from touching my skin, I'd be itchy and broken out in hives. I shift. Faux leather squeaks as I cross my legs. A gap between the hem of my sweatshirt dress and the top of my boots exposes a slash of thigh to the frosty night air. My skin taps the regal crisscross, infinity-style holes of the long bench seat. A thermoplastic coating doesn't prevent the metal from freezing. Shock stiffens my spine as the underside of my thigh makes contact with it. In an effort to play it off, I readjust and fidget with the edge of my dress to maneuver more fabric underneath me. There's a lot of that. Squirming. I rub chilled hands up and down my lap.

"Hope you don't mind the stop." Justin clutches the edge of the tabletop he sits on, which is right beside my head, where I'm sitting on the bench. I jolt as if electrocuted. "Sorry," Justin apologizes. "Jumpy much?" He laughs. "When I'm having a bad day, or a tough one with Grammy, I come here," he informs me, laughter dying. "It's quiet. Helps me think. Gain clarity. Thought you could use peace tonight."

How to respond to that? Here I am having a full-on internal melt-down, and he's considering me. Still, there's so much I need to do. For the first time, I get to call into work. I should give them super last-minute notice like they do me. Then I have to find a way to get my poor burgled car out of Petty's parking lot before it suffers more than missing battery cables.

A strong finger taps my shoulder. My heart rate accelerates as if a lion is chasing me. "Out of your head, Babe," Justin commands.

"You're right. Sorry." I exhale, trying to push my worries out with it. "This is nice," I compliment, gazing into the dark expansive park. I don't know if this is considered a true park. It'd seen better days with its neglected lawn, and no slides or jungle gyms. Other than the picnic table we're sitting on, there's only one more table across the barren field. There are goalposts at each end of the pitch, sans net. The parking lot is a stone's throw away. A dim streetlight provides no meaningful illumination. But, the stars...I peer up at the cloudless, starry sky. "Thanks for sharing your sanctuary with me. I can't believe somebody took my battery cables. Who does that? If it's not one thing, it's another."

"Yeah, that's random as hell. I'm glad you like it here," Justin says with a smile evident in his voice. "You seemed like you needed it. The sky's the second most beautiful thing out tonight."

The stars hold my attention captive. I nod in agreement. It's so clear the Little and Big Dipper are visible if I tilt my head... I heft my legs onto the bench seat. Thank God for small miracles. Literally, if I were any taller than five feet two, my entire body wouldn't fit on the long rectangular bench. I stretch out on my back, my head at one end of the seat and legs straight, heel-to-heel locked closed, at the other. Good thing my sweatshirt dress is knee-length.

"Stargazing is one of my favorite things. It's like—this is going to sound so stupid," I warn, keeping my gaze on the sky. "But anytime lots of stars are visible. It's like God's personal gift to me. My specific blessing. Almost like they're whispering all the secrets of the universe. Telling me that even when everything is *caca*, everything's going to be okay. It's mesmerizing."

Quiet stretches between us. Too much silence. Awkward silence. Oh, no! I've said too much. My heart palpitates, and I gaze up at Justin.

Who is staring at me?

"Umm... I'm not crazy. I swear," I defend. Wow! This saying every thought floating through my head when this man is around is annoying.

"It's fine," Justin sympathizes. "I understood what you meant. Gimme a second."

At his request, my gaze returns heavenward. The picnic table shakes as he gets up. A vehicle door opens and slams in the distance. My mind wanders to the events of the night. Stomach muscles cramp. Pain streaks through my temple. What am I going to do about my car? Spending extra on a tow service isn't in my budget.

Bass drops, and a guitar sounds. A deep, dirty, raspy southern male voice overlays the beat. The picnic table shakes. A thud against steel vibrates through me. Alerts me to the presence of someone, Justin, reclaiming his spot on the tabletop.

♪ *"Dick you down, dick you down, dick you down..."*

My brows furrow, trying to place the lyrics. Music recognition isn't where I shine, so it takes a few bars.

Kevin Gates "D U Down".

Wouldn't have known it if I hadn't doom scrolled short-form content on social media one night and seen hundreds of men's thirst trap videos where they danced and lip-synched to it.

Although I'm lying down, a heavyweight sinks into the pit of my stomach. Suddenly, I'm hyper-aware of being at a deserted park, God knows where, with a man I don't know. At night! I rode in his truck to the park. It wasn't super far from Petty's that I remember, but still. No one—not that there's anyone I could have told—knows where I am or who I'm with. And I'm supine on a metal bench in a dress.

Smart move.

As cute as he is, I can't believe this is his idea of mood music. A man waxing poetic about banging a chick every time she calls to prove he does it better than the other guy she's banging or the guy she was previously banging. Who knows? This is why I don't listen to popular rap or any music, unless it's in a movie.

Stars shine bright above me. They twinkle. Some blink. Those must be airplanes.

An odd sensation washes over me. Thousands of pinpricks. It isn't goosebumps, but something similar.

Justin's face enters my line of sight. He peers down. Stares at me.

I gaze into his bourbon eyes. Smile.

He is tight-lipped. Serious. Too serious.

Crap!

This isn't staring. It's gazing. Longingly.

Between one heartbeat and the next, he leans in.

I want to scream.

Firm lips press into mine. Long seconds pass.

Alarm bells aren't an apt description for the warning that blares inside my head. My palms sweat as my fingers clutch at the regal infinity metal holes of the bench seat and gain purchase with a claw-style grip. My stomach somersaults. Both arms remain firmly at my sides.

Kevin Gates moves on. Croons about the joys of finding a partner who enjoys public sex as much as he does. Far too much of my attention is on the song than it should be at the moment. He D's down someone in this song too. Awesome! Mutual interest is great...unlike what's happening now.

He pecks my lips. Once. Twice. Three times.

Noisy smacks accompany each peck. The whiskers of his thin mustache stab my upper lip. Pointy lips jab my fuller ones. It's a movie kiss packed with all the action. Head tilts—on his part. His eyes drift closed as if he is dreaming. Mine squeeze so tight that an unintentional tear slips from between my lids, and blazes a fiery trail as it flips ass over teakettle down my frigid cheek. I can't take any more, I turn my head.

Sharp lips glance across my skin, gliding through moisture from the renegade tear. They skim my hairline and the shell of my ear. Waffles threaten to re-emerge as my stomach lurches. I struggle to keep disgust from mangling my expression when my internal dry heave manifests physically.

Justin pants, and bile rises in my throat. I gulp it back and crack my eyes open one lid at a time. He's still on the table. Thank God. Everything in me worried he might get down and attempt to lie on top of me. I'm too vulnerable in this position. I jackknife into a sitting position, forcing him to move or risk being headbutted. He watches through half-mast eyes. I watch him in stark trepidation.

All the innuendos of coming to my house flash through my mind. The inappropriate pet names. His casual mentions regarding our meetings being destiny. I brushed it off before, but now it all congeals, forming an ominous gargantuan three-headed monster. That's how my nervous system interprets his words. Portentous. Not sweet. Not meaningful. Scary. And the way he regards me?

His dark blond brows crease in question.

For lack of anything better to do and out of discomfort, I give a tight smile.

Resolve sets in Justin's jawline. It's as if a decision has been made, and I witness the byplay in real-time. Hints of uncertainty. Hurt. Glee. I don't know what outcome is reached or what the options are, which terrifies me. Cold has nothing to do with the shivers racking my body.

Justin leans forward. I avert my gaze and fold my hands in my lap. Cool lips press against my forehead. My head jerks up. He mistakes my stupefaction for ardor.

A bony finger tilts my chin. The pad of his thumb brushes the corner of my mouth. I can't speak. Something lodges in my throat. Panic. Maybe? Immobility is me. I am immobile. Sweat beads dew on my forehead. Every muscle in my body locks. As he dips his head, he holds my head hostage, using the crook of his finger. We stare into each other's eyes. His glaze in anticipation. Mine widen in unadulterated terror. From the way I slant up, a pinch starts at the base of my spine. My stomach cramps. Thin lips mash into mine. It's impersonal. Hard. Dry. My skin crawls.

Teeth nip at my lips.

I thaw. "Stop!"

Justin pulls back. Frowns.

Guilt rings in my ears. He can't know what effect his kisses have on me. Can't know the mental gymnastics going on inside my head, the conflicting emotions. Confusion sets into his squinty gaze, confirming my assumption.

"I'm sorry," my apology rips from my soul. All this time, I lament over my loneliness, whine about the lack of romantic options in my life. Then, here comes a handsome all-American man who hits on me, gazing at me with unabashed lusty adoration, and I stop him. Freak out when he's been nothing but nice. What's wrong with me? I'm so damaged. "It's been a weird night. I have a stress-induced mental block or something. It's not you. We should go."

Pink floods his cheeks. Either he's cold or embarrassed. I believe it's a bit of both. My heart still hammers in my chest. If I weren't gifted with such brown skin, I'd redden as much as he does. His eyes search mine.

"No, I'm sorry," contrition deepens his voice. "This is obviously not the night for this." He sighs. "I actually saw you a few times," Justin admits. Going off what I'm positive is confusion written on my face, he drags in a deep breath and then expels it slowly. "Before we were introduced, you were always leaving campus late. You'd be staring straight ahead. Like, totally focused. Your car was always the only one in the lot. You never saw me. You were this ethereal enigma I never thought I'd meet. I was always rushing back home after my last class to relieve the caregiver, so I couldn't stop to talk to you, even if I wanted to—And I wanted to, FYI. What would I have said, anyway? You were this unattainable vision. Then Phillip told me about this extra credit. Truth be told, I didn't wanna do it. I was gonna drop. I'd totally planned to on the night you bumped into me in the hall. Electricity surged through me when we touched. It's, like, we were supposed to meet. You know you're beautiful, right? Sorry."

His confession enables me to relax—a little. I roll my shoulders, releasing some tension. It explains some of his intensity.

"It's cool." I attempt to alleviate his guilt.

"I'm serious," he insists. "You might not notice, but every time you walk by—move through a room—some guy stares at you. You don't know how that..." he pauses a beat, then, through gritted teeth, finishes, "affects me."

His obvious agitation gives me pause. Warning sirens ricochet around my mind and kickstart my nervous system. Cortisol and adrenaline shoot through my veins. My heart rate accelerates. Heat engulfs me. A shiver runs down my spine.

"It's just..." How to let him down gently? "If it were any other time, maybe... But I have work that already takes up an enormous amount of time. I need to focus on school. Personal time?" I shake my head. "I don't know. I get distracted easily and—"

"Can't you have both?" Justin interjects. He shifts his head into my eyeline, demanding to be my focus. Light brown eyes implore my face.

My honey eyes scour his, searching for the man I ran into in the hall, the one who tied my tongue and frazzled me in all the good ways that brought butterfly wings fluttering in my stomach. His perfectly finger-combed blond locks aren't as coiffed. They're tousled and hang over his forehead. The ends of his hair flirt with his eyebrows. He looks wild—Not Tarzan wild, but Scar from *The Lion King* wild. It's this feral nature I've glimpsed lurking under his handsome, too-put-together facade that triggers my sympathetic nervous system.

I don't want to see this other side. My eyes probe for more. His eyes grow hungry again, intense. Once more, he closes the distance between our faces.

I cringe away before he can kiss me again and look down. "No, I can't," I answer his forgotten question. "I've tried. Having both, I mean. I'm not a good multitasker. I'm barely juggling work, sleep, and school now."

He chases my gaze. I don't see it. I'm still staring at my hands, my boots. I feel it. Feel his hot scrutiny of me. There are many reasons for its heat, and I'd rather not ruminate on any of them.

Long, quiet seconds pass. My heart pounds in my sternum. This should be a relief. Him not kissing me. Me not having to look at him. I hope he's considering everything I've told him. Maybe in time things can be different. He is the epitome of the boy next door. Or rather, the man next door. Being with him isn't a hardship. Attraction is there. In time, we'll know each other better. I look at him out of the corner of my eye. He stares at the side of my head as if he wants to drill in and literally change my mind.

Minutes pass. We're at a stalemate. He exhales loudly, breaking the silent standoff.

"I'll take you home," he capitulates.

The first real sigh of relief bows my back. I allow my head to drop back loose on my shoulders, and I send a quick prayer to God for delivering us from this awkwardness with understanding and decorum.

Justin swoops in, smashing his lips into mine. Whatever relief I gained sprints away faster than it settled in.

I jerk away from him.

He forces me back towards him. Fingers tunnel through the hair at my nape. In his fist, he clasps a chunk of ponytail and hair from the crown of my head. My scalp stings. He yanks my head back by the roots of my hair. A scream rolls up my throat and bubbles to the surface, only to be trapped... In Justin's mouth.

His tongue thrusts into mine along with too much saliva as he seizes the opportunity my loss of control grants him. Sweat pours down the sides of my face. He snatches at my waist, granting me the opportunity to push him, to shove his shoulders. Caught off guard, his lips slip off mine. Hopping to my feet, I gag and spit out slimy, excess saliva. The ground disappears.

I'm flying.

No. I'm being lifted. He whisks me off my feet. My spine meets the metal tabletop as he slams me down. Breath whooshes from my lungs in a rush. We tussle for control of my hands. I raise one arm defensively, and his pale fingers wrap around my tiny wrist. Yanking myself free causes his short nails to slice my skin. He throws the other arm over my head. I punch him in his ribs, and my heart races, and my legs flail, pedaling hard as if I'm going uphill on a gym stationary bike. Fight-or-flight is at the forefront of my mind.

This can't be happening.

How is this happening? Things were okay. We reached an understanding.

I rip my right arm out of his grasp. He straddles my body. Real panic seizes me. His mouth is set in a firm line, one hundred percent absorbed in our struggle. Beneath alabaster skin, his jaw muscles work feverishly. This was his plan. It's evident in his concentration. Anger boils inside me and seeps from my pores. His weight holds my bottom half nearly immobile besides a few fruitless kicks. I don't know what comes over me, but I pull back my right arm. It snaps forward like a rock in a slingshot. My hand connects with his solid jaw. Tingles dance over the skin of my palm. Blond hair, completely devoid of gel, now moves freely as it flops to the side when his head whips to the right. Justin recovers quickly. What I thought were sensual lips now curl. This smile isn't charming. It's malevolent.

The change in his appearance stuns me. I was wrong. Tears fall in earnest. Once again, I misjudged a person. Loneliness brings disaster. This lesson isn't unfamiliar to me. Attention. Faith. Accepting kindness. The universe always exacts a price for trust. Craving connection never ends well.

Justin takes advantage of my distraction. He thrusts both my arms above my head and shackles both wrists in one of his large hands. Breathing hard, he leans back, taking in his handiwork. His other hand skates along my hip. Up. Down. Goosebumps break out across my bare flesh. Bare flesh? My sweatshirt dress rose during our struggle. I hadn't noticed. Now I do. Cold air brushes my lower back. Buttocks. Upper thighs.

"Your tears are beautiful," he says, cooing as if calming a baby. "Sadness is beguiling. So underestimated. So much more multifaceted than happiness. What is it they say?" His eyes squint, trying to remember. "Can't have a rainbow without a little rain. I prefer a lot of rain."

He grins, then leans in and bites my breast through the fabric.

I scream.

A crack rends the air. For a minute, I'm unsure where the sound originates from. Stars blur my vision. When he slaps me a second time, my cheeks burn.

"No!" He shouts. "No screaming." Justin wags his finger in my face. Or I assume he does. I can't tell. So many tears have collected in my eyes that they obscure my sight. "You'll wake the neighbors," he says in a hushed tone. Fingers caress my belly. It quavers.

"Please don't. Please. Please," I whisper. "Please! I won't say anything. Let me go. Please."

Justin bestows a grin upon me that the Joker would envy. Not Jared Leto. Jack Nicholson.

"You're begging me," he says, although it sounds like an awed question. His grin widens. "That just makes me want you more."

My eyes bulge. Terror blanks my mind. Screaming isn't allowed, but I scream. And scream. And scream. Blow after blow rains down on me. I thrash. Blood vessels rupture in my eyes. At least, it feels that way. A salty metallic taste coats my mouth.

"No! No!" I shout. "Help!"

Justin slaps a hand over my mouth. Sweat from his face drips into my eyes.

"You wanna die tonight?" he asks.

His hold on my mouth is so tight it's a fight to shake my head. I manage, though. Self-preservation is strong in me tonight. For all the disappointment life has brought me, I have no desire to die tonight.

Justin's glare is murderous. "If you scream again. It will be the last sound you make."

Silence follows his proclamation. Metal clinks. Justin adjusts himself multiple times. The quiet sound of a zipper unzipping is deafening.

I shake so hard it's like I'm convulsing. "No," I whisper against better judgment. My head feels stuffed with cotton. Appealing to some latent humanity within this monster seems pointless, but I can't accept this. "Please stop."

A muffled thud sounds in the distance.

Chapter Eleven

*W*alter McGinnis

"Shake a leg, Agnes," I shout through Petty's open rear door. "Assholes and elbows! I can see my breath out here."

God! She's slow. That's for sure. But, she's still as pretty as the day I met her forty-five years ago. Her hair is more silver than black and pin-straight. She used to be five-six. It'd break her heart to realize she shrank two inches. She'd probably attribute it to giving birth to my three big-headed spawns like she does everything else regarding her mood and her physique. Who am I to judge?

I watch from a distance, where I hold the door for her.

She bends to retrieve her taupe coat. Her rump's gotten bigger. Wider. Way rounder than the petite young thing she once was. It jiggles this way and that. Nope! I'm not complaining at all. The years have been kind to her. Unlike me.

My thick brown hair is long gone. My bald head is as smooth as a baby's bottom, and cold too. I yank my skull cap out of my coat pocket, pulling it over my head and forehead for good measure. The strapping young twenty-four-year-old army man stationed in Korea, she hitched her to long ago, is a distant memory. He's been replaced by this geri-atric liver-spotted, pot-bellied old cuss.

"If you don't stop yelling at me," Agnes fusses. She walks past me. "I ain't hard of hearing."

I am. Just another reason I love her more every day. Loyalty. Faith-fulness. Come hell or high water, she's got my back, and vice versa.

I gaze into her lovely dark eyes, taken with her as always. This job at Petty's washing dishes and cleaning can't end soon enough. My dogs are barking! I never intended to work into my later years. Didn't want Agnes to either. That woman can try the patience of a saint when she sets her mind to something. It's the only way we're going to save for our dream RV, and we've almost reached our goal. Another month of graveyard shifts and we'll be set. We'll close up the house and drive away in a fancy shmancy motor home, able to spend time with grandkids and enjoy our golden years.

"Got everything?" I ask. My job is to lock this door. Every other night we work, it never fails that she forgets something from that big bag of tricks she calls a purse. We wind up turning right around for some doodad she's left here by accident.

She stops. I halt my progression, too, to allow her time to search her bag. Our emperor-blue SUV, across the almost-empty lot, came with a nifty feature. I retrieve the key doohickey from my pocket and press the button to start the car remotely. The thing's amazing. I had it installed for Agnes's benefit, but why would she drive? I'm always with her.

Agnes lifts her head from her purse and pulls the strap over her shoulder. "Yep. Looks like everything's in here." She pats the bag.

Arm propped on my hip, I wait. True to form, Agnes slips her small hand through, taking my arm as we continue to walk.

"Oh, shoot!" Agnes exclaims. She yanks me to a stop. "Left the cobbler on the counter."

"Woman! You had me standing there for a good ten minutes and only now—"

"Wait!" She demands in a hushed tone.

"Of course, I'll wait, I want that—"

She wallops me in the arm twice. Her head swivels left and then right, searching the darkness.

"What's wrong?" I ask. For some reason, I adopt her quiet tone as if talking too loud will disturb the night.

"Shh..." Agnes demands, pulling on my jacket sleeve. "Hear that?"

"Help! Please. Help."

I heard it that time. An agonized voice so low I see why I missed it at first.

"Where's it coming from?" Agnes asks.

"Please. Please."

Several empty spots away from our mid-size SUV is a Silver four-door compact vehicle. Squinting proves there's something dark on the ground around the other side. I remove my glasses from the inside pocket of my coat and slip them on. Leaning forward doesn't help anything, but I do anyway in hopes of making heads or tails of what I'm seeing. It's a person. A barefoot person. It's hard to discern details from here.

"Oh, my God!" Agnes gasps.

She must see what I do. I don't check as I beat feet across the lot, moving quicker than my hip and bum knee allow on normal occasions. Rounding what I now know is a Hyundai Elantra, I freeze. The pitter-patter of small feet on damp leaves ceases a few seconds behind me.

"Dear Lord!" Agnes breathes beside me. "Who would do such a thing?"

To avoid startling the poor girl, I approach slowly and crouch down. Her brown face is so swollen that even if I knew the gal, I couldn't tell. Blood, some dry, some wet, is all over her face and caked in her long, wavy, disheveled hair. Eyes hide behind two bloated purple lids. One hoop earring appears to have been torn from her ear. She's no bigger than a minute. Welts and bruises mar every visible inch of her. I'm afraid that if I touch her, she'll break, but I can't see the rise and fall of her chest. Given how cool these autumn nights have gotten, or how long she's been out here, she could be suffering hypothermia.

"Don't, Walt," Agnes cautions. "Not her wrists. See her arms? Dear God."

Unfortunately, I do. They're both sprawled at odd angles. Broken.

"Should I put her shoes on?"

That brings me up short. I gaze around the immediate area. A pair of tall black boots lay on each side of the woman's body.

"No," I say. "I think we should avoid touching her too much. I gotta take her pulse though. Can't tell if she's breathing."

"Preserve her modesty a bit," Agnes says, "pull her dress down."

Uh… I don't know. "Can't tamper with too much evidence. Do fingerprints stay on clothes?"

Agnes clucks her tongue. Rustling sounds above my head. "I'll take a picture. We can show 'em how we found her. They'll understand."

A flash goes off behind me. Illuminates the scene. My stomach rebels. It's more gruesome in the harsh mobile phone lighting.

"Please. Please. Help."

"Call 9-1-1!" I bark unthinking at that hoarse plea. "Help's comin', sweetheart. Just hold on." Aiming to comfort her as best I can, I gingerly stroke her forehead.

Her head nods ever so slightly. Then slumps to the side on her shoulders. She's unconscious.

Indistinct chatter comes from behind me. Agnes must not have taken offense to my yelling this time.

"They're on the way," she says, confirming my thoughts. "What's that?"

"What?"

"Up there. Next to her left hand. Are those cords?"

Hadn't noticed. Squinting, I lean over the young woman's motionless body, careful of her injuries. She'll yowl something fierce if I touch her skin or broken arms.

"What in the world?" I say to myself.

Touching those definitely constitutes tampering with evidence.

"What?" Agnes asks, reminding me I'm not alone.

Two words befuddle me. The items confuse me with their presence. "Battery cables."

Chapter Twelve

*A*mina Raichand

An intermittent electronic whir nips at my consciousness. It's the umpteenth time it's interrupted an otherwise peaceful, dreamless sleep. Weeks. Days. Hours. Not sure how often it occurs. I've ignored it every other time, able to find sleep again with ease. This time, though, my eyelids flutter at the vise-grip squeeze on my biceps. Tingles shoot through the bottom half of my arm and down to my fingertips. It smells weird. My nose wrinkles at the scent of...

Nothing.

Cold. Not that there's a particular scent to cold, but if there were, this would be it. As if someone scrubbed the presence of everything away. Its absence. No lingering identifiers to hint at life. Living. Lavender plug-ins and air fresheners are always on deck in my apartment. Sterile. I perform what I hope is an imperceptible wiggle, ooh, my back. That hurts. Whatever mattress this is, it doesn't have the same firm memory foam I'm used to at home.

Scraping comes from somewhere beside me. On the same side, the squeezing is on, on the right. It's a chair against vinyl tile.

"You're awake. How ya feelin'?" a soft, unfamiliar feminine voice asks from beside me.

My eyes snap open. Where the heck am I?

I jerk my arm, or try to jerk my arm, but I'm attached, connected to all sorts of wires attached to sensors stuck to my body, I discover as my gaze travels up, up, up, and to the side. A vital sign monitor. Heart rate. Oxygen saturation. Blood pressure. Now, I know what the buzzing and squeezing was all about. There's a blood pressure cuff on my right arm. And it's noisy here. How didn't I notice the incessant beeping? The pulse oximeter is on my right finger. An IV is taped into the crook of my right arm, as well. Wow! They loaded up my right arm, didn't they? Trying to move my left arm answers that mystery.

It's broken. Plaster extends from my hand to below my bicep. Stiff covers and a thin top sheet are draped over my body. I flip them back. Ooh... No wonder I felt pinned down. My right leg is broken. Toes peek out of the top, and the cast ends just below my thigh. Aware of the IV and countless other things attached to me, I reach out and tug the metal pole the monitor is on a bit closer. Pain streaks down my armpit to my ribcage.

Ooh...

Patting my side reveals another treat. My ribs are taped. Meaning they are cracked or broken, I assume. Fun. What happened to—?

"You don't look so good. Are you alright?" The woman beside me asks again.

Consumed as I've been with my self-inventory, I forgot she was here. It would be a comfort, but I have no idea who she is. Since she's sitting, I can't tell how tall she is, but she's slender. Black horn-rimmed glasses accentuate beautiful hazel eyes with brown, green, and even gold closer to her pupil and bronze around the outer edges. Long brunette hair with long layers frames her round face. She wears a black business-professional A-line skirt and an orange silk blouse. Stockings and black pumps finish the look. The tablet she holds in her lap screams official. Yeah, I don't know her.

"Umm…" I clear my throat. Or try. It's like I licked sandpaper. "Kinda stiff," I answer. Moving my one good arm and leg, I amend my assessment. "And sore. A little loopy too."

Nameless Barbie nods. Everything about her staid expression says caring and understanding, which would ease my anxiety if I knew who the heck she was. Clutching her tablet to her chest with one manicured hand, she reaches towards me. Hand making slight contact with the bed, as if that somehow provides me comfort. "You've been through a lot. I can only imagine how you're feeling right now. You've been out off and on for over a week. Do you remember what happened?"

As if the question were a valve release, memories, ugly memories slam unbidden through my mind, one after the other. Petty's. Parking lot. Park off the beaten path. Justin. My chest caves as if I were kicked.

"Ms. Raichand, would you like me to call your nurse?"

My eyes narrow without my conscious thought. "Do I know you? How do you know my name?"

The woman's answering smile is apologetic. "Oh! Sorry," she says, extending her hand again. "My name is Megan Safford. I was informed of your situation and asked to visit with you. I hope that's alright. I'm the hospital Social Worker."

I accept her handshake awkwardly with the unencumbered fingers of my right hand. "Why are you here?"

"Like I said, in situations like this, I get sent to speak to patients," Megan says.

I must have missed it when she said it before. Possible. When she inquired about my memory, I was inundated with images and freaking out. She could have said she was Miss Piggy, and I wouldn't have heard. Being in the hospital isn't smart. I have to get out of here. Playing dumb is my best bet. For all Innocent Treasures's flaws, adequate insurance coverage isn't one of them. They provide their employees with excellent medical, dental, and vision insurance. I'll give her my medical card and get discharged. Everything else can be worked out. It's legal to get an Uber home from the hospital, right? The less information I can give, the better. How did I get here? Something Megan said replays in my mind.

"Situations like what?" I ask, watch her for telltale signs of deception.

Megan shifts back in her seat and adjusts her glasses. "Fragile situations," she says as if that explains something to me. "It's important to get as much information as we can while your memory is fresh."

Pretending to appease her, I nod in understanding. But what I understand is that I'm not saying a darn thing. If there's one lesson I've learned in life, it's street code. Yes, I'd prefer Justin to be hanged for what he did. However, I know what happens to informants once it gets out that they ratted on someone. I want no part of those consequences.

Megan glances at the screen of her tablet. "You said the young man's name is Justin Beale. Correct?"

"What?!" My eyes bulge, and my mouth falls open. Didn't she say I'd been out for over a week? When did I—? Where the heck did she—? I can't think. "When did I say that?" I ask, grabbing onto one thought.

"During one of the few lucid moments you had," Megan answers. "You were in pain. Confused. Many of your injuries have healed, but they were quite severe when you were brought in. You stated that he's in your Sociology class?"

My answering nod is stiff.

Dang! Wasn't I a chatty Kathy?

How could I have said all of that without any recollection of it? Their believing me is ridiculous. This falls outside the scope of a social worker's job description. It's what I'm receiving my degree in, although I'm not that far along. Random rantings of a patient seem more like the doctor's job. My chest hurts. This couldn't be going more wrong.

A plump middle-aged man in olive-green slacks and a white button-up shirt that is holding on for dear life to stay buttoned, pushes the door behind Megan open. He saunters in like he can't be bothered to pick up the pace. The drag of his much-abused brown loafers on the hospital floor accompanies each of his steps. The shield clipped to his belt identifies him as a law-enforcement officer. Even if it didn't, his thinning sandy brown hair, dull brown eyes, and ' 70s-porn-star-thick mustache scream "cast me in your next crime drama".

Megan glances over her shoulder at him.

"Ms. Raichand, good to see you awake finally," he greets in a gruff voice.

Sheesh! He even speaks in a lackadaisical manner. They say it takes more muscles to frown than smile, but they never met this guy. His lined face doesn't appear to have ever smiled. Its creases must be from scowling.

"Amina, this is Detective Pilcher," Megan introduces. She conducts the pleasantry since the man doesn't seem to feel the need to introduce himself. Or she notices the glare I send his way. "He's working your case. Trying to catch the man who did this."

Detective Pilcher walks around to the foot of my bed. "Speaking of apprehending the man. We scraped your fingernails. Took samples from your clothes. Ran the results of your rape kit against the DNA in our system. There's no match."

An involuntary gasp slips from between my parted lips. My eyes either cross or my vision blurs. What I know is that the word used to describe my assault triggers a visceral response. The word applies. I know it does. It is a logical description of the events, but it also makes me feel vulnerable. Victimhood doesn't sit well with me. Once I survived my childhood trauma, trauma inflicted on me at the hands of so many people, I vowed never to be anyone's victim again. I avoided entanglements when what I wanted and craved was love because I refused to give anyone else power over me. I feared it on a profound level, and here I lie. In a hospital bed. Someone's victim. Wetness slides down my cheek.

"Detective, can this wait till later?" Megan asks. "Amina's just woken up."

When did we get on a first-name basis?

Detective Pilcher grimaces. "No. I can't. The more details we get now, the better our chances of finding him. We've already lost nearly two weeks."

"Does no match mean he gets away with it?" I ask because I have to know.

The way he said it before sounds like that was the issue. If Justin gets away after I've said this much, and he finds out I said this much...

"It's more complicated than that. Justin Beale doesn't exist. Best I can guess is he was using an alias," Detective Pilcher says, like he's relating just the facts and only the facts. I guess police detectives don't need to worry about bedside manners the way doctors do. Good to know. "All his info was false."

I'm not prone to hysterics. Whenever women break down at the slightest hint of unease in movies, I cringe. I'm like, all right, pull yourself together. Figure your stuff out! But today, tingles wash across my eyelids and a distinct prick hits the inside corner of my eyes. Water springs to life, brimming in my waterline, like it was waiting for a moment like this. A WTF, head-spinning moment.

"He has a scholarship," I inform the pudgy detective that I can't imagine doing any actual "leg work," so it's highly likely he didn't truly check.

Detective Pilcher reaches into his back pocket and retrieves a smartphone. He taps the screen a few times. "Didn't exist. His tuition was paid in cash. Records falsified. With the right tech-savviness, anything can be forged these days," he says again, matter-of-fact, as if he's spit-balling ideas with a colleague and not talking to the victim of a *violent crime*.

And I'm not even going to think the R-word because that's irreconcilable to my already conflicted mind.

"It's as if he never existed," he continues, still swiping at his phone's screen, not looking at Megan or me. "This is why, in the wrong hands, technology is dangerous. Only your professor described him. The elderly couple who found you saw no one but you. They didn't even see you get dumped."

Because you're garbage. And garbage gets dumped. Like you, who is garbage. My mind conjures the unsaid preferential ending to his statement, given his tone. Only a modicum of professionalism seems to keep him from expressing the thoughts written across his nonplussed face.

The tectonic plates that are my bones and muscles shift, causing my own personal earthquake. I'm not cold per se, but my body shakes. Tears, barely held in check, spill. They drench my cheeks, chin, and the front of my borrowed hospital gown. A lesser part of my brain realizes the irrational response. Ish happens after all, I learned that lesson well before that night nearly two weeks ago, and today, but my body reacts against my wishes, as if this were the first time life proved just how unfair it can be. My nose runs. I don't bother with a tissue. My mind reels.

"You're never gonna find him," I surmise aloud, astonished.

How could they? If Justin possesses enough intelligence to forge transcripts and whatever other records to enroll in college, he's smart enough to evade police capture. As they say, when someone is caught for a heinous crime, it isn't the first time he's committed one; it is just the first time he got caught. Or close to being caught in this situation. I've never given much thought to what it takes to get a fake ID or procure illegal documents, but I imagine if it can be done once, it can be done twice. Three times. Four times. However, many times they needed to live life on the lam as Justin—or what's his name—needed. And if he's never caught...

"He's coming back for me," I choke out.

If I hadn't been so chatty in my there-but-not-quite-there moments and knew what I know now, I wouldn't have given such a detailed accounting of the events before, or even during...what happened. My mind stumbles over the memory. It won't allow me to focus too hard on the actual assault. Still, even through its active refusal to recount the experience, snapshots of park benches, perfect masculine features, blond hair, and pain shoot across my mind unbidden. Like the stars we watched. An innocent, sweet hobby morphed into my nightmare. Mental drawers where past traumas, abandonment issues, sadness, anger I'm not permitted to express, and other unpleasantness are stored, which allows me to be the "yes, ma'am," easygoing woman I'm known for rattle. Ugly things ooze around the cracks, clouding my over-medicated brain. There's too much. This is too much. There's nowhere to smash this situation.

Snitches get stitches.

Justin is Dexter-levels of creepy and adept. He'll know I went to the police, or more correctly, know the police came to me. He's obviously a pro at covering his tracks and quite a go-getter. He will get me. I'm a loose end. An unintended loose end? Who knows? I don't want to find out, but now he knows I'm vulnerable. He's untraceable. Justin is free to find and silence me so he can continue whatever it is he does.

"I want to meet a pwince," Kaylee's little voice filters through my mind.

Me too. At least I'd hoped to someday. My solitary life might not be anything to write home about, but it's my life. It's a life. One on the cusp of being snuffed out once Justin—*What's His Name*—discovers my whereabouts. Which hospital is this? The park hadn't been that far from Petty's or Hillard Brand Community College. I search around the bed with my eyes. My arms are useless thanks to the IV in the crook of my right arm, the pulse oximeter on my right pointer finger, and the blood pressure cuff attached to that arm's wimpy bicep. Megan and Detective

Pilcher are having a conversation, but I'm far from following it, only vaguely aware of it in the back of my mind. Did Justin go through my purse? Find my address and other personal information? I do another scan of my surroundings. My cell phone? It's password-protected, but this guy knows his way around electronics.

"Ms. Raichand?"

Usually, personal effects are placed in those clear drawstring "Belongings" bags. No such thing is here as far as I can tell. My car. Is it still in Petty's parking lot? It's warm in here.

"Ms. Raichand," a distant, delicate voice calls. Or the ringing in my ears only makes the voice sound farther away.

Too warm. Hot. Had Justin gotten into my car somehow and found discarded mail with my address? If he didn't strike here, what's going to happen once I'm released? Weight presses into my mid-section, then disappears.

"He's coming for me." I feel the words vibrate my vocal cords, but I don't know if the sound passes my numb lips.

"Yes, nurses' station. What do ya need, hon?" An unfamiliar feminine voice with a Southern accent asks. Again, it's caught with only a fraction of my focus.

The room spins. Or is it the bed? Walls, once stoic, unassuming sentinels, whirl. Yep, the room is spinning. My head is too heavy for my neck to support.

"Ms. Raichand is going to need something to calm down, please. Maybe Ativan," Megan says over the ringing and upbeat circus-esque blues.

"Her nurse'll be right in."

Seconds. Minutes. Possibly hours pass, and dinging comes from somewhere behind me. My personal earthquake intensifies.

Penny whistles and a bassoon layer the circus blues. Music?

♪ *"...Really, I'm sad, oh, I'm sadder than sad..."*

"I'm gonna have to ask you to leave, Detective," drawls the unfamiliar Southern voice.

Oxygen must be in short supply here. It's hard to breathe. Fluorescent lights flare brightly. Too bright. Do hospital rooms have dimmer switches? This one's broken. My eyes squint of their own volition. No! More vulnerability. This is Justin's plan. Blinding me. Whatever *it* is, I won't see it coming.

♪ *"Like a clown, I appear to be glad (sad, sad, sad...)."*

"Sorry, Meg, you too," a Southern accent orders. "Hon, you in there? Can you describe how you're feelin'?"

"I'll be around later," Detective Pilcher says.

Tugging on the IV in my right arm, but like the voices—and singing? A male singing in falsetto?—The sting is dull. Faint.

♪ *"...they're some sad things known to man..."*

"Amina?"

♪ *"...But ain't too much sadder than..."*

"Amina! Can you hear me?"

♪ *"...The tears of a clown...when there's no one around..."*

AFTER

Chapter Thirteen

G *arrett Kaplan*

    In the corner of the large, carpeted basement, on an oak tripod easel stand sits a whiteboard. The words "WELCOME TO GREENER PASTURES SUPPORT GROUP" are written in elegant script across its surface.

A hodgepodge of individuals occupies thirteen black metal folding chairs with padded seats. Various degrees of distress mangle each person's features. It's as if the zombie apocalypse interrupted everyone at various stages of life. They're like the Village People without the stereotypes, cultural insensitivities, and flamboyant undertones. There's a lean cowboy with boots, stonewashed Wrangler jeans, and a brown Stetson included. A long, white butcher's coat and black striped bib apron fit snug on a pudgy, bald man in navy trousers and boots that scream comfort and non-slip. An older grandmother-type woman in an obvious wig full of red curls wears a floral housecoat and knock-off fuzzy grey Ugg booties.

A young kid wears royal blue and black Nike basketball shorts and a large white hoodie. Maybe describing the guy as a kid is unfair, but he looks younger than my thirty-five years. Anyway, he's a smooth, dark-skinned, black man. He's tall if the way his long legs intrude halfway into the circle of chairs is anything to go on. His black, royal blue, and white Jordans with the blue Jumpman logo on the soles are bigger than my size fourteen. Now, I'm considered tall at six-three, but this kid could dwarf me if he were standing. It's like he didn't get the memo; it's the middle of June. His fingers lace behind his afro as if he owns the world, or the room. The twenty-something blonde woman to his left and the brunette dressed in Army fatigues to the right are close to being brained by his elbows due to his wingspan.

No matter how often I do this, I hate it. Multiple pairs of expectant, unfamiliar eyes watch me. Damn, Mrs. McQueen's emergency for keeping her from facilitating St. Augustine's weekly meeting. St. Vincent's is forty-five minutes out of my way, and even though these things have the whole confidentiality situation on lock, confessing my inner demons to strangers isn't my forte. Their direct eye contact unnerves me. Well, direct except for one set of eyes. A nondescript, deep-brown-skinned woman diagonal from me refuses to meet anyone's gaze. The hood of her lavender sweat suit zip-up hoodie covers her entire head. Drawstrings pull so tight the cloth pinches her makeup-free face. I can't see her hair, so her straight nose with its wider tip, heart-shaped lips, big heavily-lashed upturned honey eyes with green flecks, and high cheekbones are all I have to go on to determine sex. She curls in her chair as if she's trying to become one with it.

A throat clears, and I remember I'm just standing here staring.

"Hi, my name is Garrett. I'm not a survivor, but my best friend," I say, all business, "was raped and murdered three years ago. I've suffered from nightmares ever since that night."

Several gasps from fellow victims and survivors greet my admission. After so long, the basic details don't affect me. Sometimes the experience seems so removed it's like the memories are clips of a movie that happened to someone else. Then, times like today, the anniversary, the details are in technicolor, more real than the present.

Lost in the past, I force myself to continue. "I was supposed to meet her. Lisa insisted that when we were both single, we'd meet for dinner and a movie or some other outing to combat loneliness—her words, not mine. Lisa was something else." My head shakes at the many memories. "No one said no to her for long. Plus, dating apps weren't either of our things. So, going out was our way of putting ourselves out there—again, her words, not mine. Being single never bothered me, but it did her, which was weird."

"How's that? Two young people out together enjoying a meal? Especially, a nice guy and a gal? Wouldn't everyone think you were an item?" A stout man with grey hair, jowls, and a weathered face sitting beside me, asks.

"Your curiosity is appreciated, Ben, but Garrett is sharing," Patricia, the light-skinned, middle-aged black woman sitting at the top of the circle, who'd introduced herself when I first arrived, reproaches gently. "In an effort to keep from triggering others or asking someone to share more than they're comfortable with, we don't ask questions."

"Don't worry about it." I brush off her concern with a chuckle and faux nonchalance. Truth be told, the support group is triggering. No amount of questions will make the feeling worse, but the healing and logic behind sharing and hearing others' stories are not lost on me. "Yeah, umm...I thought the same thing. We worked out a system to make it clear that we weren't together. Lisa would even talk loudly about how single she was whenever she saw someone checking her out. There were times she'd mash my face with her hand and be, like, '*eww...*' to drive the point home." I pantomime Lisa's abject disgust and gesture.

"Anyway, I was running late the night it happened. So, we agreed to meet at one of those huge outdoor mall movie theaters a few cities away. It was the only theater with late showtimes. It's crazy, the things you remember. I don't know what movie we were gonna see or what caused me to be late. What I remember is pulling into the almost empty parking lot. The theater times Lisa found must have been old or off since the entire mall was closed. With all the exterior lights, the lot wasn't that dark. Even still, a parking lot light pole stood over her candy apple red Mustang. Lit it like a spotlight guiding me, beckoning me." A knot clogs my throat.

I swallow hard several times, attempting to get through this, needing to get through this. Lisa can't tell her story, so the least I can do is lend my voice to her. It's why I do this, why I rush through traffic to attend these meetings as often as my schedule allows.

I cinch my steel grey slacks above the knee and sit without a word or glance at the pity I know is present in the eyes of my audience; however, something calls my attention to Ms. Velour-Sweat-suit-In-Summer. She isn't looking at me. Hasn't looked at anyone the entire time we've been sharing. Anger spikes inside me. Making matters worse, she chooses this moment to pull her sneakered feet onto the chair with her. Damn! She's petite. Has to be short to accomplish such a task.

"We have about... Five more minutes," Patricia says, gazing around the circle. "Would anyone else like to share?"

Wrapping her arms around her upraised legs, she rests her chin on her knees, oblivious to the fact that everyone can see and feel her callous disinterest. Or, maybe she knows and doesn't care. This is probably part of her community service or something. Mommy and Daddy bought their princess' way out of punishment for a crime. She looks like the type to have driven drunk and killed someone. Stuck-up rich girl is too good for jail. Everything about her pisses me off. She's making a mockery of these people's pain, of my torment.

Ben, the older man beside me, pats me on the back, breaking me out of the glare I hadn't realized until now that I'd been giving the woman across from me. Blinking away my irritation, I look up at him and offer a tight smile. I pat his large liver-spotted hand in return.

He clears his throat and stands. "I'm Ben." Ben pauses as if waiting for us to return his greeting in unison, like one of those television support groups. "My wife, Jackie. Boy, she was something to look at in her day. A beautiful gal, wouldn't hurt a fly. Well, some jackass took her years ago. I hadn't wanted her to. We'd agreed she wouldn't work outside the house. Especially after the babies. It was my responsibility to be workin' and providin'. Hers was lookin' pretty, convincing me to buy things we ought not—lettin' me spoil her—and rearin' our little ones. My daddy did that, and my ma stayed home with us. It's the way it should be. But, we were gettin' behind on bills." Ben stops and runs his thumbs through his black suspenders. He needs a minute to collect himself. He takes a deep breath, then blows a raspberry. "Waitin' tables was an easy way to make ends meet, just for a bit. We agreed. Just a month or so. In that time, that's when the fella must've saw her. S'ppose he'd had an eye on her for a while and was mighty frustrated I always picked her up. Then she worked an odd shift for a friend. Her parents watched the kids. I was still at work when she got off, so she decided to ride the bus. That's when he got her. Bastard attacked her in broad daylight. Raped her. If I'd been a better man, that never would've happened. All these years later, when she's quiet. Sittin'. A haunted look creeps into her eyes, and I know I did that. I failed her." Clearing his throat again, he retakes his seat.

Tears blur my vision, but blinking holds them at bay. A glance at everyone else shows they're in a similar state, except Velour-Sweatsuit. She's unmoved. I'm enraged. My skin tightens, and heat suffuses the back of my neck. Ears. My face is on fire. This woman is cold. Even if she doesn't want to be here, how can she not acknowledge what this man feels, the metaphorical vein he sliced open in front of her? Is sympathy beneath her? Is her life so privileged that another's emotions have never touched her? If I were a different man or at a different, more impulsive time in life, I'd confront her right here, right now.

Ben sniffles. I clutch his wrinkled hand in comfort and fix my scowl on the sociopathic woman.

Chapter Fourteen

*A*mina Raichand

"Thank you, everyone, who shared," Patricia says, standing. "It looks like our time is up. Please, throw your trash out on your way out. I'm here for a few minutes afterward for anyone who may need to talk," she offers all in attendance, but her chocolate eyes stare dead at me. "See you all next week."

Everyone stands, grabbing whatever discarded items they'd placed on the floor beside their chairs. I breathe a sigh of relief, grateful to be done. Finally!

Six months of meetings—groups—didn't make me enjoy them any more than I told those... *People!* I would.

They don't help. Nothing helps. My stomach knots, and my skin crawls at the very idea of preparing to attend each week because I'm forced to come here, forced to relive the horror of that night here. It plays on a loop in my head, filling me with dread. The memory grips my entire being, my soul. All thanks to me. People are drama. I knew people were drama. They excel at it.

Life will be going along. Monotonous, but going. Then some un-foreseen element waltzes in and destroys my carefully constructed illu-sion of peace. Justin Beale wasn't welcome. In my gut, I knew something was off. A twinge of unease would slither up my spine and coil in my belly whenever he texted or called. Spidey senses tingled in the base of my skull. He wasn't quite right, yet I bought what he sold. So, I invited that man into my world out of boredom. Loneliness. The desire to interact. To be noticed. Human interaction, the ultimate drug, drew me in, and like a moth to the flame, I flew into my demise, eyes wide open.

I'm the architect of my own personal hell, undeserving of the sym-pathy these attendees are owed. They're owed much more, but at a minimum, they deserve sympathy, dignity. No matter whether they were perpetrated on or impacted by the blowback. They didn't deserve it. I did. I courted disaster. Accepting that partnership sealed my fate.

Looking them in the eye, pretending to be one of them, is a disgrace, disrespectful. So, I keep my head down and mouth shut to honor their pain. I count the minutes until I'm free. I don't want to be here. Don't want to be at home...or wherever it is.

Nothing feels right, and no one's listening! It's gone on for so long that I don't waste my breath trying to convince them anymore. Funny, I used to be so lonely. Now, all I want is to be left alone. I miss the kids. My apartment. My stuff. Not much was there, but all of it was mine. Ignoring my intuition in favor of someone else's comfort bites me in the ass once again. People pleasing got me into this situation, condemned me to this punishment. The people here deserve absolution of their guilt. Their shame. They didn't deserve the atrocities visited upon them. I did.

Coming here does nothing for me, but I pray there's something in it for them, which is all I can give them. My prayers. Also, space to exit before me. As the last person exits, I stand to make my escape.

"Amina?!" Patricia calls after me.

Dang it!

Turning around, I face the beautiful light-skinned Black woman. She wears a smart, tailored plum pantsuit and designer red-bottom stilettos. The definition in her natural, above-the-shoulder, brown, springy curls surrounding her striking face inspires awe. Not one wrinkle dares to mar striking features that don't suggest the slightest hint of her age; however, I know her to be in her mid to late fifties, if her preposterous claims have any validity. Straight posture, even shoulders, and a graceful, elongated neck speak of proper breeding. It's evident why she and that...woman...are close. They carry themselves with the same air of refinement, only Patricia is softer. Kindness and true concern bleed from her gentle brown eyes.

"Could I have a word with you before you go?" She motions towards a chair beside hers. "Have a seat."

"You know what'll happen if I'm late," I remind.

"Please?" she asks again. "I'll let your mom know when you're on your way." Patricia pats the seat cushion.

With a shake of my head, I roll my eyes. "So, you didn't want to talk then?" I approach the empty chair and sit.

"Amina," Patricia says, censure in her voice, pitching it lower. "Let's put a pin in that discussion. I wanted to touch base with you. How are you?"

Lifting my feet onto the chair, I hug my legs to my chest. "Fine."

Disyllabic and sarcasm. My new norm. When I can, I limit speech to as few words as possible. If I'd taken that stance before, fear wouldn't dog my every waking moment. I wouldn't be worried Justin will find me and finish what he started.

"Amina..." More censure.

"I'm fine, Pat." I glower at her from the corner of my eye. "Don't worry."

The look she casts me says my monotone answer wasn't convincing. She frowns.

"You told me your story. That is so brave of you. I'm honored by your trust," Patricia says with false gratitude. Reaching out, she lifts a slender manicured hand to rub my back.

"Don't touch me," I command, shrugging out from under her touch.

"I'm sorry," she apologizes, snatching her hand away as if afraid I'll bite it.

I might. Being touched, just the prospect of being touched in even the slightest non-threatening way, locks the breath in my lungs and seizes my muscles, triggering a visceral fight-or-flight response. The calm I prided myself on before is gone. Putting on a mask of rational civility for the world is impossible.

"I forgot, Honeycomb," Patricia continues. "Forgive me. Sweetie, you've been coming here for six months. You don't share. Don't make eye contact. You don't speak when spoken to. This group can provide emotional support. Coping strategies. It can be very beneficial to your mental health. It's an amazing resource. But, you've got to share. Obviously, I cannot, and would not, force you. I'm just saying... I can't even tell if you're listening a majority of the time. This is a safe space. Don't you want to share?"

How can she not understand? Sharing my story would only highlight how much of a fraud I am. Expose my duplicity. Pretending to be one of them when really I'm an emotional vampire.

"I'm not ready," I answer to the best of my ability. "I wouldn't be here if those people weren't demanding it."

I'm so sorry.

"What?" I ask, whipping my head from one side to the other at the whispered words.

Concern creases Patricia's plucked brows. Her stare is penetrating. "Honeycomb?" she asks. "I didn't say anything."

When you are, you'll understand.

The echoic voice whispers again. I glance at the ceiling. To the side. The ground. Where's that coming—

"You okay?" Patricia asks, studying me through narrow eyes. "Are you still taking your medication?"

My head swivels towards the well-meaning, uppity woman. I glare. "Those..." pausing, I search for the right word for my predicament, "pretenders...make me whether I want to or not every single day. Serve it to me on a saucer each morning during forced breakfast."

She exhales deeply. Eyes lift heavenward then return to me. "Hold on a second."

Rising from her chair, Patricia strolls to the back of the room where a metal desk with a faux walnut laminate top sits. She rounds it, reaches into a side drawer, and retrieves a black Birkin bag. Digging inside, she grabs a few items obscured in her hands then returns to her abandoned seat.

"Tell me what you see," she orders, offering a clear plastic vinyl picture holder to me.

Taking the six-page trifold from her, I glance at the first wallet-size picture. The picture shows signs of age around the edges. I don't remove it from its sleeve. Wrapped in a pastel blanket and a pastel-colored striped beanie, a chubby-cheeked, confused-looking, honey-eyed newborn baby girl. There's no obvious tell that it's a girl. I know it is because the baby is me.

Flipping to the next page, a picture of a toddler—maybe three years old—sits in a miniature white wicker chair. Fine curly brown hair is slicked into a ponytail, and she is wearing a frilly red dress with white lace trim, white ruffle socks, and shiny black patent leather shoes. The diamond studs in her ears are at least half a carat each. She has the same chubby cheeks, mirthful honey eyes with flecks of green, but a wide, toothy, dimpled grin is plastered across the little girl's round face.

"Keep going," Patricia encourages, reminding me of her presence. "There's more."

My heartbeat quickens at the sight of the next picture. Silk-pressed golden-brown hair hangs just below even, feminine shoulders. Delight upturns red-coated lips into an affectionate grin on a light brown-skinned face. Moderate glam makeup accentuates naturally beautiful features. She wears a designer V-neck spaghetti dress. Looking past one shoulder, she stands back-to-back with a hazelnut-skinned preteen dressed in a matching dress with alterations befitting her age. What sped my heart rate...

The preteen...

She's me.

I don't have any memory of this picture being taken. No inkling. Nothing. Although, given my age in the photograph—eleven or twelve—I should remember this day. Its worn top edges, lightly curling, where the picture's corners peek out of the plastic pocket, denote its authenticity. The picture's real, has to be. Who keeps wallets anymore? Storing images on your cell phone is much more effective. Besides, what's the benefit of falsifying twenty and thirty-year-old pictures?

Defrauding me for my millions?

Unlikely.

Chuckling under my breath, I trace the image of myself and a younger Patricia with the pad of my forefinger. This isn't a likeness. It's actually her. Me. Us. Yet...*nada*. Zero. My memory of Patricia started six months ago when that woman, Nora, introduced us. Introduced is a strong word. Standing over my hospital bed while I was still recovering, she decreed I attend the rape survivor support group run by her best friend, my "godmother". When I didn't react as expected, my "godmother" materialized in my room. Concern was etched into her sophisticated features, much as it is now. The only difference is that I know her. Now. Then, I hadn't known her, or our professed shared history, from Adam.

I still don't recall our past, but I have an affection for her. To look at her, one wouldn't believe she cares about anything but money. Her perfume permeates from her as if it were being emitted from her pores. Its overbearing scent screams expensive. Her erect posture and natural curls, artfully and intentionally wild, all show that Patricia is poised. Yet, her brown eyes that seem liquid, ever shifting, express a softness and genuine care. They make it hard not to feel cared for and, in return, make it difficult not to care for her.

"I want you to see this," Patricia instructs, offering her iPhone up to my inspection. "Many underestimate the long-reaching effects trauma has on the psyche. They manifest in several ways. Your mind is so miraculous that it's built a barrier between those overwhelming emotions and your conscious mind. It's shielded you from the unpleasantness of the experience, and with that, it's somehow muddled some of your memories. Those memories will return in time, though. Until then, look at this."

Glancing at her phone screen, my breath catches. She does keep pictures on her phone. In this picture, Patricia doesn't look much different from how she appears today. Her hair is in a slick, elegant bun, making her high cheekbones seem even sharper than usual. Her lips spread into a closed-mouthed, composed grin, as if showing teeth would be indecorous. A stylish charcoal-grey herringbone wool-blend three-button midi skirt suit is tailored to flatter her slender frame. One arm hooks through a petite, darker brown arm propped on a jeans-covered hip. My jeans covered hip. The fact I'm wearing jeans isn't the only surprise. It is disturbing, though, because...I do not wear jeans. Leggings? Yes. Cotton? Spandex? Sweats? Velour? Yes, to all. But jeans? Heck, no!

Years ago, I watched some dumb documentary about how women weren't meant to wear jeans. It was stupid then and now, but it's a challenge I undertook. I stopped wearing jeans and sold all three pairs I owned. I haven't worn jeans since.

"When was this taken?" I ask in a voice barely above a whisper.

Patricia swipes her screen, keeping it from going dark. "I can't— I thought you'd— It'll come back. In due time, it'll all return. Sorry, Honeycomb. This," she says, gazing at the picture with an unreadable emotion, "was last April. That science fiction show you love."

Brown eyes peer into mine. Implore. Probe for something. What? I don't know. The brief frown that downturns Patricia's red lips denotes I should know or that I've failed to meet expectations. She recovers quickly.

"Uh... Every year," she pauses, clearing her throat, "since you were ten or so, we've gone. Goddaughter god-mommy quality time." Patricia titters. "Our deal...? I'd go to your comic convention with you, walk around to different stalls looking at merchandise, and go to panels for your favorite television shows. In exchange, you visit the theater with me to see a play of my choosing. Whether after or before, you allow me to maintain your refined palate by taking you to one of my bougie restaurants."

I chuckle at how the word sounds foreign in her hoity-toity Mid-Atlantic accent. Bougie is a term I use. She qualifies as bougie. As with most things lately, I don't remember calling her that. No matter what I think, I don't usually judge people or name-call.

"Comics? Are you sure?" This doesn't make sense. I assume Comic-Con is what Patricia is referring to, but I've never been. Between my work schedule and ticket prices, I wouldn't even allow myself to hope I could go. "What TV show is my favorite?" I ask, and I'm genuinely curious.

"Oh, no, you don't," Patricia says, cackling. For the first time since our first meeting, her smile is sincere, not the ever-prevalent pity. Her laughter is light, joyous. "Fool me once, shame on you. Fool me twice, shame on me, young lady. I'm not falling for that again."

I scowl. Half a year ago, cheeky evasiveness would've provided the levity it was intended to. Now, I want to throw her phone out the window. This isn't helping me piece together my whereabouts for last April. One thing I know for sure is I wasn't in Indianapolis and darn sure not at Comic-Con. What is going on?

"May I?" I ask, inclining my head towards her phone.

She looks at her device, then casts a curious gaze at me before handing me her phone.

Once again, I examine the picture—the woman wears a long-sleeved black mesh shirt with a black tube top underneath. Her hair is in a half ponytail, half down do. Upon closer inspection, the jeans aren't just any jeans. They're Dolce & Gabbana high-waisted, indigo blue, skinny cut, and running from thigh to ankle on each outside leg is floral lace detailing. Beige patent leather Christian Louboutin pumps. If I were a betting woman, I'd bet the entire outfit cost over three grand, and that's not including the silver hoops and other jewelry. No way on God's green Earth could I afford those clothes, and not live in a cardboard box, on my barely-above-minimum wage income working at the shelter.

I'm no slouch in the makeup department, but I'm no makeup artist either. In this picture, my makeup is flawless, expertly applied yet natural. And I have lash extensions. Only in my dreams could I afford them, and maybe not even then. The price for such a service is astronomical. Unabashed happiness, as my smile displays in this picture, is incomprehensible. If I used drugs, I'd swear I was high. That's the only explanation my mind conjures, and if I weren't painfully self-aware, I wouldn't dismiss it. However, knowing myself as I do, and seeing my clear honey eyes, further disabuses me of the notion.

Decorating my apartment with expensive furniture took years. Mini sacrifices were made over long periods—Not extravagances like the clothes in this picture. Like the clothes I'm wearing? I would never. These aren't mine. Those aren't mine. I don't know where *my* clothes are.

Patricia removes the phone from my grasp. Concern is again prominent in her soft, angular, arched, and furrowed brows. Her lips are set in a firm line, and her brown eyes watch me with caution.

"It will come back," Patricia repeats in a soft voice. "The human mind is strong and fragile all at once, with immense defense mechanisms. It did what was necessary and needs a little time to reboot. There's no predetermined timeframe for the grieving process or how it manifests. You are an intelligent, incredibly brave woman. You will get through this." She reaches as if to clutch my hand in a comforting gesture but wisely retracts it. She pats the back of the chair I'm sitting in. "I'll be here with you every step of the way. Your memory will work itself out. And if you get uncomfortable, agitated, confused... Whatever the emotion, you can talk to me if you can't talk to your parents. Even if you talk to them, you can talk to—"

"They are not my parents," I interrupt, glowering.

Her shoulders slump infinitesimally, then straighten to their perfect posture. Patricia flips to another page of her six-page trifold. She hands me two plastic sleeves folded like an open book.

"You recognize this adorable chocolate drop with pigtails, don't you?" she asks, expectation obvious in her tone.

I nod. Of course, I recognize myself no matter my age.

"And this beautiful, Black woman?" Patricia asks, knowing the answer without having to ask.

The woman is younger, with skin a shade or two darker than mine and eyes the color of a top-shelf bourbon. Her dark brown hair is in an elegant chignon. Like Patricia, the woman's posture is stiff, suggesting proper breeding. This woman has the art of the smize down to a science.

Lips curve up the barest amount, and her eyes squint to the slightest, alluring degree. No denying it, the woman is breathtaking.

My nod is slow in coming. Defiant.

Her answering grin is smug. "What about the man? Hard to believe he used to be considered a lady killer, huh? Even with the glasses, surprisingly. A few shades lighter and he'd be the spitting image of that Bollywood actor, Amitabh Bachchan, in his slightly younger years, or a taller Shah Rukh Khan. Mm-hmm... Ladies loved the look of him."

I roll my eyes. The way her voice goes all airy... Sounds like she liked the look of him a little too much. She speaks with an endearment I assume is supposed to be comforting, or maybe to increase relatability. Whatever effect she hopes to have is lost on me. I feel nothing for the cultured, debonair young Indian man with short, slicked black hair and thick, black-rimmed glasses over amber eyes. My alleged "father". There's significantly less grey hair around his temples and in his beard, but it's the man I awoke to in my hospital room six months ago, with a younger, less severe version of the woman.

Gilbert and Nora Raichand.

The little girl in the picture is me at four years old, another family picture I don't recall. Given the age of the photo paper, it's not photoshopped and hasn't been altered. Just like the picture of Nora holding a swaddled baby—me—in her arms after giving birth in the neighboring plastic sleeve.

My head hurts.

Wish there was a way.

Patricia didn't say that. Her mouth didn't move. Glancing over my shoulder, stabbing pain lances through my skull and streaks behind my right eye.

"Honeycomb?" Patricia says, worry making her statement sound more like a question. "Are you okay?"

No.

But I can't admit it. Acknowledging it makes the whispers real. It encourages people to want to talk. All these strangers in this strange place. Nothing is familiar. I can't take it.

Pain slices through the top of my head.

I'm so sorry.

"We done here?" I ask, whipping my head towards Patricia. Her eyes widen at my sudden move. "My," I hesitate to continue, "parents are expecting me. They time my comings and goings to the minute."

Patricia stands. So do I.

"I'll call them. See ya next week?" she inquires as if I have an option. I don't respond since we both know the answer. "Please, consider sharing, okay? If it won't help, it can't hurt."

Chapter Fifteen

*G*arrett Kaplan

Thirty-fuckin'-minutes. I slide my phone into the back pocket of my slacks. For the umpteenth time, I chastise myself for standing out here, leaning against the grey brick building just outside the entrance to the church sanctuary. Cement cools my flesh through the fabric of my shirt. I'm waiting for her. Velour Sweatsuit.

Something compels me to confront her. At first, I figured my irritation would simmer. The longer I stood, watching each support group member leave, the more it definitely ratcheted up. The evening, brisker than I'd expect for a summer night, further increases my ire. Stars litter the dark sky. My wrath is irrational. It's not like I'll ever see this woman again. This isn't my usual meeting location. Plus, lately, I've missed more meetings than I attend, causing my outrage to spike because missing a meeting feels too much like betraying Lisa. Again. Forgetting her, like I'm betraying her memory. If agitation weren't riding me so hard, I'd appreciate the beauty of such a starry evening. Another glance at my cell phone brings indignation hurtling to the surface with a vengeance.

What the fuck is taking her so long? Leave voyeur! Emotional vampire. Your food source is gone. Maybe there are some transients or other people down on their luck, she can syphon misery from. Stepping away from the wall, I pace down the sidewalk.

A door creaks.

I don't need to see it to know it's the heavy, oak door at the back of the church. It leads to the parking lot. I should have considered that. Of course, she chooses the exit furthest from where I wait.

Coward's way out.

The clomp of my loafer's striking pavement interrupts the quiet night and reminds me of Lisa complaining about how heavy-footed I am. There's no time for self-consciousness now. If I don't hustle, she'll get away. That outcome is unacceptable to my—

Not many cars remain in the lot. My metallic, obsidian black Mercedes SUV and a luxury, blue, full-size sedan. If I were to venture a guess, I'd say it looks like a BMW. Near the front of the parking lot, as close as possible to the cathedral without people parked in the yard, sits a white mid-size Subaru. The substantial spacing between the vehicles indicates how packed the lot was earlier.

I round the corner, but she doesn't see me. Yet. She walks at such a fast clip that she might as well be running. Green sparkles flicker in and out around her, wrapping her in an ethereal heavenly glow, making her look mysterious. If I were being logical, I'd acknowledge the glimmer as fireflies. Witnessing how her velour sweatpants cup her ass, rationale eludes me and redistributes some of the heat from my anger.

I'm a red-blooded, heterosexual man who appreciates the female form and more than appreciates hers. As suspected, she's short, but her legs are long. The sweatsuit isn't frumpy; it's one of those designer form-fitted ones that make it appear as if the fabric were painted on her slight frame.

I almost trip over my feet watching her figure instead of planning our confrontation. Her hood is still snug on her head. She could be bald. Not that a bald woman couldn't be attractive. Some pull off the look beautifully.

But not only should I not care about attraction...

She could be bald.

Every couple of steps, she checks over one of her shoulders then the other. Her hand dives inside her purse. Searching. For what, I don't know, and neither does she seem to. She doesn't pay attention to what she's doing. Her entire focus is on scanning her immediate area. It's a shock *she* doesn't trip. Something about the way she moves is haunted. She's frightened. Watching her evident fear gives me a moment's hesitation, but I won't switch course. Even the Devil can do a good deed, evoking sympathy. Her tuning out everyone and avoiding their gaze plays on a loop in my mind. It pricks at the base of my skull.

Taking pity on a woman capable of ignoring the pain of others? Good or bad. It's not in me to do. A dose of reality, fear, is healthy, character building even. It may motivate her to become a better person.

She still doesn't notice me. I avoid every burst of light. From my vantage point behind her, I anticipate her motions. When she turns this way, I slide to the other side, out of her line of vision. I put more of my weight into my footfalls, making them heavier, more pronounced against our silent backdrop. I kick a loose pebble in the gravel. She inhales sharply, jumps, and picks up her pace.

I knew it! Of course, the Subaru is hers. It's not far away, a couple of yards max, but her split focus makes her trek longer. This isn't safe. Anything could happen in a deserted parking lot on a moonless night. Visibility is limited, nonexistent when not paying attention to your surroundings. I'm well acquainted with the dangers that can befall a lone person—a woman. Someone could catch her unaware in seconds. As small as she is, a scream wouldn't bubble up her vocal cords before the worst happened. No one would be the wiser. St. Vincent's isn't in the worst part of town, but it isn't the safest either. If I cared, which I don't, but if I did, I'd spank her ass for taking such risks with herself. Anger engulfs me. Propelling me forward without my conscious decision. I'm behind her when she takes off.

Sprinting.

Igniting some doormat, predator-prey compulsion I'm helpless to ignore. I chase her.

The hood of her jacket falls, revealing thick, long, dark waves that flow behind in the wind her escape creates. It's gorgeous. The desire to reach out, run my fingers through its thick mass, and tug rides me. It pushes me past her and stops me in front of the driver's side door.

Pulling up short, she jerks backward. The outrage and shock distorting her beautiful features is hilarious. Her lips purse, and her jaw tightens at hearing my laughter. Crossing her arms, she lifts an exquisite, high set of ample breasts that defy her stature.

"Excuse me, Your Highness. Were we boring you with our trauma? Disturbing your life of leisure?" I say, chuckling without humor. Her eyes widen at my assessment, and her head rears back as if slapped. "What're you, a social media influencer or something?"

She ignores me. Her gaze travels this way and that, trying to find a way around me. With a little over a foot on her and more than 150 lbs., she can't move me unless I want to move, and I don't want to move. My resolve must be evident in my harsh expression because she backs away. Two arm lengths between us isn't enough distance, obviously.

"Is that fun for you?" I ask, pointing a thumb towards the church. "Tapping the glass of the zoo exhibit, even though a million signs prohibit it."

Her glare is adorable. Her silence, however, is another fuckin' story. Mousy doesn't fit her when everything about her is clearly meant to stand out. It isn't as fun antagonizing someone who won't speak. I'd think she'd want to defend herself if nothing else. Or maybe it's my frivolous hope that someone as beautiful as her isn't pure evil. That also pisses me off because I shouldn't want to redeem her. Some people are unredeemable.

She slides the shoulder strap of her purse off one arm and flings it onto the other. Illustrating her indignation. Her gaze turns glacial. Startling flecks of green in the depths of her honey-brown eyes mesmerize me.

"Please move," she says. Her raspy voice is so low I almost miss her request.

Although I'm positive she intended to be harsh, her words were sultry without trying. She may as well be asking me to take her to bed and spread her legs.

With a deep breath and shaky exhale, I shake my head. Looking me up and down, she taps her toe.

"She speaks," I taunt. "Unlike everything else in your world, you're not going to get your way with me. Your being here is disrespectful. These people are divulging their deepest, darkest fears and hurts. How dare you treat other people's pain as entertainment? Was this an easy way for you to work off some community service hours? Might I suggest picking up trash on the freeway instead? At least your insolence won't be so flagrant there."

Narrow honey eyes meet mine. Our stare-off lasts for what could be an eternity or seconds. Time stands still. An insane desire to hook an arm around her narrow waist and draw her in swamps me. Widening my stance anchors me in place. I cross my arms over my chest to keep that particular impulse at bay. She's a heartless tourist. And if she wasn't, this isn't the time or place. I should've left an hour ago.

Rob's waiting for me, and this hasn't been a good week. He and Dad both had episodes. He's liable to think I've been abducted or am plotting against him. I don't have time to waste. Yet here I am.

"Why are you here?" I ask, annoyance with her and myself makes my tone gruff.

"Please. Move," she says again through clenched teeth with more force.

Leaning against her car door, I smirk. "You're not going to answer my question?"

"Get off my car."

Her toe taps a rapid tattoo against the asphalt. She's mad. Behind her intense glare, I see the internal struggle she wages to keep it from showing, and I want to push her. Not physically. Well, I wouldn't mind pushing her in the way a man pushes a woman to explore. What I want is to force her to unleash the rich brat I know is pent up inside her. The brat that got her this cushy sentence instead of the jail time she undoubtedly should be serving. This quiet, timorous act is insulting.

"What perverse joy are you getting from exploiting the victims here? You have a vlog channel or something? Or do you bitch about it in rant stories, reels, or whatever they call it? Monetize?"

Creaking snatches our attention over her shoulder. The church's back door opens. Patricia sticks her head out.

"Everything okay?!" the older woman yells.

I'm not sure she can see us at this distance, but if she can... This isn't a great look. I move away from the car. Velour Sweatsuit uses the millisecond to squeeze past me and get into her vehicle.

"Yeah!" I yell. "Was making sure she got to her car safely. It's dark out here. Need some more lights."

"I've let them know. Were you waiting to talk? I'm locking up in a minute, so..."

Catching the hint, I shake my head. Which I'm sure she doesn't see, but she ducks her head back inside. The door drifts closed behind her.

Velour Sweatsuit's engine starts, revs. I approach her window, close enough that if she were to attempt to put her Subaru in drive, she would have to run over my foot. It's a big risk, but I'm too deep into this to stop now.

She stares forward for several heartbeats, then slowly turns her head towards me, unamused. The window slides down a bare inch—if that.

"What?" she asks with a loud exhale.

Time to change tactics. "How are you?"

She blinks once. Twice. Three times. She arches an eyebrow and stares flatly. "Do I have a sign on my forehead or something that says, 'Ask me how I'm doing?'"

I pretend to search her face. "Not that I've seen. I'm Garrett, by the way."

"I know. You said it in group."

Maybe she was more observant than I thought. I smirk. "I know. Usually, when someone introduces themselves, custom dictates you then reciprocate by supplying your name."

Her eyes roll. "That's need-to-know information. And why introduce yourself now? Are you a guy who believes negging women gets them interested? You pick up vulnerable women at support groups?" She snickers. "Just when I think men can't get any lower... New low unlocked."

"I see your car makes you brave," I tease, only half joking. "So?"

"What?"

"Your name...?" I prompt, bracing my arm on the roof of her car and leaning in.

She leans away as if there isn't steel and glass between us already. "You don't need to know. Please, get off my car?" she asks in exasperation.

My cell chimes. Digging it out of my pocket, I move. "See you next week, foxy lady."

Chapter Sixteen

*A*mina Raichand

"How is your group going?"

Stainless steel clinks against Flora Danica porcelain as my fork hits my dinner plate. My gaze rises slowly. I chew each grain of rice with deliberate care, a gimlet stare trained on my alleged mother. Nora.

Eyes annoyingly similar to mine meet my stare head-on. Lifting my elbow, I rest it on the lace-covered table. Check. Mate. Passive-aggressive? Maybe. Immature? Definitely.

Of course, my stomach knots. Why wouldn't it? Sweat dampens my forehead and underarms. The hint of confrontation still causes my nervous system to rebel. Somehow, I thought suffering a life-altering event would irrevocably change me, untie my tongue, and make me someone who could advocate for myself to express what comes to others so easily. Sheesh! These are my "parents". Shouldn't there be a measure of comfort in telling them where to go and how fast to get there? Familiarity? There isn't any, no matter how many family pictures and home videos they show me—

From my place, sitting between their seats, one at each end of the long, ornately-carved mahogany refectory dining table, my glare travels the length of the table to my left, zeroing in on the pretentious woman. Champagne silk blouse tucks into a modest knee-length black pencil skirt. A simple strand of pearls wraps around her graceful neck and matches her pearl earrings. Nora's dark brown hair is pulled back into her signature chignon. Her posture is rigid as if she's being held at gunpoint and forced to eat the meager helping of rice, black beans, broccoli, and grilled lemon pepper salmon. Even when eating, she looks high-strung. However, I can't fault her for that. If I were served these tiny portions for God knows how many years, I'd be tense too. Where's the flavor?! The woman is suffering from food deprivation. She's hungry.

My gaze skates down the long table to my right. Gilbert Raichand. My "father". Or as I've come to know him over the last several months, King Oblivious. Either he's the most unbothered man in the world or the most clueless. Jury's still out on which one it is. Given that he's one of the highest-paid pharmacists in Indiana, a fact my "mother" mentions anytime anyone new is within earshot, I'm leaning towards unbothered. He wears what I'm becoming familiar with as his nightly uniform. As soon as he gets home, he changes out of his suit and into a fresh kurta pajama. Tonight's kurta pajama is beige. He isn't as stiff as Nora, but the way his butterscotch gaze shifts behind his black-rimmed glasses every so often, I can tell... He's hungry too.

So, no matter the family portraits dating back to my infancy hanging all over the house, the candid photographs, or the distinct, identical features that mark us as parents and child, these are not my parents. I don't know these people.

Nora clears her throat. "Don't ignore me? Group?"

I release a huff of breath. Dog. Bone. Ugh! "If I say horrible, will you allow me to stop going?" She shakes her head. Of course! Picking up my fork, I pick at my salmon. Pull it apart and scoot pieces around my plate. "Group's great, Nora!" I say heavy on sarcasm.

Nora glares at me, but not too much. Wouldn't want her face to be marred by crows' feet.

"That's good, lovebug," Gilbert says absently, not catching the mood.

Mine and Nora's heads whip around to stare at him. Dumbfounded.

"Anyway…" Nora says, waving off his thoughtlessness. "Pet, there are items on your agenda we must discuss. I've made a hair appointment for you with my girl. She's fantastic. While you're at it, get a mani-pedi. Those nubs are unsightly. Are you biting them? Not only is that unsanitary, but it's disgusting." Her grimace punctuates her unsolicited opinion. "Acrylics will fix that. Maybe some of that gel polish, too. Then contact some of your old high school friends and go out."

"Mm-hmm…" Gilbert mumbles around a mouthful of food. Both our gazes snap in his direction again. He nods.

Incredulity seeps from my pores and fills the weighted pause that passes before I'm able to form a coherent thought. The things these people do are absurd, ludicrous to the eighteenth degree. What friends? I didn't go to high school here. And why high school? If this is my home, where are my work friends? I've yet to finish my bachelor's degree, yet one is framed and hung in the room they tell me is my childhood bedroom. I won't get into the fact that the room is painted some deep shade of pink. Eww! Now, I'm supposed to have friends. Anyone who knows me knows I'm an introvert through and through. My friends are my movies. Then *Rain Man* is over here with his outbursts of off-topic ridiculousness.

"I'm so sorry. This is my fault," an echoic voice whispers in my ear.

Turning this way and that, I swat at the air beside me.

"I will atone," whispers the voice again.

"What happened?"

"Amina!"

Nora calls, breaking into my hysteria.

The voice fades. I turn towards my "mother". Heat suffuses my neck and face. Her expression is an odd blend of horror and disappointment. Resignation droops my shoulders. Clutching my fork grounds me to the here and now. I'm only able to hold her gaze for a moment before embarrassment sends my gaze scurrying away.

"Pet?" Nora asks, displaying rare hesitance. "You took your medication today." Glancing at her watch. "We can get you something for anxiety in an hour. Okay?"

"I don't need anything."

The look on her face says she doesn't agree.

"Why would I go out?" I ask, diverting to our previous, safer topic. "I have no money, no friends, no job..." Dropping my fork, I tick off each point on a finger. "What? You guys don't have fun with me around?"

Nora turns the prongs of her fork down on her plate. Resting her elbows on the table now that her meal is finished, or appetizer, considering how small a serving it was, she steeples her fingers over her plate and eyes me with narrow speculation.

"Amina, what happened to you was..." she pauses searching for the right adjective, "unpleasant. But you need to regain your independence. It's high time you took steps towards that goal. Five months since you were released from the hospital? That's enough wallowing. Stop entertaining these flights of fancy... It's beneath you."

My jaw drops open so far it feels as if the actual bone will detach and hit the floor.

"Whatever's within my power."

"Why are you whispering?"

The blink-blink stare Nora bestows me with is all the answer I need. It's the feminine whisper again.

"What? I'm not— What are you talking about?" Nora asks after a couple of false starts.

With a shake of my head, I return to the more pressing issue. The last thing I need is for her to think I'm crazier than she already does. Their guardianship is a sore subject. Mentioning the whispers will only strengthen their claim that they should have permanent conservatorship over me.

"Is this another demand, or do I get a choice this time? I already came here to be with you people. What more do you want?" I snipe, latching onto my irritation at the situation instead of freaking out over my impending loss of sanity.

"You people?" Gilbert scoffs.

"You're claiming to be my family."

It's Gilbert's turn to drop his fork.

"We're your parents!" Gilbert and Nora exclaim at the same time.

"What more proof would you require?" Nora asks, voice rising in offense. "I have a cesarean scar I can show you."

Shrugging, I shake my head. I'm not sure that would prove anything to me. If the pictures haven't inspired any faith in their cockamamie assertion, what will? Anyone can get surgery. My favorite red teddy bear that I won from one of those claw machines when I was three, which I swore I lost, is in my bedroom. It was there when I arrived here from the hospital and hadn't been in my apartment or life for almost twenty years. Only someone who knew me would have that particular keepsake, unless *Toy Story* was real, and it traveled here itself. Yeah, even that idea is too outlandish for me in my present state of mind. Still, Rosita the teddy bear, in her blue floral Chiapaneco dress I stole from a doll when I was younger, didn't sway me either.

Nora sneers. "Either meet the requirements we set for you—Do something, anything more than living in this perpetual state of doom and gloom. Haunting this house with your negative energy—Or...be admitted to Serene Meadows for inpatient treatment. Your choice."

"Are you serious?" I stare without blinking.

There's no way I share DNA with such a cruel woman. She acts as if I chose to be here, chose to be assaulted and to lose my job. How can she threaten me? Mothers are supposed to care more. Or at all. Aren't they?

Nora's smile is smug. "As a heart attack."

"Heart attack." Gilbert snorts. "Who's having a heart attack?"

He lifts his fork and resumes eating.

"You're enjoying this guardian-conservatorship thing, aren't you?" I ask, although I know the answer.

My mother's smile widens.

Chapter Seventeen

Once again, the parking lot is almost empty. The glow of the full moon casts an eerie light, draping the foliage surrounding the cathedral and the lot in mystery. It's a setting better suited for a horror movie. Screw almost, it is empty. If Patricia's BMW weren't here, then my crystal white pearl Subaru would be the only vehicle. My parents decree that I return home immediately after group without delay, and every group Patricia keeps me afterward. I don't know whether to be mad at the delay or thank her. Whatever keeps me out of that house longer. I can't breathe with them hovering over me day and night. Gratitude, it is then.

It's unseasonably cool tonight. However, my assessment might not be entirely on the mark. Since Justin stole my dignity, I can't get warm enough. Regulating my body temperature is impossible. I'm cold all the time. No amount of clothing is protective enough. Speaking of clothes...

None of my clothes are mine, which is fine. My usual leggings wouldn't be warm enough now, anyway. They tell me the clothes in the closet are mine, but just one of the designer sweatsuits costs more than a month's rent. Tonight's little number is a white Gucci sweatsuit with red-and-green web stripes on the cuffs, hem, and down the pant legs. $1800.00 price tag. And that's just the pants. I couldn't find the tag for the top.

Quickening my steps, I tuck my chin and make my way across the lot. This outfit doesn't have a hood. I prefer the extra barrier between me and the world, but such is life. Anytime I ask for my clothes, they lie to me and tell me these are my clothes, but they aren't. They can't be. Awareness skitters down my spine. If I were the type to give in to hysterics, I might jump, run. Pull my shirt over my head to be sure nothing crawled inside my clothes. My skin prickles. Someone is following me or watching. A covert glance over my shoulder reveals no one. If I were wearing a hood, my hair wouldn't slide over my face and block my view, wouldn't have me ready to rip it from my scalp each time it slithers down my back and touches my skin, the way Justin did.

Shivering at the memory, I pick up the pace and clutch my purse to me. If I have to run, I don't want anything in the way. Thank God, with this car, which isn't mine either, all I need is the keys to be close enough to my person to start it. My car, my Hyundai, was old-school and needed the key in the ignition. It never used to bother me until the night that turned my world into a waking nightmare. Night used to be my time, made for me. Stars. Nature. They were all my gifts from God or the universe, whichever one chooses to call it. Now, the lightning bugs that fascinated me well into adulthood scare the stuffing out of me as they wink in and out around me. My own footsteps frighten me. They are too loud against the quiet night.

Did this church have to be so big?

The distance from the side door to the parking lot is the size of a football stadium. If I chose the exit everyone else uses, the walk would be longer. Better lit but longer. Once upon a time, I didn't mind being alone. Not being the tallest woman or trained in any meaningful form of self-defense, I didn't take safety for granted and I stayed as alert as necessary to be proactive against possible danger, but I also didn't assume danger lurked around every corner. I did things alone all the time. Whether I wanted to or not, that was my life before. Now, after Justin, being alone causes as much anxiety as standing up for myself does, yet I crave solitude more…with other people in close proximity, just in case. The contradiction is not lost on me. Why did the other attendees leave so fast? If they were milling about, but not interacting with me, I'd feel more at ease going to my car. I'm outside of a church for goodness's sake. This should be the safest walk.

Something crunches behind me. Nope.

Feet don't fail me now. I run as fast as my legs will move. Heat burns my thighs. Flinging my car door open, I hop in and lock the doors. Squirrel? Harmless homeless person? Patricia? Offense be damned. They can see me lock the door. I'll feel bad later about hurting their feelings.

I toss my purse on the passenger seat and press the start button.

Tap. Tap.

Two hard knocks on the window scare the bejeezus out of me. My heart stops. For how long, I don't know, but it stops. Whipping my head to the side is involuntary.

Finally, my heart beats.

Pressing the button, I let the window lower almost halfway. The barrier is needed for several reasons. Hand to my heart, I ask my intruder, "Is this, like, an every-week occurrence? Don't you have hobbies?"

Greenish-blue eyes spark with amusement and mischief. He leans down, getting too close for comfort. Although given his enormous height, over a foot taller than my five-two, it makes sense. Hearing isn't possible from way up there, not that I intend to hold much of a conversation with him. I lean away from his intrusive position.

"Is it my breath?" Garrett asks, frowning in mock horror. He puts his palm to his mouth and exhales an exaggerated breath.

Shaking my head, I lift my eyes heavenward.

No, it's not his breath. His breath smells minty-fresh all the time. And he smells...Mmm...woodsy. Amber and sandalwood. Over the last month, he's proven himself to be a nuisance—a total ass. Why anyone likes him is beyond me, but when he's close? Nights spent under a soft, warm blanket, watching a thriller or scary movie by the fireplace, drinking hot cocoa, come to mind. It's comfortable, cozy. All the joy of the night I lost...wrapped in a person. And his voice? I'm surprised my window is still intact. It's filled with so much bass, it ignites something deep within me. Familiarity? I'm unsure. What I am sure of is it's the last thing I need in my life right now.

Justin lulled me into a similar false sense of security. I will not make that same mistake again.

Garrett laughs. A rich, earthy sound, causing his prominent Adam's apple to bob up and down. It vibrates through me, sending a different type of chill down my spine. His nose wrinkles, accentuating freckles across the bridge of his aquiline nose, adding a boyish charm that contrasts with his rectangular, strong jawline. Large fingers rake through close-cropped copper-brown hair. His slate blue button-down protests the action, looking as if his impressive biceps might burst the seams. Not just his arms are big, either. He works out. Business attire doesn't mask the way his clothes hug each well-defined muscle of his broad chest or his behind.

"My eyes are up here." Garrett winks.

Busted! "What do you want?" I ask, more bite than necessary in my tone.

Turquoise eyes traverse my face, long ponytail, shoulder, and lower as if he can see through the door, returning my lecherous once over.

"Don't play dumb, foxy." He levels a glare at me. "You know what I want. Five times a charm."

I purse my lips in thought then shake my head. "Not quite. Try six."

"What?!" His mouth falls open. Arms cross over his wide chest. "That's not fair. Last week, you said try five times."

Shrugging is all I can do to keep my laughter at bay. Our weekly banter is the only time I feel alive. His indignation at my staunch refusal to tell him my name is hilarious and provides the light I need to navigate the dark in my life. It makes sense when nothing else does, and everything is foreign.

"You're lucky I even talk to you at all," I say, gripping the steering wheel.

"Why are you always in such a hurry? This is possibly the longest conversation we've had," Garrett complains.

"What's it matter to you? You don't think I belong here, anyway. How goes your mission to get me kicked out? Since you want to talk so badly." My smirk is humorless.

His accusations sting and aren't far from why I believe I shouldn't be here. I put myself in the position that led to what happened. It isn't right for me to be amongst this group of true victims. They have no idea I'm a fraud, that I basically asked for what Justin did, led him on with my attention. If I had a choice, I wouldn't be here, but I don't. So, I come and try not to interfere in their grieving process. At least I thought I wasn't interfering until Garrett confronted me a month ago.

"Tell me why you belong here," he demands. His features grow taut. "Do that, and I won't bother you anymore."

"You don't even go here," I snap. "Weren't your meetings somewhere else? I'm pretty sure I heard you tell someone that a couple of weeks ago. Go there, and then you wouldn't have to worry about my motivations for being here."

"This group needs to be protected from people like you."

"Are you being racist?"

He balks at that. "I don't care if you were—"

"Purple," I interrupt, not believing what I'm hearing. A vision of Quentin comes to mind. What am I? Cursed to have contact with white men with weird racial hangups. "I gotta tell you, if you or anyone else were purple, I would notice. Gonna tell me you don't see color next?"

"What?! No!" He exclaims, looking thoroughly insulted by my presumption. "How did we get here? I'm talking about vultures who love nothing more than to pick at carcasses decimated by the vilest traumas. People who get their jollies from exploiting others' grief. I don't give a fuck what color you are, lady. Someone needs to look out for the people who attend these meetings and bare their souls."

"That's Patricia's job, Captain Save-A-Victim! No one here is under eighteen. We're all adults able to make our own decisions about what to share and what not to share. I'm not forcing people to divulge anything."

His answering glare is glacial. "Sounds about right coming from someone like you."

"What does that mean?" I ask with narrow eyes. My stomach knots, yet I don't get a headache or the sweats that accompany any form of confrontation.

"It means the world is your oyster. Everything and everyone bows down to you. You've never heard a no. Money buys everything, including your way out of whatever the hell you did that got you doing community service here. I wasn't sure before, actually considered I might be off base, but after hearing you say something so privileged and cold, I know I'm not too far off the map."

The nerve of this man! I'm on Lexapro for a short mental break, yet he's out here on the loose, being bipolar and unmedicated. One minute he's flirting, the next he's lobbing off-the-wall accusations. Somewhere there's a padded room with his name written in feces on the wall.

"What about me gives that impression?" I ask in a voice a lot calmer than the chaos in my mind.

He looks me up and down. No overt sexual undertones in his leer this time. "Your car, for one. Your outfit costs more than most people can afford for a mortgage in this economy."

I arch an eyebrow and scowl out my windshield at his SUV. "Pot, kettle, sir. What's that? The latest Mercedes SUV? I don't even know where this car came from, but I don't think it's anywhere near as expensive as yours. Meanwhile, you dress like some high-paid tax accountant. What? Only the homely corner the grief market to you?"

His glare softens. Freckles spread like bird wings over the bridge of his nose and cheeks as his full lips curve. Then he tosses his head back, releasing throaty laughter up to the starry night sky.

"Touché!" He says sobering. "Financial Manager is my proper job title, thank you very much."

Keeping my smile at bay shouldn't be so hard. Not a lot gives me reasons to smile, but more often than not, I find myself fighting it during our verbal jujitsu.

"You're really not going to tell me your name, are you? Gonna make me drive forty-five minutes out of the way again, six weeks in a row, to get it?"

I put my seatbelt on. "I'm not asking you to do anything," I say, putting my car in gear.

"That's because I'm coming whether you ask me to or not." Garrett's response is low, almost a growl, and full of innuendo.

Oh, my gosh! "I gotta go."

Chapter Eighteen

All thirteen chairs are full this evening. Indistinct chatter swirls around me as everyone socializes. Everyone's gotten really good at ignoring me, just like I prefer it. The less they interact with me, the better for them. As I told Garrett, some topics are need-to-know. No one needs to know how I played a party to my assault, how my wanton behavior delivered exactly what I deserved. They're right to allow me my emotional distance. Over the last seven months, everyone has perfected the art of navigating around me as if I'm nothing more significant than the refreshment table against the side wall. The corkboard is covered with flyers advertising various resources. Avoiding direct eye contact with me is involuntary now—a reflex for everyone.

Everyone except one attendee.

Garrett's taken his favorite seat diagonal from mine. I pick at my nails as if the secret to life is underneath them, and he stares a hole in my forehead. I don't need to look up to know. There's a sensation of being watched that's undeniable. Heat washes over me. He's several feet away, but I smell him as if he's beside me. Sandalwood. Cardamom. Amber. It's intoxicating.

There's a compulsion I can't deny. Against my better judgment, I glance up.

Greenish-blue eyes full of expectation greet mine. He was waiting. The glint in his eyes and smirk say it loud and clear. He winks. I narrow my eyes in response.

Patricia stands, blocking our view. "Hello, everyone!" She claps her hands together. "My name's Patricia." Patricia scans everyone's faces. "Since I don't see anyone new, I can forgo my usual spiel, and we can get started. Who would like to share first?"

"Aye!" says a tall Black man, raising his large hand. As he stands, the full magnitude of his height is glaring. Spring green Nike joggers seem to go on forever on his long legs. His white T-shirt is so crisp and clean, I'm sure he's never worn it before, and I'm positive he would never wear the same white T-shirt twice. He strikes me as the basketball type, especially with his huge black Nike Air Max Dn sneakers. "I'mma take my shot at the sharing thing today if that's aight," he says, making the statement sound more like a question.

Taking her seat, Patricia nods. "Absolutely. Remember, state your name. Share as much or as little as you'd like. No one is here to judge. What you say goes no further than these walls," she says with conviction while pegging everyone in attendance with a pointed gaze.

The young man pats his perfectly shaped low afro and clears his throat. "My name's Cameron. I hoop. Been hoopin' since I was young. Shot my first layup at seven years old. We wasn't rich, but my parents made do. Moms is a nurse. Dad does construction. I got two younger twin brothers and an older sister. Even though we wasn't rich, they made shit shake. Sacrificed so all of us could do what we wanted.

Someone snickers.

"Ooh... My bad."

"Share however you feel comfortable," Patricia consoles. "We're all adults. Don't get crazy with it, but if a 'shit' or a 'damn' slips out...you're fine."

"Ballin' is all I ever wanted to do. Went to camps and clinics to learn. My grades weren't the best, though. Then I got this scholarship to work with one of the top coaches. This man said he could get me on a European team as soon as I turned eighteen. Of course, going pro—to the NBA—would've been optimal, but shit...playing ball was playing ball. And if he could get me there...so be it. First, he bought me shoes and gear. Started taking me to games, too. He introduced me to folks I never would've met on my own—my idols. I didn't think anything of it. He was being nice. I was seventeen, a couple of months out from eighteen. That's when he took me to his house after practice one day. I didn't think anything of it; I'd been there with other teammates and on my own many times. This time, though... He said, 'There's a price for everything.' Told me all the greats went the same route. If I wanted to be the next LeBron...Sacrifices needed to be made. I likes me a beautiful, thick woman. I ain't gay!" he almost shouts, voice rough with emotion. "Seven years later, it's all I think about. I can't pick up a ball without thinking about what he did to me. I'm a man!"

The fire in his fervent plea cuts through me like a knife. It takes every ounce of restraint I have in my body not to jump up and hug him. Or find the person who violated this young man. My heart cramps. No one deserves to have their trust betrayed, especially not in such a vile way. I'm disgusted. Not with Cameron, but with the situation he was forced into when he was just a boy. No boy, man, woman, or child should be preyed upon.

"Your identity is yours," Patricia declares softly, but firmly. "His actions have everything to do with his depravity and nothing to do with your sexual identity. Your coach abused his power. By standing here today, still being here today, you're taking back your power. It takes an enormous amount of strength to do that, and I'm so proud of you for taking this step. Just so that you're aware...if you were gay, it still wouldn't give anyone the right to touch you without your consent. What he did is called grooming. You were a child."

"I was seventeen when it happened," Cameron interjects defensively.

"When did he start coaching you?"

"Twelve."

"A child," Patricia reiterates. "And seventeen is still a child. You couldn't have consented in those circumstances even if you'd said yes."

From what I can hear, Cameron retakes his seat. I want to gaze up, connect with this man who's experienced such demeaning injustice, but he'd misconstrue my watery eyes as pity. I won't disrespect him that way, so, my eyes remain on the wall, on a chair, to the side. Anywhere but on any particular person. Plus, the distinct sensation of being stared at hasn't dissipated.

"Thank you, Cameron, for trusting us with your story. Anyone else—"

"I'd like to share, if that's okay?" a soft female voice with a slight southern drawl interrupts Patricia.

"Absolutely," Patricia agrees. "The answer's always yes."

"Hi, my name is Katerina."

Out of my peripheral vision, I see the brunette with her hair in a tight bun and wearing Army fatigues standing. By her introduction, I would have known it was her, but I'm surprised by how gentle her voice is. It belies her rough exterior and severe features.

"Bein' a woman in the military, no matter how progressive they claim they are, there's still a stigma attached to it," Katerina continues. "I never wanted to present myself as weaker than my male counterparts. So, during my first year, I worked like I had somethin' to prove. Cuz, I did. Never used my female issues as an excuse to underperform. That includes when I was havin' excruciatin' endometriosis pain. Or when I was crampin' real bad from PCOS. Did what I had to do without complainin'. The guys were nice. Treated me like I was one of 'em. It got so, they didn't apologize anymore for making off-color jokes. I was Kat. Cool Kat. That's my nickname, the one they gave me, anyway. So cool that three other PFCs asked me to hang out," her voice cracks. "I didn't want to cuz I'd been bleedin' pretty heavy for two weeks. That, coupled with my regular duties, left me dog-tired. When I was off duty, I was in my room with a heating pad on my abdomen. But... You know... Cool Kat cain't say no. Sayin' no—admittin' to weakness—a female weakness to boot... I went," she sniffles.

My gut tightens. There isn't any positive way this story can go. If there were, then none of us would be here. Given the context clues... A rock sinks in my stomach. I lift my legs onto the seat with my feet flat on the chair cushion and wrap my arms around my legs.

"But they didn't plan to go to the bar. Not, really. Not for long anyway," Katerina goes on explaining in a hushed tone. It's as if everyone, in an effort to hear, makes a silent pact not to allow the sound of breathing to interfere with her soft-spoken words. "Soon as we got there, they bought drinks. Wouldn't let me go to the bar. Had me sit at the table with two of 'em while one got shots. We did Jägerbombs. That's the first and last drink I remember havin'. Disgustin' taste of black licorice. Clips. Flashes of my clothes bein' torn off. Snatches of my feeble, uncoordinated attempts to fight 'em. It's all the memory I have. With my exemplary service record, you'd think they'd investigate my side of things. I had bruises. Was black and blue in spots. Whole handprints left on my skin. Yet they didn't believe me. Rape kit showed micro-tears that prove something happened. In the end, I gotta see the men who violated me every day on base. I've been warned," she says in a tone that suggests it was more than just a warning, "against any further pursuit of these men or discussion of these allegations due to the negative impact it could have on my military career. Bein' in the military is all I ever wanted to do. My family is full of career vets, men and women. Knowin' this happened would shake my family's foundation. So, I'm here. All the heck away from my base to maintain confidentiality. Tryin' to make sense of nonsense."

The shifting of fabric indicates Katerina must be finished.

An oppressive silence suffocates the room. I don't know what everyone else is thinking, but if their thoughts align with mine, then their hearts are breaking. From what Katerina says, or from what she doesn't say, it seems she plans to stay in the army, to stay at the same base with the men who drugged and raped her. Something has to be done. Having no idea how the military works, I'm not sure what, if any, civilian advice would help her situation. Not that she'd appreciate advice from a fraud like me. She had to know that there was nothing any of us could do for her, yet she drove from God knows where to do what little was in her control—Share.

"Katerina, is there any way you can stay for a few minutes after group?" Patricia asks in an ultra-gentle, compassionate tone. "Would anyone else like to share?"

Since Patricia went on, I assume Katerina must have given a nonverbal answer. More silence stretches. I continue to gaze anywhere but at the other participants, but then...

Pain like no other sears my intestines and steals my breath momentarily.

"Anybody," Patricia prods the group. Silence reigns. "Come on, guys. You don't really want to hear my story again, do you?"

My stomach churns. Sweat dampens my brow, my underarms. These symptoms aren't new. A lethal battle of anxiety and guilt is being waged inside my digestive tract. Their stories are getting to me. I'm already wishing a hole would open in the floor beneath my chair and swallow me whole. A sharp knot of fraud clogs my throat, and I still feel eyes on me. It's too much. The pressure. Garrett's right. I don't belong here, and it's time everyone knew. I'm a tourist—a succubus feeding off other people's pain. I look towards Patricia standing in front of her chair.

"Come on, people. Any takers?" She gazes meaningfully at each person in the circle. Wags her fine-plucked eyebrows like a cartoon villain.

My heart slams against my sternum.

"Finally!" Patricia sighs.

Chapter Nineteen

*G*arrett Kaplan

My eyes can't bulge any further out of my head. They're stuck open to what must be a comical degree. Or it would be humorous if everyone else's expressions weren't frozen in similar shock.

She's not only looking around the circle for the first time, but Velour Sweatsuit is standing. Actually, that's not totally fair; she isn't just Velour Sweatsuit today. Today she's in a garnet velour sweatsuit, which, with its faux-leather trim, looks just as expensive as all the others. I don't think this foxy lady has ever heard of casual clothing.

Patricia, taken completely aback, hasn't returned to her seat as she usually does after a volunteer shares. She gawks, blinking her dark eyes as if they're deceiving her.

Part of me is intrigued. Who am I kidding? A large part of me is curious. She confounds me, and I find myself wanting to equally strangle her and delve into her depths to discover her every secret. What could the ice princess have to say? Part of me worries she'll be just as rude to the group as she has been to me in the past when I've tried to initiate conversation with her. I'm not a man who would ever lay hands on another human without adequate provocation, and I'd never hit a woman, no matter how she provoked me, but if this woman dares to stand up and disrespect this group, I can't be held responsible for my actions.

"Remember the rules," Patricia warns, bringing me out of my ruminations.

Clearly, I'm not alone in my concern over what she may say, which piques more curiosity? From what I've seen of Patricia over the last several weeks, she is kind, compassionate, and genuine. The group's members are her top priority. She is hyperaware and conscious of everyone's needs. As my mother would say, she's a bleeding heart. Why she allows a parasite to infiltrate her group is beyond me and intrigues me. Are Velour Sweatsuit's pockets so deep that she can bend such an ethical, empathetic, refined woman to her will? Everything about this mystery woman draws me. The more she denies me and withholds from me, the deeper my obsession with her destruction grows. Ms. Velour Sweatsuit has become my Roman Empire.

She fidgets with the hem of her sleeves and shifts from booted foot to booted foot. Whether it's an act or not, I'm unsure, but her honey-brown eyes grow round and large as she gazes around the circle. Green flecks freeze. To anyone else, it looks as if she's looking in the eyes of everyone. Since I have made it my mission to study her every action and reaction, I know she's looking above people's heads rather than focusing on anyone in particular. Her obvious anxiety is alarming. Nothing but cool detachment has greeted me for weeks. Biting words. Now, she's in distress? Every protective instinct in me roars to life. This doesn't make sense. She doesn't make sense.

"Umm..." More fidgeting. "Hi! I didn't expect to be doing this." She shakes her head. Her long ponytail swishes back and forth. "I shouldn't d-d-do this," she stammers. "It's only r-r-right."

It's at this moment that I realize I'm right. There's no internal celebration as I expected. She is a fraud. What I saw before was so much more than detachment. Callousness. Deeper.

"My name is..." She pauses, looking me directly in the eye. Her stare is unnerving. Unmanning if I'm being honest. "Amina Raichand." Amina smirks and gives a barely discernible wink.

I'm positive no one else caught it. I do because I'm acutely aware of everything about this woman. And riveted.

"Shoot! Son of a biscuit-eating bulldog!" she exclaims with a slight stomp of her foot. Her features pinch adorably. "Sorry. Nobody else gave their last name. That's supposed to be a secret, right?"

Bouncy, brown curls subtly streaked with grey caress Patricia's light brown cheeks as she shakes her head. "You're okay. Last names aren't necessary, but no one here will tell." She casts a pointed look at each member. "Everything revealed here is confidential."

"Okay," Amina agrees, then inhales a deep breath. She holds it for a second then releases it.

Her gaze finds mine again. Before it skates away as she's apt to do, I mouth, *"Seven."* And hold up seven fingers in my lap for her eyes only, illustrating the fact that it's taken seven weeks, almost two months for her to give me her name. Yes, I'm aware she technically gave it to the group, but I know in my gut it was meant for me. That's why she included her last name. It's our secret, our private joke. Strange things happen to my stomach at the fact that no one is privy to our secret, but we can allude to it in public. Maybe it's a latent form of exhibitionism or something. Either way, it excites me.

"I-I-I am," Amina stutters, and I like the way it feels to say her name even though it's internal. "I'm a rape survivor. But I'm not like you all. I'm a fake." Tortured honey eyes make direct eye contact with each person in the group. They glisten and plead for patience. "It's been almost ten months since it happened, and it was my fault. I barely knew the guy. Actually, I...uh...didn't know him at all as it turns out. And what I thought I knew was fake. My professor introduced us. Two way-too-old-for-college students in jeopardy of failing. That's what I thought we were. All we were supposed to do was extra credit. But I was stupid. Stupid and desperate. He was nice to me," her voice breaks.

My heart follows suit.

A single tear traverses the slope of her deep brown cheek.

I could kick my own ass. Again, I'm struck with the realization that I'm right. She is a fraud. Not in the way I thought, though. Her cold, aloof behavior had nothing to do with disrespect. It's because she cares too much, feels too much. She carries guilt much like my survivor's guilt, but worse. I didn't suffer the rape Lisa did. That Amina did.

She thinks there could *ever* be a reason for someone to take advantage of another, to use their power differential to forcibly take from another what is perceived as just due. No amount of kind actions or words entitles someone to another person's body or time. And I'm no better than the douchebag who took her rights. I had no right to demand her story or act on assumptions influenced by my bullshit. No wonder she refuses to engage with me. I deserve to have my fuckin' head caved in. I'm a dick. I admit it. I hadn't thought I was this much of an asshole.

Doin' yourself proud, man! My head shakes at my stupidity.

"The first person to be nice and considerate," Amina continues. "The first man to give me attention in years. I dressed up. Did my makeup and hair. Made him think he stood a chance. Then, when he took his shot, I rejected him. I led him on because I was desperate for human contact. I used him. Used him because he thought I was pretty. And I liked that. Intuition took a back seat to my ego. Because I felt something was off. He was over-eager. Over complimentary. It's called love bombing, I think. Everything was, like, triple time with him. And unnatural. Since I spent so much time alone and hadn't dated in forever, I hadn't been hit on in even longer. I wasn't sure. Ignored my gut. Fell for the manipulation. Gave the benefit of the doubt where I shouldn't, which encouraged him. He invited me to study. I knew he thought it was more. That he wanted more, and I thought, let's see what happens. I was stupid. Brought it on myself. Asked for it, and he was fake. Fake interest. Fake name. Fake records. And they can't find him." She clears her throat.

Swallowing hard, I fight to shove enough saliva down my throat to dislodge the lump. A mass of shame clogs my esophagus with each condemning word she speaks. I couldn't be more thoroughly chastened than if she yelled at me, which I deserve. She should have hit me with her car.

"He dropped off the face of the earth after beating me to within an inch of my life," Amina says, nodding as if she's coming to terms with the facts again. Her bottom lip quivers. "I uhh...keep thinking it's my fault. I know it's my fault. And, while you all have been sharing, I've been listening. Commiserating. Knowing I don't belong here because, unlike you, I asked for what I got. Deserved it." She sniffles, yet no more tears fall. Amina rolls her shoulders back. She stiffens her spine and shifts her gaze to encompass us all in as direct eye contact as possible. "You all didn't. I am so sorry I crashed your group. I won't come back."

A chorus of dissenting voices sounds. Amina retakes her seat and crawls into her shell as she draws her feet onto the chair and wraps her arms around her upraised legs. She makes herself as small as possible.

She's more than a foot shorter than me, but she's an insurmountable force. The way she stood stiff-backed and strong is the type of courage—no matter how misguided—that makes royalty, the type that fells nations. The strength she holds in her petite frame makes her ten feet tall, and I am in awe. New level of obsession... Unlocked.

Patricia gets to her feet. She throws a sympathetic smile Amina's way, but Amina is beyond paying attention and doesn't see it.

The chubby woman beside Amina scoots closer to her, hand extended to pat Amina's back. Amina shrugs away from the contact without a glance in the woman's direction.

"Okay, well—"

"Did you say something?" Amina asks in a startled voice, interrupting Patricia.

Her head jerks up from where it was resting on her knees. Frantic eyes search the gathered faces and bulge in accusation as they land on the woman beside her.

Everyone stares at Amina's uncharacteristic outburst.

Amina jumps to her feet as if tased.

"Thank you to everyone who shared," Patricia continues hurriedly.

All eyes volley between Patricia and Amina, unsure of what to do and how to react. Patricia seems determined to power through, but I don't know what to make of it. Amina looks frazzled. Unaware of her surroundings.

"If no one else has—"

"Who is doing that?" Amina interrupts again in bewilderment. She scans the group.

She's agitated. Where nothing else about her made sense to me before, this makes sense. If there's nothing else I'm good at, de-escalating agitated states is my specialty. I want to console her, but given how she jerked away from the comfort the woman beside her offered, I don't believe I'd fare any better. A calming exercise would help her now.

"Amina, Honeycomb, are you okay?" Patricia's soft-spoken question creates the illusion of a warm embrace.

Wild eyes search the circle, plead for understanding.

My soul weeps for her anguish. I want to help, but again, I don't believe it would be well received. So, contrary to every protective instinct welling inside me, I remain seated.

"Someone keeps whispering," Amina says, rubbing her hands up and down her pants anxiously. Her eyes never stop scanning.

Patricia shakes her head. She approaches Amina in the way a dog catcher edges towards a rabid animal. Within a hairsbreadth of Amina, Patricia stops. It's as if she uses her nearness as a soothing balm.

"No one said anything, Honeycomb. I was actually just about to release the group. Would that help? Then maybe we can talk a little when it's just the two of us? Okay?" Patricia asks in a low voice.

Amina's honey gaze darts to Patricia's, scrutinizing her words. Patricia maintains a direct, non-threatening stare. Biting her lip, Amina gives a subtle nod, then slowly lowers herself back into her seat.

Chapter Twenty

A mina Raichand

Walking at a brisk pace, I shove my hands deep into the slanted front pockets of my velour jacket. Once again, due to Patricia holding me back, it's dark out. Against the backdrop of night, my pearl-white car is a homing beacon, especially since it's one of two vehicles left in the church parking lot. The full moon provides sufficient light. Yet, inside, where emotions swirl out of control, it is pitch black.

How could I lose control like that? It's bad enough that I hear the whispers, but now everyone knows. I couldn't play it off this time. Everyone staring at me, judging me, inspired a break. Adrenaline flooded my system, and each face in the group morphed into grotesque, sinister things.

Foliage crunches underneath my booted feet. I know it's dry leaves and sticks from the trees, but it frightens me all the same. I glance over my shoulders. Left. Right. Tonight is such an off night. It totally backfired on me. Sharing my story was supposed to help everyone understand how much of a fraud I am, make them understand that I've taken advantage of their vulnerable states and intruded on their private moments. Instead, they offered me kindness, warmth.

Their compassion was misguided. Yet I accepted it. For some reason, they think I fit in, and they encouraged me to continue coming. Offering not to attend anymore was a bluff. My "parents" won't allow me to stop attending. I suppose I could go somewhere else for the hour-long session time, but then Patricia would likely rat me out.

"I found his journal. If only you could understand," a woman's dejected whispered words filter through my mind.

Not again.

No one's there. I know no one's there.

Quickening my steps, I adjust my purse strap and give a sideways glance left and right.

Why do the parking spots have to be so far away from the back door?

My foot stumbles over a pebble. It might as well be a boulder from the way I trip and nearly fall.

"Still no change," a serious, deep man's voice whispers.

I drop my purse. The clunk on the asphalt is deafening.

Shaking, I bend over to retrieve it. It tilts, and the keys fall out. Clinking and jangling as they too hit the ground.

"Shoot!"

This has to stop. I can't live like this. None of the voices is familiar. Yet, everything they say sounds important, like I'm missing something vital. I don't understand. The trembling has nothing to do with the weather. It's still summer. It's fear. Whatever they're meant to communicate to me, I don't catch. Is it my imagination? I don't think so. I'm creative, but I've never been this imaginative. Children have imaginary friends. Adults don't, nor would I suddenly obtain one at thirty-two years old. Plus, if I'd decided now was the time to embrace my inner child, I wouldn't create multiple voices. The whispers are sometimes from the same people. Sometimes they're different men and women, all of which seems to filter that speech through a long, echoic tunnel.

Footsteps sound behind me.

I straighten. Stiff. Slow.

Keys in hand, I pick up the pace. I'm almost at my car.

The footsteps are loud and fast.

"It's never easy. When someone you love…" The same feminine voice as the first whispers.

Forget it! I take off at a full sprint or as close to a sprint as I'll ever get.

My pursuer's feet beat the pavement.

Heart hammering, I push myself faster.

Strong arms come around my midsection and lift me off my feet. I scream and scream…

"No! Stop!" I beg. "Please! Let me go!"

A large hand clamps over my mouth.

I struggle to break free from the crushing hold. My pulse thumps loudly in my ears. Kicking and scratching at the grey-sleeved, heavily muscled forearms does nothing.

"Shh…" A man says, attempting to soothe me. "It's okay. It's me, Garrett."

His hand drops away from my mouth.

My fight slows but doesn't stop. I wiggle and jerk my shoulders. Elbows knock into his firm chest. He's hard everywhere. His woodsy, amber, and sandalwood cologne fills my nostrils. All the tightness in my limbs and muscles melts away as his comforting scent washes over me. And it infuriates me. Why do I respond this way to him?

"Is that supposed to make it better?" I ask through gritted teeth. "Let me go."

He complies immediately, but I sense reluctance in his capitulation.

Because of our height difference, it's a long way to the ground. The heels of my boots hit the ground hard. Unprepared for the impact, my knees almost buckle.

I turn on Garrett. He reaches down and picks something up. My keys. I didn't realize I'd dropped them again.

"I don't care who you are," I snipe, leaning forward and snatching the keys out of his hands. I'm careful not to touch his warm skin. The feelings his nearness elicits are confusing and too much at the moment. "What're you doing following me? Haven't you heard of announcing yourself? You were chasing me."

"Sorry," he apologizes with a smirk that is anything but. "It wasn't my intention to scare you. I actually wanted to thank you."

With a frown and a shake of my head, I turn back and approach my car. Opening the door, I turn and stare, lifting a confused brow.

"Thank me for what?" I ask. "I didn't do anything for you."

Garrett's grin exposes the whitest and straightest teeth. Even in the dim light of the moon, the freckles littering the bridge of his nose and the tops of his cheeks are evident. They give him a sort of boyish charm. However, there is nothing boy-like about him. He's tall. Legs and arms are ridiculously muscled. Once, I watched an interview with baseball players after they'd gotten off the field and showered. They were dressed in nice suits. You could tell the way the suits fit that these men worked out or were athletic. Garrett's body reminds me of that. His grey dress shirt and slacks are fighting to contain his ripped form. I'm not an ass woman, but as tight and round as I know his is, even without seeing it... Quarters could bounce off of it.

"Yeah, you did," Garrett says, interrupting my inappropriate thoughts. "Amina." His grin turns into a full-wattage, breathtaking smile.

I fight the smile his smile attempts to pull from me with a smirk. Then get into my car, shut the door, and push start it.

Out of the corner of my eye, I see his large arms cross over his strong, wide chest. His teal gaze stares in expectation at the window. I truly must be going insane. A few minutes ago, I was on the verge of pulling my hair out by the roots, then I was so scared it felt like I might have a heart attack, and now I'm ready to laugh. My mood's all over the place.

Pressing a button, I roll the window down all the way.

"Progress," Garrett comments in his cocky bass. A copper brow arches.

"I've got to go."

"Wait! Not so fast."

Garrett leans into the open window. I lean away.

"What now?" I ask, unsure of his motives. Anytime we're together, things seem to go left. "You should be happy. I told on myself like you wanted."

"Come get a drink with me?" Garrett asks instead of responding to anything I said. "Next week after group."

The look he gives me is so intense. His eyes seem to glow against the dark. What I said to him before about finding women in a support group is true, in a way. I meant it as a dig, but after what happened with Justin, or Whatever His Name Is...

Indecision must be written on my face. Garrett's brow furrows, then his mouth turns down into a puppy dog pout. Reminding me of... Justin.

"No!" I say—nearly shout—more forcefully than I've ever spoken to another human being in my life. "Not now. Not ever. Don't ever look at me like that again, or I can't talk to you anymore. I'm sorry, but I mean it. You can't do that."

For the first time during our acquaintance, Garrett actually has the good sense to appear contrite. He flinches too, as if my words hit as I intended.

"Okay. Sorry," he apologizes. His bass goes impossibly deeper with remorse.

We trade stares. His teal gaze searches mine. I don't know whether I'm sorry or not for snapping. He should tread carefully when dealing with someone as unhinged as me. Danger isn't something I exude, not physically, but after tonight's group, I'm volatile. Mentally. And I have to go home to those people—my *parents*. Nothing makes sense. Going on a date with a guy from a rape survivor group just seems like one of those frowned-upon, unspoken rules.

With a sigh, I say, "I gotta go."

His mouth opens. Before he can protest, I roll up the window. Garrett taps the window with his knuckle and steps back. Disappointment tightens his jaw. Turning the wheel, I throw the gear shift into reverse then drive away before the people-pleaser side of me surges forward and agrees.

Chapter Twenty-One

"*not sure. She may never...*" A man's grim voice whispers.

Formal living room. Who has so many living rooms that they require specific designations? My alleged parents, that's who! It's said that I grew up amidst the mix of modern elegance and antique old-money, that is this posh, furnished house. The staid family portrait, with Nora looking a picture of Black aristocracy and a dapper Gilbert in all his high-society Indian glory, suggests they've lived here for many years. Somehow, I'm part of the painting too, and I look constipated as ever, sitting prim and proper, staring at an unseen artist or photographer. Not totally sure how families work, but I feel like a family should look happier and less like they're being held at gunpoint. None of us appears pleased to be there. I thought these paintings only existed in television and movie depictions of the rich. Yet here it is, hung on the wall alongside several landscape paintings by famous artists.

Unlike my apartment, which is homey, although its decor is antique and dark Gothic, this house, this living room, is sterile and cold with its wall-to-wall, almost white Anso nylon carpet and stark white walls, coffered ceilings, crowned molding, and a built-in-the-wall fireplace.

Most of the furniture is antique, dating to the 19th century, such as the carved walnut Victorian settee. Louis XIII Secretary Desk complete with stained glass bookcase and a hutch. A stunning mahogany antique tea trolley doubles as a bar stocked with cut-crystal decanters and glassware. Even the grand piano in the corner doesn't warm the room. It aids in the pampered experience. Next to a vase of calla lilies on the coffee table is a short stack of pristine leather-bound books I can't imagine anyone reading.

And I sit here in the middle of one luxurious, plush, Gainsboro grey couch. I curl my arms around my upraised legs and lose my mind. It's been happening all day. The whispers. They're more urgent. More insistent. I can't stop it. And there's no ignoring them. They're everywhere, surrounding me.

"...it D.I.D...so sorry..." a forlorn woman whispers. *"I tried. I will fix this."*

No one is here in the living room with me. I know it, but I scan the room, anyway. A tear escapes down my cheek, and I do nothing to slow its progress. This is it. This is what it feels like to go insane. Sanity is crawling away while you're helpless to drag it back. It claws at the tile and kicks at your rationale. Screams echo through the void that is your once logical mind. I fight to hold on to what I know, what is verifiable?

The matching grey couch across from me is real. The four walls with priceless artwork are real. My body is solid. I'm Amina Kimberly Raichand, five-foot-two, one hundred and fifteen pounds. My favorite color is burgundy. Movies are my jam. I'm real.

I'm real.

I'm real.

Unwrapping a hand from my leg, I rake my fingers through my hair and scrape my nails down my face.

Tangible.

Real.

I am Amina Kimberly Raichand.

"I had no idea... There are so many. I'll find them," the distraught woman mutters.

I'm real.

"Hello, *beti*," Gilbert greets, using the Hindi word for daughter and drawing me from the downward spiral. "Your mother hates it when you put your feet on the furniture. What are you doing here alone?"

My—I can't bring myself to refer to him as my father—Gilbert swats my legs playfully with a rolled newspaper. Unfamiliar with teasing touches, I flinch away from the contact. His bronze features pinch. Of course, he doesn't express his irritation aloud. The older man is the definition of avoidant. Behind his thick-framed black glasses, crow's feet spiderweb from the corner of his eyes. Wearing one of his signature brown at-home kurta pajamas, he saunters over to the second couch and sits.

He unfolds his newspaper and begins to read, oblivious to my prior distress. Gilbert's complete unawareness of most of what is happening around him continues to perplex me. However, at this moment, it comes in handy, since he doesn't see the tear streaks on my face or the agony, I'm sure, is stamped on my expression.

Shrugging, I try for casual, although he isn't paying attention to me.

He props one leg over the other, getting comfortable.

Nora sashays in, dressed to the nines, which I believe is for her but looks stuffy to me. A black, curve-hugging, A-line skirt to her knees is paired with a beige silk blouse that's topped by a black blazer. She's wearing nude pantyhose and beige kitten heels pull the outfit together. Of course, her jewelry is chunky. Chunky pearls adorn her neck and ears. Her greying, dark brown hair is in a severe knot and her makeup is immaculate. Loud, expensive perfume wafts into the room, steps ahead of her. Again, the question drifts through my mind. How is this woman my mother? She's so pompous, hoity-toity even. Her clothes are what you would expect to find at Saks Fifth Avenue or some boutique too expensive and exclusive to have a name.

Gilbert floats through life with blinders on. Reminds me of Phoebe from *Friends*. He personifies the idea that ignorance is bliss. But what gets me is the riches. They're loaded. They live and behave like the high-falutin parents on television. Which makes this entire situation more maddening, more surreal.

A pounding pulse takes residence behind my left eye. Great! Whether it's from stress or anxiety, I don't know. They're super prevalent during the whispers or when I'm dealing with my "parents".

"You like?" Nora asks, with a gleaming hazelnut-brown gaze on Gilbert. "It's new." She twirls a full circle for his inspection.

Gilbert doesn't lift his gaze from his paper. Instead, he mumbles, "Keep spending my money. Stupid new clothes all the time. Bank of Gilbert. That's what I am." Mimicking Nora's tone, he goes on. "Gilbert, I got this. Darling, I bought that. Hmph!"

Her brown eyes freeze, turning glacial. Placing her hands on her hips, Nora stares at her husband, eyes squinting, then turns her attention to me. Scrutiny replaces anger, of course. Judgmental seems to be a permanent state of being for Nora.

I groan inwardly.

"Weren't you instructed to go out?" Nora reminds me unnecessarily. "Serene Meadows is just a call away, and this is not a hippy commune. Your bare feet do not belong on the furniture. Where are your slippers? This living room isn't for lounging." With the last jab, she shifts her eyes between Gilbert and me.

"Slippers on the couch are better than clean feet?" I grumble, sliding my feet off her precious sofa. "Okay."

Nora splutters, stumped by me using her words against her. Clearly, sarcasm isn't a language she's familiar with. Since she's comfortable threatening to institutionalize me, I take perverse pleasure in ruffling her perfectly preened feathers. Either way, in a few short months, her court-ordered guardianship will end, and her threats will mean nothing.

That prospect delights and frightens me. Innocent Treasures won't allow me to return. How could they? It's one thing to be a no-call, no-show for a day or two. With my work ethic and extreme overtime—not to toot my own horn—I'm an irreplaceable employee, but I haven't had contact with them in months. When I woke, the items the hospital presented me with weren't mine, not the clothes, nor the purse. Facial recognition unlocked the iPhone, but I've never owned one. None of the programmed numbers was recognizable. Innocent Treasures wasn't even listed in my contacts. No one memorizes phone numbers anymore, so there isn't a way for me to inform them of what happened. They haven't called me either, not that that would matter either way since the phone number attached to the phone isn't mine. This also means my mystery caller can't get a hold of me either. I don't know how I feel about that one, though. I'm more upset than I should be about a wrong number. Google doesn't deliver any search results when I try to find Innocent Treasures' number online. And my apartment...

God, my apartment! Rent was already a luxury. They've more than likely thrown all my stuff on the street corner or sold it at auction for back rent and court fees. Where will I live when I regain my freedom? My bank is my bank, but it isn't. The guardianship gives Nora and Gilbert control over my finances, anyway. Guessing the PIN gave me access to my online banking information, but the app on the phone isn't my bank, yet the name on the account is mine.

Ugh...

My head throbs. Pressing my thumbs into my temples, I rub in firm circles. None of this makes any sense. The more I try to force the puzzle pieces together, the more agitation floods my system and irritates my head. Sanity slips my grasp again.

"Pet?" Nora's voice yanks my attention to her and out of my spiral.

"Yes, mother?"

"Are you trying to force our hand?" she asks in that snide way she's perfected to grate on my nerves.

Anxiety boils through my intestines, and sharp pain twists my gut. I'm not prone to violence, but the level of uncertainty of my own reactions unnerves me. My skin itches and feels tight. This woman doesn't know me, isn't aware of how close I am to snapping. Given that I've never snapped before...

Who knows what I'm capable of? Crying? Throwing a fit? Throwing hands? All options are on the table at this point. She doesn't realize it, but she's forcing my hand. I'm a hazard to myself, and I'm scared.

"Do you understand, pet?" Nora asks.

Lost inside my mind, I don't know what she's talking about. What I know is I need to get away from her, stat.

"Uh..." I scramble to come up with a valid excuse to get out of the situation. Bingo. "Actually, a friend from group invited me out for coffee last week. I hadn't thought to ask to go, but you just reminded me of your stipulation. So, I guess I'm getting coffee tonight after group."

The shock on Nora's face is priceless. "That's not quite what I had in mind, and you know it. Friendships with the unfortunate souls in your little group aren't the type you should be cultivating."

Lurching to my feet, I say, "Should have specified that earlier. A win's a win. I'm gonna go shower."

Chapter Twenty-Two

Garrett Kaplan

Rickety squeals and squeaks of hard rubber wheels rolling on linoleum give way to intermittent sounds of blenders blending ice. Electronic beeps chime every few seconds.

The brunette Barista dressed in a black polo shirt and green apron glances up through the bill of her black cap, scanning the area.

"Zack! Grande Iced Caffè Mocha," she calls from behind the counter.

Ignoring the hustle and bustle of the big-box retailer, I observe my gorgeous companion. Suspicion narrows my gaze. Yes, I'm thrilled at this turn of events. Given how we parted ways last week, I half-expected never to see her again, but here she sits, in all her blush-pink velour sweatsuit glory. It would not surprise me to learn that she owns a factory that churns out these sweatsuits for her daily. This one, of course, is expensive—it's obvious without having to touch the fabric, which I'm sure feels like butter. It's what all those sweatsuits with *Juicy* or *Couture* written in rhinestones across the ass aspire to be.

Her heart-shaped mouth, with its thin upper lip and a fuller bottom lip, holds a green straw in its grasp. Her small, even white teeth nibble on the rare plastic straw. The extraordinary lengths the young, gangly male cashier went to find it for Amina, when she mentioned she disliked the Eco-friendlier paper straws, shocks me. That's all it took. A throwaway comment about preferring a different straw, and the kid made it his duty to find Amina a plastic one. She thanked him with a grin that nearly caused the poor guy to pass out. The woman has no idea the power she wields over others. Her clueless nature makes her all the more alluring.

Given her height, her feet are nowhere near reaching the ground. Her black boots barely reach the looped metal footrest of the bar stool she occupies across the pub table from me, which is probably why her legs swing loosely back and forth. Elbows propped on the round wood-grain table, drink in hand, Amina watches people mill about and shop. She looks sweet and innocent. She looks...anywhere but at me. If avoiding eye contact was equivalent to one of my MMA bouts, she'd be the undefeated division champion. Despite her disregard for her appearance and me, she sits there, the definition of beauty, making me want to carry her out of here just to get a second alone with her.

Shit! Jealousy over something so trivial as her thanking another man almost made me violent. Fighting is usually reserved for the cage when I'm able to spar with friends. I don't need to register my hands as weapons or anything, but I'm too old for testosterone-fueled rages. It's a hobby. But witnessing her smile at the cashier had me re-evaluating my profession. Not that I could fight him if I were a full-time MMA fighter, but I could invite him to a bout and mistakenly bring him into the cage. Things might happen... You never know.

Damn! What am I thinking? This is very un-Garrett-like behavior. Something about Amina brings out the protective beast in me. However, beating a cashier doesn't necessarily fall under protection. That's more for pleasure and all caveman-like.

Said cashier—chooses the heels of that thought and this moment—to steal a glimpse of Amina. Her back is to him, so she doesn't see the smirk on the moron's face or how his hazel eyes turn hooded the longer he stares at her.

In a show of—I don't know—dominance, I stretch my arms over my head, twist my head from side to side, and crack my neck. Leaving my arms extended, I interlace my fingers, drawing out my ridiculous stretch, so the cashier and all the men gawking at Amina know that yes, my biceps are almost as large as my head. Inside, I castigate myself over such macho, dickish behavior. Outwardly, I allow this to go on way longer than necessary. Guess The Bloodhound Gang is right. We're nothing but mammals. I'm all animal at heart when it comes to Amina.

Intellectually, I know she can't control the world's response to her. She's not doing anything to cause it. I just wish there were fewer people around. Beggars can't be choosers, as my grandmother used to say.

Taking in her visage, an eerie feeling strikes me. It's as if I've done this before in a way. Déjà vu isn't a phenomenon I have overt familiarity with, but when I'm with Amina—talking to Amina—it's as if I know her, as if this or something similar has happened before. Our energies recognize each other. An almost physical tug on my spirit draws me to her.

Yeah, those ultra-intense sentiments would send her running through the automatic doors if I shared them ten minutes into what I'm sure she doesn't consider a date. Moving too fast and intimidating her is the last thing I want. That's why I've let her set the pace of our *interactions*. That was true before hearing her story last week. Letting the object of my affection take the lead... Again, another example of un-Garrett-like conduct. Now, I won't allow anyone to disrespect her boundaries or cause her anxiety, including me. However, being less than myself is inauthentic and not a practice I subscribe to. But I try. For her, I'll try.

"You hijacked my date, foxy."

Amina lowers her drink to the table, her honey eyes dart towards me. "What? What do you mean?"

"Target?" I say, waving my hand at our surroundings. "This is one step away from a grocery store. I was hoping for something a little more intimate than an in-store Target Starbucks."

She snickers and fingers her straw, absently swirling it around in her drink. "Trust me, this is more intimate than either of us needs right now," Amina remarks, grumbling the last part.

It's my turn to chuckle. She has no idea how intimate I want to be with her. "I still can't believe you're here."

"Why?"

"You went from, 'no, never,' last week to, 'let's go, I know a place tonight.'" I quirk a brow.

Amina shrugs. "I'm a woman. Changing our minds is one of those innate gifts we're blessed with." Honey eyes taunt me, holding my gaze prisoner for seconds that seem like hours. Straight white teeth drag the corner of her full bottom lip into her mouth and nibble the plump flesh before allowing it to slip from their grasp. She lifts her drink and takes a sip. Glancing down, she finally releases me from her saucy jail.

So many inappropriate scenarios for Target and the public run through my mind; all I can do is nod to keep them at bay. I don't taste the sip of coffee I take. It could be unleaded gasoline for all I care. To divert my attention from the lascivious thoughts begging to burst out of my mouth, I struggle to think of a non-sexual topic.

"So... Umm... The sweats. Are they a uniform of some sort? Should I be in sweats, too?"

"Not unless they're grey," she mutters.

I almost choke, trying to keep from showing I not only heard her but also understood what she meant. She does that a lot—mumbles under her breath. It's a nervous habit she's unconscious of, but it's one more interesting facet about her to deepen my infatuation.

She sighs in exasperation. "If I answer, will you stop interrogating me?"

Crossing my heart with a finger, I mash my lips together.

"Attention isn't my thing. Not that I don't like dressing cute and doing more with myself, it's just that with my schedule, it hasn't been an option. Plus, I'm more of an in-the-cut kind of girl who likes to watch. Anyway, the night... Umm... *it* happened, I dressed up. Normally, I wore nothing fancier than leggings and a top, but as soon as I met him... He always looked like a million bucks, literally." She shrugs. "Maybe I wanted to impress him, to be worthy of his attention. Heck, if I know. I started dressing up to study with him, and then we went out that night, and I was dressed up... I ignored the red flags with him. If I even get an inkling to change something about myself due to who I'm around, I refuse now."

"Even if it makes you happy? Something empowering you want to do?"

"I won't go through that again," she answers in a tone bespeaking finality.

Her expression is crestfallen. Again, the desire to protect her, embrace her, swamps me. She should be in my lap while I pull out the hair band holding her long, dark waves in a ponytail before I run my fingers through those tresses.

"Foxy—"

"Why do you still call me that?" Amina asks, pulling her straw in and out of the cup lid, as if she finds comfort in the squeak it makes as it rubs against the plastic. "You know my name now?"

I place my hand over hers, halting the action. My nerves can only take so much. Reminding myself of my decision to take things slow, I remove my palm from her silky-smooth skin when I'm sure she gets the drift.

"I dig all things '60s and early '70s. Music for the most part. Joplin. Morrison." She stares blankly. My heart drops. How could she not have heard of these legends? "The Rolling Stones?" Still nothing. "The Who?" Thick, long lashes sweep down, then back up, blinking. She shakes her head. "Ray Charles?" Disappointment sours my stomach. Her lack of knowledge of music history devastates me.

"If it's not from a movie, I don't know what you're talking about."

"You wound me," I say, feigning hurt with a hand to my heart. "First, you turn me down, then you treat me like some tramp and bring me to Target on our first date. Now, this... You don't know Hendrix?" I hang my head, mocking dejection. "Jimi Hendrix has this song, 'Foxey Lady.'" Again, nothing. "It comes to mind around you."

Nodding, Amina counters, "This isn't a date."

Leaning forward, I capture her gaze and look her head on so there's no misconstruing my words. "You're absolutely fuckin' right about that. This," I wave at the meandering store patrons, "isn't a date. Wasn't my idea either."

"Hey, I'd rather be having a Ménage on the Beach. If it wasn't for those people always in my business and alcohol negatively interacting with my Lexapro, that's what I'd be doing. So, this is all you get with me."

Her interruption catches me completely off guard. I know a lot about health—mental health in particular—context clues have me thinking she's referring to medication. However, the mention of a ménage has my entire attention now.

"Ménage on the Beach? Aye, get down how you get down, you just didn't strike me as a woman who got down like that." I chuckle. "I'm not a man who plays well with others. I do have a couple of friends who—"

"What?!" She exclaims, shaking her head and grinning. "No! You lunatic! It's a drink I created messing around one night. It's so good, though. It looks like the perfect Tequila Sunrise, but there's no tequila in it. It's actually more like Sex on the Beach with its vodka, orange juice, and cranberry, but there's a secret ingredient. It's a twist I randomly thought of, 7 Up. Since it's two different drinks, with a third included... I thought that was a good name. It's *sooo* good." She moans.

I almost ejaculate in my slacks. Slumping on my barstool, I rely heavily on its backrest for the strength to keep me upright. The fervor with which she talks about her made-up drink, and the way her eyes roll to the back of her head in euphoric bliss... It's the most animated I've seen her behave outside of arguing with me. Damn, she's dangerous!

"What's Lexapro?" I ask, staring into her eyes, into her soul and wishing I could burrow in deep and read her every thought.

"Long story short, a mood stabilizer. Good thing this isn't a date, huh?" She snickers, wagging her eyebrows. "Not really date conversation."

Oh, if she only knew...

Chapter Twenty-Three

I resume my previous position. Given my bigger frame, I invade her space even with the small, circular, wood-grain table separating us. The move must surprise her because she lifts her drink and scoots away on her bar stool. With the backrest, she's unable to go far. I'm close enough to catalog each green fleck swirling in her honey eyes. Hers are the type of guileless eyes a man, or woman, can get lost in. There's intelligence in their depths, and curiosity. Yet, the honest openness makes a person want to both protect her and destroy her, all at once. It's intoxicating.

And depending on the person making her acquaintance, it could spell danger for Amina.

Poor woman has no idea the beast her words have awakened inside me.

I could get lost in her eyes, but I need to make a point.

Lowering my voice, I say, "I heard what you said in group, took note of every detail, and I listened to everything you said and didn't say now. The *monster*," I growl, unable to keep the guttural sound at bay, remembering what she divulged in group, "that took advantage of you

was a coward. A manipulative, dishonest...coward. A waste of fuckin'
space that doesn't deserve the right to breathe. I may be a lot of things, a
touch judgmental—"

Amina's incredulous, wide-eyed arched expression interrupts and
reprimands me.

Clearing my throat takes some of the heat from my proclamation.
"Okay, a fuckin' lot judgmental. I was wrong, completely wrong in my
assessment of you, and I'm man enough to admit it and apologize. I'm
sorry. You didn't need to do something you were uncomfortable doing.
You don't need to prove shit to me or anyone else. I'm a random asshole
who doesn't know shit from Shinola. I had no business calling you out.
That had everything to do with my bullshit, not anything you did. You
provided a convenient outlet, and that wasn't fair. You should've cussed
me out and slapped me."

Amina scoffs. "I almost did, which is not like me." She regards me
speculatively. "You bring out the flippin' worst in me for some reason.
All these uncharacteristic traits. No one's ever gotten me to respond to
them the way you do. It's freakin' annoying."

"What's that about?" I ask, laughing.

I'd noticed her cringe a few times when I cursed. In group, she
winced when a few members used more colorful language. Each time it
caught my attention, but something else diverted it. Now, she has my
undivided attention. Not that she didn't before, something just always
got in the way, like a car window.

"What?" she asks, sounding slightly offended by my laugh.

I lift a brow. "Flippin'?" I ask, stealing her word. "What else have I
heard you say...? Shoot. How old are you?"

"Thirty-two. Why?" she asks, voice rising an adorable, offended octave. "How old are you?"

"That's not really what I was..." I stammer, not sure how to answer.
I didn't expect her not to get it. "Thirty-five. I wasn't being literal.

Umm…" I'm at a loss for words. "Freakin'? Flippin'? You use words like that all the time instead of—"

For some reason, I'm so uncomfortable that I stop mid-sentence.

Luckily, realization lights Amina's beautiful eyes. "Oh! I've worked with small children for years, specifically, children in the foster care system. Being around kids all the time, I've learned to watch my mouth. It takes a lot for me to curse. And, anyway, it's easier not to after so long."

"Groovy," I compliment, tone going husky. Just another captivating bit of information to store away about her. The way she plays with her straw again, careful not to make a sound, shows her discomfort at the topic. "What about when you're with your peers or friends? You don't ever let loose then?"

Sadness flashes in Amina's eyes. She drops her gaze.

I'd do anything to erase it. Being near her is so natural and familiar that I forget to be mindful of the emotional landmines I've often glimpsed while we verbally spar, like the fear that darkened her expression last week when I asked her out. I don't know for sure, but I believe the look I gave her set something off. Maybe a memory from her assault? Whatever it is, I log it away to ensure I never repeat that mistake.

"What are those?" she asks in a soft voice. She chuckles without humor.

"What do you do in your free time?" I ask mimicking her lower tone to avoid causing distress.

"What is this free time you speak of?" She laughs. "Before *everything*, all I did was work and go to college classes. On the off chance I get a few hours to myself, I watch movies. Movies are my jam." She scrunches her nose, grins, and performs a shoulder roll of excitement.

I fight not to drag her across the table and into my arms. Pressing my back into the backrest to create distance and force myself to behave, I ask, "So, no rugrats for you? No husband waiting at home?"

Her brows wrinkle. She shakes her head. "Nope. And I wouldn't be here if I weren't single. But I might as well have kids for how much I work—" A deep frown mars her gorgeous brown face. "Worked," she corrects as a veil of sorrow clouds her gaze.

Dammit! How I manage to land on every taboo topic, I'll never know. I can't seem to keep my foot out of my mouth. Everything I bring up devastates her. How to make this better?

"I can't wait to have kids," I say, trying to lighten the mood. "A bunch of little girls that look like you and sons as handsome as me."

Amina flinches. She sets her near-empty drink on the table with more care than necessary, as if she's being careful of her own strength.

"Are we going to pretend last week didn't happen?" she asks calmly. "That you didn't witness me lose my crap and act like a complete psycho? Why would you want anything to do with me? I have issues. My issues have issues. There are red flags, and then there are *red* flags." She deepens her voice to illustrate the severity of her point.

"What? That!" I wave her comment away as if it's no big deal. "I talk to myself, too. All the time."

She pegs me with a gimlet stare. "I wasn't talking to myself. People talk to me. They whisper to me all the time. I can't stop it. Even when they aren't talking, there's this low-level buzz like they're waiting for the perfect opportunity to speak." Looking down, she groans as if she's said too much. Her shoulders slump. "Talk about man repellent, huh?" she grumbles, scrunching her nose and giving a self-deprecating laugh.

I return her laughter. Mine's genuine though. She's playing with fire and has no idea.

"Oh, foxy..." I drawl, kicking her booted foot playfully under the table. Needing to connect with her somehow. "If I were a different man, that'd scare me the fuck away."

She flinches at the curse, but I'm happy this time.

I want her to feel this point. "You have no idea how much hotter you just got. And I already thought you were gorgeous. I didn't realize there were levels to this shit."

She laughs. A true laugh this time. The most outrageous honking sound I've ever heard comes from deep inside her throat. It's not a cute or dainty snort. It's foghorn level, impressive. Reminds me of a movie my parents made me and my brother watch when we were kids, *Revenge of The Nerds*. I laugh hard. She covers her mouth, doing nothing to muffle the sound, and her eyes bulge in mortification. I nearly fall off my chair. People push their red carts more slowly past the coffee shop. Tears drip from my eyes; I'm cracking up so hard. The honking increases. It's like being at a park with a gaggle of geese. Swarmed by a flock of seagulls. Or being beached with a colony of seals. It's the most unattractive noise I've ever heard another human being make. And I don't ever want it to stop.

I want to tickle her so that I can hear more of it. But a crowd is forming, and I don't want to embarrass her more than she already is by her inability to stop laughing. I work to calm myself. Amina follows my lead. And isn't that sexy as hell? The erection that causes surprises me. At this point, I don't think this woman can turn me off. Even as I accused her of being a grief-group tourist, I found her attractive.

Other than a few stragglers, the crowd disperses, and Amina's gaze flits around us uncomfortably. "I'm so sorry."

Rubbing my stomach, I tease, "Hey, I'm honored you chose to honk your horn at me." A wayward tear trickles down my cheek.

She narrows her eyes and purses her lips, giving me her best evil eye, but humor swims in her honey gaze, giving her away.

"So, did your voices convince you to go out with me?" I joke. "If so, I'm on their side. Whatever they want is groovy to me. I need every ally I can get."

Her gaze lingers on mine a moment, then falls to her lap. She's ready to bail. I can almost hear the thought going through her mind. That can't happen. I'm laying it on too thick, applying too much pressure. I'm having way too much fun with her. Plus, if I let her leave this way, she'll never come out again. She already fought me tooth and nail not to ride here with me. Forced us to take two cars five miles down the street. Taking her to a second location will be impossible.

"Come walk with me?" I offer out of pure desperation. Her honey eyes narrow at me. Skepticism is a living, breathing thing between us. "We won't leave the parking lot. Promise."

Chapter Twenty-Four

Amina Raichand

"Damn! Who was the last person to sit in here? A midget?" Garrett grouses.

The way he folds into the passenger seat of my Subaru is comical. His knees scrunch so much it looks as if his large kneecaps might burst through the material of his steel-colored slacks. His shins press into the dashboard, and his fingers molest the side of the seat. I assume he's looking for a way to adjust the seat, but I can't help him there, since this car isn't mine. Well, it is. But it's not, even if the registration and title are in my name.

His shoulders curl, and his head of dark copper hair bends at an awkward angle so that he can fit inside the car without his head bursting through the roof. Oh, if there was ever a time to need a moon roof...

"That is not an acceptable term anymore, sir." I reprimand him, stifling my laughter. "They're called little people."

He tilts his head to side-eye me. Irritation hardens the greenish blue of his eyes, and not for the first time, I notice how his eggplant-colored dress shirt intensifies the green in them.

"Oh, this is funny? Clown cars have more room than this. If you weren't so difficult, we could be in my truck."A garbled sound rents the air, and his seat slides back. His posture relaxes minimally since he's still too big in my tiny car.

"Who's difficult now?" I quip.

"My shirt is gonna be all wrinkled by the time I get out of here," he complains. "There's more legroom in my truck. I'm claustrophobic in here. Let me pull around right next to you, and we can sit in there."

So... Tempting.

Really, it is.

But I can't do it. I still don't know for sure that I want to be out with him now. This is too much like Justin. Only, it's not. Something about Garrett is cozy. Maybe it's his compelling earthy sandalwood scent. When he's this close, it wraps around me like a glove and confuses my mind when I should be wary. He makes it hard, though. That's why I made the horrible mistake and unleashed my real laugh on him inside the store. My neck and cheeks burn at the thought of the spectacle I made of myself. I'm always in control of that laugh. Ever since I was made fun of in fifth grade, I have hidden it behind a demure giggle. Then, after thirty minutes in his presence, I let it rip.

Shaking my head at my thoughts, I say, "Either we sit here, or I leave. I think it's late enough for me to go back."

A thick brow quirks. "So, I'm an item you needed to tick off a list or something?"

Oops! Didn't mean to make it sound harsh.

Truth be told, it's an empty threat. Not the part about getting into his car. I won't do that. I'm surprised I let him in here. Trust is a luxury I can't afford, but I don't want to leave. And doesn't that make me the dumbest decision-maker ever? I might as well be the woman in the scary movies who investigates the scary sound even though she's home alone. Or she peeks around a corner, knowing the killer is a step behind her.

That's me right now, and I can't change it, or rather won't change it because the feedback is gone.

Funny, I didn't notice until a few minutes into our coffee. It's a constant hum in the back of my mind, like picking up interference on a two-way radio or walkie-talkie. When I'm with Garrett, it's gone, as if it never were there. I didn't even realize it until I'd been with him for an extended period, and I fear I'm addicted to the mental silence. The stillness within my body. To him.

Garrett.

I steal a glimpse of him out of the corner of my eye. He fidgets with the seat and doesn't notice me ogle the way his dress shirt hugs his biceps and triceps. I don't know what he does in his spare time, but it must be something aerobically effective. The man is built like a baseball player. He even has a small, yet cute, baseball player butt. He fills out his business-casual attire like nobody's business. I'm not entirely sure what a Financial Manager is, but clearly, it's the type of job that allows him the freedom to work out.

Suddenly, he turns and winks at me.

Crap!

"See something you like?" he asks in his bone-rattling bass.

Busted!

I narrow my eyes. "You're pretty full of yourself for a guy who was ready to have me formally kicked out of group two weeks ago. Run a little hot and cold, don't you?"

His grin loses a fraction of its flirtatious edge. "Sorry, foxy. What can I do to make it up to you? You want to hit me?" Garrett offers me his shoulder. "Hit me. I can take it. You said you wanted to kick me before. Punch me. I get punched all the time. It won't hurt."

"Umm... No, thank you," I say, scooting against my driver's side door.

"I can take it," he insists, slapping his shoulder. "One good time. Right there."

"No. I'm good. You get punched for fun?"

"Sometimes," he answers with an odd nonchalant shrug. "I give as good as I get. That's where the real fun is...punching. Flesh against flesh." There's a double entendre I pretend not to catch. The way his mouth moves and his bass dips lower is impossible to ignore, though.

After what happened to me, I didn't think I'd ever be... Interested. Again? Normal? I don't know if it's too soon to have these feelings. It feels too soon, but in a way, it's natural. Me. Around Garrett, I feel like myself. No, not quite me. An altered version of myself. A version I'm way more comfortable with than when I'm at those people's house surrounded by familiar yet unfamiliar things. Garrett's familiar in an odd way, too. I can't put my finger on why, but he's soothing.

And largely annoying.

Justin confused me too. He made me uncertain of myself and my reactions. This isn't that, but it is disconcerting.

"Know anything about MMA?" Garrett asks, breaking into my reverie.

I shake my head. "Uh... Not...really. Isn't that where guys kick and hug each other in booty shorts?"

"No! I don't know whether to be offended or horrified by your take on a sport I hold near and dear to my heart. It's mixed martial arts." Garrett laughs without humor. "It's full-contact combat, not kicking or hugging. You grapple and ground fight. We use techniques from various combat sports. You're going to one of my bouts sometime. It's a hobby of mine you need to get acquainted with. How are you going to cheer me on with that attitude?"

There he goes ruining a fun moment with futuristic talk again. He did it earlier, and I tried to course-correct him. As much as he gives me these unexpected feelings, I can't be what he wants, even if he's not like

Justin. I don't know how to respond. Playing with the threads of the leather steering wheel, I ruminate on what to say.

Silence stretches between us.

"So, are you one of those guys who watches only movies about sports? What's that one called...?" I pause, trying to remember the name and avoiding his probing turquoise stare. I can tell he doesn't appreciate the topic shift, but there's nothing I can do about it. "*The Iron Claw*? It's based on a true story, right?"

Garrett raises an eyebrow, appearing as if he doesn't want to answer. "That's wrestling, not MMA. Came out a few years ago, but yes, it's based on a real family of wrestlers. But I don't watch much TV or movies. Movies are your jam, aren't they? That's what you said. What's your favorite?"

"Too many," I say, sitting straighter in my seat, excitedly. This is a conversation I can get into. "*Fight Club. The Jacket. Shutter Island. Tenet. Looper. Takers.*"

"Damn! Don't get too sentimental on me now," Garrett says, sarcasm oozing from each deep word. He chuckles.

"What?"

"I don't know. For some reason, I thought you might have some softer tastes. Chick flicks, maybe. Something sweeter."

"Because I'm a woman? Women can like other movies," I assure him. "I like movies that make you think."

Garrett watches me. It's not a total lie, even if he doesn't seem to buy it. His shrewd gaze takes in every minute change of my expression. I try not to let the fact that I don't completely believe this hogwash show on my face. Eclectic tastes in movies are healthy—I guess. Although, before Justin, my tastes weren't so action-intensive. With his firm lips set in an equally firm line, Garrett continues to study me with astute eyes.

Not for the first time, the freckles across the bridge of his nose garner my attention. They're so incongruous with his sharp, hard, masculine features. And he's still staring.

"Okay," I relent. "Sheesh! I used to like other movies—"

"Before the assault, right?"

I swallow hard. "Yes."

"Our experiences were totally different," Garrett says, voice taking on a gravelly, serious edge. "You remember what I said happened to my best friend Lisa?"

I nod.

"Seeing her broken like that. Learning what happened to her, I can't imagine what that's like on any level. Knowing you experienced something so similar and are still here is awe-inducing. Against all odds, you survived. The guilt I feel pales in comparison to both your experiences, and it's hard for me. I struggle daily with the knowledge. I want to tell you it gets better, that you'll wake up and be good as new, but that'd be a lie. What I can tell you is that it gets different. You gain space to hold the experience and the lessons you garnered from it. You can live. Don't allow that jackass to take more from you than he already has. Time does heal all wounds."

His strong, warm hand engulfs mine, squeezes it. The strength of his conviction seeps deep within me and touches my soul. It invigorates my spirit in a way I didn't know I needed, waking me from the nightmare state I've persisted in for months. When he releases my hand, loss overwhelms me. I mentally shake off the ridiculous response.

"It truly does," Garrett continues. "I promise." He crosses his heart with a finger. "And I haven't broken a promise to you yet." He winks.

"Out of the one you made, like what...? Seven seconds ago." I giggle.

"Uh... Two. This is the second promise. I promised we wouldn't leave the parking lot, and look," he says, looking out the passenger window, then the front windshield, illustrating his point. "We're in the parking lot. Now, what's your real favorite movie?"

"*The Jacket* has a romantic element to it, FYI," I correct.

The arch glare and nod he gives screams...yeah, right!

"Okay!" I relent with a sigh. "Like a lot of women, especially when they're young, I saw *Cinderella* and was hooked. Then there's *The Sound of Music*, *Beauty and the Beast*, *Mad Love*, and *Neo Ned*. But my all-time favorite is *Romeo + Juliet*—the 1996 Baz Luhrmann version, not Franco Zeffirelli's 1968 version. Baz stayed closest to Shakespeare's script. It's amazing."

Garrett frowns. "I don't think I've seen any of those. I'm sure I probably saw some Disney movies when I was younger, but I was always more into superheroes and comics. Shit like that. I'm a music buff. I remember reading Shakespeare in high school, specifically *Romeo and Juliet*. We watched the movie, but fuck if I remember which version. All I know is it's morbid as hell. Not romantic if you ask me."

"That's because it's a tragedy," I explain. Excitement zips through my veins. I'm in my element. "It is romantic and beautiful, though. Romeo's and Juliet's deaths brokered peace. And the only way they could be together was in the beautiful embrace of death. That's symmetry. A beautiful symmetry at that. Life is love, loss, and beauty. Haven't you seen *American Beauty*?"

He nods.

The way he's focusing on me so intently is a good sign. He's paying attention, which means he can be taught. I'm all for expanding his horizons and teaching him about the art of cinema.

"You know how Ricky stares in wonder at the plastic bag? He's almost moved to tears watching how the wind tugs the bag through the sky. The way the bag dances in the breeze. Then, when Lester lies dead in the garage, Ricky stares into his glassy, sightless eyes. He takes in Lester's perfect stillness. Whatever he last saw..."

Garrett stares like I've grown a second head.

My stomach falls. This is another reason I stay to myself. Being a thirty-two-year-old woman who doesn't cuss is embarrassing enough. Now, I'm a morbid, weirdo movie nerd. Attention never works out in my favor. I know this, but being around Garrett is so easy that I forget my normally introverted nature.

"I'm sorry, I know that sounded—"

"Go out with me. On a *real* date," Garrett blurts out, interrupting me. "Somewhere we can't also buy toilet paper and fruit." He grins.

I take a deep breath before bursting his bubble.

"Garrett. Surprisingly, I've really liked talking to you. But I have to admit a couple of things to you. First, I agreed to go out with you on such short notice because my..."

Ugh! How to say this without explaining this? "My *parents*," I say, unable to stop my eyes from rolling at the ludicrous term.

Garrett quirks a brow. "What's that about?"

"What?"

"You rolled your eyes when you said parents." Of course, he caught that. It's not like I hid it—or that I could hide it. "Aren't they your parents? Are you in some kind of trouble? Do you need help?

Hmm... How to answer that without sounding like a lunatic. "Do you want the truth? Just know that if you do, the answer will really ruin the date mood," I say, settling on just a hint of transparency.

"If inside of Target wasn't a date, then sitting in your car definitely doesn't qualify as one either. So, there is no mood to be ruined. So, explain away." He waves his hand to let me know the floor is mine.

I sigh. Nothing left to do but to rip the band-aid off. "Those people aren't my parents. I don't have parents. Yet, somehow, they're my parents. And this car," I say, waving my hand at the interior, "isn't my car. I drive an older-model silver Hyundai Elantra. But ever since the incident, this is my car, and now I have parents. There's proof and everything, apparently," I say in a rush without pausing to take a breath.

I sneak a peek at Garrett through my lowered lashes. Nothing I said made sense. I know it. That's why I kept my gaze fixed on my lap or just past his shoulder. Garrett's expression is stone-cold sober. Usually, even when he's irritated, there is a liveliness behind his turquoise eyes. Now, they stare blankly at me. Now, I regret saying anything—no wonder I'm always alone. I have no people skills. Now that I'm crazy, I don't even possess cordial, polite society people skills. My head droops. Closing my eyes, I scrub my face with a hand. What does someone even say to—

"Hey," Garrett's voice breaks into my self-conflagration.

I ignore him.

"Hey!" He says louder.

Head in my hands, I turn and regard him through one eye.

"You have nothing to be embarrassed about. I'm nobody's judge. I haven't gone through what you have. Plus, my brother and my father are schizophrenic. Wild shit can fly out of their mouths at any given time. There's not a lot that can shock me."

"Really?" I ask, my voice muffled by my hand.

He moves as if he might remove my hand from my mouth but then lowers his hand as if thinking better of it. Or he stopped because he thinks I have psycho cooties and he doesn't want to catch them.

"Yes, really. And we'll get into everything you just said. So please don't think I'm just brushing it under the rug." He checks his cell phone. "It's getting late, and I want to give your disclosure the attention it deserves. There is a fair in town starting tomorrow. Do you like rides?"

I sit up straight. This new turn in the topic startles me.

"Yes," I answer, slowly drawing out the word. "Why?"

"Because you should let me take you out on a real date tomorrow evening. We can ride some rides, eat funnel cake and deep-fried Oreos, and talk. Doesn't that sound fun?" He smirks and winks.

I sigh. "That brings me to my next point. I'm damaged, like Cuckoo for Cocoa Puffs, certifiable. Like, all the lights are on, and I'm on the roof, nuts. And that doesn't include the issues I have from the rape. I don't know if I can ever be in a relationship or even be physical with a man again."

"I totally get it, and thank you for giving me a head's up. I'd be lying if I said I wasn't physically attracted to you," he says. He salaciously looks me up and down.

I startle a little at his forthrightness; however, I don't know why. Garrett seems to be one of those people who is unapologetically himself and says whatever comes to his mind.

"I would love nothing more than to lean over there," he says, and does infinitesimally, "stroke your cheek with my thumb, then kiss the shit out of you. I want to feel you in my arms, feel you on top of me and underneath me."

Well, shucky darn! It's hot in here. My sweatsuit is oppressive. I flushed with warmth. I gulp and stare into his hooded greenish-blue eyes. It's like he's imagining every word he's saying, or, maybe, experiencing every act he's describing.

"But I know how much rape affects people, and I respect your feelings. Everyone's healing journey is different, and I'd never force myself on you or do anything I didn't explicitly know you wanted me to do. However, that doesn't mean I won't hope that one day you'll change your mind and trust me enough to allow me the honor of skin privileges."

I chuckle. "Skin privileges?"

"Yeah. Skin privileges. I won't touch you or cross any boundary you set until you tell me that I have skin privileges. Just know, once you give me skin privileges, I'll have free range to touch and kiss all over your tight body."

Okay. Now, he's being lewd on purpose. No man is this understanding, hot, and smooth.

I'm struck mute for a moment. His uninhibited words do unbidden things to me mentally and physically, things I'm not ready to deal with.

After a beat, I say, "You might wanna bet on a surer thing. Because I'm not it. And if—and that's a big if—it's possible for me to trust someone to that degree... It'll be a long time."

Garrett smirks. "Good thing I'm a patient man. You're already mine. You just don't know it. What's any measure of time when we have a lifetime together?" He shrugs. "You're worth it. Just remember, I don't play fair. As long as you understand that, then we'll be fine. Now, what time am I picking you up tomorrow?"

"Umm..." I'm thrown off and don't know what to say. "Around seven-thirty?" I say, the statement comes out more like a question.

His answering smile is blinding. "Works for me. I need two things from you, though."

"Shoot."

"Exchange numbers with me so you can text me your address."

He hands me his phone. I input my contact information and address to my alleged parents' house. I place his phone in his waiting palm.

"Next, the sweatsuit thing... I mean, they're cute and accentuate your best attributes, but... Are they a uniform of some sort? Should I wear one too?"

I giggle. One part funny. One part uncomfortable. It would be hilarious to see him in a velour sweatsuit like mine, but I'm also still ashamed by actions that led to my rape. Since I'm all about ruining the mood tonight, I may as well power through. I take a deep breath. "Before the rape, I always wore understated clothes, not because of low self-esteem or anything, but because I'm more of a wallflower. I've never liked too much attention on me. Attention usually leads to disaster for me. Just look how you reacted to me when you saw me in group."

Garrett pulls air through his teeth. It produces a sound like one would make when they're stung by touching something hot.

I fidget with my sleeves, but go on. "When I met the guy who hurt me, I was immediately attracted. He had that all-American boy look going for him. After that, I started taking more pride in my appearance. Wore makeup. Wore cuter clothes. Dressed with more care and attention. Maybe if I hadn't done that..." I shrug tears well in my eyes, but I don't let them fall.

"Hey!" Garrett says, raising his voice a little.

I'm staring at my lap again. I didn't even notice until he spoke. I return my gaze to his. It's like he sees right to my soul.

"You're allowed to feel confident and dress in whatever makes you feel good. Nothing you could've worn gave him the right to do what he did. That asshole deserves to be buried underneath the jail. He's a piece of shit and did what pieces of shit do. That has nothing to do with you. I know I keep saying it, but things will get different, and time will heal those wounds. I promise. And I haven't broken a promise to you yet. So, it looks like I'd better go shopping. I need a sweatsuit to wear for our date."

Him and his promises. I roll my eyes. A genuine smile curls my lips. I actually do feel a tiny bit better, but I won't tell him that. His head is big enough. "You don't have to do that. I'll wear...whatever I wear. You just be you," I say.

"Good deal," he says, opening the passenger side door. "You get home to your not home, safe. I'll text to make sure. See ya tomorrow, Foxy."

Chapter Twenty-Five

Garrett Kaplan

Shit! I check the clock on my navigation screen.

7:10 p.m.

I'm going to be late. Traffic is nutt-to-butt. I didn't even change out of my work clothes. How could I not plan for this? St. Vincent's is forty-five minutes away from work. It makes sense that she lives close to the church. From what she told me, she's kept on a short leash. So, of course, her house would be near it. *Stupid!*

This is the worst look. Showing up late when I had to bribe her to go in the first place. Why did I pick the fair? I'd seen signs for it off the highway on my way to group a week ago, and it was the only thing I could think of that wouldn't scare her. Clearly, and rightfully so, she has issues surrounding being alone with men. I figured the fair would provide the illusion of being in public while keeping us as far away from it as possible. My showing up late will feed her narrative about bad things coming when she adds people to her life.

Plus, if I hadn't thought of something fast, she would have created more reasons for us not to explore whatever this pull is between us. She hadn't finished her first admission for why she decided to go out with me at the spur of the moment, but I'm not a moron. I'm sure it had something to do with her being threatened. If that's true, I see why her not-parents would force her out of her shell. She's obviously gorgeous without trying. However, there's heavy sadness in her feline-shaped golden-honey eyes. There's loneliness, an emotion I'm intimately acquainted with. I don't think she realizes how much fear radiates from her. Fear of living. Fear of being. Her self-imposed isolation seems to have become a self-fulfilling prophecy. It's not like I'm trying to fix her or change her. I want to root her on from the sidelines while she discovers her place in the world. I don't want to be another person who lets her down.

"Hey, Google!" I shout at my navigation system connected to my cell phone. "Text My Baby Doll."

"What would you like to say to My Baby Doll?" The electronic voice asks.

> "I know we said around 7:30, but I'm running late. Fuckin' traffic is worse than I expected. And I..."

A grey Tesla decides it'd like to slow down at a green light. The light turns yellow, and it goes impossibly slower.

"The fuck, bro! We both should have made that light, Grandpa! Sorry, Foxy," I say, apologizing for my outburst. "As I was saying, I should have timed things better. I'm on my way, but I'm probably going to be five or six minutes late. I *will* be there."

As soon as this motherfucker decides to drive!

It's already 7:20 p.m.

She hasn't texted back. Shit!

I can almost hear her giving up on our tenuous connection, her window rolling up in my face.

*A*mina Raichand

My heart is pounding in my chest. I stare at my reflection in the full-length mirror fixed to the back of my bedroom door. I'm doing it again. Why am I doing this again?

A few bantering sessions and one amazing pseudo-date, and I'm dressing up and calling attention to myself like the entire Justin thing never happened. To top it off, I gave this man I barely know my non-address, and somehow, I agreed to a date I'm still not sure how I got roped into. I'd been fighting the good fight, explaining why I can't be with anyone, then suddenly I'm programming my info into his cell phone.

What is wrong with me? I ask myself for the umpteenth time while smoothing my hand down my black, off-the-shoulder peasant-style dress. I hope it's not too short. Since the closet is full of clothes that aren't mine, I don't have many options for date attire, at least, not options that fit my style. The dress's skirt only reaches mid-thigh. I'm not trying to give the presumptuous Garrett any ideas, which is why I paired the dress with tights. Although they don't really do the job I want, seeing how they're too sheer for my comfort and have roses etched up and down their length. Hopefully, the gargantuan sunflowers printed all over the dress give it more of a friend vibe than an "I want you to do everything you said you wanted to do to me" date vibe. I do a little makeup but not a crazy amount. It's just enough to fit the outfit. Silver hoops and black cowboy boots bring the look together. I do my hair in a half-up, half-down ponytail to pass the time.

I don't want to seem all excited by being ready earlier than necessary. It'll give time for anxiety to strangle me, and whether I truly want to go on this date or not, I agreed. It's too late to back out now.

Sitting on the ridiculous—Who am I kidding? I might not recognize this room as mine—even though I'm told this is the room, I've occupied my entire life, but this bed right here is amazing. It fits my entire Gothic appeal. It's a queen-sized hand-carved black Rococo-style four-poster made of solid wood. My favorite color, burgundy, appears on at least 1,000-count Egyptian cotton brocade sheets. This bed is the only thing that brings me happiness. Rosita and I have never slept in such comfortable luxury, definitely not Rosita. After all, I lost her at three years old. Yet, here she is, in my faux room, at my faux house, and living with my faux parents. I swing my legs back and forth, fidgeting with the bell sleeves of my dress for all of two minutes.

I can't do this. I'm too nervous. It has to be close to time. The last thing I want is the Absent-Minded Professor and the Ice Queen to answer the door. Hopping up off the bed, I grab the Coach clutch that is but isn't mine. I pull the iPhone that isn't mine from the charger and shove it inside the clutch. That simple act causes momentary panic.

The identification shows my picture, albeit a better one than on my actual driver's license. It's still not me. The address on it is not mine. If I get pulled over or stopped, I won't be able to verify anything about myself other than my name. I guess the birthday is the same, so I'll have that, but that's pretty much it. A muffled ding sounds from somewhere.

Oh! It's the not-my-iPhone.

I retrieve the foreign object from the clutch, and for logic-defying reasons, my face opens the phone. A text notification from Baseball Butt flashes across the screen. Trepidation skitters through me. I open it.

> Baseball Butt: I know we said around 7:30, but I'm running late. Fuckin' traffic is worse than I expected. And I—The fuck, bro! We both should

have made that light, Grandpa! Sorry, Foxy. As I was saying, I should have timed things better. I'm on my way, but I'm probably going to be five or six minutes late. I will be there.

Harsh breath burst through my lips. Of course! I was just a curiosity for him, a puzzle he wanted to figure out. An enigma. I guess I gave him more than he'd bargained for. More than likely, he set the date to escape the crazy woman without incident. All his understanding was malarkey. Fool that I am, I fell hook, line, and sinker.

I look at the clock.

7:30 p.m.

Son of a got down sat on a bench!

I toss the clutch and the phone on the bed and fling the bedroom door open. Unfamiliar people. Unfamiliar places. Unfamiliar family portraits. New mental health issues...Same inconsiderate people. Is "waste my time" written on my forehead?

I'm so easy to disregard, to dismiss. Kind words and sweet gestures don't mean I'm a priority. I should know that. I do know that. Even with this faux family, one thing remains consistent. Amina does not matter. They can hang up pictures of a girl who looks like me and call it family, call it love, but it's cold—unauthentic. Fake smiles. Fake hugs. Fake sentiment. The only thing real about this new life—the one constant—I don't matter. I should've never rolled down my window, never engaged in a battle of wills with a man that was hard in all the right places, smelled like Heaven, and is debauched as Hell.

Gilbert enters the living room at the same time as I do. *"Nee romba azhaga irukka* (you look very beautiful), Lovebug. Going somewhere?"

"Are you?" I ask, looking him up and down.

He's traded in his lounge-around-the-house kurta pajama for a nice, crisp black one, and he wears shiny black loafers without socks. His salt-and-pepper hair is slicked back. The greying hair at his temples gives him an extra look of refinement. His grey goatee appears neater than usual.

"Your mother and I have a pharmacy awards ceremony to attend this evening," he answers. "She did not tell you?"

I shake my head. "Bert, I don't talk to her unless I absolutely have to and vice versa."

"Bert..." he mumbles under his breath. "It is either *Appa*, *Baba*, or Papa. These are the only acceptable names to call your father."

That's a landmine I'm not looking to step on. My emotions are already raw. I have to stay on my guard in this upside-down world.

"And where are you off to, Pet?"

Ugh... Her voice causes me to shiver inwardly.

Perfume enters the room before its wearer. Nora saunters into the living room again, dressed to what I'm sure to her is the nines. Under her dark-violet blazer is a flattering golden blouse tucked into a dark-violet knee-length A-line skirt. For the first time since I met her, her dark hair isn't in a severe bun but a much more semi-loose one with curled ends tucked under. A 2-ct. round-cut diamond and gold tennis bracelet provides blinding icing for her dainty wrist. Nude pantyhose and black Louboutin heels round everything out.

She looks down on me. If I had any self-esteem left, I'd be offended by the disdain present in her perusal. "Your father and I won't be home until late. You didn't need to get dressed up on our account. However, I am happy to see you make more of an effort with your appearance. You look halfway decent."

"Actually," I say, mimicking her pompous tone, "I was supposed to have a date. I didn't even know you were going out until Gilbert—" Gilbert clears his throat. "I didn't know you were going out until *Appa*," I say, stumbling over the word, "told me just a minute ago."

Gilbert scoffs. "Why was that so hard? She's called me that her whole life," he murmurs.

"Well, sorry it didn't work out," Nora says with no remorse. "We have to go." She checks her watch and puts her black clutch under her arm. "Try to do some skincare tonight."

With that, she and Gilbert open the front door and...

Garrett.

He stands on the doorstep in grey slacks and a blue dress shirt—a crooked grin on his face. I want to slap it off. "Why are you here?" I ask slowly through clenched teeth.

"Young man?" Gilbert questions.

"We're going to be late. Didn't anyone teach you any manners when encountering your elders? Or etiquette when visiting a stranger's home? Are you selling something?" Nora snipes.

Her curt tone should embarrass me, but what do I care? She's not my real mother, and I'm angry, anyway.

"Nope, not a salesman. I'm here to pick up Amina. Garrett Kaplan," Garrett introduces himself, extending his hand towards Gilbert.

"No, he's not," I say, contradicting him. "I was supposed to go out at 7:30, but plans obviously changed."

He pulls his cell phone out of his back pocket, taps the screen, then puts it back.

"Amina, it's 7:38. I texted you."

"7:38," Gilbert interjects. "We need to get going." Gilbert tries to usher Nora out by the elbow past Garrett. Garrett steps aside to let them pass.

Nora stops just outside the door in front of him. Even in heels, she's shorter than he is. She looks up her nose at him. "And where exactly did you meet my daughter?"

"That's between the two of us, ma'am," he answers with a devilish grin.

Dagnabbit! His rudeness makes me want to grin, too. Someone needs to take some wind out of that woman's sails. Unfortunately, it's the time-suckage douche delivering the verbal smackdown.

Nora scowls. "You're from the group, aren't you? You're supposed to be healing, not using it as a dating service," she says.

"Please excuse me, I'm about to overstep," Garrett says. Mine and Gilbert's jaws drop, but Garrett leans against the door frame. Should I close the door? Look away?

"First," Garrett says, ticking off his points on long, thick fingers, "we didn't start as friends, let alone use group to troll for dates. Secondly, I had to twist her arm for her to agree to this date. Third, and probably the most important thing is... I'm not dating your daughter. I'm too old for that shit. I'm courting your daughter." Garrett turns pointedly towards me. "My time management wasn't the greatest today. But make no mistake, I'm here to take you out."

Nora's head jerks back as if slapped. She stares slack-jawed.

"That answers that, doesn't it?" Gilbert mumbles. Louder, he says, "We'll meet again, Garrett. We need to go." Then he guides a still-frozen-in-astonishment Nora down the walk and out of sight.

"Ready to go, Foxy?"

I scoff. "You were late."

"By eight minutes. I'm here now." Garrett shrugs.

"I don't expect you to understand why timeliness is so important to me, but...timeliness shows intention and respect. Being late for a first date tells me all I need to know. You don't respect me, or maybe you're only here out of some false sense of obligation. You don't want to be the bad guy who backs out of a date because the woman is a head case. Thanks, but no thanks. I have no interest in being your pity date."

I slide the front door closed or start to. His palm and foot stop the action.

"I knew you were going to take this wrong. I live forty-five minutes away from St. Vincent's. My job is even further away. I know I should've, but I didn't consider travel time. Maybe I was still so damn excited you said yes. I don't know. I'm sorry. This isn't a good look, but I wasn't bullshitting about what I told your mom."

"That lady is not my mom."

"You are a perfect blend of those two people. No DNA test needed."

"She's not my mom, and that's not my dad."

Garrett sighs. "Amina..."

"Come inside real quick," I say, turning away from the door and leaving no room for argument.

His footsteps are so heavy on the tile floor, I know he's following. I stop in front of the large framed "family" portrait. My doppelgänger, or changeling, stands in front of a younger Gilbert and Nora, each with a hand on one of her shoulders. Everyone is dressed like a million bucks and smiling. It's fake. Not the photograph but the "happy family" facade. A chill seems to waft from it. There's no love, no happiness.

Garrett stands beside me. "Is that you? What're you, fourteen or fifteen here?"

"Exactly!" I shout. "That's supposed to be fourteen-year-old me. I have no memory of this being taken. I've never even had my hair braided. My hair is too fine for braids. They damage my hair. I tried once when I was twenty, and they broke off different sections of my hair. This picture cannot be me, no matter how it looks."

He's staring at me again. Unlike the vacant stare he gave me yesterday, he looks deep in thought. He takes a more speculative glance at the portrait.

"You have to remember stuff from when you were fourteen," I say, but it sounds like a plea. "Fourteen isn't four. I have lots of memories from my teen years. None includes this house, these people, or this picture." I pause.

It's silent for several beats. I can't stand it.

"What are you thinking? I'm crazy, right? I mean, it has to be me. Same eyes, same nose, same teeth, same braces. But it's not me, and I don't have an identical twin."

Garrett sighs but does not immediately indicate what he's thinking. Finally, he says, "Both my father and brother have schizophrenia. Their crises can be really bad at times. They both suffer from auditory and visual hallucinations. They explain the wildest things in such vivid detail you'd swear what they're seeing, or hearing, was real."

"I knew. At the very least, speculated. I should have addressed it sooner. Prevented this..." a woman's voice whispers.

"1-2-3 eyes on me," a deep voice comes from somewhere, calling me.

"This is my fault. I will do everything in my power to make this right," the woman continues to whisper.

Large, strong hands grip my shoulders.

"1-2-3 eyes on me, baby doll," the deep voice says with more urgency.

Greenish-blue eyes enter my line of vision. Garrett.

The feedback that seizes my mind as the whispers start begins to recede.

Garrett gives me a crooked grin.

I shake my head. "No skin privileges."

He drops his hands. "Thought I lost you there for a minute."

Heat envelops my neck and cheeks. I'm so embarrassed. If only a hole would open in the floor and suck me into it. "I'm so sorr—"

His well-groomed brow pulls down. He shakes his head. "Stop. You don't need to apologize to me. As I said, I've experienced when someone is having a hallucination, or an episode. I'm well-versed in them." Garrett shrugs. "For some reason, I believe you. If you say it's not you, then it's not you." My shoulders droop in relief. Someone believes me. "We'd better get movin'. I think the fair closes at ten. We'll only have a couple of hours."

All I can do is stare for a second. "Didn't you hear me? See me?"

"Yes. And you heard what I told you. I'm courting you with intention. Now, let's go on our first date."

I shake my head and scowl. "Garrett, you don't—"

Firm, demanding lips press against mine, shutting down my entire thought train. Before I can really get into it or reprimand him as I should, he pulls back, cocky grin in place.

"You really don't listen, do you?" I sigh.

"You look gorgeous, Foxy. I couldn't resist. Let's go." He motions with his head towards the front door.

"Umm... I haven't forgotten that you were late and that you don't—"

He steps close, invading my space. Feeling his body heat, I crane my neck to look him in the eyes. It's a battle of wills.

"Woman," he states between clenched teeth, "you are driving me insane with all these excuses when we both know how it'll end. You are my insanity in living form. Stop being difficult." He winks.

Chapter Twenty-Six

*G*arrett Kaplan

"What in the Lord's good name is this?" Amina asks from the passenger seat.

Damn! I wish she'd grip me the way she's gripping the seat. You'd think I'd just gotten my license with the way she's behaving. The woman is absolutely terrified for no reason. She wasn't this afraid on any of the rides we went on at the fair three weeks ago. She ate a humongous pickle and funnel cake with strawberries and powdered sugar, then baited me into getting on a ride that not only shot into the sky but also flipped us upside down, dropped us, then went back up and started spinning. I know my face had to be green when we got off that ride, but hers? Cool as a fuckin' cucumber. She laughed and wanted to go again. But today with me driving...

She's scared for her life.

It might have a little to do with the fact that I didn't tell her exactly where we were going or who would be there. I've come to learn that Amina is a stickler for information. She wants to know everything and have everything planned to the second. She's annoying as hell. I wasn't kidding when I told her she's my insanity, but I'd have her no other way.

"I told you this song reminds me of you, remember?" I say, answering her question. "Ooh shucks, foxey lady..." I sing in my best Jimi Hendrix impression. I glance at her. She stares blankly at me. "It's Jimi Hendrix," I say. Her expression remains impassive. "Let's try something else, hold on." I scroll through several songs on my playlist before landing on a song she must know. "You have to know this," I say as "California Dreamin'" by The Mamas & The Papas. Still nothing. "This do anything for you?" She shakes her head. I scan through my playlist again. Janis Joplin. Everyone's heard of her. I play "Piece of My Heart". Golden-honey eyes squint as if in recognition. Thank God! I was beginning to think this woman was an alien. Everybody knows this—

Amina shakes her head.

What in all the fuck? Not only do I have to get her accustomed to MMA, but I also have to expand her entire music catalog. We need an entire week of music appreciation. Thank God she found me when she did. Poor girl was out here barely living. There has to be one song from the '60s or '70s she's heard. I fast forward to Creedence Clearwater Revival's "Bad Moon Rising". This time, she shakes her head before I can ask. I shake my head in disappointment. One last try before I deem her a lost cause, I press play.

She bounces in her seat. I'm bestowed with a beatific, dimpled smile.

"The Beach Boys, 'Don't Worry Baby'! It's from *My Girl*. I love that movie. The first and second one. I had a huge crush on Austin O'Brien. He played Nick Zsigmond. Your freckles kind of remind me of him."

"*My Girl*?" I snort. "Of course, you know it because it was in a movie. It's classic 1964 Beach Boys. You should know it for them." Amina sways to the music. I roll my eyes.

"Hey! I told you I didn't know any music unless it was in a movie. Movies are my peanut butter and...JAM!" she says the last word in a faux deep voice.

I laugh. She is too cute for her own good. Amina is effortlessly alluring. Captivating to the extreme, yet she thinks she can be a wallflower, thinks she can move through life without drawing attention to herself. Her very being is attention-grabbing. Shit! She grabbed me while wearing a sweatsuit with her face obscured.

"Well, my jam is music from the '60s and '70s. I'm a music connoisseur. New school stuff is all right. There are a few groovy songs and artists, but nothing beats the '60s and '70s. Back then, music had heart, soul; it all had meaning."

Amina grunts. "*Heart & Soul* is old, but it's a really good movie." I toss a glare at her out of the corner of my eye, and shake my head.

She giggles. "I know what you're trying to say. I feel the same way about movies. They can transport you anywhere, even places you never thought existed. When I'm watching movies, I get to be part of the world—many worlds—without having to deal with the world and all the ways people can hurt you in it."

Weighty silence fills the space between us. There's a wealth of meaning in what she said and what she didn't say. At some point in Amina's life, she'd been hurt. Emotionally and mentally, I'm guessing. That's why she's so closed off. The way she explained her personality before being assaulted seems like she was still just as closed off. Movies are her literal escape. Most people use them as a break from the real world, but for her, they are quite literally her escape. She lives through them. It wouldn't surprise me if she learned all her morals and values from television and movies. And that makes me sad for her, deeply, but not pity her.

As children, we rely on our parents, teachers, friends, and extended family for a sense of security, safety, and belonging. They're how we find our place in the world. I don't know why I feel it, but I don't believe

Amina's ever felt safe. Our identity comes from these very important people in our lives. Maybe that's the reason she doesn't see herself in family photos and doesn't recognize her parents. It's possible they neglected her during her formative years.

Amina clears her throat. "So, what cologne do you wear? You always smell so...expensive."

"So, you dig my vibe?" I say, chuckling.

"You are the cockiest man I've ever met."

"Tom Ford Oud Wood," I answer. "It's all I wear. What about you? You always smell..." I struggle to find the right way to describe her scent. "Mysterious. Sexy. Dark."

"It's body spray, Into the Night," she says with what I suspect is a little bashfulness. "I have extremely sensitive skin, so I don't wear perfume."

"Hmm... That tracks. You always draw me in. Night perfectly describes you."

She laughs. "You're so weird. Tell me more about you. When's your birthday? Where were you born? Are your parents still together, or were they never married?"

"I turn 36 on May 9th. I'm a Taurus. I was born in Minnesota. My parents are still married. Have been for many, many, many years. Neither side of my family does divorce. We Kaplans play for keeps. So, don't get any ideas. There's no way out for you." I wink at her. She laughs, but I'm dead serious, which is part of the reason I wasn't totally honest about where we're going. She scares easily. This is my spin on immersion therapy. I know she'll be fine.

"Are you close to your parents?" she asks.

"Uh...Yeah. For the most part. It's always just been my brother and me."

Amina's silence is loaded. Uh-oh! I've said too much. She's too perceptive. I'm forcing a lot on her. It's only right that I be open with her. I take a breath deep enough to reach my toes.

"I love my family. My mom is one of the most supportive, ambitious, and committed people I know. And she's so loving. She has to be with all she's had to deal with. Remember, I told you my brother and father are schizophrenic. They can have really good weeks and really bad months. We never know which of them will have an episode. So, life was always eventful for me growing up. I know my parents love me, no question about it, but it's easy to feel invisible when you're not the person who needs such focused care. I don't resent them at all. My father and brother require a lot of time and resources. My mom has dedicated her life to their care, and mine. I stuttered when I was young, and she threw herself into figuring out how to help me. She'd do tongue twisters with me." I shrug. "Eventually, my stutter went away except for when I'm nervous. She's so strong. She's written several books about Schizoaffective disorder and living with someone who suffers from it. She authored a book about parenting a Schizophrenic child. She and my father co-authored an autobiography about his struggles and life living with a mental health disorder."

"Wow! That's impressive. She's not just strong, she sounds like a superhero."

"Oh, she is," I agree. "Both of them are amazing. It's not an easy life, but they're committed."

"It sounds like it," she says, then she pauses. The pause seems loaded, not in a good or bad way, just like there's a lot more to be said. I glance askance at her. She's staring at me, a little crease forms between her finely plucked brows.

"I also see how that could make a child feel pretty lonely, or maybe, unseen. It doesn't mean they don't love you, and you don't love them. You were all in it together. Your family sounds very strong. Doesn't mean your feelings are selfish or invalid. I mean, I don't know you that well. I'm as messed up as can be now, so I'm in no place to judge, but I can tell there were events they probably missed because of the episodes you mentioned. Maybe there were even times when instead of a hug, you had to self-soothe, or you might not have said anything about what you were going through because, in your mind, what you were dealing with wasn't as important as whatever was going on with them."

It takes me a moment to respond. A lump forms in my throat, and tears glaze my eyes. Somehow, she's 100% right. I'd never put it into words before because I didn't want to be a burden or come off as selfish. It's probably why I've been a serial monogamist. Searching for the companionship I missed when I was younger. I have friends, best friends, but there's always a missing connection. I want to be the center of someone's world, like my dad and brother are for my mom. Freud would have a field day with me.

"Sorry. I didn't mean to psychoanalyze you or anything," Amina apologizes. "I'm far from a therapist, although I've taken a lot of psychology classes. Before everything happened, I wasn't too far away from a BA in Social Work."

All I do is shake my head. No apology is necessary. She hit the nail on the head. I know she would have been an amazing social worker. If I have anything to do with it, I'll help her realize that dream if she still wants to pursue it.

"It's taking forever," she says, changing the topic. "Where are we supposed to be going again?"

I chuckle. Sneaky, sneaky girl. "We're almost there, and I never told you exactly where we're going. So, sit back and enjoy the ride." Glancing at her, I add, "You're looking real tense over there, hugging the door and 'oh shit' bar. Relax."

She cuts a sidelong glance at me. "It's never advisable to tell a woman to relax. I don't like surprises. In my experience, they rarely lead to anything good. I prefer plans, sir, maybe an itinerary. Something. I need time to prepare mentally."

"Amina, not everything is an ambush. This will be fun. It's my best friend's birthday party," I say, providing the same information I told her three days ago when I invited her.

"Where's your gift if it's a birthday party? Don't guys give each other presents for their birthdays?" she asks, a wealth of suspicion coloring her tone.

"If you're not too afraid to let go of the door handle," I say, jokingly, "there's a long black drawing tube on the seat behind you. Reach back there and grab it."

She rolls her eyes, then unbuckles her seatbelt, turns, and reaches into the backseat.

I'm not mad at all at the view. Her knitted peach-colored mini sweater-dress rides up her thigh, almost exposing a nice apple booty. It's not big, but it's enough for a man to grab a firm hold of. If she weren't wearing black tights, the view would go from perfect to magnificent. Although, if I'm being honest, the view from the front is also pretty great. The V-neck of the dress rides the line between classy and sexy. The Lord outdid himself when he created those breasts. A hint of her plump brown globes' crests over the top like the sun rising between two mountains. Scrumptious!

"Stop staring at my booty, buddy." Busted! She glares at me from over her shoulder. "Eyes on the road. I don't want to fly out of the windshield if you have to brake. No eye privileges," she says, but her soft giggle belies her serious tone.

"Then hurry up. It's on the seat."

"There are two of them."

"It's the one with red threading on the adjustable strap."

"Ah," she says, plopping back into her seat with the nineteen-inch black tube. She refastens her seatbelt. "What kind of present comes in this? Is your friend an architect?"

"Open it," I offer, "Be careful not to bend it or touch it too much." When silence greets my warning, I glance at her. Amina arches a brow and bestows me with a snotty eye roll. "Just be careful," I caution.

With a huff, she unscrews the cap and pulls out the rolled pastel mat paper. She sets the drawing tube on the floorboard, resting it between her thick thighs. Ugh! I've never been more envious of an inanimate object in my life.

She unrolls the paper. And gasps.

A mina Raichand

Oh, Mylanta! "You drew this?" I ask, not even trying to hide my astonishment.

"What do you think?"

"That there's some art gallery missing one of their best pieces," I quip. "Ohmygoodness! Garrett! Wow! Why would you ever want to be punched and hug guys for fun? This is your calling. You might break your hand or something doing that other crap. This is amazing."

Here I was thinking Garrett, dressed down in a thick maroon flannel over a white shirt, wheat Timberlands, and dark denim jeans, was a work of art. Well, I'm still right about that, but this picture is gorgeous.

If I'm not mistaken, it's done in oil pastels and is so lifelike. I can almost smell the ice. There's so much detail. The deserted hockey rink is mysterious, with overhead lights that brightly bounce off the slick ice.

Under the ice, two blue lines divide the rink into three zones. A thick red line divides the rink in half; thin red goal lines are at each end of the ice, and small lines are perpendicular to the end-zone faceoff circles. There are nine face-off dots and circles; and two painted blue semi-circles in front of each goal. There's everything one would expect to see at an actual hockey rink, including reflections in the glass surrounding the rink, the stands, and the *pièce de résistance*, a white Zamboni at the fair end of the rink waits to shave and resurface the ice. No words in the English language can adequately express the picture's grandeur.

I look at Garrett in a different light. He may be hyper judgmental, cocky, and a bit dominant, but he's so much deeper than I ever would've imagined. And, not that it matters, but dude has some serious money. His Mercedes-Benz SUV smells like expensive leather and him. It must have been washed recently, because the metallic obsidian-black exterior is sleeker than usual. Every gadget one could want is mounted somewhere: a dashcam, and a wide navigation display, for example. The front seats are heated and ventilated. I've been struggling not to use the hot-stone massage feature, one of eight massage programs. No wonder he's always so self-assured and full of himself; he lives in a constant state of chill.

"Why exactly are you a Financial Manager? You should focus on your art. You're talented as all get out," I say.

Red creeps up his neck and suffuses his cheeks. Aww... He does have a shy bone in his body. He rubs the back of his neck with one hand, then runs his fingers through his short, dark brown, and copper hair.

"I'm good with money. It's a stable job. Drawing is something I do for fun," he explains. "It's a passion. If I did it for work, that would suck all the joy out of it."

"Hmm... I can get that. You're really good at it. You should draw something for me sometime. Anything that comes to mind. I'll love whatever it is."

"You love me, huh?" He gazes at me with heat in his greenish-blue eyes and his signature smirk on his lips.

Ugh! Of course, he'd pick that word to focus on.

I re-roll the picture with great care, put it back in its tube, and screw the cap on. Instead of throwing it in the backseat, I return it to the floorboard and keep it steady between my knees. Trying to think of anything to say rather than address his whole love obsession, I stare out the window.

And I am met with more beauty.

Just outside the window sits an idyllic, quaint suburb. It reminds me of Stars Hollow from the show *The Gilmore Girls*. It's adorable. All this time I've lived in Indiana, and I've never once seen this town. It looks like a dream, so lush and green, like you can walk everywhere. It's the kind of place with farmers' markets where you'd run into your neighbors or the mailman, the kind of city where they have town hall meetings that the entire town attends and live music in the town square. It's so inviting.

"What's this place?" I ask, pointing out the window.

Garrett glances out the window. "That's Carmel. It's beautiful, huh?"

"I want to live there. It looks like it's a city out of time."

"What's that mean?"

"You know, like it preserved the old school feel. Did you ever see the movie *Pleasantville*?"

"You and movies," he grumbles. "No, I haven't seen *Pleasantville*."

"You should see it, it's good. These teenagers get transported into this black-and-white 1950s TV show. The town is very *Leave It to Beaver*. It's awesome. That's what this city looks like to me. Time and corruption haven't tainted it. It's perfect."

"I didn't understand most of what you said. You are a fount of television and movie knowledge," he says, laughing. "But on the good news side of things... we're almost there. You'll see a grey and white house in about five minutes."

Chapter Twenty-Seven

Garrett Kaplan

"Where the heck did you bring me?" Amina asks through gritted teeth.

Getting out of the car, I go around to the passenger side. Amina opens the door before I can reach for the handle. The way she steps out in her knee-high boots screams pissed. She doesn't know quite where we are, but there is suspicion in the depths of her golden eyes. Flipping her dark brown unbound hair—which looks incredible; I've never seen it down before—over her shoulder, she pegs me with a piercing stare.

"You said birthday party," she says in a hushed tone. "This looks like a family thing. People are grilling, and they look way older than us. See those people over there setting out plates and refreshments? I thought this was going to be more like s'mores and beer. You lied."

She slams her door. I reach out to guide her with a hand to her lower back as we make our way to where everyone mingles behind the short wooden fence. Amina sidesteps my touch.

Should've known. I laugh. If she could, she'd probably speed up and walk away from me, but she doesn't know where she's going, so she's forced to stay beside me.

"I didn't lie to you, Foxy," I rush to correct her before her imagination can run wild. "This is a birthday party for my best friend, who also happens to be my cousin. This is our family beach house. The older people don't hang out long. It's only aunts, uncles, and my parents."

For the first time, Amina grabs my wrist and pulls me to a stop. Or tries to pull me to a stop. I'm 215 lbs. and 6'3". She's not stopping me unless I want to stop. And I stop.

"Your parents!" she whisper-shouts and stomps her little booted foot. "I don't want to meet your parents. We are nowhere near a step like that."

"I met your parents," I retort.

Her jaw clenches, her lips pucker, and she squints up at me. "Those are not my parents, butthead! We went through this. Which ones are your parents?"

I can't help it, I laugh. She flicks me in my stomach. Luckily, my shirt prevents her from making contact. That might have hurt. I laugh again.

"Don't laugh at me. I'm serious. I don't like surprises."

"Baby doll, you agreed that they sound great, right?"

"Yes, but that—"

"No buts," I interrupt, "they're awesome. You'll love them, and they'll adore you. I don't bring women who don't matter around my family."

She stands silent for a beat. The longer she searches my eyes, the more I notice the flecks of green in her golden-honey eyes. Fuck! She is so beautiful, and she doesn't realize it. To know her is to love her. As cornball as it sounds, there's just something about her. Maybe it's the mix of vulnerability and contrasting strength that emanates from her entire being. It makes me want to protect her and provide her with a sense of safety. She can be mean sometimes, but I know she won't hurt me.

"Look... out towards the open sliding door. See it?"

"Yeah."

"An average height woman is wearing a white turtleneck and brown flannel, her hair up in a messy bun. She's to the left of the door. And the tall dude over at the grill."

"Yeah. The man in the denim jacket?"

"His hair's dark auburn, cut like mine. Goatee."

"Mm-hmm..."

"Those are my parents. Totally innocuous. The people further into the beach are family and friends of the family. They're our age, very cool."

Amina sighs heavily. "Okay. Fine."

And doesn't move an inch.

Hmm... I thought her answer was capitulation. Yet here she stands, hands wringing and gaze fixed on something in the distance. Too far in the distance... She is not here.

Shit!

Knocking her hands apart, which she doesn't so much as flinch at, tells me all I need to know. She's hearing the whispers again and trapped somewhere I can't reach her, lost. to me. Unlucky for her, my entire life has prepared me for her, for this. I may have often been ignored, but I learned a myriad of tricks and tools by watching my mother fight invisible demons and dragons. Watching her crawl over landmines and through shrapnel on reconnaissance missions to retrieve my father and brother from the POW camps, where their minds held them hostage. Choosing this woman, her stubbornness, her horrible laugh, her passion, her mystery... Choosing her means I will be honored to save her from any monster, even if that monster is her.

She's going to be pissed, but *que sera, sera*. I've become a seasoned veteran at dealing with her anger. Placing my hands on her shoulders,

I turn her to face me. Her movement is wooden; she doesn't jerk from my touch. And she stares through me. Her lips quiver. Sweat that has nothing to do with the crisp March air glistens on her forehead. I gently shake her shoulders.

"Amina! 1-2-3 eyes on me."

Her expression remains blank, yet her light brown eyes shift back and forth as if she hears something. Whether it's me or the whispers, I'm not sure. I stroke her arms up and down, admiring the softness of her knitted sweater-dress.

"1-2-3 eyes on me, doll," I repeat in a calm tone. "Come back to me, Foxy."

Amina blinks and shakes her head. She uses her eyes to scan her surroundings but doesn't look at me. After several deep breaths, she looks at her arms. No, that's not right. She glares at my hands where they're still caressing her upper arms.

She glances up at me through impossibly long lashes. "No skin privileges, buddy."

Laughing, I drop my hands and put not as much distance as she'd prefer between us.

"Nobody noticed that, did they?" she asks. Her eyes bulge, and her lips tighten into what I'm guessing is mortification.

"If they did, all they would have seen is me loving on my lady," I say.

Amina rolls her eyes. "Don't call me that. You never even asked. That type of declaration is usually made after a question is asked."

"Would you say yes if I asked you?"

"No."

"That's what I thought. That's why I didn't ask."

"Proclaiming it doesn't make it true."

Winking, I give her a salacious grin. "I get what I want. Stop fighting it."

She cuts her eyes at me.

"Are you two going to join the party or stand out there making out all evening?!" my dad shouts.

So engrossed in one of our usual sparing matches, we hadn't realized we'd gained an audience. We turn and see several of my friends and my parents watching us from the other side of the fence. This time, Amina walks beside me, allowing me to guide her with my hand on her very rigid back. Baby steps. I'll take it.

"Oh, shit!" I stop. "I forgot Keith's present. I'll be right—"

"Nope. You're not going to leave me here with all these people I don't know. Give me your keys. I'll get it," Amina demands, holding out her dainty hand. She snatches the keys and quickly walks off in the direction of my car.

As soon as her back is turned, I turn to stare at my family, who have all congregated around the old wooden fence. I give the universal wide-eyed warning and head tilt to the side, instructing them to scatter.

Amina returns to my side a few seconds later. I turn to her with a grin. She didn't stop an arm's length away. For the first time, she's where she belongs, right beside me, waiting for me to guide her over. With a big shit-eating grin, I place my hand at the small of her back, and together we walk over to meet my family.

*A*mina Raichand

I want to pull away immediately, but Garrett is grinning like the cat who got the cream, and I don't want to embarrass him in front of his family.

Ugh! Family!

I wish he had told me we would be meeting his family. I was nerve-wracked enough thinking I would be meeting a bunch of his long-time friends. But... family! That's an entirely different beast.

I'm no good at families or parents. Children are simple. They'll love you as long as you feed them and play with them. Some want to be held. Other than that, they don't care about what you look like or about your past. It's easy to make a good impression on them, and I love children. I don't love being looked over like some show pony. Everyone will be probing for information and combing through everything I say, searching for hidden meaning.

Too much pressure.

I haven't had a ton of serious relationships, but the one I had where I met the guy's parents was a disaster. His mother, literally, broke down in tears talking about how I wasn't who she wanted for her son. The dad said that girls like me were only good for one night. I left that restaurant in tears. Every eye and ear was on me. That's exactly why I hate attention and being around people. My life will be moving along nicely, and then, the moment I reach out for something that should be normal or real, I'm reminded that I'm not allowed true happiness or people in my life. People bring drama. That's why I forced myself to be content with random booty calls from trusted pillow pals—that's what I affectionately call what most refer to as F buddies—to scratch my carnal itches, should I have any, and it's been a long time since I've had one of those. When I want romance, I watch one of my favorite movies, and I find joy and happiness in those characters' lives. This... Meeting Garrett's family is a recipe for disaster, even if they like me. Something will destroy it. And what if I like them? My heart can't take any more disappointment and pain. Every woman has her breaking point. I had no choice in this. But here we go. People part like the Red Sea as Garrett unlatches and holds open the short wooden fence's door. Everyone smiles like mischievous lunatics. Great!

I plaster on my best pleased-to-meet-you smile—or I hope that's what it is. It could also be my Donner-party-of-one smile. Who knows!

Garrett's mother approaches, smiling from ear to ear. Dark freckles spread across the bridge of her nose and apples of her cheeks like wings of a bird. Her messy copper-red bun bounces with each step. Her smooth skin doesn't so much as hint at her age.

"Well, well, well," she says, putting her hands on her hips. She eyes me up and down. "You are just as precious as Rett said. I'm so happy you agreed to come. Rett said he wasn't sure if you would."

I leer askance at Garrett. "Oh, Rett said that, did he?"

Garrett clears his throat. "Foxy, this is my mom, Gwendolyn, but everybody calls her Gwen. And my dad, Trevor, is over there playing grill master." He points towards the grill not far away.

Gwen offers me her hand. "I assume your name is not Foxy."

Shaking her proffered hand, I say, "No. Garrett seems to forget my name a lot. I'm Amina. Nice to meet you. Do you prefer Gwendolyn or Gwen?"

"Gwen is fine. One day, maybe you can even call me Mom," Gwen says, nudging Garrett. He grins. I groan inwardly. He does not need her to give him ideas.

"Where's Rob?" Garrett asks, looking around. To me, he adds, "Rob's my older brother."

Gwen waves a dismissive hand. "Oh, inside, of course. He refuses to stop watching whatever show he's been binging for the last week and a half. You know how he is when he's hyper-fixating."

"What about Ma'ma-ma and Nampa?" Garrett asks.

Balking, I ask, "I can kind of figure it out, but for clarification's sake, who's Ma'ma-ma and Nampa?"

"His grandparents," Gwen answers, laughing. Humor twinkles in her green eyes. "They're Trevor's parents. When Robbie was little, he couldn't say Grandma or Grandpa, so he settled on Ma'ma-ma and

Nampa, and since he was the first grandchild, it stuck. That's also how Garrett got his nickname. Thank goodness, we didn't go with what his dad wanted to name him. Otherwise, his nickname would sound more like Shrek."

"Thanks, I guess," Garrett says.

"Shush!" Gwen scolds Garrett. "It wouldn't have been Shrek. It started with a 'D' or something."

Watching the interplay between Garrett and his mother is hilarious. I see where he gets his attitude from. They're so lighthearted and easygoing with each other, further proving that Nora and Gilbert can't possibly be my parents. Oil and water blend better than we do.

"You thirsty, Amina, honey?" Gwen asks. "Or hungry? Trevor's just grilling some extra odds and ends, but there's food inside that I was about to bring out before you and Rett showed up?"

I shift from one foot to another. "Umm... I could use a drink, thanks."

"Don't thank me. Rett's going to get it," Gwen says, leveling Garrett with an expectant stare. "Aren't you, Rett?"

Garrett looks down at me. His turquoise eyes ask what his mouth can't. *"Will you be okay if I go get drinks?" they ask wordlessly.*

"No, don't leave me." That's what I want to say. Instead, I shrug and offer a closed-lip, compliant smile.

He rubs a quick, gentle circle against my lower back. "I'll be over there," he says, jerking his head, "where that big group of morons is." He and Gwen chuckle.

Following his head gestures, I see a group of about 9 or 10 people a few yards away, near a large circle of stones. They're dressed in what I can only describe as a walking Carhartt fashion shoot. Some wear beanies to match their outfit. I'm so out of my element.

Garrett slides the drawing tube strap down my arm and takes it from my fingers in a way that's absolutely inappropriate in front of his mother.

And the lip bite and hot look he tosses me over his shoulder as he walks away is...

Frickin' hot!

And also, super unacceptable for my body to get all shivery.

Gwen's laughter alerts me to the fact that not only did she see what he did, but she also witnessed my saucy glare. Warmth suffuses my neck and cheeks. If ever there were a time to be grateful for brown skin, it was now. Otherwise, I'd be blushing from my head to my toes.

"Incorrigible, that one is," Gwen says, laughing nonplussed. "Come have a seat with me over here, I want to talk at you for a minute. Get to know the amazing woman my son keeps bragging about."

Nodding, I follow her a short distance to a long table covered with a navy-blue tablecloth. Gwen pulls out a long wooden bench seat. We sit beside each other. Instead of rushing right into the conversation I think she wants to have with me, she gazes at me with a silly smile on her thin pink lips for far too long, longer than I'm comfortable with.

"So..." I sigh. "Garrett tells me you're an author. You and your husband, actually. He's so proud of the two of you. I'm impressed with all of your strength. You sound like a close family."

Gwen rolls her eyes and grins. "We are. I love my boys, but I want to know about you. Rett's only brought one other girl home, and that was when he was in middle school. He was positive little Courtney Rogers was gonna have all his babies. Then she heard his stutter when he got nervous. Broke his little heart into a million pieces. He must have played 'Close to You', 'Love Hurts,' and 'When a Man Loves a Woman' a billion times." Her laugh scrunches her nose, and her green eyes sparkle.

I follow suit—laughing in my, polite public laugh instead of my real *Revenge of the Nerds* laugh—although I'm not sure I've ever heard those songs, but context clues tell me they're cheesy breakup songs.

Sobering, she continues, "It was a rough three weeks in our household." She looks around us conspiratorially. "We'll keep that between us.

We'd almost gotten his stutter under control, but any bouts of nervousness, and it'd rear its ugly head. I used tongue twisters to help him with it. Then I realized they worked to calm Trevor and Robbie during their crises. But enough about that. I don't want to embarrass him or any of them. These'll have to be our little secrets. So, what do you do for work?"

The topic change throws me for a loop. After a short pause, I answer, "I work." My gaze drops to my lap. How easily I forget. Taking a deep breath, I start over, "I worked with children who are wards of the court in a group home setting. The state system is very flawed and oftentimes does more harm than good to children. My goal was to get my degree in Social Work and implement change from the inside."

Gwen squeezes the hand I hadn't even realized I'd gripped the hem of my sweater-dress with. Her hand embodies warmth, comfort, and her smile is sympathetic. "That's an admirable goal. Keep after it," Gwen advises. "It sounds like you speak from first-hand experience."

I nod. Gulp. "Yes. It's a very personal passion," I say, trying to convey as politely as possible that I'd rather not talk about it.

"And would you like to have children someday soon?" she asks, again giving me whiplash with her ability to jump topics without warning. Her smile is blinding. I can't decide if I'm happy, she picked up on me, subtly shutting down the discussion of my childhood, or mortified because I absolutely know why a man's mother would ask this question.

"Umm..." I don't know what to say.

She waves her question away. "Look at me being Miss Nosy Rosy, giving you the third degree on your first time over. I'm so excited you're here that I don't know how to act. Excuse my manners, Amina, honey."

"No worries. I didn't know I'd be meeting you today. I'm a little off balance," I say unbothered.

Gwen's eyes bulge, and her mouth falls open. Then she laughs, shaking her head. "That sounds like Garrett."

"What sounds like me?"

Chapter Twenty-Eight

"Noneya," Gwen says with a smirk. "But it would be nice if you gave your girlfriend a heads up before throwing her to the wolves."

Garrett's mouth forms an "O," and his eyes widen.

Turning to me, he says, "You told on me!" His lips turn down into a pout. "That's a party foul, baby doll. And here I was being sweet and making you a special drink." Illustrating his point, he holds up one of two grey solo cups in his hands.

"Hush!" Gwen says. "You were getting her that drink, no matter what she did or didn't tell me. You're the host. You're supposed to serve your guests and make sure that they're comfortable."

"Says who?" Garrett asks. "This is Keith's birthday party."

"That's ridiculous, your cousin can't host his own birthday party," Gwen states emphatically. "What would that look like? He'd order pizza and a keg, and you all would be sitting on bean-bag chairs."

"Auntie Gwen, that's just cold," Keith, I suppose, says, walking over to stand at the end of the table next to Garrett.

A mocha-skinned beauty sidles up to Keith and Garrett, forcing her way between them. They almost spill their drinks. She has to be the shortest woman I've ever seen. I know she is a woman and not a child because her curves go on for days. Her pink coat with a white fur hood, form-fitting brown dress, black tights, and knee-high boots do nothing to mask her curvaceous frame. Nutbrown doe eyes outlined in black eyeliner look deceptively innocent. Her plump lips are outlined with dark brown pencil and filled with clear gloss, making them perfect, kissable lips. I wouldn't kiss her, but I'm positive many others have and would. She wears her hair free-flowing in what appears to be long, natural, dark brown curls, but the two attention-commanding things are her blue money pieces framing her face and her height.

I'm no one to comment on height. I'm five-two on a good day. With five-inch heels, I reach a smooth five-seven. A runway model, I will never be. I'm the shortest person in most rooms, except out here. I know she has to be wearing heels, and she still only looks about four-foot-eleven. I'd be a giant next to her.

"Who invited the tiny terror?" Gwen asks, no heat behind her insult.

"The question is who wouldn't invite me, Gwendolyn?" the short woman asks in a raspy, haughty voice. "I'm a delight to be around. And who is this sexy chocolate thang next to you? I never forget a gorgeous face," she says, leaning in and licking her lips. Her brown gaze lands on my respectable cleavage.

"This..." Gwen says, throwing her arm over my shoulder.

It takes Herculean strength to keep from throwing her arm off me. Not that she's being forceful or anything, I'm just not in a place where touching doesn't cause a fair amount of anxiety.

"...is Amina Raichand," Gwen pauses as if waiting for a drumroll. She gives another blinding smile. "Rett's girlfriend. They've been seeing each other for a few months now. I have a good feeling about this one."

"He brought her here. That says a lot," Keith says, adjusting his black beanie. It rests on his dark, thick brows, accentuating his piercing grey eyes.

"Can you get up, Mom?" Garrett asks, interjecting. "I'd like to give my lady her drink. The ice is gonna melt, and then it'll taste off." Gwen—blessedly—removes her arm from my shoulder. I take an easy breath for the first time since she placed it there. "Is that any way to speak to your life bearer?" Gwen says, tittering. "Mom, may I please sit beside the love of my life?" She adds, trying to mock Garrett's deep voice, but failing.

Garrett's voice is bone-rattling deep. The deepest singing voice is *basso profondo*, which best describes his normal speaking voice. It's so deep and resonant, no one could ever mimic it. And that's saying something because Keith's voice is also deep. It must be a family trait.

Gwen slides off the bench and stands. The short woman pushes Garrett out of the way before he can move to take the seat.

I chortle at the outrage on his handsome face.

"You'll have to excuse Varinka," Keith says. "She hasn't been the same since she moved to Arizona." He shakes his head, and a moue graces his lips. "No home training."

"Honey, help me with this lid!" Trevor shouts. "I must've latched the fuckin' thing somehow. I'm burnin' the steak. Rett, you and bonehead get the really burnt ones."

"Uncle Trev, it's my birthday!" Keith shouts over his shoulder. "I should get the best one. Give the burnt one to Rob or Mighty Mouse."

"Fuck you, Keith," Varinka says. "I don't eat steak. I suck on meat. Big. Tender. Meat." She flicks her long, pierced tongue out like a snake.

I blanch at the lewdness of the inappropriate conversation. Is this what it's like when parents hang out with their adult children? Manners be darned! Everybody says all their inside, intrusive thoughts out loud. These people are closer to each other than I am to myself.

"Was this drink for me, honey?" Gwen asks Garrett, reaching for one of the solo cups he's holding.

He hands her the cup in his right hand. Garrett extends his free hand towards me.

"Let me get you away from all these perverts, Foxy."

I take his hand without hesitation. I'll think about the implications of skin privileges later. Although he'd been holding a cold drink seconds ago, his large, warm hand envelops mine. Gazing into his eyes, I sigh in contentment. Garrett does his sexy grin while applying steadying pressure to my hand. I'm almost in a daze, rising from my seat. Something is happening here, and I'm not sure I like it. Am I feeling safe? Pampered? Affection? Or is it that he's the only person I'm familiar with here?

"Don't take her away," Varinka whines. "I haven't had a chance to get acquainted with this delicious surprise."

I scoot between the small space between the long table and the bench seat, past Varinka.

"Ne-ver mind," Varinka says. She grunts. "I hate to see her go, but I love to watch her walk away. Damn, girl."

Once I'm beside Garrett and far from his pint-sized friend, I toss a momentary quizzical glance Varinka's way.

We walk a short distance away around the side of the house. The view of the ocean from over here is breathtaking. I'm not a nut for water, though I can swim. It reminds me of a few scenes from movies like *Dear John*, *Grease*, and *The Notebook*. I appreciate the water's beauty. When we stop, I tug my hand from Garrett's. He releases it without complaint then winks at me. He thrusts the grey solo cup towards me.

"What is this?" I ask, guard up. I survey the cup with suspicion.

Garrett rocks back on his heels. "A little urine mixed with Rohypnol." He laughs.

I grab the cup, narrowing my gaze at him.

"Just take a sip. It's your favorite. You'll like it. I promise." He winks. "And I haven't broken a promise to you yet."

Rolling my eyes, I take a hesitant sip.

Ooh! That's yummy.

"Mmm... that's good, but I can't. Remember? Lexapro. Klonopin." I hand him the drink.

"What?! I made it special for you. It's your drink. The Ménage on the Beach," he cajoles. "C'mon, it's one drink. There isn't that much alcohol in it. What'll it hurt?"

"A lot, if Heath Ledger has anything to say about it."

Garrett grimaces. "Don't be dramatic. It's only one drink, and it's not even full."

I hit him with a droll stare and snatch the cup. "What are you? Some poorly written after-school special bully peer-pressuring the quiet kid."

My lips curl around the aluminum cup's rim, and I stare suggestively down the cup's base.

Garrett steps closer, invading my personal space, and tips the bottom up with a finger.

"All the cool kids are doing it," he teases. "Chug, Foxy."

"Here you two are," Varinka says, rounding the side of the house. Three tall men trail her.

Most people are taller than Varinka. She's not an accurate metric. Gauging their heights against Garrett's or his cousin Keith is a better comparison. The two blond men are an inch or two under Garrett's 6'3". The man with short-cropped brown hair is about the same height as both cousins. If one hadn't spent any time in Varinka's presence, it would look like these men were kidnapping her. From what I can tell so far, though, what Varinka lacks in height, she more than makes up for it in personality. She's the biggest in that group.

Garrett doesn't move until my drink is more than half gone. Then he steps back.

"Baby doll, this is a friend of ours, Chuck," Garrett says, gesturing to the brown-haired man who bears a striking resemblance to Ian Somerhalder, if Ian Somerhalder were modeling for a men's camping magazine.

"S'up, Baby doll," Chuck says, extending his hand to me.

He's all smiles with his straight and startlingly white teeth. That's one heck of a Colgate smile.

Garrett swats his hand away. "It's Amina for you."

"Nice to meet you, Chuck," I say, offering him my hand. Garrett swats my hand away, too.

"Don't flirt with my woman, man," Garrett growls. And not in that sexy way they describe in books, he actually growled a low rumble emanating from his chest. Chuck's answering laugh is good-natured.

"Who are these guys?" Chuck asks, arching a brow at the two men with Varinka. "This is an invitation-only shindig, no strangers."

"Don't be jealous 'cuz you can't tap this anymore," Varinka says. "We had our moment, boo. It wasn't that deep. Literally," she adds with a saucy yet condescending grin. "This," she says, linking her arm through the blond with the goatee, "is Caleb. His soulful brown eyes won me over. And this," she says, linking arms with the arm of the clean-shaven blond with hazel-blue eyes, "is Hayden, and well, look at him. What's understood doesn't have to be explained. They're my dates. I needed one, and they were both nice enough to agree to come with me."

"In more ways than one," Chuck grumbles. He sips from the beer bottle I didn't realize he had at his side.

Letting go of each of her dates' arms, Varinka saunters towards me. I brace myself. This is a woman who openly brought two dudes to a friend's birthday party—and insinuated that she slept with one of her other friends at some point. By the animosity I can feel between them, that might not have been that long ago. Then there's how she looks at me...

"I don't mean to be rude, gorgeous, but I must say your skin is beautiful. It looks so soft. May I..."

Please, don't ask to touch me.

"...inquire about your ethnicity? I know you're Black, but there's something about you," Varinka says, her lecherous gaze skating up and down my body.

I shiver, and not because it's cold. "Umm... My birth father is East Indian, and my birth mother is Black," I say.

Varinka's attention becomes bolder. She bites her lip, perusing my body like I'm some gourmet meal. "Too bad Garrett got to you first. I'm jealous," Varinka purrs. "We should exchange numbers just in case." She reaches into her bra and retrieves a card then hands it to me. "If he fucks up—and he will—call me."

Garrett makes a noise from beside me.

"Kidding. Kidding," Varinka says, "I'd never poach a friend's person. Maybe we can hang sometime if you ever want a break from corn and scarecrows and want to step into the Valley of the Sun. I bet you'd glisten under the Arizona sun." She winks. "Come on, guys, I need a drink," she says, sashaying away with her dates.

I glance at Garrett. "Uhh... Was she serious?"

Chuck throws his head back and guffaws.

"Maybe. With Varinka, you never know." Garrett chuckles.

How do I ask this question without seeming phobic? I'm not. To each their own, but... Varinka has two male dates, and no one bats an eye at it or her crude manner of speaking. She's a lot. Then she's coming on to me... My head is spinning. I don't understand.

"Don't analyze it too much," Chuck says. "Varinka's a blast."

"She's down for whatever and whoever. She likes genitals. All genitals," Garrett further elaborates. "No discrimination."

Well, that answers that. I don't yuck her yum. I inspect the card Varinka gave me. "Varinka's a divorce attorney?!" I ask, unable to keep the shock out of my voice.

Both Chuck and Garrett burst into laughter. "Varinka is a very complex being," Garrett says.

Chuck slings his arm over my shoulder, tucking me under his arm.

Not again! He's not sweaty. He actually smells good. But why? Why is this group of people so handsy? I was starting to like Chuck.

"All right, all right," Garrett admonishes, "You're making my lady uncomfortable."

"A and me are buddies now," Chuck says. "She digs it." Garrett punches Chuck in the opposite shoulder, then slaps his arm off me. Unfazed, Chuck chortles. "You hit like a bitch, Rett."

Shattering glass sounds from somewhere. I guess that it's inside the house.

"Robbie, honey, it's okay," Gwen shouts. "I'll be right there."

A boom of something falling or being thrown rends the air.

"Shit!" Garrett and Chuck say in unison.

They run towards the open sliding back door of the house located behind the long table.

"Wait here, Foxy," Garrett commands over his shoulder.

Garrett Kaplan

Fuck my life!

Chuck, Keith, Mateo, and I all come through the open sliding door and into the family room at the same time. We stop short, taking in the scene unfolding before us. The lesser part of my mind wonders about Mateo, a Brazilian man who'd been a friend to not only me but everyone here since childhood. He must have gotten here when I was around back with Amina.

What a homecoming!

And what a birthday for Keith.

The house is a wreck. The flat screen has a ten-centimeter hole through it. Decorative vases and flowerpots lay scattered in a million pieces. The solid oak coffee table is broken into unfathomable pieces. I don't even want to speculate how Rob managed that. Blood-splatter paints the walls. Ma'ma-ma and Nampa are gonna shit a brick.

When Mom said Rob was inside, fixating on a TV show, I was relieved. He was way less likely to have an episode when he was hyper-focused on building something, reading, or watching a TV series. This isn't how I want Amina to ease into meeting my family. I'm embarrassed, and then steamrolling right over that emotion is shame. Shame because this wasn't intentional. If Rob could control it, he would. He's not an embarrassment to me.

That's my big brother. His petrified blue eyes and wild, dark-red hair are not indicative of who he is. Thank God, Mom forces him to keep his nails short. Even with that small blessing, there are tears down each side of his face. Blood wells from the gouges in his skin. He must have been pulling his hair because it is sticking up in every which way. This isn't my brother. This is his illness. Like a broken leg or the flu, his schizophrenia doesn't make him less not to me or any of us here.

I just know he'll feel horrible about this once he comes down, and he'll be mortified when he finds out it was while Amina was here. When I told him about her, he couldn't have been happier than if it were him who had met someone. That's why I told her to wait for me. He protected me in school when people bullied me for my stutter. He taught me how to build houses since carpentry and construction are his passions.

I never want to blame or shame him for these outbursts. They're like my stutter, part of him. Society wouldn't judge someone who broke out in chicken pox, or with a rash from an allergic reaction. No one should judge him for this. I don't. I love him.

Mom pushes through the four of us blocking the entrance. She's slow to approach him, all the while speaking in a low, calm tone. "Hey, what happened? Did your show go off?"

Rob turns crazed eyes on our mother. She doesn't back down, nor does she move closer.

"Mat," she says, talking to Mateo in the same level tone without turning around, "could you do me a favor, honey, and turn off that kitchen light? Turn on the lamp on the one side table, beside where the couch usually is."

When she says that, I notice for the first time that Rob flipped the couch over. That's been in the family for years, as long as I can remember. Rob will enjoy refurbishing it...later.

"Keith, go get a few chairs from the dining room," Mom says in the same tranquil voice.

Mateo and Keith go their separate ways to do as they were instructed.

"Now that your show is over, do you want to eat?" she asks Rob. "Rett or Dad can go get you a plate."

Big mistake.

Rob bellows, stabbing my mother and me with a glacial glare.

"I'm not a baby!" Rob yells. "You don't need to feed me. I can get my own food. Or are you trying to put something in it? That's why you don't want me anywhere near the food. I heard you whispering earlier. You're trying to drug me."

Only a lifetime of dealing with these types of episodes keeps me quiet. Reacting in anger or irritation would only feed the flame. He has acute psychosis. That, coupled with his natural penchant for challenging, can cause him to lash out to provoke a negative reaction in others. At the end of the day, he's still Rob, and he has just as many quirks and personality flaws as any of us.

The overhead fluorescent kitchen light goes off. Warm light from the lamp bathes the living room in a more natural, calming glow. Keith carries three large chairs in from the dining room. He places them against the far exterior wall of the kitchen bar since it's the only area not littered with shards of glass or splinters of wood.

Glass crunches under Keith's and Mateo's booted feet as they make their way past me and back outside. They are also familiar with crisis protocols. The more people who are in the room, the worse Rob's agitation can get.

Mom sits on the chair between the other two chairs.

"Come sit with me, Robbie," she says. "I'm not wearing the right shoes to be standing on glass. I know you always tell me to wear sturdier footwear when I'm near your workshop or any building zone, but today I chose fashion over common sense."

Rob doesn't move. He stands looking part pensive, part terrified.

"Sit next to me, Robbie?" Mom asks again, in no hurry.

Longing fills Rob's eyes as he gazes at the chair.

Then all hell breaks loose.

He stomps on bare feet through the glass over to the chairs. Bloody footprints stamp taupe Berber carpet in his wake. Mom doesn't flinch. I hold my breath. Rob grabs the antique chair and lifts it over his head. He roars, and I ball my fists at my sides. I might have to tackle my brother if he throws that chair at my mom. Rob caterwauls.

"Haaave... Yooou... Ever gone fishin' on a bright and sunny day with all the little fishies swimmin' up and down the bay? With their hands in their pockets, and their pockets in their pants, all the little fishies do the hoochie coochie dance. Sha lalala la, sha lalala, with their hands in their

pockets and their pockets in their pants, all the little fishies do the hoochie coochie dance."

Rob spins around and roars...

In laughter.

Chapter Twenty-Nine

"I-I-I'm so sorry," Amina says, stuttering her apology. "I didn't mean to interfere. It's just that I heard it getting worse, and you had mentioned the thing about tongue twisters. I don't know any tongue twisters, but suddenly a little song I remembered from nursery school popped into my mind, and I really wanted to help, so..." She shrugs, gazing around with the widest eyes and bewilderment etched into her expression. "I'll wait outside. I'm sorry."

Turning fully towards her, I reach out an arm and hook her around her waist, drawing her close to my side before she can escape. Her struggles against my hold are meek. I know it's only because we're in front of my mom and brother, or she'd extricate herself expeditiously.

Mom, Rob, and Dad are still chuckling.

Never in my wildest imaginings would I have guessed she'd be the one to calm Rob. It can take hours to calm Rob and my dad. I'd told her to wait outside because I didn't want her to see the uglier sides of what life could be like with me. Or maybe I had her wait because I was afraid of what she'd think of me, my family. Other women I've dated proved they couldn't handle the more real parts of life before we'd gotten to the "meet the family" phase. Their reactions, the look on their faces, when I told them about my father and brother, told me everything I needed to know. If they couldn't deal with hearing about it, what would they do when one of their crises lasted days or weeks? Yet, this skittish, petite woman with a big heart and insightful mind managed to do it with a well-timed children's song.

A wealth of emotions rushes through me. They almost spill out of my mouth right here in front of God and everybody. It takes tons of strength to keep them at bay. She's not ready to hear them yet. What I feel for her has grown so fast that it surprises me. She's not just *any* woman. And although she's unprepared for the feelings I have for her, I can't help but love her. Call it trauma bonding, ill-advised, or too fast, but it's real. I'm in love with Amina.

Rob places the chair on the floor beside Mom and sits on it.

"Fuck! My feet hurt," Rob says, picking each foot up and inspecting it.

"Damn!" Mom exclaims. "Amina, honey, thank you. That was definitely creative. I'll have to remember that. Let me get the first aid kit." Mom pops up from her seat and heads down the hall to the bathroom, where the first-aid kit is kept.

We always have one of those stashed away. Situations such as these aren't rare. Thankfully, it wasn't both this time. When they're both in crisis, it's an all-hands-on-deck sort of situation.

"I'd better get a broom, mop, the carpet cleaner, and bleach," Dad says, entering through the doorway where he must have been standing when Amina rushed in. When he comes upon Amina, he offers her his hand, "You must be Amina," he says, in his deep, gruff voice. "I'm Trevor Kaplan, this one and that one's dad. You can call me Trev or Dad. I prefer Dad." He laughs.

If I know him—and I do—he's serious.

"With what you did there," Dad says, nodding towards Rob, who's still inspecting himself, "you're family now. You can't get rid of us. We're like a bad case of jock itch. We'll always be on 'ya."

Wow! That's my dad for you—a real wordsmith.

"Dad, take it easy," I say. "You're not supposed to be weird until you've met someone at least twice. And give her her hand back."

Instead of a normal handshake, he'd held her hand hostage in his meaty grip. It surprises me that she took his hand at all. He lets go.

Amina tries to extricate herself from my arms at the same time, but I grip her tighter. I can't help it with these emotions swirling in my chest. I don't want to let her go. She stiffens noticeably but doesn't try to flee again. Amina gives my arm an inconspicuous pinch to show her displeasure. Above her head, I grin.

"Aww... look at you two," Rob remarks. "Like peas and carrots," he says, impersonating Forest Gump. "Sorry you had to see that, gorgeous. I'm not always like that, promise." He winks at Amina.

And there's the smooth big brother I know and love. I learned my signature wink and lop-sided grin from him. It gave him a naughty, boyish quality that girls went nuts for. Of course, I had to adopt that one and work it into the rotation.

"It's totally okay," Amina says to Rob. "I understand more than you'd realize. Plus, we all have our bad days, right? You only threw the couch and a couple of vases." Then, as if divulging a secret, she says, "I want to throw Garrett across the room, like, eighty times a day. But look at me and look at him... He is humongous. I'd probably give myself a hernia."

Dad and Rob get a kick out of that. Mom returns from the bathroom laughing.

"You and me both, honey," Mom says, reclaiming her seat beside Rob. She drags one of his long legs onto her lap, taking over the injury inventory. "Let's see how bad these cuts are."

"You, missy, are every bit the doll Rett said you were," Dad says.

The compliment must make Amina shy because she fidgets. She pushes up my sleeve and plays with my arm hair.

And now I'm hard.

Good thing she's in front of me. Well, good for me, bad for her. I'm positive she can feel it by the way she stands up straighter. The closeness and open affection aren't inappropriate, but it's still intimate in a way I've craved since I kissed her to silence her arguing with me. Although her posture straightens, I swear she backs her ass on my erection. Or maybe that's what I want to believe she's doing. Either way works for me, it would appear.

"Rett, why don't you take Amina outside with your friends?" Mom suggests. "After we get everything cleaned up here, we're probably going to take off. Aunt Sheila and Uncle Noah left a bit ago. And I think I see Keith and Mateo taking wood down to the fire pit for the bonfire."

I follow her gaze out of the open sliding door. True enough, Keith and Mateo are walking out of the back gate towards where we've made a large circle of large, comfortable Coleman Quad camping chairs. Mateo, Keith, and I have to use the Coleman Quad II chairs. We're big men and need the oversized cushioned steel chairs that support our weight and larger frames.

"You sure?" Amina asks, "I'd be happy to help if you need. I'm really good at cleaning up messes."

"Now, that's a good woman," Dad says, laughing. "Don't fuck this up, Rett."

I gasp, truly affronted. "When have you known me to screw up a relationship? It's not my fault women can't handle perfection."

It's Amina's turn to burst into laughter. One of her seal noises squeaks before she can catch it. She slaps a hand over her mouth and shrinks against my chest. We all crack up.

"Oh, honey, what was that?" Mom asks between guffaws.

"Sorry," Amina says, her voice soft. "I tried to hold it in."

"You're definitely part of the family now, gorgeous," Robs says, laughter subsiding. "We have good blackmail material on you now."

"And with that, I'm taking my lady outside before you can embarrass her anymore," I say. "It's not her fault that she honks when she laughs. It's endearing."

Amina breaks my hold and stomps out of the back door. Laughter erupts behind her retreating form.

"Nice meeting you, honey. We'll meet again soon," Mom yells.

*A*mina Raichand

Standing on the fringes, I pull my arms into my sweater-dress's sleeves. It's colder than I thought. Everyone socializes several feet away. They're so at ease with each other. Laughing and smiling. They've all known each other forever. People-watching isn't a concept I'm unaccustomed to. It's literally been what's kept me sane throughout my self-imposed solitude all these years. But, watching them all gathered around the bonfire... Some are sitting in camping chairs, sipping beer. Others stand to the side, engrossed in more intimate conversations. Flames flicker, and embers drift on a gentle breeze, creating a relaxed ambiance. It's like a scene straight out of an Abercrombie & Fitch or Eddie Bauer late Spring or early Winter beach advertisement, except all the men are in flannels of varying colors, and Carhartt is stamped somewhere on their clothing.

Everyone looks so comfortable, like they belong to this secret society. Most of my life, I've been fine being a voyeur, apart but not a part of a world filled with interpersonal relationships I didn't understand. I spent my time people watching from afar, never wanting to be part of inside jokes or to reminisce about days long gone. With no knowledge of how to even begin to form those types of bonds, I'd convinced myself I was fine alone. If I had my TV shows, books, and movies, I was perfectly content to live vicariously through my favorite characters. Now, watching these friends laugh and banter with each other, something stirs inside me. Longing?

I want that. I want to be in the in crowd.

Voyeurism no longer appeals to me. Right now, Ariel from *The Little Mermaid* is super relatable. My personal musical rendition of "Part of Your World" fills my mind.

Unshed tears haze my vision. No way on God's green Earth will I allow them to fall. I blow air out of the corner of my mouth like I'm blowing my bangs out of my eye, but it's really my covert attempt at drying my tears. For some reason, I'm frickin' emotional suddenly. Something's going on with me.

A need for connection draws my attention to where Garrett is sprawled in one of the black, oversized camping chairs. For such a big guy, that chair is doing a manful job supporting his tall frame. He's the definition of chill. Long limbs stretch, demanding all the space not only in front of him but in front of the people sitting to his right, like he's the king of his domain, and his domain is wherever he says it is—an amber beer bottle lounges in the cup holder. I'm impressed. Everyone else is on their fifth and sixth beers while he's still babysitting his second. The control that takes has to be enormous, considering the atmosphere. I'm not too surprised, though. The man exercises control in everything. He's so together it makes me a little envious. I'm over here an emotional nut basket while he's Buddha on the mountain top.

I didn't dare have another Ménage on the Beach since the first one, which Garrett pressured me into drinking. To be fair, it didn't take too much arm-twisting. I'd been craving one for the longest, and it lived up to everything I thought it would. It was like a party in my mouth, and everyone was invited. I lick my lips in remembrance of the delectable drink.

At that second, Garrett turns. He winks at me, and my heart skips a beat. He smirks and slightly arches a copper eyebrow. Then pointedly stares at me, pats his lap, and spreads his arms wide. It's an invitation.

"Warm lap with your name written all over it," Garrett says, quirking his brow higher.

Narrowing my eyes, I shake my head. My feet, however, don't get the memo because, against my conscious decision, I amble over to him.

When I'm within arm's reach, I don't know which of us is more shocked. He loses a bit of his cool, and his eyes widen infinitesimally. I chew on my bottom lip, staring into expectant turquoise eyes. Thick brows waggle in challenge. The entire party goes silent, most likely watching the interplay between us. Or it could be my anxiety, reading more into things than there is. The silent standoff between us is weighted as if things we don't even mean to say are being said with just our eyes and his lifted arms. A self-conscious moment passes. Before embarrassment melts me into goo, I sit cautiously on his thigh. I plant my booted feet firmly in the sand, not wanting to surrender too much of my weight. I'm not particularly body-conscious, but one never knows if they're retaining a little extra lunch bloat. His muscular arms immediately engulf me, knocking me off balance, and I slide back, coming to a rest with my butt pressing into his pelvis. I'm no longer able to reach the ground. He adjusts me. Snug against his warm, broad chest. Butt right against his groin.

He doesn't have to say he's happy about my chosen seat. The evidence is growing by the second. "Do you want me to get up?" I ask, turning and whispering between clenched teeth close to his ear.

Garrett squeezes me tighter. Grinding his bulge into my behind. "Too late," he teases, giddily. "No turning back now, Foxy. You made your decision." He nips my earlobe. "You're mine."

It's cold. My shiver has nothing to do with the zing of excitement that shoots through my body when his breath tickles my ear, and his bite unfurls something within me. Ah! Self-delusion. I know thee well. "We're in public," I reprimand.

His chuckle reverberates through me. Once he's done amusing himself, we sit in companionable silence listening to conversations and light-hearted banter that swirl around us.

Wood crackles as flames lick the bark of the logs. I've never had such a "normal" time with people my age. Scanning the faces of everyone gathered around the bonfire, I feel out of place, like an impostor—a child sat at the adult table for the first time at a family get-together, out of place. At thirty-two years old, and considering my traumatic past, I'm mature. To me, anyway. But I know, given my reclusive nature, there are many experiences I've yet to have. Plus, I wasn't rebellious by any stretch of the imagination as a teen. I didn't cut loose in my twenties. Having to provide for myself at such a young age, with no safety net to rely on if things went to crap, I had to work—no partying—not that I was invited to any parties. One would need friends to receive invitations to parties. Outside of work friends, I had none. I still don't have any. Working two full-time jobs at seventeen, instead of going to college, didn't provide opportunities to make friends.

Despite the fire and Garrett's body heat, cold seeps through my mini sweater-dress. Scrubbing my hands up and down my black tights, I seek to generate some warmth. Leaning so far back exposes more of my legs to the cold. Larger, pale hands dwarf mine. As brazen as their owner is, they take over the action.

"You cold, Foxy?" Garrett asks, his mouth scant inches from my ear.

Chills of a different nature race down my back, stiffening my spine. "It's nippy out here."

Garrett rakes his meaty fingers between mine. Well-groomed fingertips trace an invisible path over the backs of my hands, between my fingers, and then the length of my forearm. Tingles spiderweb up my arm and through my body, sending quivers to places inappropriate in mixed company.

"Hey," Garrett calls with a jerk of his head, "Mateo!"

Mateo glances in our direction, smirking as if he knows something we don't.

"Pass me one of those blankets on the cooler," Garrett orders per usual.

A beige faux fur throw blanket flies towards my face. Of course, Garrett is not only tall, muscular, and gorgeous, but he also has excellent reflexes. In a startling feat of athleticism, one hand darts past my head, catching the blanket before it hits me, which saves me the embarrassment of not having caught anything thrown at me now, nor ever. Dropping things is so regular for me that it's become a physiological imperative.

Reaching around me, he expands the blanket. It makes a *thwap* sound. He covers both of our legs. The blanket is huge. It reaches his ankles and drapes over the armrests. Everything's so idyllic—everyone standing around the roaring fire at dusk, drinks in hand, conversing like a Hallmark movie moment. The inherent intimacy of the moment isn't lost on me. I snuggle closer to Garrett's strong, hard chest.

"Enjoying yourself?" his bass asks near my ear.

I giggle. "I've only ever seen this in Nicholas Sparks movies. Everybody's so..." I search for the right word, "normal."

"You must've missed where my brother had an entire schizophrenic episode." He laughs. "That was *so* normal."

Lifting away, I turn and nail him with a haughty eye roll.

His teal gaze grows serious, and he raises his hand to hover above my shoulder. "Skin privileges?"

"Hmm..." Narrowing my eyes and pursing my lips, I mull over his question. There's a lethal amount of challenge in it, and there's trepidation in my answer. "Temporary skin privileges."

"Uh-uh! You're in my lap, Foxy." Garrett points out, quirking a brow. "Full skin privileges are part of the deal. I have to touch you."

This is a trap. I know it, but I can't think of a strong enough argument against it, or any loophole. I am in his lap. We're with a ton of people. Not just people, but his friends and family as well. It's not like anything can happen.

"Temporary full skin privileges—until I get up," I acquiesce. "Within reason."

His nod is a little too enthusiastic, triumphant.

"So, where'd you guys meet?" Varinka asks, plopping into the lap of a tall, blond, attractive, lanky man whose name I don't remember. "Or did I miss that story?"

I exchange a strained look with Garrett. Even if his friends know about his counseling, I don't want them to know that's where we met. I'm not ashamed— Okay, maybe I'm a little ashamed considering my life's previous trajectory. After all, I went to college to be *the* counselor—a social worker—not be the one who needs counseling. With my life plan up in the air, this is the first time I'm adrift, aimless. Garrett's this ballin' out-of-control Financial Manager, and for all intents and purposes, I'm a scrub. Topping that off with admitting I'm a traumatized, emotional nut basket isn't the image I want to portray.

"I stalked her. Followed her around until she agreed to give me a chance," Garrett answers with a laugh.

"Poor, Amina," Mateo says, chuckling. "Hey, do you have a nickname or something?"

"Yeah, Mrs. Kaplan," Garrett rushes to answer for me at the same time I shake my head.

Caught so off guard, I try to get up. Garrett tightens his hold on me and presses down—Snug against a very evident bulge in his pants. "Skin privileges," he whispers in my ear. His whiskers graze against the sensitive skin of my cheek. I fight to keep my eyes from drifting closed at the unexpected erotic sensation.

Mateo laughs. "You've been hoodwinked by his pretty-boy shit. The freckles. He's like old gum. You're never gonna get him off your shoe. You're doing the Lord's work, girl, taking one for all of womankind."

"He brought you to a family party on a first date?" Varinka asks with an incredulous gasp.

"Did he kidnap you?" Keith asks. "If you're here against your will, blink twice."

"Y'all can suck my dick," Garrett growls, jostling me in his lap in an attempt to make a lewd gesture.

Whether consciously or not, his cloth-covered erection settles in the exact wrong place, which can't be comfortable for him since I'm now sitting so far back that I'm almost on his lower abs. I try to move, but a steely grip around my waist stops me. His other hand slithers underneath the blanket covering us and latches onto my upper thigh, effectively, stilling me.

"It was actually love at first sight—thank you," Garrett continues.

"Yeah, right!" several of his friends exclaim in unison, uncaring or not noticing our little power struggle.

"Butthead," I grumble low enough for only his ears. "You're a gosh darn liar."

"OMG! I'm in love," Varinka shouts, informing me that I wasn't as quiet as I thought. "She is adorable. Can I keep her?"

My shoulders slump and tighten. I cringe—just another glaring example of how I don't fit in. I know what's coming next—another reason why I'm a poser.

"Shut the fuck up, Var," Garrett admonishes his friend, saving me from embarrassment.

"What?" Varinka asks, unperturbed by Garrett's rudeness. "I think it's cute. Don't corrupt this one."

"First, I've never corrupted anyone that wasn't already a little twisted," Garrett says.

So many questions run through my mind. What does he do to women? Is he into something perverted? Or is he just a little kinky? Dang! Now, I'm curious.

"Second, she's a grown woman."

"And you're a lot," Varinka adds. "More than most people can handle with your caveman ass. We tolerate you because we've known you forever, and it couldn't technically be deemed a crime of passion if we murdered you."

"Uh... Speak for yourself. It's genetic for some of us," Keith corrects. "I'm predisposed to giving a shit about this motherfucker."

"I'm gonna need all of you to take turns kissing my entire ass," Garrett commands while his fingers sneak further up my thigh. "You guys aren't helping my case. It was hard enough getting her to tell me her name."

"I knew I liked you," Mateo says, winking at me. "She's smart."

"Yeah, she is," Varinka comments, and something about her sultry, husky tone leaves a lot of room for interpretation. "So, he *did* kidnap you?"

Shaking my head, I say, "No. We came to an understanding after our first date."

"Ooh..." she exclaims. "This is the second date. Don't waste no time, do you, Kaplan?"

"Stop scaring my lady," Garrett demands.

"You mean, we shouldn't tell her about the other women you stalked and kidnapped?" Keith asks, chuckling.

"Didn't you insinuate that my girlfriend of *two years* was a stripper?" Mateo grouses. "At Thanksgiving dinner with our families in attendance. Your ass deserves this. You know he has a jerk-off station in his house? He reclines in this old, beat-up leather recliner, plays smooth jazz, and has lube and extra-soft Kleenex on a side table. Straight romancing himself."

I glance over my shoulder at Garrett and laugh at his chagrined expression. Heat reddens his cheeks, making his freckles more pronounced. Garrett glowers at his friends and then at me, causing me to laugh harder. A large hand latches onto a hunk of my thigh, wraps around it, and squeezes. I nearly jump off his lap, but his arm still pins me in place.

"Ah, so prejudgments aren't reserved for only strangers," I muse aloud. "Good to know."

"OnlyFans, stripping," Garrett defends unrepentantly. "Close enough." His outward shrug is casual, masking the fact that his meaty fingers have found their way to the juncture between my legs.

Turning my head to him, so he's the only one who can see, I mouth, "What are you doing?"

Garrett leans forward, his chest against my back, alerting me to how oversensitive my skin is. The assault on my senses is overwhelming. His fingers caress my vulva, and his larger body swamping mine from behind heightens my awareness. I'm almost too warm now, but I don't dare move the blanket and expose what Garrett's doing.

"Do you want me to stop?" Garrett asks, whispering in my ear.

Goosebumps spring to life, causing the hair on my arms to stand on end. I'm torn between hopping off his lap and running or letting my head rest on his shoulder and melting into his touch.

I nod in response.

His fingers press more firmly, making contact with the swollen bundle of nerves between my folds. Liquid dampens my panties and seeps through my tights. On second thought...

I shake my head.

"Good girl," Garrett praises me with a low chuckle. "Sit back, baby doll, and let me make you feel good."

Against my better judgment, I don't protest. He widens his legs ever so slightly, which spreads my nether lips, and he begins to stroke in earnest. Unbidden, my hips subtly swivel, seeking more attention.

"Aww... You two look cozy," Mateo teases, popping the false bubble of privacy our murmured words and secret touches have created.

"You mad?" Garrett taunts. "Be jealous. My woman's beautiful."

"I told you, girl," Varinka says. "Caveman. Run if he lifts his leg around you."

Laughing is a struggle. It's more of an uncomfortable, strangled sound. Garrett presses his finger firmly against my clit, rubbing in tight circles.

"In the shower doesn't count, right?" Keith asks. "Cuz I might be guilty of that."

"Of peeing in the shower? Eww..." Varinka groans.

"Dude!" Garrett and Mateo exclaim simultaneously.

I'm hearing their banter with a lesser part of my brain. Garrett manages to maintain communication while doing his best to finger me through my tights. Meanwhile, I'm here, ears ringing, body tingling, and on the cusp of a public orgasm. If his rigid length weren't rubbing the area close to my entrance, I would think he wasn't as affected as I am by his ministrations. His covert grind into me feels way more intimate than it should. How?

Turning towards him, I ask through gritted teeth, "Where are your underwear?"

Leaning forward, he nips my ear. Then he grinds his palm into my mound. "In a drawer at home," he answers, nuzzling my cheek. His hot breath against my ear. "Where are yours?"

Chapter Thirty

*G*arrett Kaplan

Damn! Busted.

To her, this probably seems sleazy and premeditated. Well... It wasn't premeditated, and it was—a little. In the months since we'd grown closer, I increased my commando days from maybe once a month to every time, I know I'll be spending time with Amina. It's not that I'm being presumptuous, but this woman excites the shit out of me. On every level, she turns me on. I wouldn't ever rush her into being physical after what she's been through. She's made it clear that she's not sure she'll ever be ready for that type of relationship. While I don't agree that, she'll never be able to be physical again, I do respect her boundary. That being said, just in case her boundary around physical activity changes, I wanted to be ready. The early bird gets the worm, so to speak.

She's also not getting up. I'm not forcing her to stay. Should she truly want to get off my lap, I would let her, no coercion and no questions asked. And right now, knowing I'm not wearing anything under my pants, she nestles into my lap, into my embrace.

Under the blanket, my fingers lightly graze her knee, caress her thigh, and stroke her juicy upper thigh. My digits wander to the scantily covered "V" between her thighs. Heat comes in waves from her most sensitive area. I want to touch her there with no barriers. I want to taste her.

Amina shivers once again. I know it's not due to the cold. The fire and the blanket keep her plenty warm and shield us from inquisitive eyes.

Since she's so short, the beginning of her tights reaches past her navel. So, I'm shit out of luck if I want to work my hand down them. Everyone would know what was happening, and I want to retain her dignity. I have to be more creative. And she still hasn't stopped me. On the contrary, she leans more heavily into me. So much so, I can feel her measured breaths. Using my knuckles, I skim up and down her swollen folds. Her breath hitches.

"Amina," Keith's girlfriend, Tamsyn says, "are you from Indiana or are you visiting? We went to college with Varinka briefly before she abandoned us for tumble weeds and rattlesnakes in Arizona." She pins Varinka with a narrow glare.

"Oh, darling, don't cry for me, Argentina," Varinka says, saccharine-sweet, "we'll always have our night in the sauna." She blows Tamsyn a kiss.

Shaking her head, curly red hair bouncing back and forth with the action, Tamsyn rolls her eyes.

"Are you for real?" Keith asks, looking between Tamsyn sitting in his lap and Varinka draped across her dates' laps. "Varinka Shaw, you better not touch my woman again."

Going lower, the warmth coming from Amina's channel scorches the knuckle of my middle and ring fingers. I want to tear through these flimsy tights. They aren't thick enough to protect against the cold, anyway.

"Anyways," Tamsyn says, breaking the stare-off between Keith and Varinka. "You guys interrupted Amina. She's part of the group now, and we need to include her. So, are you an Indiana native or a transplant?"

Amina swirls her ass against my dick as I apply more pressure to the small hole in the tights I've found near her opening. Unfortunately, it's covered by panties and tights. Straightening her back, she wiggles against me, then pushes more firmly into my erection.

A triumphant grin curves my mouth. Barrier or no, my fingers are still effective, but we might get caught if...Kissing the side of her neck causes her to roll into my hardness. I lick around her earlobe, then nip it.

"They're talking to you, angel," I croon in her ear. "Don't be rude; answer them." I pinch the side of her ass.

"Umm..." Amina says, searching for her voice. "I'm homegrown, from Lake County. That's a little more than two hours from here, I think."

"Cool, I've been that way," Shea, Mateo's on-again, off-again girlfriend—fiancée—or whatever says, flipping her long black hair over her shoulder. "Is that where you're living now?"

"Damn, Babe," Mateo says, jostling Shea on his lap, "do you want her social security number next?"

Bringing my palm between Amina's legs forces her to spread them wider for me. I cup her sex.

I widen my sprawled legs ever so slightly. Given that each of her legs rests on top of mine, her thighs open further. Amina tosses what's supposed to be a scrunched-nose glare over her shoulder at me, but I'm way too familiar with her expressions, especially anger and irritation. This isn't either of those. When her golden eyes meet mine, her gaze softens, goes dreamy. There's heat, but it's of an aroused nature. She wants me.

"What are you doing?" she whispers between tight lips.

"Foxy, the way you're rubbing against my dick is killing me," I whisper in her ear. "Your ass is so soft. Why'd you have to wear these fucking tights?"

Her nostrils flare. "What. Are. You. Doing?" she whispers once more.

"Getting caught if you don't play it cool." She narrows her eyes. "Enjoying my skin privileges," I tease. "But if you want me to stop, I'll stop," I add seriously. To illustrate my point, I stop kneading her petal smooth folds. Ice enters her glare. Grinning, I ask, "Do you want me to stop?" Through her tights and underwear, I use two fingers to delve into her center as much as possible. She arches her back, and shock fills her wide eyes.

"Do. You. Want. Me. To. Stop?"

Her nod makes my stomach drop through my ass. Smirking, she shakes her head and relaxes against me. My heart pounds in my chest. She'll pay for that.

"Good girl. Relax and let me make you feel good," I murmur. "They're talking to you. Answer, or everyone will know I'm playing with your fat pussy."

Amina turns forward and trembles.

"I'm sorry," she says, "what did you ask?"

"Not for your social security number, contrary to what others might think," Shea turns a pointed glare at Mateo. "I wanna know where you live, so we can maybe hang out, if you want to. If you don't want to, that's fine. But if you want to, that would be so great. Me and Tamsyn would love for you to come out with us." She grins in her ditzy way.

"Yeah. Of course, we can hang out. I live on the Greenwood Center Grove border along the Bluff Road corridor," Amina says.

"Ooh!" Varinka quips in a high-pitched voice. "Miss Thing has some money, honey."

Everyone chuckles while Amina shakes her head and snuggles into me. She's so wet. It saturates her panties and tights. My erection strains against my zipper. These damn tights are in the way. I dig my thumb into a small gap where underwear doesn't quite meet the crotch of her tights. Then, I wedge my middle finger into a spot right below her tights' covered entrance and pull and twist, hard, ripping a wide hole for my fingers in the flimsy material. Amina jolts.

"Relax," I whisper.

"What. Are. You. Doing?" she mutters.

"Getting caught," I reiterate, "if you don't play it cool, dig? You'll like this."

Now that everyone is engrossed in their own side conversations, I can concentrate better. My hands aren't cold since they've been luxuriating between her thick thighs. I move her panties to the side and subtly thrust my hips at the same time as I thrust two fingers inside her liquid core. She wiggles on my lap, and I curl my fingers inside her in a come-hither motion. I kiss a path up her neck. Amina grinds on me, and I roll my hips. Each grind brings her plump ass in contact with my cock. Her head drops back onto my shoulder.

As much as I fight it, I know my eyes are hooded. I am hard to the point of pain. If I lift Amina, I'm certain my dick would drill through my jeans. Across the way, Varinka glowers daggers at me. The flickering flames make her look sinister. She smirks.

Smile all you want, Var. It's my fingers massaging her clit and coaxing the spongy flesh within her. I grin.

Wrapping her hand around the back of Caleb's head, Varinka yanks him forward and crushes her lips with his. All the while, her nutbrown eyes stay open, glaring at me.

Amina's tight heat clamps onto my fingers. Head rolling against my shoulder, she bites her lip. If I were a younger man, I would gloat about getting the woman Varinka, with her young Lil' Kim look-a-like ass, thought she could steal from me. But I'm not a younger man, and I respect and value the treasure I hold in my arms. Amina doesn't trust easily. Those weeks of her unwillingness to roll her window down to speak with me are cemented in my mind. Her trusting me with skin privileges, allowing me to pump my fingers in and out of her sopping wet cave... It is an honor. It's a gift I don't take lightly.

"Fuck," I say into her ear. "You're tight, baby doll. You feel so good, gripping my fingers. Mmm..."

Her fingers wrap around my wrist under the blanket.

She is mine for all time. I will protect her with my life and after. Death won't be strong enough to keep me from her—my angel. And my angel loves dirty talk.

My dick is desperate to touch her, to fill her. The combination of hot and cold—hot because I'm burning from the inside out, and cold because of the ambient temperature—wreaks havoc on my system.

I pump slower. Amina licks her lips. If only I could kiss those generous lips. Unfortunately, that might make what we're doing obvious. Right now, she looks like she could be relaxing and taking in the serene environment.

Her breasts rise and fall in quick succession. She's close. If her breathing doesn't give it away, the way her pussy milks my fingers is a dead giveaway.

The blood from my brain rushes to my manhood. I snap, ripping the hole in her tights bigger, granting my hand more freedom of movement. She bears down on my fingers and, in turn, on my cock. Her hips rock in a restrained way that tells me she's still partially aware of our surroundings. I'm about to explode, to ruin my pants like some out-of-control teenage boy. My vision blurs as Amina's entire body quakes.

"I-I can't...here, Garrett," Amina says in a hushed tone. Then nips my earlobe closest to her mouth.

Shit! She's killing me. Fuckin' kill-ing me.

I growl in her ear.

"Aren't you gonna…you know…in your pants?" Amina asks breathlessly before she wiggles her hips. Her clit collides with the base of my fingers, causing delicious friction.

"This is about making you feel good," I remind her. "I'll be fine. I can rub one out later."

"That's not cool. We can stop," she says, but her bucking hips tattle on her.

I lick her neck, then bite down. She jerks as if she's being electrocuted. Fluid gushes around my intruding digits and into my hand.

"Cum for me, Foxy," I say, blowing in her ear.

Her head moves back and forth against my shoulder. "I can't, it's not fair. And I need more."

Reluctantly, I pull my fingers out of her, and she whimpers.

I tap the outside of her upper thigh twice.

"Grab the armrests with each of your hands and lift just a little for a second." She looks back at me with an arched brow. The green flecks in her eyes are more prominent when her eyes are glazed with lust, as they are now. "No one will see, I promise. Have I broken a promise to you yet?"

Indecision passes through her expression. Bracing herself, she lifts, using her upper arms to support as much of her weight as possible. With quick motions, I tear her tights more and free myself from my jeans. I'm so hard, my dick springs out and sticks straight up.

Perfect.

I grip her waist on each side and position her just so. Her lips suck the head of my cock. Holding my breath, I slide her down my shaft inch by painful inch. Amina's body convulses. My jaw clenches hard enough to break a tooth. Her walls clutch me in a vice-like grip. Fluid drowns my dick. Before I know what's happening, my load shoots from me with brutal force. I'm forced to bite into her shoulder to keep from shouting.

How embarrassing...?

Her head whips around so fast our foreheads nearly collide. Eyes wide, she asks, "When your parents left, did they leave the house open?"

I nod.

Amina hops up, and the blanket slips to the ground, and I have .01 seconds to tuck myself back in as she sprints towards the house.

*A*mina Raichand

Kegels don't fail me now!

Ohmygoodness!

My thoughts are a mess, just like my tights and underwear. A jumble of incoherent musings runs through my mind. I'm going to have to take both off. The tights are a lost cause. They're totally ruined. I can wash my underwear, but what the heck am I going to wear on the ride home? Garrett has leather seats.

Passing through the darkened living room, I notice it's completely cleaned and a lot barer. The TV is gone. There isn't a splinter or chunk of wood remaining to hint that there ever was a coffee table. I think they might have cleaned the carpets, too. Hopefully, I'm not leaving boot prints in my mad dash to the restroom.

Once in the bathroom, I slam the door and lock it. Then I flip the light switch on.

I'm taken aback by the image that greets me in the mirror. My hair is flat from lying on Garrett's shoulder. The little makeup I put on has held up, thankfully. There is a purple hickey on my neck. I don't remember him even sucking that spot. I thought he was kissing me.

Running my fingers through my hair a few times brings it back to life. My peach sweater-dress is in order. Underneath is where the real war zone is. Speaking of which...

A trickle of something slithers down the inside of my thigh. I flip the toilet lid up and plop onto the cold seat before any more can escape. Cold bites into my skin and clears the last vestiges of post-coital haze from my mind. What just happened? One minute, I'm relishing digital exploration. Next, I'm having full-on intercourse. UNPROTECTED! I'm not on any birth control. Why would I be? Abstinence is supposed to nullify the necessity for prophylactics, and I had every intention of keeping my vow of chastity.

Deciding everything I can force out is out, I stand and flush the toilet. No use in pulling up my underwear or tights. I remove both and ball them up. I search under the sink for a bag or something. Given how unexpected Rob's and Trevor's crises can be, I'd think they'd keep a healthy stock of kits for all different needs.

As much as I didn't intend to be physical because frankly, I didn't think I could, it happened, and it was way easier than I thought it would be. Garrett makes me feel so cherished and safe. It's hard to imagine not trusting him with any facet of myself. For goodness's sake, he knows about the whispers and knows the craziness surrounding my parents, "not parents," and he hasn't run screaming yet. I've been meaner and more expressive with him than I have with anyone in my entire life. He takes it all in stride and gives as good as he gets. Everything with him is so natural. Garrett is familiar to me on a molecular level. But am I betraying my healing journey because I'm horny?

I suffered a very traumatic event. A traumatic intrusion?

Yet I survived. Somehow.

Is this what enlightenment is supposed to feel like? An "ah-ha" moment. While I did survive what Justin did to me, he's still out there somewhere, which scares me. Despite that very real fear, I've made room for something good, no matter how unexpected it may be. My entire world is upside down. Nothing makes sense, except Garrett. And bonus, I had fun tonight, actual fun with humans. Besides some awkward conversations, nothing bad has happened. Yes, Rob had his meltdown, but for once, me being around, helped someone. It didn't cause drama.

I also don't feel bad about giving myself to Garrett. Am I freaked out about the possibility of an unplanned pregnancy and cooties? Yes, totally. Have I become an exhibitionist? Not at all. I prefer more privacy than a blanket provides, but I don't feel taken advantage of.

The doorknob jiggles and turns several times. My heart rate skyrockets. Garrett opens the door. Stepping inside the small room, he closes the door, as if he has every right to be in the bathroom with me.

"Wasn't that door locked?" I ask, gazing up from where I'm crouched, searching through the cabinet under the sink.

"What're you doing?" he asks.

Lips puckered, I scan my surroundings. "Writing me manifesto," I tease. "I thought I locked that door."

He takes a deep breath and runs a hand through his hair. "I picked the lock. This is my family's home. I've been doing it for years," he says.

Note to self: Find more inventive ways to lock doors when Garrett is around.

I stand and close the cabinet, taking a moment to inspect Garrett's taller image in the mirror. For as happy as I am, he looks horrible. His eyes are bloodshot. He avoids making eye contact in our mirrored reflections. There's a noticeable dampness near the fly of his jeans. They're dark jeans, but there is still an obvious darker spot.

I cringe inwardly. How many people saw that? And why does Garrett look like he's being framed for murder?

"What're you doing?" he asks again. "You ran away."

"Umm...yeah. I had to clean up. You tore a hole in my leggings."

"I know," he says, voice so low and gravelly, I almost need to read his lips. "I don't know what happened. I'm so sorry. I didn't mean to trigger you."

Trigger me? "What makes you think you triggered me?"

"You made it clear that you didn't know if you could ever be intimate again. Then I go so far past your boundary that I do worse than that demon did. I fucked you in front of my friends. I'd totally understand if you hate me forever. Please know that wasn't my intention. I mean...I wanted you, still want you, but I shouldn't have been so eager and careless."

My stomach plummets to my toes at the mention of "that demon".

"See?" Garrett says. "You're trying to keep from crying. What can I do to make it up to you? I'll do anything."

Mole hill, meet mountain. Here I am, having this deep, insightful revelation, and he thinks he hurt me.

"You're either really strong, or you were really horny. I did *not* realize my tights were of the breakaway variety." I giggle.

Garrett frowns. "What's funny, Foxy? I broke my promise."

"Did one of your friends see us?"

"No! Amina, I broke my promise."

"No, what you're doing is destroying the mood. I'm not mad at you," I say, then I think better of it. "I'm mad I don't have underwear or tights to wear, but I'm not mad at you. You said you'd stop if I asked you to. You checked in with me. I gave you the go-ahead and you..." I pause, struggling for the right word, "went ahead."

His eyes widen. "You're not mad?"

I shake my head.

"I really would've stopped," he vows.

"I know. Do you have a plastic bag or something?"

"Why?" he asks, quirking his brow.

"You literally tore a hole in my favorite leggings, and my underwear is ruined. I'm not going to walk out with them in my hand. What am I going to wear now?"

"Your dress is fine," he says, shrugging.

"Are you crazy? It's freezing."

Observing me, his greenish-blue eyes hood and smolder. "You are my insanity. My little diamond in the rough."

Chuckling, shaking my head. "I can't believe you did that."

"You liked it," he says, full of masculine pride. "As you said, you could've stopped me anytime."

"Right... Like you would have been able to. What you would've ended up doing is putting out one of your friends' eyes if I hadn't been sitting on you."

Big hands grip my shoulders. Garrett spins me around. All previous playfulness flees from his eyes. It's as if it never existed. "I would have absolutely stopped. I will never force you into anything. I'll jerk my dick every day if you want me to. But I will never force myself on you. With me, you always have a choice, and I'll respect it."

He's killing me.

He is kill-ing me.

And melting my heart.

I back out of his hold, and he lets go immediately.

"Skin privileges are now limited, buster," I say through narrow eyes, wagging my finger.

Chapter Thirty-One

*N*ora Raichand

"...My stepfather. Like you, no one wanted to believe me."

Patricia's hand hovers in the space between the young man with a well-shaped afro's chair and hers. It hangs above his rich brown hand resting on his leg.

"May I touch you?"

The young man nods.

Patricia places her hand on his and holds it in comfort and solidarity. "It's difficult. You lose faith in yourself when everyone invalidates or downplays your very real, traumatic, lived experiences. But I'm here to tell you...you are valid. What was perpetrated against you wasn't your fault, and I believe you and in you. Everyone here supports you. You can get through this. Look at me,"—she waves her free hand in front of herself— "I got through it. You will too."

I wait on the short staircase at the mouth of the ramshackle basement, listening. Patricia's story is one I'm quite familiar with. I'm one of the few people whom she confided in about her stepfather violating her. During our sophomore year of high school, I witnessed how many people didn't believe her, how many blamed her in one breath while proclaiming her a liar in the next. They disparaged her character and said she was exaggerating, storytelling. They called her dramatic. No one took her allegations seriously. If not for a nosy guidance counselor, Patricia might never have been removed from her mother and placed with her grandparents.

Silent tears roll down her cheeks and drip off her chin. The woman's capacity for sympathy inspires awe. Patricia often cries tears that others can't. Which, by the stiff posture and flex of his tight jaw, is what she's doing for the man beside her, allowing his emotions to filter through her.

My eyes sting at the sight. If I were a different woman, I might cry too. However, stoicism is bred within me. As a child, I was trained that a woman of breeding must always contain her emotions. To expel more than a token tear at an appropriate time is to give way to hysterics. No one respects a woman prone to hysterics.

"How long until it stops replaying in my head?" asks the man. He sniffs, yet no tears fall. "My manhood's in question. How am I gon' tell females this? My boys find out? It's a wrap for me, man."

"Did you ask your coach to do what he did?"

"No."

"Did you want it?"

He shakes his head.

"Did you do everything within your power to stop it?"

He nods.

"Then your manhood is well and intact. You're human. Your strength is limited. When someone with authority over us abuses that power, that's on them, not you. And, if your *boys*," Patricia says, placing extra emphasis on the word, "don't understand that, then it's time to reevaluate your friendships. When will you stop thinking about what happened? Never. It's part of you, part of our story. How those thoughts affect you will change. Over time, they won't be as invasive. You'll be able to think around them. And when things get overwhelming, talk about it. Are you still meeting with the counselor I set up for you?"

"Yes, ma'am." He nods. "Once a week."

"Good. Keep doing that and coming here. I'm encouraged by your progress and by how you're handling your feelings. Before, you would have done something reckless. Today, you came to me with your concerns. Those are positive coping strategies."

"Thank you," he says, his voice gruff, solemn. "I appreciate you talking to me. I'm sure you have other shit to do."

Patricia snickers. "No thanks needed. Anytime. Nothing is more important than this. I clear my night every so often for occasions such as this."

The young man rises from his chair and scoots back. Before either notices me eavesdropping, I back away, reverse until I'm on the top stair of the staircase. Patricia would give me an earful about confidentiality if she knew I overheard her conversation. Though, if she hadn't wanted anyone to hear, she should have made sure the entry door was locked.

"S'cuse me, ma'am," the young man says, passing me. Offering a nod and tight-lipped smile, I press against the brick wall, allowing the extremely tall man to get by.

Once out of sight, I close the interior door behind him, as Patricia should have if she expected privacy, and descend the stairs to enter the basement room proper.

Patricia throws out Styrofoam coffee cups and red plastic stirrers. She wipes down the long imitation-wood table with a disinfectant wipe. I take a seat in one of the abandoned cushioned folding chairs. Shaking my head, I set my purse on the floor beside me.

Why she persists in demeaning herself with this menial work? I'll never understand. Involving herself with these poor, damaged people when she has a thriving private practice catering to high-class clientele... It's incomprehensible. Patricia has always been a bleeding-heart sort, but she carries herself with dignity, grace. That's one of many things we have in common. It drew us together in our youth, carried us through high school and well into our college days. Then she reminded me of a young Phylicia Rashad. Now, in our mid-fifties, I watch her in her plaid, red cashmere sweater, black slacks, and red-bottom heels, like mine. She gives off poised Clare Huxtable energy. It may be a conflict of interest to send my daughter to my best friend for help, but Patricia has unimpeachable, impeccable moral integrity. Ever the professional, there's no one I trust more with my daughter's mental health.

"And to what do I owe the pleasure?" Patricia drawls in greeting without turning. "Seems we're seeing more of each other now than we have in the last ten years."

I scoff and cross my legs. "You're quite busy with,"—A wave of my hand encompasses the space. — "And I'm busy attending to Gilbert. He's a full-time job. We should have a spa day sometime soon. Do brunch and mimosas, too. The whole shebang."

Patricia spins around. Her chin-length, springy black curls bounce with the movement. Her brows arch, and a smirk spreads across full lips. "You think copious amounts of alcohol and mani-pedis are enough to pay me off? We're not in college anymore." She approaches, bends, and engulfs me in a side hug before sitting in the chair next to me. "How are you doing?"

"Alright." I sigh. "Hanging in there. And you?"

"Good. Good. What brings you to the slums?" She gazes at me deadpan.

I roll my eyes. "I was mad. It was over a year ago, and I don't believe I referred to it as the slums."

"Actually, you likened it to a third-world country," Patricia reminds me.

For such a sympathetic person, with her hippie-dippie natural hair out, forgiveness sure isn't part of her vocabulary. No one can be held liable for words uttered in anger.

"I've entrusted you with my child's mental health," I point out. "That counts for something."

Patricia crosses her arms and frowns. "Not an apology. Anger is insidious, Nor, and highly unproductive when not tempered with rationale. Your sharp tongue has wrought steep consequences."

How can I forget? Children aren't born with instructions. Those helpful nurses don't go home with you once you leave the hospital. A common misconception is that once you become a mother, some mysterious instinct manifests. I'm proof it doesn't, yet no one talks about that. The gut-wrenching terror that seizes a woman when she gives birth. Not fear because she doesn't want to be a mother. Horror at the idea that you have to expose this defenseless, tiny extension of yourself, your heart, to the cruelties of life. You wish you could force this person back inside your womb, where you can protect it forever. Imagine the internal conflict I, someone who never wanted children, with no maternal bone in my body, was thrown into.

I was twenty-two, studying medicine at Rutgers University, and loved my boyfriend with a fierceness bordering on obsession. We had a plan for our lives. Children weren't part of it. When I discovered I was pregnant, I visited the clinic to get pills to rectify the situation. Unfortunately, my menstrual cycle hadn't ever been regular. I was past the pill solution point, which meant medical intervention was the only method available to take care of it. Gilbert agreed with my plan until his parents got hold of him. My parents withdrew their financial support. On the day of the abortion, Gilbert proposed. I pride myself on being honest, tactful but honest. Honestly, I often mourn the life I should have had. I love my daughter, but I wanted so much more than the life of a housewife. Thank God, I made sure pregnancy wouldn't infect me again.

Unfortunately, Amina overheard one of these honest moments ten years ago. Because she couldn't grasp complex concepts, she misinterpreted my meaning. In retaliation, she squandered her potential and her psychology degree and moved to a godforsaken town to live well below her means to work with downtrodden hoodlums. The stubborn girl refused all my gifts and refused to speak to me. She's like her father that way. Her penchant for grudge-holding...It's infuriating, and the reason I missed ten years of my daughter's life. Yet, as horrific as her mishap was, it was also the catalyst for our reunion. Some say a strained relationship with Amina is a consequence of my candor. I say her unfortunate circumstances are a small blessing.

"That's why I'm here," I say, course correcting our conversation.

"Because a devastating twist of fate provided you a second chance with your estranged daughter?" Patricia snidely remarks.

"Hilarious." I wrinkle my nose. Narrow my eyes. "I'm worried about Amina. She hasn't been herself since we brought her home. How's she doing in group?"

Patricia shakes her head. "I can't talk about group with you. It's confidential. You know that," she chides.

Her and her morals. Annoying.

"She's talking to herself. Hearing voices," I inform her.

"I know," Patricia confirms.

"You know?!" Incredulity raises my voice. "And you didn't say anything? She's gorgeous. Smart. Too intelligent to be insane. Is it time to talk about Serene Meadows?"

"She's suffered an extreme trauma. Every day that monster evades capture is another day of stark fear for her," Patricia advises. "Yet she's walking and talking. Living. Thriving."

"And cursing like a sailor. It's uncouth."

"She's coping and seeing a therapist. She needs time. Plus, it's been ten years," she continues with more unsolicited advice. It's as if she wants to push the knife that is my daughter's rejection deeper. "Amina is grown-grown with life experience now."

"No. It's the random strangers she's around and poor life choices."

"That's,"—her brows crinkle—"Random strangers? With her previous schedule? I doubt toddlers are responsible for her expanded language skills. Plus, I wouldn't call what she does cursing."

I return her queer expression. "Toddlers?" This generation's slang confounds me. "Is that code for illicit encounters pursued with strangers over the Internet?"

My friend cringes. "Wait. What?" Features pinch. "What are you talking about?" She chuckles without humor.

"What in the Devil are you talking about?" I counter.

"Nora!" Patricia grumble-yells in irritation.

She hates being put off, has since we were teens, but she's not indulging in my queries. It's only right she shares in my vexation.

"When we arrived at the hospital after Amina was found, the inept detective wanted a recounting of her normal habits and acquaintances," I explain. "You know Gilbert is useless when it comes to details. All these years of freezing me out with their Sunday father-daughter dinners, and he doesn't know a thing about his only child's friends or hobbies. Amongst her belongings was her mobile phone. It was locked." There is no reason to feel guilty. A mother seeks information about her children at all costs. Privacy doesn't exist in a parent-child relationship.

My tone is grave as I continue. "Her childhood diary's code was her birth month and day. Apparently, she hasn't gotten any more creative. I unlocked the phone, and we discovered she'd been using some newfangled dating button—"

"App," Patricia interrupts. "Dating app."

An unladylike sound emits from the back of my throat. "I don't care. The detective seems to think she met someone from one of these sites. His supposition was further confirmed by an application in which the messages disappear. It displayed photographs and messages from her, alluding to their meeting. It couldn't be verified because the gentleman's messages had vanished. Something about settings." I shake my head. "The time frame matches, though. Now, she's cavorting with another strange toddler from your group. This isn't supposed to be a singles group."

Patricia narrows her dark eyes. "That's not—" she stutters and shakes her head. "Toddler doesn't mean. When I referred to toddlers, I meant..." She sighs. "Never mind. I can't talk to you about group members. It's a breach of confidence."

This is why we butt heads occasionally. If she had children, she'd understand. Clearly, barren-of-womb is synonymous with barren-of-loyalty.

"You pledge fealty to these," I pause searching for a proper descriptor, "sad, mentally ill individuals and heathens fighting their sexuality and down-low proclivities. Yet, for your cousin? Nothing?"

Patricia's mouth gapes. Aghast is the only way to describe her expression. No, I hadn't intended to confess my eavesdropping. She should have closed the door. It's her own fault. Why are others so averse to reality? It's baffling.

"Remember what I said about your sharp tongue? I'll say this once. There is a firm boundary surrounding my work and our friendship. Friendship," she reiterates, noticing my wide-eyed disbelief. "That preposterous ancestry test is meaningless. We're eighth cousins. You're more related to your mail carrier. However, if you would like to keep the tenuous thread of our friendship intact, do not disrespect my profession, nor my moral and professional integrity, or my clients. Do we have an agreement?"

Deep sigh. Patricia is so dramatic. I nod.

Patricia grimaces. "Did you confirm your conjecture with Amina? About how she met her attacker?"

"Her telephone was confirmation enough." Something about her question strikes me. "Why? Did she share that information with you?"

She frowns and lifts a well-plucked eyebrow.

"At least tell me about this Garrett?" I ask, pretending nonchalance.

Patricia glares. My false nonchalance is lost on her. "I can't tell you anything more than whatever Amina's told you, other than they seem to get along."

"And?"

"What do you expect me to say?" Patricia laughs, gaining joy in my frustration. "You know what I know."

"It's been months," I prompt. "You haven't noticed anything more about their interactions? Is it serious?"

She shrugs. "I know what you know," she says in a sing-song tone.

I retrieve my purse from the floor and stand. This isn't getting me anywhere. Patricia's smirk is one of total mirth. It appears sympathy is an emotion she reserves for her clients.

"You wanted her to go out," Patricia says as I reach the door.

I turn at that. "With other women. Cultivating female friendships is healthy, given her condition. She doesn't need to be involved with another toddler."

Patricia snickers. "Calm down. It's been—what?—five months. Maybe? How serious could it be?"

Chapter Thirty-Two

A mina Raichand

Mr. Man has some stuff up in here!

"Why do I feel like the poor girl who lucks into the billionaire in one of those cheesy romance novels or something?"

Garrett laughs. "What are you talking about?"

"You know," I explain, perusing his space as if I have every right, "those movies or books where the woman is from humble beginnings and then somehow bumps into a billionaire. Those movies are always on the Hallmark channel. Of course, those girls are usually blondes or wide-eyed brunettes who 'aren't like the other girl', but they're model gorgeous, and every dude is in love with them. Guess I don't fit the bill on any of those fronts, huh?"

"You're so silly," Garrett says. "Luckily, I haven't seen any of those ridiculous movies. I prefer more action, less cheese, when and if I watch a movie." His large leather sectional couch squeaks as he takes a seat. "I'm thirty-five, Amina—"

"Amina?" I ask, injecting faux shock into my tone. However, his calling me by name bothers me more than I will ever admit aloud. I've been Doll, Foxy, Baby doll, but not Amina—well, Amina, when he's being super serious or when he's irritated with me. Right now, after everything at the beach, calling me Amina? For some reason, it seems like he's distancing himself from me. I don't like it.

"That *is* your name," he says from behind me.

I almost wet my pants. He's a literal giant to me, yet when he wants, he moves like a smooth hunting panther.

"May I touch, Doll?" he asks.

He stands too close, way too close. His heat overwhelms me, and his scent fogs my mind. It's leather, spice, rich cologne, and him. It's everywhere, surrounding me. It's been a week since our beach encounter, and now I don't know how to act.

"Yes," I say, a little breathless.

His wide, chiseled front presses into my back. Muscular arms wrap around my waist, and his fingers interlock over my abdomen, trapping me against him.

"I'm a single man—no responsibilities outside of what I choose. I'm in banking. Fiscal responsibility is my bread and butter. I know a thing or two about money management. Plus, if I didn't, my grandparents left my brother and me a substantial inheritance. That, added to the savings my parents put aside that neither of us could touch until we were twenty-five, makes me comfortable. Hardly a billionaire." His deep abiding laughter resonates in my ear.

Garrett sways us side to side.

"Single man, huh?" I ask because I have no comprehension of the life he describes. No one ever made sure I was financially set. Yes, he works, but I've had to grind for everything I have or had, no matter what those people, my alleged parents, say.

He squeezes me. "Was a single man."

"You're still single," I assure him, giggling. "You still haven't asked me anything. Don't get excited."

"Oh, I'm excited," he growls, rubbing what is obviously an erection against my back.

I roll my eyes, although he can't see, and step out of his hold. He allows it without protest. I continue inspecting his bachelor pad. One full wall is dedicated to an enormous record collection. An antique record player sits in the center. This is more than music appreciation. It's an obsession. I'm way too short to see half of his records. Not that I'd recognize any of the music if I could. The long wall opposite that one has a huge mural, I'm sure he painted, on it.

"You listen to all of these?" I ask, turning to face him.

He smirks. "Not at once."

"Why not download them? Don't you have Spotify or something?"

His brow quirks. "You know I do, but nothing beats the authenticity of a record. That's how music is supposed to be enjoyed. Especially in the '60s and '70s. The crisp crackle. The soul. If you close your eyes, you can envision all the musicians in the studio recording on actual instruments, not machines and auto-tune like today's bullshit music. Most of these new so-called musicians don't know how to play an instrument and couldn't spot one in a line-up." Garrett speaks with such passion. It's sweet.

Reaching up with his big hand, he strokes the jacket of several records.

"'Tears of a Clown' by Smokey Robinson & The Miracles would sound like trash on a music streaming platform. I don't want to imagine Skeeter Davis's 'End of the World' on Amazon Music." Pausing for a beat, he admires his collection. "Take your shoes off. Stay awhile." Garrett offers.

My stomach drops. That's a bit on the nose for what I'm attempting tonight. Bending, I unzip my boots and step out of them. Hmm... Kinda lost my advantage here. Not that there was much of one. In five-inch heels, I'm still way shorter than him, but still. Slinky walks of seduction are better suited for long legs. Mine are stubby without shoes. It's giving sex gremlin instead of sex kitten.

He toes out of his shiny, humongous dress shoes. Two of my boots could fit inside one of his shoes.

I pick up both of our shoes and pad down the entryway to the door, place them beside it. The light oak hardwood floor is cold on my stocking feet.

"How about a tour?"

Hmm... I take a shuddering breath. That might make this easier. I'm not new to sex, but I'm new to it this way. At this time in life. With my baggage. There are insecurities I didn't have before.

"Maybe later. Do you have wine?" I ask. Wine is sexy, right? It's a mood creator.

"I have beer, hard liquor, and pop, maybe some juice... And pre-workout. What happened to, 'I can't drink. Lexapro, remember'?" he asks in a poor imitation of my voice.

I flash a sardonic grin. "Oh, you're funny." I laugh without humor. "Wasn't it you that said one wouldn't hurt?"

"That was a special occasion," he says. He sits on the couch and stretches his long legs across the coffee table. "Come. Let me hold you." He opens his arms.

Enticing, but I stay rooted to my spot.

Garrett frowns. "C'mon, Foxy. What happened to our progress?" When I don't move, he continues, "May I hold you?"

"Don't," I admonish. "New rule. You don't need to ask permission anymore." I wave a hand from my head to my toes. "You, Mr. Kaplan, have all the skin privileges."

His eyes pop wide, and his jaw drops. "Do I now?" Garrett's voice grows husky with implication. "In that case..." He hops up from his seat and prowls towards me.

I run.

Just take off.

He gives chase.

Each of his footfalls rattles anything not heavy enough to stay in place. To anyone able to see through *all* his windows, we must look ridiculous—my heart pounds. Then I slip.

Note to self: Stockings and polished hardwood. Not conducive to quick getaways.

Garrett catches me before my head kisses the floor.

"Whoa! Careful. Why are you running?" he asks, short of breath. "You said game on. Don't toy with me."

I laugh so hard I can't breathe. He looks adorably crestfallen. His freckled nose wrinkles in bewilderment. It's a minute before I'm calm enough to speak. "Sorry. I swear it is, just slowly."

"I have been on hard since the day we met." With this solemn confession, his greenish-blue eyes darken. "I'm a grown-ass man, Baby Doll, but an animal at heart. Gotta be careful when you let the beast off the leash."

That sends me into another fit of giggles.

His lips stop my laughter in its tracks. Before I know what's happening, I'm stepping backward as he advances without breaking the kiss. Something hard greets my back—a wall. Garrett lifts me as if I weigh nothing. On instinct, my legs wrap around his waist. He devours me. Then he leaves my mouth to kiss a sizzling trail up my neck to my ear. He sucks the lobe into his mouth and nips it. I whimper. Masculine moans vibrate through his chest and into me. A gasp is all the permission he needs to invade my mouth again. His tongue is insistent, demanding. Our kisses are sloppy, urgent. Our teeth clash a few times.

I don't care. I'm panting. I want this, him.

But I need control. It's stupid. Yes, women can initiate intimacy. I support a woman who owns her sexuality. I'm personally traditional, though. My normal preference is for aggressive yet considerate men.

Garrett is a perfect balance. He's dominant in his stature. Personality and his presence. Yet, this moment feels too similar to what happened. Those memories don't belong here between us.

I'm unsure how to ask for what I need. Wanting something in the abstract is super different from wanting it in reality, craving the release of submission but needing a sense of control. It's a heady contradiction of needs I can't adequately express.

I tear my mouth away. True to form, he doesn't force me.

"What's wrong, Doll?" he asks, panting.

The strength he expends supporting my entire weight with one arm is impressive, but he's sidetracking me. "I don't know. I need..." Pausing, I search for how to explain.

He nods as if he knows my mind better than I do. "Wanna take this party to the bedroom?" I stiffen and start to shake my head. "I promise nothing will happen that you aren't 100% into." Suspicion narrows my gaze, and his green eyes study mine. "Promise," he says, emphasizing each syllable. "Have I broken a promise yet?"

"No." My smile is indulgent.

"So...bedroom?"

I nod.

Instead of placing me on my feet, he carries me down the hall. We pass an open door, which I know is a bathroom, having passed it three times, once when we first entered and the other two times, walking back and forth to put our shoes beside the front door. This place is huge. It puts my old one-bedroom apartment to shame. It's easily over fifteen hundred square feet. Across from the bathroom is a closed door. There is a small laundry room beside that, and a small closet, or what appears to be one. Another closed door looms in front of us, and finally, we approach the master bedroom to the right.

We step over the threshold, and I notice that more floor-to-ceiling windows make up the far wall, just like in his front room. City lights twinkle against the night sky. The decor is minimal and quite masculine. There's a long black dresser with silver metal handles as well as a king-sized bed with a mahogany wood frame and headboard made of evenly spaced wooden slats. The bed sits a lot lower than I prefer. Given his massive physique and height, though, it makes sense. Two matching squat nightstands flank the bed.

Garrett slides me down the length of his body. Every inch of his long, thick erection rubs against my sensitive mound. By the time my feet hit the floor, I'm a live wire. My clothes irritate my skin. I sit at the end of his bed and watch as he empties his pockets, wallet, keys. All items are placed on the dresser behind him. Leaning in, he places a hand on each side of me, caging me. His firm lips touch mine with a gentle kiss before he backs away.

"I'm not gonna say I planned for this, but I hoped." He chuckles and turns to open the top drawer of his dresser. There are a lot of clanking sounds, and then the drawer closes. "I know myself and don't want you ever to be afraid of me. Hold out your hands," he commands.

I'm so curious that I obey without hesitation. I extend both my hands palms up, as if expecting a surprise, and that's exactly what I get. Carbon steel is heavy. Cool to the touch. It isn't like I had an idea of what they'd feel like. Not in my wildest fantasies did I ever expect to be in this situation. My hands droop a little under their weight.

I stare at the steel for long moments, trying to process their presence. At a loss, I gaze up at Garrett, mouth agape.

"What?"

"Handcuffs? You thought—given everything you know about me—this was a handcuff-appropriate moment? And how exactly is this not a plan?" I ask. Either he's kinkier than I know, or he's been kinky and using these with other women. Neither idea sits well with me. "Are you crazy?" I move to stand.

He pushes me down.

"Shake it easy, Foxy," he says way more jocular than he should be. "I know what you're thinking. I haven't used those with anyone else. I bought them a few days ago."

One curiosity down. "And you thought I would be a great partner to explore this kink?"

"Yes."

Okay. "What about me screams BDSM to you? I don't want to be handcuffed."

Garrett doubles over in laughter. Strange. I didn't make a joke. I'm ready to beat him over the head with the handcuffs he finds so humorous, and he's busting a gut!

"Why are you laughing? This isn't funny. You said I could trust you," I accuse.

That sobers him. He lifts his head, his face reddening.

"While I would thoroughly enjoy tying you up. Having you at my mercy while I lick and nibble each delectable inch of your body," he says. His hot gaze travels the length of me as if he's imagining me naked and doing just that. I squirm under his intense perusal. He holds my gaze captive. "Handcuffing doesn't excite me. You're going to handcuff me."

"Handcuff you?!"

Garrett kneels before me. A hand engulfs each of my kneecaps. Peering into my eyes, he says, "I'm a big man."

I stare deadpan and arch an eyebrow.

"I'm not talking about my dick. Although..." he says, insinuation left hanging. He smirks. "I'll let you be the judge. What I meant is, I'm bigger than you, and that can be intimidating. I don't want anything we do to trigger you. If I can't get free, you can be free." Garrett winks. "We'll do it this way until you trust me."

Whatever reservations I had about tonight drift away, like a feather in the breeze of his kindness. Once again, Garrett anticipates my needs when I'm unable to. Something saucy inside me unfurls. I have the power. Although I'm almost positive it's an illusion of power, I'll take it.

"You're really gonna let me use these on you?" I ask with a grin, dangling the cuffs from one finger.

Garrett stands and leans against the dresser. His arms cross over his chest as if we're discussing something as mundane as where we want to eat dinner.

"One wrist. Around a wood slat in the headboard. The dominant one, so I can get at you like a clumsy stranger with the other hand. Skin privileges still apply, right?"

"Yes, you have skin privileges," I confirm.

"Let me know when you're ready, and we'll lock me down." He flashes his devilish smile. That mix of boyish charm and masculine mischief does exciting things to me. I agree with a nod. "Good. Bring that brown sugar to Daddy, Baby doll," Garrett says, his voice going impossibly deeper.

My answering snort is very unladylike. "Shut. Up!" I guffaw. "You are so stupid."

"Stupid for you. Now, come here," he growls. Then takes the choice from me.

The handcuffs drop onto the bed with a *thud* as he sweeps me off my feet and lifts me into his arms. Like a koala, my arms and legs instinctively wrap around his neck and waist. Large hands grip under my thighs, and his lips smash into mine. There are no pretenses, no sweet pecks. It's a clashing of tongues—a claiming—and my body catches fire. I want to feel his manhood against me again, but, with as short as I am and the way he holds me, I'm closer to his navel than his penis.

His fingers, however, are in the exact right spot. He uses a strong finger to caress me through my pants. I'm so wet it wouldn't surprise me if the polyester were damp on the outside. He groans against my lips as his finger grazes my covered slit. I roll my hips to increase the pressure of his touch. My walls pulse, clutching at air and wanting more.

"Ready to move to the bed?" Garrett asks, panting, lips mashed against mine. Beyond ready. My response is to bite his lower lip.

He tosses me into the center of the bed. Steel clinks as handcuffs bounce along with me. Garrett's hooded dark green gaze spears me. I'm riveted watching him unzip his charcoal slacks. Black boxer briefs. Nice. My expression must broadcast my thoughts because he glances at himself with masculine pride before stepping out of his pants. He unbuttons several buttons of his shirt. And then whips the material over his head, ruffling the longer locks of his copper hair. Witnessing his usual suave demeanor unraveling is a heady, erotic thing. Sucking in the corner of my bottom lip, I bite it.

Garrett groans. "Like what you see?" he asks.

Do I!

I knew he was built. The way he lifts me without breaking a sweat, and how his clothes mold to him. But, dang... His body is a work of art. Smooth, sculpted pectorals and abdominal muscles top the pronounced shallow grooves cut into each side of his abdomen, forming a "V," Iliac furrows, or, what I pervertedly call, cum gutters. Instead of a yellow brick road, a fine, dark trail of hair disappears into the elastic waistband of his boxer briefs and leads to what I hope is Heaven. An impressive thick mass bulges the cotton.

He leans forward and, before I have time to protest or even realize his intentions, yanks both ends of my wide-leg pants, pulling them off with startling ease. He tosses them over his shoulder. Barely an inconvenience.

Laughing, I say, "You could've asked. I would've taken them off."

He crawls up my body. Latches onto my chin with strong fingers, tilting it up towards him. Our gazes clash. My bottom lip somehow finds its way back into my mouth, and I chew the plump flesh.

"Not as smooth," he quips. Using a thumb, he liberates my lip from my teeth. Garrett drags his pink tongue over the seam of my lips. I sigh, and he plants a tender peck on my lips. "You have on too many clothes. Whatever will we do?" he teases. "Let me help with that."

With that, he unbuttons the rest of my blouse. All three buttons since the top two were already undone. He peels the two halves away with slow deliberateness. His frown tells me he's discovered that one of Victoria's Secrets isn't a front-clasping bra.

"Fuck, you look good." He groans while tickling my side. "Arch your back."

I do. Sure, quick, fingers unfasten my bra. Guess he's an expert at this, too. I've worn a bra for decades and haven't ever been that deft. Some maneuvering removes my shirt and bra, leaving me partially bare under Garrett. Both of us are in our underwear, he in his boxer briefs and me in my black, lace-trimmed boyshort panties.

"These are sexy," Garrett says, then shimmies them down my hips. "Even sexier on the floor." The soft material slides down my legs and disappears. I'm acutely aware and thankful to have had the forethought to shave...Everything. The previous night. "Mmm..." Garrett moans.

One finger glides back and forth over my folds, and I shiver. Tingles flutter through my abdomen and shoot down my spine. My nether lips feel engorged. On the third pass, his finger parts my lips and rubs my tiny clit. He dips into my entrance. I'm so wet that I writhe in pleasure, encouraging him to go deeper. He doesn't, and I nearly cry. One hand slides up my stomach to cup one breast, then the other. Squeezing, his fingers tweak my nipples, rousing them to taut peaks. The sheer weight of his arm effectively holds me in place. Breathing is harder to regulate. He's probing my channel with too much interest and, at the same time, intentionally too little, keeping me right on the precipice of true enjoyment. Perspiration beads on my forehead.

Irrational panic steamrolls its way through an otherwise sensual moment.

Garrett's green-blue gaze travels the length of my supple body, but catches my eyes, his exploration ceases at once.

I whimper in equal parts protest and frustration. This can't be happening. I don't want this to end. It feels so good. Garrett is the right man, but, in this vulnerable position, my mind won't stay engaged, no matter how awesome the sensations coursing through me. I'm broken.

"Hey," Garrett's bass voice breaks through my spiraling thoughts. "Eyes on me, Foxy. It's okay."

He reaches beside our bodies. I'm suddenly wary and very aware of our nakedness. I wanted this, dang near begged for it. I even initiated it with suggestive words and actions. I want this. But now... My heart thumps wildly in my chest. I don't take my eyes off his. The handcuffs come into view, dangling from his index finger.

"We have these, remember? Is it time?"

Without waiting for my answer, he stretches out onto his back beside me. Cool steel lies across my belly. He is so tall that his entire body takes up the length of the bed, and his feet hang over the edge. I look up at him. He winks as if I didn't destroy the mood with a near panic attack.

It's like he knows me better than I do. I'm not a young girl apt to fall in love with anyone who gives me attention, but the way he intuits my needs without verbal cues speaks to me. My heart stumbles. Trips. If I'm not careful, a fall is imminent.

"Ready, Baby Doll?" Garrett asks, extending his right arm upwards. It meets a slat in the headboard. With a deep breath, I chew my lip. And shore up my resolve. I grab the cuffs and lean over his body, hyperaware of the fact I'm naked. Garrett caresses my hip with his left hand. I shackle the right to the thick wooden slat. He jerks his wrist, testing its strength. It's secure. Desperate to relieve the awkwardness, I bend and kiss his lips.

True to form, Garrett takes control. He thrusts his tongue into my mouth. The mood immediately ratchets up as if our interlude never intruded. Our kiss lasts for what seems to be forever. Anticipation sizzles through me and pools between my thighs. I move to straddle his waist, to feel that bulge where it'll extinguish a bit of my need.

"Wait," he commands. "Help me get these off." Garrett struggles to get out of his boxer briefs one-handed. "I wanna feel you."

I help him remove the offending clothing and fight to keep my mouth from falling open at the sight that's revealed. Taking a page from his book, I toss his briefs over my shoulder while staring at his package. Impressive isn't the right word. It's a little longer than average, but what it lacks in length, it makes up for in imposing girth. *Unreal*. His erection stands long, strong, and proud.

Sitting back on my haunches, I admire its grandeur. His penis is beautiful. He was right when he said he's a big man. My hand involuntarily wraps around the base—the meatiest part. A substantial gap keeps my fingers and thumb from touching. I stroke his shaft and use my other hand to circle the mushroom tip. Clear pre-ejaculate oozes, weeping from the tip. My mouth waters. I want to lick it. Instead, I spread the pearl of slippery fluid around to aid as I jerk him off. Garrett's guttural moans filter through my concentration. His fingers curl around my hip, gripping me tight.

Relishing in the power I possess to reduce this gigantic man to groans and pants, I toss him a sultry smirk. Then I bend down, take him fully into my mouth, check my gag reflex, and hum. Muscles at the back of my throat vibrate around his head and shaft.

"You're playing with fire, Doll," Garrett grits out between clenched teeth. "Just wait."

Snickering, I continue my erotic torture. My breasts are full and oversensitive. Since his range of motion is hampered, I massage them myself. All while never letting him slip from my mouth.

"Come closer," he says, beckoning me with his free hand. "Let me do that."

Shaking my head, I release his manhood and lick my lips.

"You're in so much trouble." He groans.

I bend, allowing my breath to tickle his tip. My lips hover above the head of his dick. Looking square into his lust-glazed eyes, I take the crown into my mouth. Swirling my tongue around the circumference, I suck hard then release it with a pop. The curse that rips from Garrett's lips is encouraging. Giggling, I straddle his waist, lower myself, and gasp.

He has great core control because, with minimal effort, he thrusts his hips forward as soon as I'm within striking distance. I gasp as his turgid member pushes between my swollen folds. We both groan at our unintentional joining. I'm sopping wet. Even still, his bulbous head lodges at my entrance.

Garrett hisses. "C'mon, Baby Doll, let me in," he says between clenched teeth.

"I'm trying," I whine. Swiveling my hips draws him in an inch, but he's still not completely inside.

"Sit on it."

"Make me."

Wrong taunt.

His hips roll beneath me, and delicious friction knocks the breath from my lungs. He steadies me with his left hand on my hip. Then he thrusts inside me, to the hilt, and I'm sitting. His pubic mound greets my clit. My folds spread around his thick intrusion. It's pleasure and pain, an intoxicating combination. I'm full.

He doesn't move, letting me adjust to his size. Again, my comfort is foremost in his mind. "Squeeze my neck, Doll." He moans. My eyes widen, and I shake my head. He bucks beneath me. "Do it. Right on the sides."

It's salacious. Wrong. I can't.

I do.

Reaching forward unseats me a little, but I grip the sides of his thick neck opposite his Adam's apple. His groan vibrates through my arm. I slide my bottom back down his shaft slowly. Dang, that's good! Although I love control, I let go and place my hand back on his chest. I bounce on his thick member, and sparks shoot through my clit as it meets his pelvis.

"Trust me yet?" he asks, voice tight. The veins in his neck are stark against his pale skin.

Hands braced on his chest, I lift an infinitesimal degree. The glide of his shaft against my inner walls stokes the flames of my desire. I slide back down and roll my hips. *Mmm...* It's so good, I can't speak.

Yes. I trust him. He's been so patient, understanding when I know for a fact it isn't in his nature. This man would love nothing more than to stamp, **Property of Garrett Kaplan**, on my ass if he could. Yet, he holds back. He considers me in all things.

It's too soon to admit, but I love him for it. I love him.

Wood cracks.

My eyes snap open.

When did I even close them?

The wooden slat that his wrist is cuffed to snaps in half and clunks onto the ground.

Struggling to stop gyrating my hips, I moan, "You broke your bed."

"Your back's next," he says, tone almost guttural.

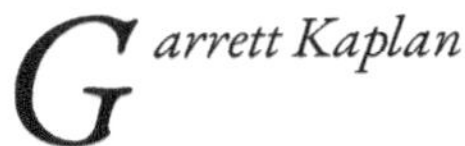

*G**arrett Kaplan*

I thrust myself as deep as possible inside her. This is nothing like the beach. I have all the time in the world, all the time to savor each stroke, to worship her the way she desires and redeem myself for being a thirty-second chump on the beach. That wasn't one of my finest moments.

Amina's walls grip my dick.

So... Tight!

Shit! Maybe I don't have all the time.

This is way too good.

Unlike the beach, I can linger on the way each part of our naked bodies makes contact. The slip. The slide. This is more than I prepared for. I knew it would be great for a multitude of reasons. Privacy is a big reason, but it's as if our souls are joining. My heart is fuller now that we're joined in this way.

I kiss along her collarbone. Loving the way her skin warms for me yet also breaks out with goose bumps.

"Mmm... Garrett," she moans my name.

Rolling my hips hits different spots inside of her, providing different sensations on my head and shaft.

Fuck! I'm close.

I deepen my thrusts, ensuring her engorged clit kisses the base of my cock.

Her body begins to shake. And her breath grows shallow.

"Kiss me," she demands.

I oblige, crushing my lips to hers in a bruising kiss.

She meets each roll of my hips with a thrust.

"Ah!" she shouts. "I'm-I'm..."

I scrunch my eyes closed as her thighs lock me in place.

Her inner walls strangle me. "Ah!" she screams as she drowns me in her juices.

"Shit!" I shout as her orgasm wrings mine from me, milking me dry.

We lay panting for a brief moment, then I roll off of her and out of bed.

"Is something wrong?" she calls after me.

In the bathroom, I grab a clean washcloth and run it under hot water, lathering it with soup.

"Nope," I say, reentering my bedroom where she lies glowing in the aftermath of our true first time. I remove the sheet covering her lower half and spread her legs.

Amina lifts onto her forearms. "Ooh... That's warm. I like it. Why did you do that?"

"No man has ever wiped you clean after sex?" I ask, confusion and irritation lacing my tone.

"No, why would they?"

I toss the washcloth onto a nightstand. Lying down, I cuddle her close and cover us with the crimson flat sheet. Our naked bodies pressed together contrast in every way imaginable, but they're so right together. She nestles her head against my chest.

"A man who values and respects the one he's with should always clean up the mess," I say solemnly. "Plus, I don't think either one of us wants to sleep in a wet spot."

"That's sweet," she says then clears her throat. "I guess I've never had that. But sadly, there won't be any sleeping in a wet or dry spot."

"What? Why?"

Chapter Thirty-Three

*G**arrett Kaplan*

"Did you just booty call me? You did it wrong. It's not booty call hours."

Swatting my pectoral, she laughs. "No, weirdo. You aren't a booty call. But those people will have two cows, a duck, and a chicken if I don't go back tonight. I can't take another threat to institutionalize me."

That makes sense, but I'm disappointed.

"Can you hand me my phone?" she asks. "It's on the nightstand beside you."

I hand her the device. She scoots up and fiddles with it for a few seconds. Then thrusts it in front of my face.

"I know you don't believe me about my parents not being my parents, but I found proof. See this picture," she says, pointing at the screen.

It's a picture of a younger her reclining in a hospital bed. Her parents are on either side of her. Her grimace, though adorable, is one of agony.

"Yes, did you break a leg or something?" I ask.

"No, this is a picture of what's supposed to be me after my appendix ruptured. Me—not me—had to have an emergency open appendectomy. I'm allegedly fourteen in that picture. Open appendectomies leave scars."

I shrug. "You're not fourteen anymore. Scars change over time. They can disappear completely as you grow."

She nods. "Right! Swipe to the next picture. Me—not me—is twenty-two here. I would never wear a yellow polka dot low-rise bikini, but clearly Faux-mina has no taste. Anyway, the scar should be right here," she says, pointing to her right hip bone in the picture.

"Faux-mina?"

Grinning, she says, "That's what I call my look-alike or doppelgänger. Either way, there's a few inches of a visible scar right there," she explains, pointing at the right hip.

Sure enough, there is a scar peeking from the low waistband of her bikini bottoms.

Amina rolls to her back and lifts the sheet off her body.

"Do you see a scar anywhere on my body? Especially, there." She asks.

Not one to pass up an opportunity to look at her naked, I click on the bedside lamp for better light.

I scan her entire body. My fingers skim over her belly button and then lower. Next thing I know, I'm massaging her mound and preparing to open her flower for digital exploration.

She clears her throat. "Umm... Sir, stick to the task at hand."

"Oh, I plan to stick somethin'," I mumble, but do as she requests.

There's no scar. Her brown skin is smooth, unblemished. It doesn't appear as if she's ever fallen, scraped a knee, had a zit, or had an ingrown hair. That's how clear her skin is. It's perfect. A scar of that magnitude would definitely be there now if it were there when she was twenty-two, yet there is nothing.

"You didn't have surgery to have it removed?" I ask, trying to make it make sense, although I know the answer.

"Nope," she says, shaking her head. "I've never had surgery. And even if I had surgery to remove the scar, wouldn't there be even the tiniest remnant that I had? Mole removal leaves a little scar sometimes, even though that defeats the purpose of the removal."

"Yeah, it does," I say, my agreement coming much slower as the wheels in my head spin.

She's right. I believe her, and she's right. The two women could be identical twins, but there are subtle differences in the way they carry themselves. The woman in the picture is posed in a very sassy way, with a regal, confident stance. Not that Amina isn't confident, but there's a humbleness ever present in her expression and shyness behind her eyes.

These are not the same person.

If Amina is lying in bed with me...

Who the hell is the Amina in the picture?

And how do I get the Amina I love away from those people who think she's their daughter?

Chapter Thirty-Four

*A*mina Raichand

Life has gotten a lot kinkier since I met Garrett. Exhibitionism. Handcuffs. And now...

Blindfolds.

Unfortunately, this time, I'm the one in the blindfold, and it isn't fun. I don't have one iota of power in this situation, but ever since I made the mistake of telling Garrett I trust him after he admitted he believed me several weeks ago, he's tested that trust. His being the only person in this upside-down universe on my side means everything to me. Garrett's belief was the last brick removed from the guard wall surrounding my heart. We haven't said the words to each other yet, but it's in our actions. He makes time to see me whenever he can. No matter if he's dragging after a long day of work, he still makes the nearly fifty-minute drive to see me for 10-20 minutes. When we can't be together, he texts and calls to check up on me every two hours. It's like now that he knows that I'm a visitor in this timeline, he's scared I'll poof out of existence.

I won't admit it out loud, but I'm scared too. What if whatever caused me to wake up here decides, without warning, to put me back where I belong? And where does that leave Faux-mina? Is she living my life? Is she as confused as me? Group and Patricia have been a Godsend for me, helping with not only the assault but also with my confidence. I'm finding my backbone for the first time in 32 years and learning to accept the idea that I'm worthy of love and friendship without convincing. I deserve happiness.

That's one thought I'm still fine-tuning. After all, Rome wasn't built in a day. Reprogramming internal speech remains a hard task for me, and old habits die hard. Speaking nicer to myself and speaking positively about myself, utilizing positive affirmations, is a struggle, but I'm dedicated to doing the work for the first time.

Much to Nora's delight, I've gone on two shopping trips with Shea and Tamsyn. If she knew they were connected in any way to Garrett, she would snub her nose at them. However, Shea and Tamsyn speak Nora's language: arrogance and money. At least they do a darn good job acting like it. Little does Nora know that the luxury cars they drive are their boyfriends' and the money they spend, at least the money I've spent, is Garrett's. I don't ask for it, but he insists.

Just like he insists on having sex anywhere he can get me. It's sweet except...

A speed bump, a pothole, or uneven asphalt...something jostles me.

"You're doing that on purpose," I say. "I know you know how much your driving freaks me out. Just because your car is all sleek and aerodynamic doesn't mean you have to drive like a maniac."

Garrett chortles.

"Why is this so funny to you?" I ask. "I don't like being sensory deprived."

"Duly noted, Doll," Garret says, cool as a cumber.

Of course, he's ecstatic at having me at his mercy.

This morning, he showed up and presented me with a soft pink rectangular gift box. I'm not the most materialistic woman on the planet, but I was excited. I mean, what woman doesn't love gifts? I ripped off the big pink bow, opened the lid, and there, on a fluffy pillow, sat what appeared to be a baby-pink satin scarf. To say the reveal was a bit anticlimactic would be an understatement.

Next thing I knew, he was standing behind me, putting the scarf around my head and eyes, then tying it. He says he has a surprise for me, even though he knows I hate surprises. I thought we went over that when he surprised me by ambushing me into a meeting with his parents. He led me by the hand to his car and buckled my seatbelt. I believe that was fifteen minutes ago.

Fifteen minutes or more without sight and very little smell since the mask squishes my nose.

"Are we there yet?" I whine like an impotent child.

"Would I still be driving if we were?" he asks.

I stomp my feet. "I don't like not being able to see. And you can check this off the list for any of your fetishes. This is a onetime deal, buddy."

"How else was I going to surprise you?"

"Not surprising me was an option too. And is this a new Mercedes? This is more than comfortable, Richie Rich."

When he pulled into the driveway in this sleek black Mercedes, I thought it was his SUV, but it appears newer and smells like a new, expensive car. Of course, I didn't get too good a look at it because I found myself blindfolded mere seconds later.

Garrett scoffs. "I'm hardly, Richie Rich. I already told you my money skills are on point, and I do well for myself. This is one of the perks of that. A lot was done to secure my future, a lot of death. But I also contributed as well. I knew I didn't want to be one of those guys who stumble into a family and can barely take care of himself, let alone a partner."

Darn! Now I feel bad for picking at him. I'm sure his grandparents left him a sizable inheritance, but something tells me Garrett would give it up to have another day with them. Apparently, Gwen's parents were loaded. Getting to know him over the last several months has given me an arcane look into his heart and soul. He cherishes his loved ones and protects them fiercely.

"Sorry. I didn't mean to bring up bad memories."

"Don't worry about it," he says. I can almost hear the smile on his face. "Nothing can ruin this day."

"Well, good for you because the suspense is killing me."

Garret chuckles. "I promised you you'd love it," he reminds me. "Have I broken a promise to you yet?"

Biting my lip, I shake my head.

*G*arrett Kaplan

"Just another few steps," I say, guiding Amina down the brick walkway.

I thought the drive would alleviate some of my nerves, but it didn't. I might be more nervous than when I picked her up. Thankfully, she listened to me for once and bound her hair with a clip, long curly strands cascade over each side of the clip like a thick dark waterfall. Her deep orange maxi dress is beautiful against her brown skin.

Caressing the back of her soft hands is what it must be like to touch clouds. The evening is meant for her. It swaddles her in its luxurious scents of raspberry noir, amber crystals, rose petal creamy patchouli, and mocha musk. She smells enticing. Amina is night incarnate.

Once we approach the front door, I drop her hands.

She swats at my back.

"Hey, hey, hey! Woman! What's wrong with you?"

"I still can't see. Why'd you let go?" She pouts. "What if I fall?"

"Don't move. Give me one second," I say, retrieving the keys from my pocket.

"What are you doing?"

Quietly as possible, I unlock the door and push it wide open. Then spin, kneel, and snatch Amina off her feet and into my arms. I cradle her to my chest. She squeals and hits my back.

And I step over the threshold.

*A*mina Raichand

A door slams behind me, and I think I may pee myself.

This is what happens in those scary documentaries, though I didn't meet Garrett on a dating app. Still, there are all those true crime stories of meeting some guy, and he's great until bada bing, bada boom, you're last seen on CCTV walking through your hotel, and he's leaving alone at the butt crack of dawn, rolling a big suitcase behind him.

My breath quickens. I only have room for one traumatic incident every fifteen years. I cannot afford another. My heart can't take it. Something hard and warm approaches my back. Just as I'm about to scream or kick, the end of the blindfold is yanked, and it falls away.

Ohmygoodness!

It takes a few seconds for my eyes to adjust, but blinking twice doesn't clear my confusion. The house is empty. Well, not totally empty.

A large, checkered blanket lies in the middle of what I'm guessing is the living room floor. A vase brimming with red roses, interspersed with baby's breath, sits in the middle of the blanket. On each side of the roses, there are crystal candle holders, each with a lit tapered candle. Two flutes of champagne sit off to the side of the blanket. Tears prick my eyes.

"Welcome home, future Mrs. Kaplan!" Garrett shouts, coming around in front of me.

He's smiling like the cat that ate the canary.

I'm frozen. "What is this?" I ask. I'm not putting the obvious pieces together fast enough, and Garrett's smile falters a smidgen.

"Our house," he answers, brow arched. "For after we get married. You said you wanted to live in Carmel, right?"

A tear slithers down my cheek. "What kinda wife can I be? I hear things, and I could be yanked out of existence at a moment's notice. Like, really, poof! No more Amina."

Head tilting, Garrett bestows me with a sad smile. He takes both my hands in his and kisses the backs of them, then drops to one knee.

"Amina Kimberly Raichand, you drive me insane," he says, then chuckles. "I mean it. I was stuffy, rigid, and domineering before I met you. And you've opened my mind in ways I never thought possible. Our meeting was in no way conventional but in every way destined. You were literally dropped into my universe. You're my gift. In a roundabout way, because of Lisa, I have you. I'm so happy I wasn't some chump who settled. I waited. Lisa and the Lord delivered me an angel. You healed my broken heart. I know you've said much of your life was spent alone before, but you'll never be alone again, Foxy. If being with you is insanity, then I never want to be sane. You will always have me. In life, death, and beyond. This is my promise to you, and I haven't broken a promise to you yet." He winks.

Tears are streaming down my face and dripping off my chin. I wipe them as best I can with my right hand.

He reaches into his pocket and produces a white-gold, four-carat diamond solitaire ring.

Lifting my left hand, he says the words that the lonely little girl inside me never dared to dream she'd ever hear.

"Will you do me the tremendous honor of being my wife? I love you."

I'm light-headed. My face is cold. And my head is full. My stomach is doing somersaults. I wet my lips with my tongue and say, "Yes, Garrett Stewart Kaplan, my prince, my sanity, I will marry you. I love you, too. To infinity and beyond." We both laugh as he slides the ring on my finger. He stands and twirls me in his arms, careful not to hit the champagne glasses and careful not to catch the long end of my maxi dress on fire. There we stand for what could be seconds or years staring into each other's eyes. He squeezes my waist.

"Would you like to dance with me?" he asks.

"There's no music."

He gives his signature grin. "I can fix that."

Swaying us back and forth, he begins to hum.

I'm positive I don't know what song he's humming, then...

"*...Like all at once, I wake up from something that keeps knocking at my brain,*" he sings. "*Before I got insane, I hold my pillow to my head and spring up in my bed, screaming out the words I dread. I think I love you...*"

Chapter Thirty-Five

*G*arrett Kaplan

Shit! Now, this...is swank!

Amina gets on to me about being "Richie Rich," but those in glass houses...

I thought these types of scenes were done for dramatic effect in period pieces, the ones where the king and queen sit at extreme opposite sides of a ridiculously long table, but, I guess it's real. If someone told me they were given specific instructions to "dress" for dinner, I'd believe it.

It had been a struggle to allow me to sit beside Amina instead of at the extreme opposite side of the table across from her. The way Mrs. Raichand throws daggers at me from the extreme right end of the table shows she's not over the slight yet. Too bad for her because I wasn't going to sit that far away from Amina in this house of... Phonies?

That's not an accurate description of this situation.

Professional portraits after professional portraits hang on any available wall space not commandeered by ugly, expensive artwork. I can create nicer pieces to display in minutes if this is their idea of being cultured. But the portraits show that they do care quite a bit about their daughter and appearances. Everywhere you turn, there's a stuffy, staged family portrait of Amina and her parents at various stages of life, from birth to early twenties.

If I ignore all the evidence Amina has shown me, and there's a lot. We drove to Hillard Brand Community College, then for nearly an hour and a half to Bumfuck, Precious, Indiana, to find a children's home called Innocent Treasures. Then we risked it all, scouring a dicey neighborhood where she was certain her apartment should be. We found the college. It is real, but there were no records of her ever being enrolled. The children's shelter existed, but the person working the day shift didn't recognize her name or face. In lieu of all that evidence, should I still need proof, I've found it here. The pictures are extra-staged, but there is a real air of superiority clinging to everyone in them. In the portraits, Amina looks like a spoiled child who's angry at her parents.

My Amina isn't anything like that. The green flecks in her honey eyes are a hair different. There's quiet strength honed by difficult life experiences behind *my* Amina's eyes. I don't think the trauma of her assault is what forged the strength I admire in her. This strength was born in her. It's innate. I can trick myself into believing a lot, but no matter how ludicrous this is, my Amina is not the Amina in the photographs. They could be the most identical of identical twins, but the soul is different; they are somehow different people.

I understand why her parents, *not parents*, think this is their daughter. It's an easy mistake to make. This is a person who would naturally come from these two people. And...

Amina is staring at me through tight lips. That's my cue. It's not like I'm going to eat this handful of food. Who the fuck eats like this? Their fancy plates aren't even full. It's like 1/3 cup of green beans, 1/3 cup of brown rice, and 1/3 cup of shrimp scampi.

After a couple of calming breaths, I say, "I know it seems spontaneous. But these things happen when they happen."

"Of course, it does," Mr. Raichand says under his breath. He takes a sip of his lemon water. "We have dinner every night. You happened to come to this one. Nothing spontaneous about that."

Hmm...

Not a lot to say to that. Looking around the table shows everyone heard him. Mrs. Raichand and Amina stare down the table with matching expressions of boredom on their faces. After a beat, they continue eating. Well, Mrs. Raichand eats. Amina moves food around her plate.

"Pet," Mrs. Raichand says.

I assume she's speaking to Amina, but it sounds like she might as well have called her a bitch.

"You're not eating. Your father works too hard," she says, then looks towards me. "My husband's a pharmacist, one of the best-paid in the United States. It isn't cheap to provide the best, freshest, and healthiest food. Amina's eaten this way her entire life, but as of late, she's become a bit pickier. Haven't you, Pet?"

Amina pinches me under the table.

My turn again, I guess.

"I wasn't referring to dinner. I was speaking of Amina and I meeting and falling in love."

Mrs. Raichand chokes on her water. She slams the glass on the lace tablecloth-covered table, and with a dainty hand, she pats the chest of her cream-colored silk blouse.

"Love, huh!" Mr. Raichand mumbles. "Kids these days don't know love. Lust is what they know. The uptick in STI diagnoses and medications prescribed for those STIs is proof." He shoves a few green beans in his mouth.

Amina and I look at each other with arched brows.

"I never expected to meet someone," Amina says, taking over the landmine of a topic. "Garrett understands me."

Mrs. Raichand taps a long fingernail on the table.

"He can understand all he wants, but I know what you're about to say," she spears us both with ruthless glares. "This isn't happening. We still have guardianship and power of attorney over you. Pretend all you want, Pet. Nothing will change without our consent."

Mr. Raichand finally makes eye contact with us.

"Men only marry a woman after five or six months for one reason," he says, then stares at me pointedly. "When is she due?"

Amina gasps, and her eyes bulge.

"What?!" she says, voice rising. "I'm not pregnant."

We exchange a quick look at each other from the corner of our eyes.

She's being honest. We don't think she's pregnant; however, we have been playing chicken with pregnancy. That's not something they need to know, though.

I chuckle at my joke.

"I haven't..." I start to say, "We just..." I don't know how to recover this train wreck. "Mr. Raichand, Amina, and I are adults. Well into our adult years. I'd say we're both responsible. I'd never ask someone to marry me because they were pregnant. It hasn't been that long, but when you know, you know. And I know I love Amina with all my heart."

Mr. Raichand shifts his gaze between the two of us.

"Don't explain to them," Amina says.

"Don't explain," Gilbert mumbles, forking a piece of shrimp. "Coming over here, telling me you're getting married, huh?" He pops shrimp in his mouth and chews slowly. "In my home. Don't explain. Hmph..." he continues muttering after he's finished chewing.

Is this what Amina's been living with? I shake my head and stare at Mr. Raichand. Mrs. Raichand says he's a well-known pharmacist, but he doesn't come across as one. The man gives it's-almost-time-to-put-dad-in-a-home. That's saying a lot considering my family. He shouldn't have guardianship over anybody or anything.

I glance at Amina. She gives a subtle shake of her head.

"The guardianship, or whatever, is up next month," she glares at Mrs. Raichand. "I checked. I can do what I want then."

Mrs. Raichand glowers back.

"Maybe before that happens, you'll already be at Serene Meadows. It'll be hard to get out of that involuntary hold. Your father and I are very concerned about your decision-making and safety. You could hurt yourself, especially, with all the voices," Mrs. Raichand says as if she's let some secret slip.

Little does she know. I'm the right man to deal with the voices and anything else Amina has going on.

Pointing a long red fingernail at Amina, Mrs. Raichand says, "Let's say you manage to go through with this, we won't be there. And afterwards, you and your hobosexual need to find somewhere else to live."

Amina scoffs, then rises from her chair. I follow suit and push in both chairs.

"Whatever floats your boat," Amina says. "I didn't plan on living here after the wedding, anyway. We're leaving."

She grabs my hand, attempting to yank me out of the dining room.

Mrs. Raichand stands as well.

"Oh, Pet," she says, all civility fleeing her tone, "your friend is welcome to leave. Actually, I demand he leave, or I'll call the authorities. It'll be hard to marry someone who can't legally come onto our property. And as you so gleefully reminded us, your guardianship ends in a month. That month's not today, though. So, goodbye, young man. Amina, go to your room."

Chapter Thirty-Six

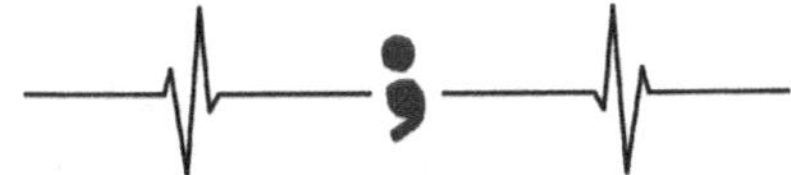

*G*ilbert Raichand

After changing into my olive-green kurta pajama, I shuffle downstairs and into the sitting room. I haven't been able to speak to Nora since the young man left and Amina stormed off to her room. Alienation is a term my wife knows intimately. Specifically, regarding our daughter. Our nearly thirty-three-year-old daughter, who, by some stroke of luck or misfortune, we've been granted another chance with.

I search through the pharmaceutical periodicals on the table. There is always something new to glean in the pharmaceutical world. Grabbing one from the coffee table, I plop down in my favorite chair and click on the lamp beside my reading chair. Flipping through a few pages, without seeing any of the titles, I toss the magazine on the side table. I adjust my glasses.

Maybe I can't rest because, for once—that's untrue, it's been more than once—I don't agree with another of Nora's unilateral decisions.

When we were first married, I believed that once she gave birth, she would return to the spirited, ambitious woman I fell in love with. Nora Vaughn was the classiest, most vivacious woman in college. Every man wanted her, and she knew it. She had this endearing small gap between her two front teeth. On most women, the gap might be distracting, but on Nora Vaughn, with her petite, coke-bottle figure, it added to her beauty in unimaginable ways. The only thing more beautiful about her was her mind. It entered the room before she did. And Nora supported my goals. She didn't mind when I would miss visits to study, and she encouraged me to reach for more. We thought we would open a hus-band-and-wife medical practice.

Then my traditional East Indian parents discovered our relation-ship. We'd kept it secret for an impressive two years. When *Appa* (father) and *Maa* (mother) came for their unexpected visit, they did not approve of my chosen fiancé. Her parents did not take too kindly to me either.

Still, Nora and I decided to continue our relationship in secret. Her friend Patricia acted as our intermediary. She aided us as much as possible and did much of the heavy lifting to keep our clandestine dalliances covert, which led to the conception of my love bug, Amina. If Nora had it her way, I wouldn't have ever known about Amina. Patricia interceded before Nora could address what she deemed a problem. Had she spoken to me, I wouldn't have forced her to go through with the pregnancy, but I did want to be consulted. I wasn't a fly-by-night lover. I was her fiancé, and I loved her—still do. Deciding to abort our child was worthy of a discussion. In my anger, I confided in my parents, a decision I'm equal measure grateful for and regretful of.

They saw to it that I did the right thing. I begged Nora to marry me and promised her that she could still pursue her dreams. I promised that a baby would not detract from our goals. With the two of us, things could be better. She fought me on it until the decision was beyond our medical control. And I couldn't be happier for that, but Nora suffered the most. Her parents disowned her. Mine began to tolerate her, and we married. Nora devoted her time to supporting me and being a mother but never fulfilled her own dreams. Out of guilt, I deferred to her about everything regarding Amina, hoping the fact that I supported her decisions would bring back her joy, but it backfired. The older Amina got, and the more her individual personality took root, the more Nora seemed to hold our daughter in great disdain. My greatest joy became Nora's greatest foe.

In one breath, she would bring Amina close, and in the next, she'd push her away with callous words and criticisms. Ten years ago, when Amina shunned all the privileges her birthright afforded her and went no contact with us, part of me died. I'd lost my love bug because I'd become a background player in her life. I didn't champion her when she needed it most. Eventually, using Patricia again, I got Amina to agree to weekly dinners. Her only caveat was that her mother knew nothing of what we discussed during these dinners. They were meant for the two of us, *Beti* and *Appa*, and I agreed.

Tonight, that same little girl who stared at me, begging me for help when her mother was cruel, pleaded with me through those same golden eyes, and I said nothing.

Nora waltzes into the sitting room, running the tips of her fingers over my back and the top of my shoulder as she passes. A few of her elegant fingers dance along the keys of the grand piano as she passes it. She drapes herself onto the Gainsboro grey couch.

"Can you believe your daughter?" Nora says with as much drama as she enters the room.

"I'm surprised you noticed?" I grumble.

"Gilbert... Speak up! I catch only half of what you say most days," Nora says, groaning.

I rest a leg over my thigh and lean forward, gaze locked on my wife.

"I said, I'm surprised you noticed?" I say, raising my voice.

Lifting out of her slouch, she straightens her posture. "Excuse me?"

"Did you notice, for one moment, that our daughter was happy?" I ask, baritone voice rising to a pitch it never has. "That in her happiness, she decided to share with us for the first time in who knows how long.

She shared with us, and you shut her down, sent her to her room like a toddler."

Nora scoffs, shaking her head. "That's not what Patricia says. Apparently, toddler means something new these days. The youth have commandeered another term."

"What?!" I shout. "Did you hear what I am saying to you? You hurt your daughter."

Her answering smile is flippant. "She'll get over it. This is a crush forged in trauma. Soon, she'll realize I'm right and we'll keep our daughter. We just got her back, and now she wants to leave already. If she persists in this foolhardy endeavor, Serene Meadows is our only recourse. She's not in the right state of mind to be making decisions for herself. Her guardianship will be extended uncontested. Don't worry. We won't lose her again."

I want to run headlong into a wall, or maybe a wall is what I'm talking to. Where did her heart go?

"This was never about losing for you. It has always been about control. You lost control when we unexpectedly got pregnant, and you've been trying to reclaim it by treating our daughter like a miniature copy of you. You want her to be everything you couldn't. The only problem is that...you could have. I would have supported you. I would have been the proud husband of Doctor Vaughn-Raichand. Instead, you allowed pregnancy and marriage to defeat you. Family is supposed to bolster you, not hinder you. We would have been your biggest cheerleaders, but instead, you chose to play the villain to your own daughter. You want her to be you. Then, when she falls short, you find no issue with crushing her under your expensive stilettos. The only way I lose our daughter is if I stay quiet, but I love Amina and want to see her happy."

Nora thrusts to her feet. "Oh, I'm the bad guy. I'm always the bad guy because I choose to face reality and not prance around in a field of dreams, delusions, and deceptions. Why is the truth so hard for people to hear? It's not mean. It's not nice. It just is. And marrying some ne'er-do-well without a pot to piss in or a window to throw it out of is a fool's errand. She may think she's happy, but what about her psychology degree? Her doctorate? I can't watch her give all of that up for love. I won't watch her give that up for love. So, if institutionalizing her is the way to keep that from happening, so be it. She'll thank me later."

I recoil as if I've been slapped, and stand.

"Where are you going?" Nora asks with a huff. "If you go upstairs now, you'll spoil her—as you always have. She gets her obstinacy from you."

"You would think that?" I nod before taking a last glance at our family portrait, walking out the front door.

*G*arrett Kaplan

I can't believe this shit. This is fuckin' insanity!

But, of course, it is. Why wouldn't it be?

"This is The Beatles!" I laugh, walk over to the sectional, and plop down. "The Beatles. The British invasion? The Rolling Stones." I toss my arm around Amina's shoulder. "Baby doll, I have so much to teach you. For the rest of your life, you will be subjected to nothing but music. No more movies for you."

Amina giggles. "Yeah, right! Your taste in music sucks. Have you ever seen *X-Men*? *The Vow*? *The Time Traveler's Wife*? *The Color Purple* is a classic."

I shrug.

"*Gone with the Wind*?" She puts a hand to her head. "'After all, tomorrow is another day,'" Amina says in a dramatic, genteel southern accent. Then she laughs. "*Thoroughly Modern Millie*? Nothing?! Nothing! Garrett, my darling, you may be versed in musical classics, but I, *mon cher*, have spanked you in classic cinema."

"Let's try some soul music," I suggest, lifting her legs into my lap. I rub the knots in her calves and thighs. It couldn't have been easy on her shins, dropping from that second-story window. "Otis Redding, 'Try a Little Tenderness'?"

Her lips mash into a firm line, and her eyes roll back and forth.

Amina shakes her head. "I don't know. Hum a little for me."

With a droll stare, I knock her legs off me and go to my record player. Finding the record, I put it on and set the needle.

"This was released in 1966," I say over the instrumental. "Dance with me, Foxy," I hold my hand out towards Amina.

Smiling, she comes to me. The lightness in her steps matches the lightness I see in her eyes for the first time, and I'm honored that I'm the one who put it there after our atrocious dinner with her parents.

We dance, holding each other tightly.

Then she beams up into my eyes. "I do know this song."

I pull back enough to look her in the eyes and arch a brow. "You do?"

"Chris Brown sings it in *This Christmas*?"

"Chris Brown...?" I hang my head in sadness.

The doorbell chimes. Leaving her to her music-ignorance shame, I answer the door, and my jaw drops.

"I assume my daughter is here," Mr. Raichand says.

"Umm..."

Leaving him standing in the doorway, I go stop the record.

"At least I knew it this time," Amina whines.

"You get half a point for that one," I say, ushering her to sit on the sectional. "We have a visitor."

"Who? Shea? Tamsyn? How'd they know I was here?" She grabs the sleeve of my dress shirt before I turn fully away. "Please, don't say Varinka. I love her, but she's better in small doses."

I chuckle. "It's not Varinka. Arizona isn't an Uber ride around the corner. I'll be right back."

Inviting Mr. Raichand inside, I close the door behind him. He follows me down the hall to the living room. Damn!He's pretty tall. I don't know how I missed it, but he's maybe an inch shorter than my 6'3". I'm surprised Amina's short, neither of her parents is—I stop that thought in its tracks. This isn't her father. Or is it? If we're playing fast and loose with physics, it stands to reason that her real parents are identical to her not-parents here. That would account for how much they favor each other. It's the only thing that makes logical sense if anything in this situation can make sense.

Amina looks as shocked as I did when I return with Mr. Raichand.

He takes a seat on the opposite side of the sectional, and I sit beside Amina.

"What are you—?" Amina starts, then stops. "How did you know?"

Mr. Raichand grins. "As a child, you were just as adept at escaping our home as I suspected you'd be tonight."

Maybe my Amina isn't so different from their Amina. I nudge her with my elbow.

"I had to leave," Amina says by way of apology. "That lady was calling a crisis team to have me carted off to Serene Meadows. I can't go there. I'm not making some decision on the fly or out of some misguided crush. Garrett and I talk a lot and have spent a lot of time together. Not that I need to explain it to either of you, but I do love him. It's real. Many couples get engaged after six months. It's not like it used to be. This isn't a shotgun wedding or a marriage of obligation."

Something akin to pain or remorse passes across Mr. Raichand's bronze face. It comes and goes so fast, I'm not sure what I saw.

"You know your mind," Mr. Raichand says. "You've known since you yanked out those bows that your mother liked to put in your hair when you were two. When you refused to let us pay for your car when you were sixteen. If you hadn't been in a coma, we wouldn't have been able to upgrade you to the Subaru. Which I noticed you didn't drive here..."

I can't help but brag. "Actually, I got her a GLS 600 Maybach as an engagement gift."

Amina gives me a lethal side eye.

"I am astonished. My lovebug is not one for flash or gifts," he says, chuckling...and maybe with some longing. "But back to the matter at hand. You have always known your mind even when it vexed your mother. I think her cruelty comes from things she feels she gave up, and she doesn't want you to make the same mistakes. I also think she's very bad at finding ways to be close to you. She doesn't realize her maladaptive behavior is having the opposite effect. I've stood by too long and said nothing, but not tonight. You will not be going to Serene Meadows, and you have my blessing to marry this man." His gaze shifts to me. "As long as you vow to keep her living in the way of life she's accustomed to."

"I think I can do better than that," I say, only half joking, because I know what her life was really like.

Having said his piece, Mr. Raichand stands.

"That's all I came to say, but I also have a request," Mr. Raichand says. "I don't know if you've disinvited us after your mother's antics. I wouldn't blame you, but would it be all right if I walked you down the aisle?"

Amina clears her throat. Looking over, I see tears forming in her eyes. She jumps to her feet and runs to Mr. Raichand. "I'd be mad if you didn't, *Appa*," she says, embracing him in a tight hug.

Chapter Thirty-Seven

*G*arrett Kaplan

Stop this train, I wanna get off...

Damn! Life has been a whirlwind these last five months. Nora actually invited me to dinner and apologized for lashing out, which caused Amina and me to nearly fall out of our chairs. Still, Amina has built a new relationship with the people she now, affectionately, calls her re-gifted parents because of that apology.

Gilbert is the best fake father-in-law a guy can ask for. Not that I need his money, but he offers to foot any bill he hears we might need to pay. He also offered a dowry for Amina, and he would not take no for an answer. She explained that she wasn't for sale, but he insisted that wasn't what a dowry meant. Also, he gets along great with both of my parents. Nora's still an acquired taste. What's wild, though, is that Rob adores her. She cannot escape him, no matter how hard she tries or where she hides. That shits funny as hell.

The wedding was gorgeous. My boys and, shockingly, Amina, did the "Walk It Out" dance, leaving the reception. I owe Varinka big time for pulling that off. Amina hates attention, but not only did she wear two wedding dresses, one traditional American and the other a vibrant, beautiful red silk saree with gold accents in honor of her East Indian heritage. I'm man enough to admit I shed a couple of tears seeing her. Everything was gorgeous, and the way they hid her growing pregnant belly was a work of art. No one knew until after the wedding.

I'm being honest when I say that I didn't know she was pregnant when I proposed. Didn't have one inkling she might be pregnant. We're both in our thirties. Though we weren't avoiding pregnancy, I figured we weren't supposed to be as fertile as twenty-year-olds at a bar. Apparently, I was wrong. We found out two weeks before the wedding, but I couldn't have been happier. It bumped our timeline a bit, but it was right on time. What I'm unhappy about is that we conceived in my one-pump-chump moment of weakness. That's not a story I want to tell our future daughter.

That's right! We found out at our twenty-week ultrasound that we're having a daughter. We painted the nursery pink with white fluffy clouds. I'm scared shitless, but Amina says it'll be great. She loves babies and children. I'm excited to see her as a mother, and seeing her carrying my child is oddly erotic. If she lets me, I'll keep her pregnant back-to-back. It's like, that's my baby in there. I did that to her! Then she waddles in, all baby, and a pang of sympathy stabs at my heart.

"Ugh! I'm a cow. I swear I'm hungry every twenty minutes."

I get up from the couch to help her sit in her special pregnancy recliner.

"But you're a cute cow," I say.

She glares daggers at me. "Shut. Up. You and all your abs make me sick. My body's never going to be the same again. And..." she says, sniffling. "I can't see my vagina anymore."

I bite my lip to keep from laughing.

"Don't laugh. You'd be sad if you couldn't see your penis anymore."

The dam breaks, and I burst into laughter. Tears drip from my right eye.

"Foxy, I can assure you your vagina is still there, and it's beautiful," I say, trying to console her. Amina punches me in the stomach, and I return to my spot on the couch, still laughing. "I can get you those jalapeño poppers you like? Or the chocolate cake and Tabasco?"

She wipes her eyes. "We still have some in the refrigerator."

"Well..." I say grimacing, "I ate that last night."

"What?!"

"You make it look so amazing with your eyes rolling in the back of your head while eating it. I had to try it."

Her eyes narrow on me. "I knew you liked all my cravings! You're not as put out as you act when you have to go get me something at two in the morning. I knew it."

"Is that a dig at my sympathy weight?" I say, rubbing my flat belly.

"What sympathy weight, jerk? You've gained more than I have, but somehow yours makes bigger muscles."

Laughing, I watch Amina's gaze lose focus. Her sightless eyes dart around the room.

Shit!

I haven't seen this in months. For some reason, I thought us being together made it better, but... I get off the couch and kneel in front of her.

"1-2-3 eyes on me."

Amina's expression grows sullen.

"1-2-3 eyes on me, Foxy," I say louder.

Watery golden eyes refocus and stare into mine.

"Are you hearing them again?" I ask, caressing her face.

She nods. "I thought it was stopping. It hasn't happened in so long. I'm sorry."

I lift her from her recliner and sit her in my lap on the couch.

"What are you sorry for? You can't control it." I shrug. "And look, I got you back. But... You know what's in your control?"

She shakes her head.

"Breaking my leg. I just deadlifted a ton. Daddy's gonna have to stretch before I do—"

Amina doubles over and slips from my lap.

"Oh, God!"

*A*mina Kaplan

Something tears inside me. I don't know how I know, but it's like when you pull a muscle, only deeper. Garrett kneels on the floor beside me. He lifts my head to meet his eyes.

"Are you okay?" he asks, voice quavering with concern.

I glance down between our bodies. Spots of blood blossom near the thighs of my maternity pants.

"No!" I say, through the tears, I didn't know were flowing. "Something's wrong, Garrett. I'm only 31 weeks today. This should be—OW!"

The next few minutes, or eternity, I don't know, happen in a blur. I'm lying on the floor in the living room of our house. Then I'm being lifted onto a stretcher with strangers hovering above me. Lights swirl around me, and sirens blare.

Someone grabs my hand.

"Garrett?! Where's Garrett?"

"Shh..." A hand squeezes mine. "It's okay. I'm right here."

I'm being lifted, and his hand slips from mine.

"Garrett? Don't leave."

Seconds pass, and then his hand is in mine once more.

"Ma'am, when did the pain start?"

"Five, ten minutes ago, maybe," Garrett answers from somewhere beside me.

It's claustrophobic in the tiny space in the back of the ambulance. Someone puts a blood pressure cuff on my left arm. It's too bright here. Is the back of an ambulance always this bright?

People are talking to me and not talking to me all at the same time.

"Mrs. Kaplan, how far along are you, did you say?" someone asks. "Mrs. Kaplan."

"She's thirty-one weeks today," Garrett answers.

It's good he's here because the discomfort in my abdomen has increased tenfold. There's an IV being placed, and my left arm is being squeezed within an inch of its life. I'd think they were trying to tourniquet my arm to prepare it for amputation if I didn't know what they were doing. I want to grab my stomach, but my limbs are otherwise engaged.

"Garrett?!"

"I'm right here beside you," he assures me.

"I'm—"

"We're here," Garrett says, interrupting me.

He always seems to know me better than I know myself.

"I'm going to let go of your hand just so I can hop out, but I'm right here."

Seconds later, heavy doors are opened, and I can barely make out the top of Garrett's dark copper red hair as he jumps out of the ambulance. After some jostling, I'm at a slant, then the side of my head tilts, and the gurney lifts. I'm out of the back and rolling before I'm positive both wheels have hit the ground.

Garrett isn't holding my hand.

Strangers run beside my stretcher, hands holding each rail. The gurney smashes through double doors. Fluorescent lights are too bright in the hall I'm being rushed through.

I can't find Garrett.

My heart hammers in my chest.

"I'm here," Garrett's deep voice says from somewhere beside me. "Right here, Baby Doll."

There are too many people in scrubs, in white coats, and EMTs in black shirts. My head movement is limited, so I can't see around any of them, but I hear his deep *basso profondo* voice answering questions. It's the sweetest, most comforting sound I can ever hear.

A man who appears in his early fifties with deep smile lines, salt and pepper hair, and kind brown eyes gazes down at me. Surprisingly, he's able to keep up. We are booking it through the hall.

"Hello, Mrs. Kaplan. Didn't expect to see you so soon. What's going on?" Then, looking behind me, he says, "I'm Mrs. Kaplan's Obstetrician. What seems to have happened?"

A voice from somewhere says, "Looks like a possible abruption. Patient presents with severe abdominal pain, vaginal bleeding, and contractions are three minutes apart."

"Isn't it too soon, Dr. Eloy?" Garrett asks from somewhere above my head.

Dr. Eloy pats my hand. I know he means to comfort me, but I cringe at the thought of contact. Only Garrett has skin privileges.

"Mrs. Kaplan, I'm going to get you back to a room so we can monitor you and baby. I'll do a quick exam, take some labs, and get an ultrasound. Does that sound okay with you?"

I nod as tears run down the sides of my face and into my hairline. What else can I do?

We make it to the room. Three EMTs hold one side of the sheets under me, and a doctor and two nurses grab the sheets on the other side. They lift me onto the bed, and I want to die.

That small amount of movement makes it feel as if shards of glass are slicing my lower abdomen, near my vagina. I scream in pain and must pass out.

When my eyes open, they're met by beautiful, worried greenish-blue eyes. Galloping sounds come from the machine beside my bed and fill the room.

"All those fuckin' breathing classes, and this is how we do it," he says with a sad smile. "I told you we should've skipped those."

I smirk. "Hmph... We never do things the right way, do we? We're trendsetters."

"If it wasn't us, who would it be?" Garrett chuckles. "We do things the weird way. Weird is different, and different is good."

I sigh. "I'm scared."

"I know you are, Baby Doll," he says, rubbing my forehead. "They say that yours and the baby's life could be in danger, but you know I'll take care of you both, right?"

I nod.

"I'm right here. I won't ever leave you. I promise."

His conviction is palpable. I want to believe him, but even some things are outside of Garrett's control. I know he'd never break a promise intentionally.

Dr. Eloy wheels in an ultrasound machine. Garrett and I glance at each other quickly, then at Dr. Eloy. "Don't worry," Dr. Eloy says, setting up the machine. "We've done this before. You know this doesn't hurt. This is only one part of determining if it is a true abruption."

"What if it is a true abruption?" Garrett asks what I'm thinking as Dr. Eloy lifts my gown and squeezes ultrasound gel on my stomach.

Hmm... They use the warm kind here. That's nice.

Dr. Eloy moves the probe around on my belly. Presses it into my distended stomach this way and that.

"And this tells you if she's experiencing an abruption?" Garrett asks.

"This, in combination with the abruption panels we ran," Dr. Eloy explains. "An abruption can't always be detected by ultrasound. Sometimes we're able to see a collection of blood where the placenta is separating from the uterus."

The probe moves further down, searching around my swollen belly.

Searching for something the doctor isn't finding. Or something it's found.

"Holy! Oh! God!"

"That hurts?" Dr. Eloy asks.

Garrett squeezes my hand. "Obviously!"

Dr. Eloy presses the call button.

I'm only aware of it with part of my brain. The other part is struggling to process the pain coursing through my body.

"What's wrong?" Garrett asks. "What'd you see?"

"We need to prep Mrs. Kaplan for surgery," Dr. Eloy says.

I assume he's speaking with a nurse. I don't know because my eyes are closed, trying to breathe through the pain.

"Also, let's get her some Dilaudid," Dr. Eloy continues, "and get Mr. Kaplan some scrubs."

"What's going on?!" Garrett asks, his voice gravelly with panic.

"We need to get the baby out. I don't like the fluctuations I'm seeing in her or her mom's heart rates," Dr. Eloy explains. "Get some oxygen for mom," Dr. Eloy says to what I assume is a nurse. "This, coupled with the abnormal abruption panels, is all I need to see to diagnose a total abruption. Don't worry, Mrs. Kaplan, we can have the baby out in thirty seconds if need be."

The room is a flurry of activity. Medical professionals come in and out. There are what seem to be spotlights over my bed. Alarms chime all around me. I'm being pricked, poked, and jabbed from all sides.

Dr. Eloy must have left the room because I hear other voices but not his.

And not Garrett's.

My eyes are open, but my vision is blurry. There's a fuzzy quality to everything within my sight. I'm awake, but it's as if I'm dreaming. Nothing feels real.

"Mr. Kaplan, we need to get you changed," a nurse says.

Garrett must not be far away, but he's not holding my hand anymore. It's been too long since he's said anything.

"I'll be by your side, always, Foxy," Garrett says, then finally squeezes my hand. "You and the baby will be fine. I won't leave either of you. I promise. Have I broken a promise to you yet?"

I'm sleepy. My lids are too heavy to hold open. Everything and everyone sounds far away.

"She might be coming to," Megan whispers.

"Wait," I believe I shout, but my tongue is too big for my mouth. A hum resounds in my mind. It's static. "Garrett, they're back. Help! They're back."

Distorted, echoic music reverberates from somewhere.

♪ *Why do the birds go on singing?*

Blinking rapidly, I struggle to make out the faces of the nurses and staff. Garrett.

"Mr. Kaplan," a nurse says, but it's framed as a question.

"She's waking," Megan whispers. "It looks like she's blinking. Or trying."

"What?" I breathe. "Why are you whispering?"

♪ *"Why does my heart go on beating?"*

The pillow is uncomfortable. My head rolls back and forth, or is it me? My head spins.

"I think she's trying to say something," Megan whispers. *"Get the doctor!"*

♪ *"Why does the sun go on shining?"*

"Garrett?" I cry. I can't find him. My eyes won't focus. "Where are you?"

♪ *"Don't they know it's the end of the world?"*

"I'll be back..." Garrett whispers, *"I promise."*

♪ *"It ended when you said, 'Goodbye'."*

SERENE

MEADOWS

Chapter Thirty-Eight

*A**mina*

Opening my eyes is harder than it should be. It's like trying to see through cobwebs, and my lids weigh at least five pounds each. I attempt to speak.

And can't do it.

It hurts like someone's been brushing my esophagus with barbed wire. "Garrett?" I rasp, swallowing a million nails. I cough several times.

"Amina?" a soft, oddly familiar feminine voice asks from beside me. Turning towards the voice, my jaw drops. I freeze.

"Can ya hear me?" The all too familiar woman sitting at my bedside asks. She adjusts her black horn-rimmed glasses, her hazel-brown eyes watch me with caution through the thick lenses.

"Amina? You, okay?" she asks, pushing a wayward layer of her long brunette hair behind an ear.

"Megan?" I ask in a gritty voice. "Where's Garrett? Is the baby okay?"

"Here," she says, grabbing a pink jug off the tray I hadn't realized until now was hovering over my lap. She pours some water into a small, matching pink cup. "You probably need a drink. I've never been intubated, but I hear it's rough on your vocal cords."

With stiff arms, I reach for the offered cup. Then I stop short, there's another frickin' IV in the crook of my right arm. My next attempt to take the cup is more gingerly.

I don't take a sip, I gulp. I spill cold water on my borrowed hospital gown then hand the empty cup back to Megan.

She refills it and sets it on the tray in front of me.

Megan stands from her chair and straightens her black pencil skirt. She reaches so close behind my head that I can see her shaved underarm through the short sleeve of her green blouse.

"Yes," what must be a nurse says from an intercom.

"Could you page Ms. Raichand's doctor?" Megan glances at me and smiles. "She's awake."

My brows scrunch. "Kaplan. Mrs. Kaplan," I correct.

"I'll do it now," the nurse says.

Megan's expression is unreadable.

"Thank you," she says, retaking her seat.

She skims a hand over mine. It's a lightest touch, but it says more than she ever could.

My heart rate skyrockets. A bell chimes on the heart rate monitor beside the bed.

"Is it the baby?" I ask, heart sinking. "Where's Garrett?"

Megan eyes me curiously. "What do you remember?"

A man, I absolutely remember, in his early fifties with deep smile lines, salt and pepper hair, and kind brown eyes, saunters into the room.

I sigh in relief. For a minute there, I thought I was losing my mind.

"Dr. Eloy," I say with another sigh, "did everything go okay? Is Garrett with the baby?"

Dr. Eloy wordlessly checks the machines. He silences the alarm. Without looking in my direction, he logs into a computer on a stand I hadn't noticed and reads through what I'm guessing are my charts.

My chest cramps.

Something's wrong. I don't know what, but something is wrong.

Gone is the kind, informative man who assured me my daughter and I would be fine, and in his place is a cold physician making the rounds on a patient he's acting like he's never seen before.

Finally, he turns to me and approaches the bed. He lifts the top sheet over my lap, then lays it down.

"Do you mind if she stays in here, or would you like her to come back after I've examined you?" he asks.

He's talking at me and not really to me, which makes no sense. At every one of my doctor's visits, he's been nothing but pleasant and inclusive. Now, he's...sterile. As sterile as the pine-and-bleach-smelling hospital I'm in.

I survey the room. There's no bassinet. No rocking chair. No pull-out bed. I'm not wearing the cozy postpartum outfit that I packed in my hospital bag. This isn't a postpartum room.

A heaviness settles over my heart.

"How are you feeling?" Dr. Eloy asks, after giving me a noninvasive once-over. "I can have her step out while I check your bandages if you'd like?"

"No!" I shout, startling everyone.

A portly, professional-looking woman with brown hair and chunky blonde streaks rushes into the room. If they were planning a remake with older versions of the characters from *Grease*, she'd be a dead ringer for Stockard Channing in her late fifties to early sixties.

"How is my daughter?" I ask more sternly than I've ever spoken in my life. "Is my husband with her? You need to tell me something."

The portly woman is the one who approaches the bed. Which isn't what I want or expect, since I don't know her.

She regards me through light caramel eyes. Their softness is meant to comfort, but nothing about this stranger is comforting.

"Amina," she says in a voice as gentle as her gaze, "who do you think Dr. Eloy is?"

My brain is going to explode. Nothing seems real. If IVs and blood pressure cuffs didn't hamper my movements, I would be pulling at my hair. I scan all three people's faces in the room, praying for an ally.

Everyone watches me with varying expressions of concern. I hate it. I hate them. They all want to ask questions, but no one wants to answer mine.

They remain quiet.

I push out a breath in frustration. Fine.

"Umm... Dr. Eloy is my obstetrician." I say brows drawn tight. *Isn't he?*

Of course, he is, but the way they're staring at me shakes my confidence. But he's had his fingers all in my cervix for months now, so he better be an OB-GYN, or someone is getting sued. Garrett will kill him.

"Amina," the full-figured woman says in her calming tone, "Dr. Eloy isn't an obstetrician. He's a neurointensivist who's been overseeing your care for the past eight months."

She places her clammy hand on top of mine.

I yank my hand away. I'm drowning on the inside.

"Eight months? That's impossible," I say, shaking my pounding head. "I remember my wedding. Garrett. My—" I clutch at my now flat stomach. "I remember my baby."

I refuse to believe the woman shaking her head.

"I'm sorry. You've been here since your attack. For a while, you were in what we believe is a catatonic state. Then you went into a coma. There is no baby. There's no Garrett. But you're safe here and healing. We'll help you get back on your feet."

Chapter Thirty-Nine

A mina Raichand

Patients in lavender scrub sets, like mine, wander through the common room. Since the building is made of brick with tile floors, everyone wears white tennis shoes or fluffy, grippy socks. I observe them without really watching. They're hard to miss, lumbering around in their medically-induced haze. To be fair, some patients sit on couches and chairs arranged without any functional layout. There are some chairs around tables for group activities, such as playing board games and assembling jigsaw puzzles. I can't understand why they think adults want to play children's games and do puzzles. Two flat-screen televisions are mounted diagonally across from each other in opposite corners of the room.

Sunlight beams through the many old-fashioned arched windows around the room and the building. This place reminds me of those old mansion asylums from movies where patients receive electroshock therapy. Heavy locking doors separate the men's wing from the women's wing. Doors slam throughout the day and night, terrifying me. Everything here terrifies me. One of the orderlies told me the doors are so heavy because they need to lock behind them without assistance, leaving less room for mishaps and escapes. For a place they don't want people to escape from, there sure is a lot of glass. What would they do if someone decided to Superman out a window?

On one side of the large common room is the door for the women's wing, and on the other side is the men's wing. Orderlies post up at both doors, ensuring we leave room for the Holy Ghost. Oops! Lunatic babies are bad for PR.

I chuckle at my own joke. And why not? Lots of people roam around here having full-on conversations with themselves. My laughing isn't anything to sneeze at.

Halfway between the wings is a split door where nurses dispense the drugs. There's a walled-in "healing garden" outside where orderlies or nurses can take us to watch as we... Touch grass? I don't know. It's not quite the hospital setting I expected. Maybe it's another one of my delusions.

If everything else about the last year-and-some-change of my life was a delusion, or as Dr. Whittemore says, was a coping mechanism my mind created to protect itself, maybe Serene Meadows Adult Behavioral Health is too.

As exciting as it is doing nothing in the common room, I shuffle across the room to do nothing in my cell—I mean room. I flash my wristband to the orderly, who slides his card in the card reader that allows me access to the women's wing. It consists of a long, bland wall painted pastel blue with doors upon doors across from one another. Each door has a small square window embedded in it, just in case we want to stare out into the empty hall. Since I'm 5'2", that's not a luxury I can partake in. However, my eccentric roommate is 5'6" and can see out of it on tiptoe without a problem. She's always gazing out of it like the hallway walls are talking to her.

Maybe she thinks they are.

Who knows?

"Amina, I've been waiting for you. You're late," Dr. Whittemore says.

She sits in a wooden chair in front of my twin bed on my side of the room.

I roll my eyes.

During the months I was doing physical therapy to regain strength in my legs after being in bed for so long, she put me at a disadvantage. I was a captive audience, literally. Free from the confines of my wheelchair, I avoid her like the plague. If I never hear the words dissociative or depression again, it'll be too soon. I know what I know. Why would I invent a world where I'm forced to go to group therapy and have crappy parents? That doesn't make sense. Creating an antagonistic relationship with a man, even if he's a gorgeous man, but one who accused me of all manner of subterfuge upon our first meeting, is too masochistic even for me.

"I'm sorry," I say, sitting cross-legged in the middle of my bed. "I can go back to the common room until your shift is over. I meant to skip today's session. It's Saturday, don't you ever go home?"

Dr. Whittemore offers me a prim, proper, tolerant smile that accentuates every crease and wrinkle on her face. With the amount of foundation she wears, it does little to hide fine lines. And the blush... It's a bit over the top.

"Deflection," the psychiatrist says as if she's found gold in a pond. "I understand how difficult it's been for you. But you have a fighter's spirit. Most people in your situation would still be unable to walk after so long in a coma. Yet, you overcame that enormous obstacle in just a few months. That strength is what kept your mind intact through your assault and subsequent struggles. The human mind is a fascinating thing. Once you're through this, you can return to your life."

This woman irritates the shit out of me.

Pulling my knees to my chest, ankles still crossed, I sway back and forth. It's the only comfort I find. She doesn't understand. We go through this every session, and she doesn't get it. There isn't a day I'm going to wake up and abandon my life—my real life. I'm a wife and mother. I've never seen my daughter's face. She thinks I'll forget all of that and return to an empty life with no family, no friends, and no hope. That's impossible. Hopelessness is what I felt before. Without knowing love and acceptance, I pacified myself with TV and movies. Being forced to give up those things, things I'd only thought existed on screen, to have them torn away, is cruel. God can't be that cruel.

A tear slips down my cheek. I wipe it away against the shoulder of my scrub top.

"There's no this," I say in a whisper. "This is hell. That was real. I'm not crazy."

Dr. Whittemore shakes her head. Pity waves from her light brown eyes.

"Amina, sweetie, you're right," she says in a patronizing voice. "You're not crazy. You suffered an extreme trauma that your mind protected you from when you couldn't protect yourself. You woke up because it's ready to confront those things from your childhood and more recent past."

"I woke up, though," I remind her. "I talked to Megan and that detective. How was that real and not everything else? I woke up."

Another tight-lipped smile. "Yes, that did happen. But finding out your attacker couldn't be immediately found, your mind went into shock. It protected you from all the implications that knowledge carried."

Unbidden tears trail down my cheeks. I don't want to cry. I don't want her to see me cry. She doesn't understand. I roughly rub my face against my upraised knees.

"I'm still not okay," I mumble. "Why would my brain stop protecting me?"

"Because it's time," Dr. Whittemore says. "You're ready to surrender your delusions."

Jerking my head up, I glare at the "good" doctor. "Get the fuck out of my room."

She rises from her chair and pushes it underneath the small desk in my corner of the room. Dr. Whittemore is always unflappable. She reaches to pat my knee.

I cringe away from the contact.

"I'll see you the day after tomorrow. We'll get through this," she assures me.

Chapter Forty

My legs ache from being bent all day, but I can't bring myself to move. Physical pain is easier to tolerate than emotional pain. The only way I'm aware of the passage of time is because the lights in the hall get brighter and their glare shines through the small window in the door. Somehow, the lights aren't intense enough to keep me awake, but my memories are.

I replay every moment of my real life in my head so often that I'm unsure I ever sleep. It's more like catnaps here and there. This twin bed isn't made for comfort. It's lumpy and dented from its previous occupants, which I don't want to think about. The sheets are clean and smell of sterility. I'm not particularly germophobic, but the idea of so many sick, traumatized heads and bodies lying where I'm curled up is disconcerting.

Thinking about that, I get up and go back to the common room. My preferred seat is a yellow pleather loveseat that's located beneath one of the televisions. It's as far away from the medication window and from where the other patients gather as possible. Is it wrong to be afraid of them?

They're just people, sick people with varying handles on their illnesses. There's no reason to fear them. I never feared Rob, even when he was throwing furniture. Maybe it's the smell here or the way we're all managed and herded like cattle. The orderlies and nurses are the sheepdogs meant to keep us all in line. We're told when to eat, when to sleep, and some are told when to go to the restroom. Some are escorted to the restroom or the cafeteria, supervised as if they're about to bolt or snap at any second. This environment is so strict and controlled that Serene Meadows, in itself, feels frightening.

In my opinion, most of the patients are over-medicated to keep them docile. I can't help but think that it exacerbates their mental health conditions. Some are unpredictable, shouting, flinching, and talking (not necessarily to anyone visible) at random moments. This facility doesn't treat people like people.

And I feel for them.

I am them.

I fear them.

"Hey, roomie!" says a maniacally chipper voice beside me.

Drawing my legs up onto my cushion, I wrap my arms around my knees. I glower out of the corner of my eye, at Bryn, my roommate.

In another world, she's beautiful. Actually, she is beautiful. With artificially plump, pouty lips, hazel-blue eyes, a thin, snub nose with a slightly rounded, upward-sloping tip, and hair so blonde it appears nearly white, cut into a long bob. A rose tattoo on her inner forearm adds a touch of charm. At twenty-five, and skinnier than is healthy, she seems younger, with her fresh face and absolutely manic personality.

After giving her a once-over, I continue to stare straight ahead at nothing in particular.

"Leave me alone, Bryn," I grumble.

Taking that as an invitation, she sits on the loveseat's other side. She scoots closer after what seems like a pensive moment, completely ignoring my personal space.

"C'mon," she says, rolling her head with dramatic exaggeration, "I'm trying to have a Winona and Angelina moment with you."

I can't make myself any smaller on this fuckin' cushion.

"I'm not here to make friends," I inform her. "I need to find my husband."

Bryn giggles.

"What?!" she says, arching a brow. "Oh... I forgot. Did I interrupt date night or something? Am I sitting on him right now?" She gasps.

I get up to leave. I'm not in the mood for this.

"Wait, don't go!" Bryn grabs my hand. "Don't leave your husband here. I—"

A loud crashing sound comes from behind me, interrupting Bryn, and I turn towards the noise.

Two big, burly orderlies burst through the heavy double-swinging admittance doors, each pushing one side of a wheeled gurney. Whoever they're transporting to the men's wing thrashes and yanks at restraints tethering him to the thin mattress. All I can see from here is a mass of overgrown dark auburn hair and unkempt facial hair. The man is so long and strong that the stretcher teeters side to side.

"I am not a pheasant plucker!" The man yells in a booming voice. "I'm a pheasant plucker's son! But I'll be plucking pheasants when the pheasant plucker's gone."

"Looks like the king of crazy's back," Bryn says in a snotty tone. "Maybe you and his majesty can go for a ride on his unicorn sometime. That is..." she pauses for dramatic effect, "if your husband won't mind."

Without any clear reason, I move closer. The orderlies are making slow work of getting him to the men's wing. I sure as shit can't help, and honestly, I don't want to. But I've never seen an intake like this before. It's wild.

My mouth falls slack.

"He is my husband," I say, eyes wide.

Bryn scoffs in disdain. "Derek Boulanger's your husband?!"

Chapter Forty-One

"**S**tephan, handsome, where've you been all my life?"

"Off." The dirty blonde orderly looks down his nose at Bryn. "What did you do to Roberta?"

Bryn gasps. "You're supposed to tell me when you're off. I thought we had a deal?"

The orderly chuckles. "Is that the same deal you have with Jake?"

I roll my eyes from where I'm hiding behind the lip of the wall in the hall. Bryn seems to have a way with every male orderly and some female orderlies. She's a Serene Meadows regular, for whatever reason. She might have explained, but I don't listen to her most of the time; she makes trips here like weekly nail appointments.

If she can pull this off, I'll owe her big time. And since we're stuck in an insane asylum, I have no idea what I can do for her.

"Jake, shmake, who cares about Jake?" Bryn says with a manic giggle. "What I care about is when Stephan and Bryn are going to spend a little time in the walk-in fridge."

"What do you want, Bryn? It's lights out."

Peeking around the corner, I watch my roommate work her magic. She places a hand on Stephan's pectoral muscle, just barely contained underneath his grey scrub top.

"I'm hungry, like near death, hungry," Bryn whines. "If you could, pretty please, get me some graham crackers, I'll wait right here and won't move. Promise."

Stephan stares down at Bryn who has tied her too-loose lavender scrub top in a knot in the back to highlight her assets—her words, not mine.

After several uncomfortable moments—for me—of appreciation, he lifts his brown gaze to Bryn's face.

"Let me poke my head in and tell Tim I'll be right back," he says then turns and slides his badge in the card reader to the men's wing.

Bryn turns, gives me a thumbs up then widens her hazel-blue eyes and pokes her tongue out.

Stephan turns around to face Bryn.

"How many packets do you want?"

"Hmm..." Bryn hums, pretending to think about it, then slips her finger between the door and frame before it can latch. "Three," she answers.

He smirks. "Be right back," he says, tapping Bryn's exposed belly button.

Once he's out of sight and the doors to the cafeteria slam behind him, Bryn signals me.

"Five minutes, chick," Bryn comments, "I don't know how I'm going to explain having to have my finger amputated to my agent. Look? It's purple."

Giving her a dry stare, I pass by and head down the hall.

The corridor's ugly blue, too. What's with all the pastels? Every paintable surface looks like the Easter Bunny threw up on it.

Bryn said Derek's room is the fourth door on the left. I don't know how she knows, but I follow her instructions. I crack open the door and squint. The lighting in this room is dimmer, which is strange since the same lights are in this wing as in the women's wing. There's the same small square window in Derek's door. When my eyes finally adjust to the different lighting, I frown. Not because he has a single room, but because he's tied to the bed with soft restraints.

"One-one was a racehorse. Two-two was one too. When one-one won one race, two-two won one too," he mumbles to himself, gaze fixed on the ceiling.

I open the door enough to squeeze through the opening. Derek turns his head to the side and looks at me.

"Are you awake?" I ask in a whisper and kneel beside his bed.

"And they say I'm crazy," he grumbles. "You think I sleep with my eyes open or something?"

He's different. Yes, his hair is longer, and he has a goatee, but there's something about his eyes.

I grimace.

"Sorry. Do you recognize me?"

His eyes roll back and forth in thought.

In thought!!

My eyes water unbidden.

"Regina? Is that you? I've been in love with you since I saw *Friday*," he says, his gruff voice wistful. "I'll be Craig, your Craig, baby."

Eww... Disgusting.

I sigh. He doesn't know me. How?

"Craig is Regina King's brother in *Friday*," I say, unable to keep disappointment from my voice. "Are you being crazy, or do you really not remember me?"

"I got some meds in me. I'm good."

"Do you remember me?" I repeat. "Do I look familiar to you at all?"

He studies me through squinted eyes.

And I notice the difference.

His eyes are now more blue than green. They're still beautiful but gone are his greenish-blue turquoise eyes.

"Nope," he answers. "Never seen you before, but I'd be happy to change that if you wanna undo these restraints."

Ah... Garrett. Still so brazen. Somehow, I know it.

He's in there.

My Garrett.

But I don't know how to reach him. Maybe whatever medication they're giving him causes amnesia?

"Okay," I say after a brief silence. "Umm... Sorry, I interrupted your little rhyme."

The door opens suddenly.

Shit!

"Amina!" Stephan chastises. "You're the last person I thought I'd find breaking rules."

Derek laughs a low, throaty laugh.

"Excited executioner exercising his excising powers excessively," Derek rambles.

"Out of here, Ms. Raichand. You don't want me to notify Dr. Whittemore, do you?" Stephan threatens.

I scramble to my feet. Taking one last second, I glance at Garrett or Derek, whatever his name is.

Derek winks at me with a devilish grin.

I think my heart stops.

Chapter Forty-Two

"**D**on't you want to get back to your life? I'm sure the kids at the shelter miss you."

I glare at Dr. Whittemore. Once again, she's in my room, and I couldn't care less. I haven't left my room except to go to the cafeteria in five days. Nurse Dettinger, with all her southern hospitality and ethereal warmth, has brought me my meds twice a day. She's not supposed to do that, but she does. With her red hair, drawl, and sweeter disposition, she reminds me of Blanche from *The Golden Girls*.

That's another thing that stayed the same.

My world might be upside down, but there's always Lexapro and Klonopin on tap. Big pharma has quite the reach. World to world, they're making money hand over fist, and this woman must be too.

Dr. Whittemore stares at me in expectation, thin lips compressed in a firm line. She's waiting for me to reply, and I have no response. I want her to leave. Nothing I have to say to her is going to change anything.

My husband doesn't recognize me. We spent months building a relationship filled with fun, easy banter, and created a life together—an entire person I never got to meet. He looks at me with eyes that aren't quite his. His hair is his, but longer. One thing that can never change about him is his height, his *basso profondo* voice, and most of all, his spirit. Garrett is trapped inside Derek. I'm the first to admit how wild and unlikely it sounds, but my heart knows it's true. My soul recognizes his soul. I'd know him anywhere, in any form. He promised he wouldn't leave me, and now, he's gone.

And this woman wants to act like none of it ever happened.

I scoot as far as I can into the corner of my bed. Drawing my knees as close to my chest as my boobs will allow, I comfort myself as best I can and hug my legs.

"I miss them," I rasp. "I do. I love those kids, but it's unlikely that the same kids are there, anyway. Shelters are very temporary placements. Plus, I was happy with my life. Happier than I'd ever been."

Dr. Whittemore shifts in her chair closer to the bed.

I want to scream.

"You can have all of that in this life. But you can't find happiness holding on to a life that doesn't exist."

"This life is painful," I croak.

Dr. Whittemore exhales loudly.

"Amina, sweetie." She runs withered fingers through her shoulder-length hair. "You can't have that life. It's not debatable."

Well, fuck you too.

"It is," I protest. "I just have to figure out how to get back to it. Get Garrett to remember."

Dr. Whittemore closes her eyes and rubs her temples.

"That is Derek, not Garrett. Don't drag him into this delusion."

"He just needs to remember. He will remember."

"Remembering would imply there was a preexisting relationship to remember." Dr. Whittemore clenches her teeth. I can tell because her cheekbones stand out sharply against her thin, pale skin.

"There was. It was strong—it's still strong," I say, correcting myself. "He helped me learn to trust another human being. Connections that strong don't just disappear because you want them to or say that they should."

"It does when it never happened, Amina," Dr. Whittemore argues. "He's schizophrenic. He has his own delusions. Don't give him yours. You need to leave Derek alone."

I bite my lip to keep my tears at bay. She doesn't understand. No one understands. Rocking stops me from slapping her.

"It's going to take a little time," Dr. Whittemore says, temper more regulated, "but you can get through this. I'll help you."

"Get the fuck out of my room." I glare directly into her brown eyes. A tear escapes down my cheek.

She stands, turns the chair out, and slides it under the tiny desk.

Thank God.

Dr. Whittemore turns before I can get too excited.

"I'll see you…" she pauses, "not tomorrow but the day after. Write in that journal I gave you. It'll help."

She leaves, and I glare at the unused brown leather-bound journal on my desk.

Chapter Forty-Three

Derek had another crisis yesterday. I walk through the "Healing Garden" to keep myself away from him. It's not the worst place to be. It's definitely more appealing than all the pastel walls inside. Two orderlies in their matching grey scrubs stand far enough away at the garden's entrance to give the illusion of privacy. Only a few patients are strolling through the garden, but they're more in the thick of the plush green grass. I walk alone on the asphalt path between rows of daisies, dandelions, sunflowers, and scattered wildflowers interspersed within the thick patches of grass.

I'd stay here all day and night if they'd let me. Near the corner of the cement barrier wall, there's an antique-looking wooden bench with black edge trim. I cut through the grass to sit there. This is as close to peace as I'll find in this strange life. Sitting cross-legged keeps others away since it's such a small space, and that's exactly why I do it. I stare up at the clear, blue, cloudless sky.

Since the walls are so tall and I haven't been outside in a long time, I don't know what season it is. The garden seems to exist in an eternal spring. There's no snow, so it's obviously not winter, but otherwise, there's no real way to tell what time of year it is.

My mind drifts to thoughts of Gilbert and Nora. Before everything turned upside down, we had been growing closer. They were excited about the baby, and Nora seemed determined to be a decent grandmother. They aren't my parents, but I was willing to let her because they felt like family to me. They behaved like the bougier families I saw on TV when I was younger.

On most of the shows I watched, none of the families were perfect. In the soap opera reruns I used to watch, siblings were always fighting and stealing each other's significant others. Boyfriends, girlfriends, husbands, and wives were like musical chairs. Some would pass off other people's children as their own to keep marriages together, or out of sheer desperation—I could never quite tell. Long-lost children kept turning up out of nowhere as adults and became thick as thieves with parents they had spent their entire childhood apart from. Even some women didn't know they had long-lost children, but once they found each other, it was always mom this and my daughter that.

There was a soap opera about a woman with a split personality who committed the wildest crimes and lived a life of her own. She was scandalous, yet after a few episodes, she returned to her normal self, and her family accepted her as if nothing had ever happened.

I figured I could do that with Gilbert and Nora. We look like parent and child; they have photo albums and scrapbooks chronicling my—Faux-mina's—entire life. No one can tell us apart. So, what does it matter if I indulge? Clearly, Faux-mina isn't willing to bear the burden of having her family. I hadn't wanted to either at first, but I was falling into the role of a disgruntled prodigal daughter pretty well by the end.

Then... *Poof!*

It's all gone.

"Hi, Amina. What's with the long face?"

Jolting in shock, a scream escapes my throat at the scratchy, rough voice struggling to sound higher-pitched. I turn to look over my left shoulder. A thick white sock with stuffed, floppy ankle sock ears and a drawn face is close enough to almost touch my nose. I jerk my head back to avoid going cross-eyed while staring at the odd puppet.

"Cheer up. You're tiny, I'm loony, we're all a little kooky," Derek says in an overly gruff, sing-song puppet voice.

I glare at his sock-covered hand. He suddenly pops up from behind the bench and jumps over the back to plop down next to me. The entire frame and the wood slats shake under his immense height and weight. It must be a sin to look this good in lavender scrubs from a mental institution. Garrett—Derek—whatever you call him still has the same athletic build, with well-defined muscles and broad shoulders. Even with his grown-out hair and scruffy goatee, his strong jawline could cut glass.

"What's up, sweet thang?" Derek says, tossing the sock puppet into my lap. He pushes his large hand through his overly long bangs to clear the hair out of his eyes. "No, you're not imagining this. I'm really here," he continues when I don't say anything and only stare.

"What do you want?" I ask, trying my hardest to act blasé.

He throws a chiseled arm over the back of the bench behind my back.

"Just checking up on my wife." His blue-green eyes sparkle, and he winks.

Embarrassing!

I close my eyes and shake my head in shame. "Who told you?" I mutter. "Does everyone know about that?"

"There's no confidentiality within these walls," Derek answers, looking pointedly at the cement walls. He grins. "Crazy people talk a lot."

"Says the schizophrenic," I retort with a grin of my own, a genuine grin. I haven't smiled since I woke up in the ICU and opened my eyes to this hell, but one lopsided grin from Derek, and I feel lighter.

Derek snorts. "2 Y's U.R. 2 Y's U.B. I.C.U.R. 2 Y's 4 me."

I stifle a laugh behind my hand and lean back on the wooden bench. His arm rests behind my head.

Garrett's in there.

Chapter Forty-Four

It's too bright in the common room today, and with the nausea-inducing pastel walls, I feel sick to my stomach. In my usual spot on the yellow loveseat beneath one of the flat screens, I watch Nurse Dettinger hand out meds from behind the Dutch door. A long queue of patients of all ages, sizes, and colors waits for her to give them their morning meds.

The cheery, buxom southern belle is one of the kindest people I've met. She must have been quite the looker in her youth because she's still gorgeous. I don't know if she dyes her hair that red, but whatever it is she does to it flatters her fair complexion, and make her deep blues eyes pop. Even her grey standard-issue Serene Meadows scrubs suit her. That drawl probably made her quite popular with whatever partner she chose. There's no ring on her left hand, so I'm not sure if she's married or not. The lack of a ring could also be because they worry one of the patients will steal it or eat it.

We're under strict supervision here. They might as well have bumper pads on the tables and corners of the furniture. If we want a pen or pencil, we have to sign it out and sign it back in. Arts and crafts is a heavily monitored timed activity. Only certain patients are allowed to participate in it. I don't think anyone will be eating glue, crayons, staples, or paper, but who knows? Someone could always cause damage with scissors, I suppose, but from what I've seen, they only give us the children's version that don't really work well. Everything being so guarded also increases my fear. It's like they want us to be afraid of each other.

"Meds time! Who needs their happy pill?!" Nurse Dettinger calls, jingling a Soufflé cup of meds like a bell.

An older man whose jowls and weathered skin make him appear angry all the time shuffles forward. Nurse Dettinger extends a cup of medication and a Dixie cup of water to him.

"Here you go, Mr. Garrison."

He snatches them from her hands.

She frowns. "Now, Mr. Garrison, you fixin' to catch these hands if you keep grabbin' thangs from me. I've had enough of you, and it's only eight in the morning."

Mr. Garrison grumbles something unintelligible and tosses back his pills and throws back the cup of water like a shot.

"Lift your tongue, please, suga," Nurse Dettinger instructs with a smile.

"I'm a grown man, not a five-year-old."

Nurse Dettinger props a hand on one full hip. "Grown men don't cheek pills and sell them to other patients. Now, open your mouth and lift ya tongue. Please," she adds with a saccharine sweet smile.

I can only see the back of his balding head, but he must comply because Nurse Dettinger nods.

He stomps away.

"Hey, Ms. Bryn," Nurse Dettinger greets my roommate, returning to her warm, pleasant tone. "Aren't you just as pretty as a peach this morning? And no bigger than a minnow in a fishing pond. You gotta eat more, suga. How are ya?"

Bryn takes her cup of meds and tosses them back. "Crazy as a bed bug, wanna come?"

Nurse Dettinger shakes her head.

"I don't know how you take those without water. I'd choke to death."

Bryn shrugs a shoulder. "No gag reflex, baby. It's a talent. Comes in handy."

She laughs. "Lift your tongue, please, suga."

"See ya tonight, Nurse Dettinger," Bryn says, hips swinging as she sashays away.

"Hey, roomie!" Bryn says in her manic, chipper voice, later today.

She sits on the tile floor in front of my favorite loveseat. I curl up with my knees drawn up and arms wrapped around my legs deliberately. My hopes that she'd leave me alone this afternoon drift away like leaves in a strong breeze. Intrusive isn't a word Bryn understands well, and she's even worse at taking hints. Thank goodness she doesn't choose to sit beside me today. My mind is all over the place since Derek and I had what felt like a moment a few days ago. It's strange how he seems to appear and disappear. Sometimes, I wonder if I'm confusing what's real, and maybe he doesn't even exist. This place has a way of distorting reality. There are entire days when I don't see hide nor hair of him. I'm not crazy. He might spend more time than I realize strapped to his bed. I haven't heard anything about him having any more episodes, and Bryn and her big mouth would definitely tell me if he's had one.

"How's your baby?" Bryn asks, kidnapping my attention. "Twelve pretend months old—right?"

I narrow my eyes at her audacity. "Why do you talk to me? Is there a sign on me somewhere that says, 'Glutton for punishment'?"

Think of the devil, and he shall appear.

Derek saunters over, coming up behind Bryn with way too much swagger for his own good. Damn, he makes a pair of scrubs look like a masterpiece. I lick and bite my suddenly dry lips. He sits beside me, leaving no room for the Holy Ghost.

Lord, have mercy! I'm about to melt into this couch like a fuckin' popsicle on a 100-degree day.

Bryn's hazel-blue eyes narrow on him. "Why does he get to sit next to you?" she whines. "I'm your best friend."

"A pessimistic pest exists amidst us." Derek grins.

I wrangle the smile that threatens to curve my lips.

"Either you're starting to make sense," I turn to say to him, and realize he's gazing. At. Me. My stomach does a somersault. "Or I'm going crazy."

"Crazy? I was crazy once, so they put me in a round rubber room. I died in that round rubber room, and they buried me six feet deep. Six feet deep has worms down there," Derek says, pinching the soft flesh of my upper arm playfully, then his gaze shifts around as if he's forgotten where he is or what he's saying. "Worms? I hate worms. Worms drive me crazy..." he says, elongating the last word. Then he grins with a wink. "Crazy? I was—"

Bryn smacks Derek's leg. "Is there a reset button on you somewhere?" she complains. "You are all types of crazy."

And with that, Bryn rises to her feet and skips away.

Literally, skips.

"Thanks."

"You're not mad I scared away your best friend?" he asks, placing his arm on the back of the loveseat.

Behind me!

"She's not my best friend," I grouse, rolling my eyes. "She's a lunatic."

He nudges me. "Hey, you're tiny. I'm loony. We're all a little kooky."

"You know why I'm here, clearly," I say, returning his nudge. "Isn't it only fair that I know why you're here?"

"With all the nosy people here, nobody's told you yet?" he asks, turning to fully face me. "Now, that's *crazy*."

I titter. "I guess you're not as popular as you think?"

"Oh, I am," he says with a cocky grin. "I'm sure you know about my little episodes."

I nod.

"I was diagnosed when I was seventeen. It's not always hereditary, but for me it seems to be. I know there's a strong genetic component because my dad is schizophrenic."

His dad? That's too much of a coincidence. It can't be. I don't want to interrupt because he's divulging sensitive information, and his expression is more serious than any I've seen him wear, but I want to ask more. I want to blurt out things that I don't know will trigger him or not. Rob is supposed to be the schizophrenic one. Well, no one is really supposed to be schizophrenic, but Rob was—or is. What is going on?

"Visual and auditory hallucinations aren't always mutually exclusive, but I've always been a bit of an overachiever," he explains with a smirk. "In the beginning, I didn't realize I was hearing or seeing anything different from anyone else. When I'd ask other people to confirm what I was experiencing, it was terrifying when they didn't understand or know what I was talking about. I'd seen my dad have episodes, but I didn't realize how intrusive the things he saw or heard were. Mine weren't that frequent, so I didn't think I needed medication. I was managing fine until my girlfriend and I got an apartment together."

"You lived on your own?"

Derek nods as if to say, 'Of course.'

That's astonishing to me. Rob lived with his parents. Once, when Gwen and I talked about it, I got the impression that living alone was impossible. I should have asked more questions. Maybe it depends on how serious it is. Asking Derek now seems rude and insensitive.

"So, one night my ex, Lydia, and I were lying in bed." He chuckles like whatever comes next is about to be hilarious. "All of a sudden, she morphs into this huge crow and starts pecking at my eyes."

Derek belly laughs. Several orderlies and patients turn and stare.

My mouth is hanging open, and my eyes are as round as saucers. "Oh. My. Gosh!"

He guffaws louder and smacks his knee. "Wait! It gets better. I tried to stab her because I can't just sit by passively and let a crow pluck my eyes out. I almost got her, but she flew out of the window. At least that's what I thought happened, but I'm sure she ran out the door."

I can't pick my jaw up. He just keeps laughing.

"Are you serious?"

"Totally. Then I'm sitting there alone, and the devil keeps telling me to dig this device the government implanted into my stomach out. But I couldn't get it. It was kinda like Neo in *The Matrix*."

"How are you talking about this so cavalierly?" I ask, staring at him deadpan. "Shouldn't you be in prison?"

He shrugs. "Remember? I'm insane in the membrane. Plus, I wasn't on my meds. When I'm on them, things are a little less unpredictable. That's when I started accumulating my Serene Meadows frequent flier miles. But, think of it this way: if I hadn't been so stubborn about taking my meds, I wouldn't have you." He waggles his eyebrows at me.

And I freeze.

Chapter Forty-Five

"P*sst... Pssst...* Amina? Amina!"

I jerk awake. Dark bangs nearly hide electric teal eyes against a pitch-black background.

Where am I? The last thing I remember is taking my medicine, and now I'm in a dark room with someone's eyes penetrating my soul. Staring, I try to piece together what's happening.

A finger taps the tip of my nose.

"Amina! Wake up!" a booming voice growls at me.

"Garrett?" I whisper, blinking hard.

"No, but it kinda rhymes with it."

"Derek?"

"Yes, wake up!"

How in the Hell? This has to be the most vivid dream I've ever had. Bracing myself with my elbows, I try to sit up.

"No, don't get up, Baby Doll," Derek says.

Once again, I'm caught off guard. This is Garrett. No matter what anyone says. No matter what he says. I don't know how it's possible. Maybe I am losing my mind.

"I believe you."

"Were we having a conversation?" I ask, shaking my head. "What time is it? How did you get in here?"

I'm totally lost.

"Amina!" Derek sighs. "It's three in the morning. I have my ways. That doesn't matter. I've been thinking about your fantasy world. Tell me more about it. How do you know me?"

This is dangerous territory. He's Garrett, but for some reason, he's not. It hurts to think about my life. I'm a mother without being a mother, and a wife without being a wife. Garrett and I got pregnant in the weirdest way. I didn't know I was pregnant when we got engaged, but we were in love. That love grew over time. Seeing him, Garrett, in Derek's mannerisms, the freckles on the bridge of his nose that extend to the tops of his cheeks, his roguish grin—it hurts not to have him when he's right here. I also don't want to trigger him, but maybe I can have what I had there with him now.

I take a deep breath. "You are—were—Garrett in that life. Garrett has a brother and a father who are schizophrenic. His mom is a New York Times best-selling author. She wrote about her experiences with her husband and son. He—you—have shorter hair and no facial hair. Your eyes are different and—"

"Stop." Derek's thick eyebrows knit, and he studies my face.

My mouth goes dry, and I bite my lip, feeling a little uncomfortable under his intense scrutiny.

Kneeling closer to the bed, almost nose to nose with me, he raises a large hand and rubs my cheek with his thumb.

I catch my breath.

"My mom wrote several books about her life with my father and me," he says, his voice as gravely serious as his expression. "My older brother and I were close before my diagnosis, but now we don't talk as much. Since my schizophrenia is more disruptive than my father's, my parents don't really know what to do with me. I don't know what to do with myself either. My mom thinks I should live at home, but what thirty-six-year-old man lives with his parents?"

"What's your mom's last name?"

"Boulanger."

My hope dissipates. I can't help the sadness that waters my eyes.

"She and my father had this weird thing when they got married. My mom wanted to retain her independence, and they made a deal. She'd hyphenate her last name, and they agreed that my brother and I would have hyphenated last names as well because she didn't have any brothers to carry on the Boulanger name. It's so stupid and ridiculous, I'd never do it. You marry me, you take my last name only. My brother's last name is Boulanger-Kaplan. My last name is Kaplan-Boulanger. It's simpler to use Boulanger instead of giving a long-ass last name. What's Garrett's last name?"

I gasp. Since I'm lying down, tears stream down my temples and into my hair. It's him. Somehow, it's really him. My heart races. I can't find my voice. We stare into each other's eyes for what feels like years.

"Kaplan," I finally respond.

He continues caressing my cheek, and his pupils dilate. Something inexplicable passes between us.

"I believe you," Derek says. "I read this book once about parallel universes."

"Parallel universes? Really? Are you making fun of me? If so, this really could've waited."

"I'm serious," he says with a harsh exhale. "I think we all may be living in another universe."

"Normally, I love your little riddles. But I'm barely awake right now."

"Have you ever heard of doppelgängers?"

Nodding, I say, "Umm...Tangentially... But aren't those supposed to be like evil twins or something? Like one of you dies if you ever meet each other."

"What if they aren't evil? Maybe they're just us in a different universe that runs parallel to this one."

At that, I sit up, and his hand falls away. I miss it instantly.

"And you're sure you're awake, right?"

"I'm not joking. I promise. I know it sounds way out there, but this isn't a moment of psychosis. I need you to believe me because I think maybe you crossed over to that other universe somehow," he pleads.

"Say I were to believe you, how do I get back?"

For some reason, his expression falls, and he grimaces. He takes several deep breaths.

"I don't know."

My stomach drops.

"Yet," he rushes on. "But I promise I'll figure something out."

I scoff. "This from a guy who talks to Satan."

"Hey," he says with a huff, furrowing his eyebrows. "Have I broken a promise to you yet?"

My mouth hangs open, and my eyes bulge. What is happening?

Chapter Forty-Six

Sitting in the common room on my favorite loveseat, a few days after Derek got into my bedroom—something I still don't understand how he managed— I read a book I found in the small bookcase by Gracie Cooper titled *Forever Luna*.

"Hey," Mr. Garrison says, sliding onto the cushion next to me.

I dog-ear the page I'm reading, then place the book on the arm of the loveseat.

Like a sketchy weirdo, he looks around nervously before saying, "You wanna buy some pills? I got some good stuff. Xanax, Valium, Soma, Klonopin, OxyContin..."

Why do I feel like I'm in a dark alley of a shady neighborhood? I glare at him. He scoots closer, and I edge so far away I might as well be on the armrest with my book.

"Get away from me."

"I'll cut you a deal," he says, twitching as if trying to shake bugs off himself or something. "I got a lot of good stuff. Stuff that'll take you to la-la land." Mr. Garrison wags his bushy grey eyebrows.

"Hey, old man, get out of my spot," Derek says, strolling over.

Relief washes over me. I've never been involved in a drug deal before, so I didn't know what to do.

Muttering something unintelligible, Mr. Garrison stands up and wanders away. I return to sitting on my full cushion.

"Thank you."

Derek shrugs and sits next to me.

"Hey, guess what?" he asks, grinning. Excitement shines in his teal eyes.

"What?"

"My brother's gonna let me move in with him. He's sending for me in a week. I'm going to help him do some carpentry work, save up, and get a place."

I smile at his infectious joy, even though my heart sinks.

What am I going to do without him?

"Congratulations. They're just going to let you leave?"

"I'm not a hostage," he says, giving me a droll stare. "And I'm back on my meds. I signed a treatment plan with Dr. Whittemore to continue outpatient care."

"I'm happy for you," I say, trying hard not to let my sadness show. This is a good thing for him. It really is, but he's all I have of Garrett, and after the other night, I thought he and I connected. "I don't think I'm ever getting out of here. I don't even know how I'm here. My insurance isn't good enough to pay for a place like this."

Derek frowns.

"What?"

He sighs. "If you're never getting out...you can't accept my offer."

I search his face in confusion. "Are we having one of those conversations again that I'm not a part of?"

"Ha. Ha!" he says waggishly, bumping my shoulder with his much larger one. "I wanted to ask you to stay with me when I get my place. You probably already have a place, but it won't take me long to save some decent money. Carpentry makes bank. I'm intelligent, but I don't know how to travel interuniversally. What I can offer you is me here and now."

My heart swells. Believing there's some parallel universe I can return to feels futile. Maybe I did make up Garrett and our daughter. I can't trust my own mind. Deciphering what's real and what's not gets harder each day. But there is Derek, and he's offering me a life I can only dream of. Still, he told me about what happened with his girlfriend, and even though I don't know this version of him, I still care. What if I'm projecting misguided expectations onto him based on a delusion? That could be harmful for him.

"Umm..." I take a deep breath then blow it out. My heart is crumbling. "I don't know if that'd be very healthy for me—recovery-wise and all."

He gazes into my eyes, a flood of emotions visible in his. He rubs my thigh, and I don't stop him. A rush of arousal surges through my veins. Part of me worries I might be cheating on Garrett, but another part recognizes his soul. I want to climb into his lap and feel his strong arms around me.

"We can make this work," he says confidently. "All the things you had, the baby, the house, I can give you those. Here. Just give me a chance to be the man you need and deserve."

"I—"

Two large orderlies burst into the common room, slamming heavy double doors ominously behind them, breaking my concentration. One of the men is Black, and the other is Latino. They're both bald and dressed in their grey scrub uniforms, looking hulking and angry. Menacing dark brown eyes scan the room.

"Oh, shit!" Derek breathes.

"What?" I ask as both orderlies spot Derek. "What did you do?"

Derek hops up like he's sitting on hot coals. He leans in to whisper in my ear, "Let's just say I left a going-away masterpiece in the men's quarters bathroom." He winks and flashes a devilish grin. His straight white teeth gleam.

"C'mon, Mr. Boulanger," the Latino orderly shouts. "There's a pair of soft restraints with your name all over 'em."

Derek runs, juking left then right. Patients skirt around the stampeding men in their game of cat-and-mouse. Derek crawls under one of the tables, his head hitting the underside because of his height. I'm in shock; it feels like a football game without the football. As he scrambles out the other side, the orderlies close in on him. Derek executes a few more evasive maneuvers, and the Black orderly comes up behind him, grabbing him in a bear hug.

"Gotcha!" the orderly says.

Derek squirms in the shorter man's arms, almost head-butting him.

"I let you get me!" he shouts.

Everyone watches the spectacle except Bryn. I don't know where she is. She seems to come and go in the same confounding way Derek does. The other orderly grabs both of Derek's legs. Since he's much sturdier than both men, it's a true battle to move him across the common room into the men's wing. The Latino orderly tries to hold on to both of Derek's kicking legs with one arm while he fumbles to retrieve his badge with the other.

"Wait! Wait...! Amina!" Derek shouts, thrashing against his captors as the orderly opens the door. He sings, "...*Like all at once, I wake up from something that keeps knocking at my brain. Before I got insane, I hold my pillow to my head and spring up in my bed, screaming out the words I dread. Hey... I think I love you...*" His booming voice echoes. "*I think I love you...*"

The orderlies pull him through the door.

My mouth drops open as I stand there, stunned and gaping. This is just too much.

I'm accepting his offer.

Chapter Forty-Seven

"If none of that was real, then I'm really losing my mind," I say while sitting on the edge of my bed, swinging my legs.

I can't sit still. So many thoughts are racing through my mind, and I don't know what's right, wrong, or real. It feels like living in a dream I can't wake up from. Nothing makes sense anymore.

Dr. Whittemore's light brown eyes examine me intently. Her nod is deliberate. "Have you been writing in the journal I gave you? Writing your conflicting thoughts can be very therapeutic. It can help you sort things out."

"I have. It's not resolving anything. Everything he does and says, even the way he moves is Garrett. According to you, none of that other life is real, but he is Garrett."

We sit in uncomfortable silence for several minutes. Dr. Whittemore writes in a black leather-bound journal of her own. She's always writing in that journal. It must be notes about our sessions, but I don't understand why she does it. I've seen her conduct sessions with Bryn before, and she uses a small laptop with her and everyone else. Apparently, I'm a special kind of insane. Thinking I jumped from one universe to another is crazy. I'm a thinking woman I wanted to be a social worker and help people, children, and here I am entertaining ideas that make no sense in a mental institution that I know my HMO won't cover. I'm no better or worse than anyone here. We're all just people trying to figure it out, and I can't let go of what could be or what might have been.

"Is there any way he read your journal?" Dr. Whittemore finally glances at me.

I shake my head.

"Did you tell him?"

I'm slow to shake my head this time. I did tell him some things. Bryn is aware of why I'm here. Did she tell him? Could this all be an elaborate game, an act to mess with me? They're fuckin' with me. My heart sinks. Are they? I can't think straight.

"But it's like he knows," I say. "I see it in his eyes. Derek may be looking at me, but Garrett is in there."

"Amina, sweetie," Dr. Whittemore says, remorseful, and with something else heavy in her tone. "It can't be Garrett. There is no Garrett. You need to stay away from Derek. He'll be leaving soon—"

"I can't," I say, interrupting her. "I physically can't. Ever since I first saw him, I've been drawn to him. He's been drawn to me. There's an invisible thread tying us together."

Dr. Whittemore grimaces. "I'm going to request that the staff keep the two of you apart for the remainder of his stay here. It's for the best, you'll see."

Tears well in my eyes. "Please don't do that."

She shakes her head. "You have to get better. It's my job to put your mental health first, even if you can't. You had a life before the rape. It's time you reclaim it."

Scooting to the corner where my bed meets the wall, I draw my legs up and wrap my arms around them.

"Get the fuck out of my room," I say, glaring at her.

Dr. Whittemore closes her journal, smooths her black A-line skirt, and lifts herself out of the rickety chair. She places it back under my small table, and regards at me through sad eyes.

Or is that disappointment?

"Same time the day after tomorrow, okay?" she asks, stopping in the doorway.

"Why do you care so fuckin' much?" I glower.

"It's my responsibility to care. There won't be any more repeats of Derek's outburst last week. I'll make sure of that. Stay away from Derek."

She turns, glances once more at me, and leaves.

"**W**hatcha readin'?"

I glare at Bryn over my book. I'm reading another Serene Meadows smash hit. They aren't really in touch with the times here. The book I found the other day was a hidden gem. I've read this one a million times. Never read it in the Healing Garden on a grassy lawn, sitting on a bench. It's the only way I can keep my mind off Derek, whom I haven't seen in over a week. It seems as if the good Dr. Whittemore is a woman of her word.

Bitch!

Bryn sits next to me.

"*Romeo and Juliet.*"

"Hmm..." She plucks the book from my hands. "I read this in high school once. It has a pretty shitty ending." Bryn smiles, her gaze lingers a bit too long.

"What? Why are you staring at me?"

She purses her lips and then sighs. "Trying to find that 'Glutton for Punishment' sign."

Bryn gives a wide grin.

Everything she does is so extra.

Shaking my head, I ask, "Why are you here?"

"A little well-timed suicide attempt and a dose of bipolar." She giggles, and it sounds just as insane as Bryn is. "It'll get you anywhere."

All I do is stare and blink for a few seconds.

I don't get this place. Everyone is so loose with how they speak about the most serious and wild things. I'm constantly off balance here.

I take a cleansing breath. "I meant why are you...here. With me. Right now. Not here like here." I look her up and down. "Can't you live in the outside world with bipolar?"

She laughs. "Normally," Bryn says with a shrug, "but mine was..." she clears her throat, "affecting my quality of life," she says, finishing in a snobby professional voice.

Given my recent intense therapy sessions, I totally get it. I nod. "Ah... I see. Can I ask you a question?"

"Yes, you can have a hug," she says, opening her arms wide.

"No." I slap her hands down. "Something else."

"We can work up to the hug thing. What do you want to know?"

"All of you talk about being crazy so casually," I say. "Isn't that term frowned upon? Insensitive just a tad."

Hazel-blue eyes roll. "Mina—"

"Amina," I correct her.

"We're best friends, best friends have nicknames for each other," she says as if I'm the crazy one. "We're taking the word back. It only has power if we let it have power. If others can use it against us then they win. If we use it ourselves, then there's nothing anyone can say to hurt us. Plus, I call it spicy brain."

She's like a tall, blonde, mentally unstable Yoda.

I nod.

Bryn nudges me with her sharp elbow. "I got a good one for you. Pete and Repeat went out on a boat. Pete fell off; who was left?"

"Repeat."

"Pete and Repeat went out on a boat. Pete fell off, so who was left?"

I groan, then sigh. "Very funny. Sounds like something Derek would say."

"He did," Bryn says, then pulls a rolled-up sheet of paper from beside her that I hadn't noticed she had. "He told me to tell you, and to give you this." She hands the paper to me.

I unroll it, and my mouth drops open. It's beautiful. There's an expert drawing of a red rose suspended in the air, encapsulated by a lovely glass lid. It's from *Beauty and the Beast*. One night, Garrett and I were talking about all the movies I love, and I mentioned it. Written at the bottom on the side, it reads: "Come see me tonight." And then Derek's signature.

He remembers.

Bryn scoots closer to see the picture. I scoot away.

She feigns offense. "I feel very annoyed when you treat me like I have cooties, so what I need from you is to stop ignoring our deep connection, so I don't feel annoyed."

I give Bryn a droll stare. She wags her perfectly plucked eyebrows and smiles.

Laughing, I shake my head.

"Check me out! Using my 'I feel' statements and shit. Oh, no! Therapy must be working." Bryn smacks her palm into her forehead.

Scooting closer to her, I let her see the picture.

Chapter Forty-Eight

"If you understand, say 'understand'. If you don't understand, say 'don't understand'. But if you understand and say 'don't understand', how do I understand that you understand? Understand?!"

I listen as Derek murmurs to himself before making my presence known. Something feels off. He sits cross-legged in the middle of his bed, rocking back and forth. His long hair brushes the collar of his scrub shirt, and overgrown bangs hang in his eyes.

Entering his room completely, I ensure the coast is clear in the long hallway of the men's wing. I slip inside and close the door with a soft click. The hall lights cast a glow through the square window into his room.

Derek gazes at me. "Love's a feeling you feel when you feel you're going to feel the feeling you've never felt before," he murmurs.

I smile, walk over to his bed, and sit on the floor in front of it. "Where do you come up with all of those?"

"They're tongue twisters. My mom used to use them to help me with a childhood stutter and then for my father and me once I was diagnosed," he explains. "When I'm anxious or freaking out, they help—even at this age—oddly enough."

Shock is a whip lashing my spine, and I try to keep the grimace off my face. I nod. "Why are you anxious? Or are you freaking out?"

He frowns and clears his throat. His large Adam's apple bobs with the action. "My brother got engaged. He says I can't live with him because his fiancée is afraid of me."

I get up and sit beside him on his bed. "I'm so sorry. What are you going to do now?"

Derek shrugs and keeps rocking, his hands gripping his ankles. "Dr. Whittemore says she's gonna get me a social worker. She told me they're going to be able to get me into some supervised apartments."

Reaching out, I rub his knee. I'm rusty at comforting people. Touching has never come easily to me. Garrett's personality was so overwhelming and dominant that he always took the reins when it came to physical contact. It was impossible not to touch him. Derek is a little more reserved, which makes sense given where we are.

"At least you get to get out of here," I say.

He watches my hand on his knee. Then he frowns.

"Yeah, right!" he chuckles dryly. "If I go there, I won't have my parents or my brother." Derek looks into my eyes. "Or you."

I give him a rueful smile. "I'm sorry," I manage to say around a lump in my throat.

Almost imperceptible tears swim in his teal eyes.

"Supervised apartments are worse than here. Serene Meadows is exactly what it claims to be, an old-fashioned mental asylum dressed up. It's designed to confine us. There's no illusion about what it is. A supervised apartment is like a gilded cage meant to make you think you're free, but in reality, staff live on site, watching. They are always watching, reminding you that you're sick and a prisoner."

"Maybe I can get placed there too," I say, trying to smile.

"They don't want me near you here. You really think they're gonna send you there?" he asks. "That's no place for you. You're not like me. Nobody's scared of you."

Derek takes my hand and interlaces our fingers. He studies our connected hands.

"I'm not afraid of you, and Bryn's too crazy to be afraid of anyone."

"Come here," he says, his voice going impossibly deeper.

Then he takes the decision away from me. He lifts me into his arms and settles me astride his lap. We lean our foreheads against each other, and he rubs his nose against mine. For several seconds, we gaze into each other's eyes and breathe each other in. My heart pounds, and although he says nothing, I know his is pounding too. No matter what universe we're in, our souls are connected. We're inevitable.

Derek presses his firm lips against mine in a demanding yet tender kiss. Opening to him, he explores my mouth, and I explore his. He's just as amazing as he ever was. This can work. We fit together in all the ways that matter, and if I ever need help with his episodes in life, I know where to get it.

"Amina," Derek says, his sinful voice oozing sensuality. "I want inside of you."

My breath hitches.

"Say yes because I'm knocking down walls tonight one way or another."

Damn! I want to laugh, but his blue-green eyes are dead serious. "How?"

With little effort, Derek lifts me and sits me across his lap, bridal-style. Equally effortlessly, he removes my elegant white tennis shoes and tosses them across the room, then pulls my scrub bottoms and underwear down and off. Derek possesses effortless strength. Lifting his hips with me still on his lap, he slides his scrub bottoms down and off.

All the while, he maintains eye contact, keeping the moment intense. He then sits me astride him.

"Amina," he says, cupping my cheek, "we have so much we don't know about each other, but what I do know is that you are the natural progression my life was meant to take. The tongue-twisters help a lot when I'm freaking out, but what's been helping the most is you. You are my sanity."

Unbidden tears roll down my face. Derek kisses each track. Then he kisses my lips. All that stands between us is his solid erection poking out of the front of his boxers. I slip my hands between our bodies to take him in hand. His hip thrusts are in time with my strokes. Our tongues continue their erotic dance as we moan into each other's mouths. My inner walls pulse with need. I grind in his lap, desperate for him to fill me.

"Are you wet for me?"

"Yes."

"I don't believe you," Derek says with a naughty grin.

He shoves a big hand between our bodies. Sitting astride him, I'm already open to him, but he manages to open me wider with the sheer size of his hand.

"Mmm... You are wet," he says, circling my clit with his thumb.

Two of his fingers find their way to my sopping entrance and push inside. I gasp at their thick intrusion. My stomach clenches. He pumps his fingers in and out. Derek wraps his other arm around my back. Rolling my hips sends his intruding fingers deeper. I moan, and Derek catches it in his mouth. I stroke him faster.

"Ready for me, Baby Doll?" Derek asks, removing his lips from mine.

I run my fingers through the back of his hair. It might be long enough to touch his nape and appear messy, but it feels like silk. He leans his head back into my hand. With his Adam's apple exposed, I lean in and kiss the knot. The wiry facial hair on his jaw tickles my nose. Derek runs his hand up the back of my scrub top. It should be offensive for his shirt to hide his hard abdomen, but I understand the need.

In a different place, we'd have time to fully undress and appreciate each other, but we both know why that can't happen. Time is ticking. I didn't see this coming, but I want it.

"I want to feel you," I say in a breathy voice.

Derek withdraws his fingers from inside me. Our eyes lock, and he brings both fingers to his mouth, licking them clean. My head spins from the heady sight, and I almost faint from how hot that was. He holds me up by my waist and slowly lowers me onto his hard length. I gasp as he gradually enters me, inch by delicious inch.

"Is that what you wanted?" He growls.

I only nod as he slides me down the last inch of him. We both take several steadying breaths as we rest our sweaty foreheads together. He has his arms around my waist, and I have mine around his neck. There is so much emotion in his eyes, and I'm sure it is reflected in mine. This isn't just sex; this is a joining, two souls becoming one. I rock hips and he meets me thrust for thrust. Our heavy breathing is the only sound in the room.

"Thank you," Derek whispers into my ear.

Chills skitter down my spine. My orgasm is building.

"For what ask?" I ask in a whisper.

"Showing me love and support," he answers.

Tears fill my eyes. I really do love him. It doesn't make sense, and I thought I might be transferring my feelings for Garrett onto him, but I'm not. Garrett once asked me if he felt the same as others who'd hurt me, and he didn't. Derek feels like Garrett, and I would love him just the same, no matter his name.

Holding my hips steady, his thick length hits a spot so deep inside me I nearly short-circuit from how incredible it feels. He kisses a hot trail up and down my neck. We grind and rock against each other at a feverish pitch. Soft moans and groans fill the dark room. Then we explode together, breathing hard.

"Knock. Knock," Bryn's voice comes from the other side of the door. It creaks.

"Stay out! Give us a second," Derek tells her.

I hop off him and snatch up my clothes from the floor.

"There's Kleenex in the top drawer of my dresser," Derek offers while tucking himself in and putting on his scrub bottoms.

Going to his dresser, I find the Kleenex and clean up as best I can. Then I get dressed and put on my shoes. I don't know how to navigate this situation. Do I turn and leave? Say thanks for the sex?

Derek spins me around, and I bump into his chest. His arms wrap around me. He lifts my chin. There's a wealth of meaning in his penetrating gaze. He lifts me off my feet and brings our mouths even. His kiss is deep. Passionate. Urgent.

"Woohoo! Look who gets her prince," Bryn says, her head poking into the doorway.

I hop down and step away from Derek. "Weren't you supposed to be keeping a certain orderly busy?"

"I did," Bryn says with a saucy grin.

"You fucked him?" Derek asks.

"Of course, I did," Bryn says, rolling her eyes. "How do you think you got so much time? I did you a favor."

"Thanks?" I say, but it sounds more like a question.

That's definitely taking one for the team.

Derek quickly goes to his bed.

"What are you doing?" I ask Bryn.

"I hate to break things up in the love shack, which, FYI, smells like sex. But the orderlies will be doing bed checks in a few minutes."

"Shit! I gotta go," I tell Derek.

He reaches under his pillow and turns toward me.

"This is for you," he says as he hands me a folded sheet of paper. "It's a picture. Don't open it until I leave."

I frown. "Just give it to me the day you leave."

"Tick Tock, psychos. Time waits for no one," Bryn reminds us.

"I might forget," Derek says, answering me. "Plus, we're not allowed to talk to each other. Just keep it and open it when I leave."

I roll my eyes. There has to be a way to see him before he leaves. It seems Bryn is a team player. I'm not trying to pimp her out or anything, but we can figure something out.

"Fine," I acquiesce. Then I kiss Derek on the cheek. "Bye."

Bryn and I hurry towards the door.

"It's not the cough that carries you off. It's the coffin they carry you off in."

At the door, I turn around. "Don't freak out. It's gonna be fine. We'll see each other again, I promise."

"You can't know that," Derek says, looking forlorn.

"Yes, I can," I say with a smile. "Have I broken a promise to you yet?"

Chapter Forty-Nine

It's difficult to stay still. I fluctuate between crossing my legs and letting them sway over the side of my bed. Dr. Whittemore sits across from me in the chair she always pulls from the desk.

"That's not possible. While we can't stop it, we strongly discourage it," Dr. Whittemore says, attempting to dash my hopes.

"It's not up to you, right?" I ask. "It's up to the other place."

Dr. Whittemore narrows her eyes. "No. However, I could note it in his chart. I'm sure his new psychiatrist wouldn't approve either."

I glare. "Why would you do that? I thought the goal was for everyone to get better and live normal lives."

Dr. Whittemore groans. "Normal for you isn't normal for him. He has a serious, life-altering mental health issue. You had a psychotic break caused by trauma. You'll get better."

She persists in seeing everyone here like they aren't people. As if they aren't more than their mental health conditions, it's no wonder they act out and get scared. This place drains life out of people. There may be a genuine need for facilities like these, but they shouldn't treat people so inhumanely. Derek was left for hours tied to his bed with soft restraints.

He couldn't get himself free in an emergency. Even if she is a salaried employee, Dr. Whittemore can't be worked to the point of exhaustion. In my time here, I've only seen her. Are there no other psychiatrists? Whoever the administrators or owners of Serene Meadows are, they don't see patients or their staff as people.

"You said he could live a normal life. He was going to live with his brother," I persist.

The doctor sighs. "Amina, no. You can't visit him or see him after you leave here. I'll make sure your name is on the list of people not allowed to visit Derek."

Why is she so determined that I move on? If Derek and I are released from Serene Meadows, she can't control what we do. We would both essentially be private citizens. Why should we be denied the chance at happiness? I despise this woman.

Scooting to the corner of my bed, I bring my knees to my chest and wrap my arms around my legs.

"Get the fuck out of my room. I don't want to talk anymore."

Dr. Whittemore rises and pushes the chair under the desk.

"No, Amina. No visiting Derek. Focus on getting better and returning to your life. Forget the delusion. It's not real. The present moment is real. You were a productive woman before, and you will be again."

I scowl. "I forgot the delusion. But I can still have a life with Derek. We both deserve to be happy."

"Your recovery is the only thing you need to focus on. I won't tell you where he's going. No one will. It's a confidential placement."

Rocking back and forth, I tune her out.

"Your entire life, you've prioritized others. While that's commendable, don't you think it's time to consider yourself? Your resilience has brought you this far. It will help you move beyond your time here. I will support you."

With those parting words, Dr. Whittemore departs.

"Crazy people talk a lot. I'll find him," I murmur.

It's another endless spring morning. This garden is such a conundrum. Blue skies always, and lush green grass. I've been here for seven months. Not a single day of rain or snow. I just don't understand.

Bryn skips over to where I'm sitting on the bench and sits beside me.

"Hey, roomie! You know Romeo and Juliet kill themselves at the end, right? There's not one spicy scene," she complains.

"It's supposed to be symbolic. The only way they could be together was in death. That's why they're star-crossed," I say, trying to explain to someone once again the brilliance that is this tragedy.

Bryn scoffs. "I think Shakespeare might have been a little nutty himself. Writing all those tragedies is crazy work."

"Ladies," Nurse Dettinger says, approaching Bryn and me. "I'm gonna need y'all to go to your room. We're on lockdown."

Bryn and I exchange worried looks.

"Has this ever happened before?" I ask.

We've been in our rooms since Nurse Dettinger came and got us earlier this morning. I had no idea we could be forcibly locked in our rooms and told to sit on our beds with our legs crossed. This feels like an adult timeout. I'm surprised they didn't make us stand in the corner.

Bryn bounces up and down on her bed, restless.

"Only once in the eight months I've been here," Bryn responds.

"Why do they keep us locked in?"

She shrugs. "I guess so we don't get in the way being crazy."

There should be some sort of rules list we're given, but I wasn't. One minute, I was in the hospital ICU; the next, I was transferred here under Dr. Whittemore's supervision. I didn't sign anything. My personal effects weren't handed to me, and I have no idea what my job thinks happened to me. Hillard Brand probably dropped me from school. Someone who hasn't shown up for nearly a year without any call or explanation couldn't be counted on to save space for. That means all that tuition money is gone. It's as if, once I was attacked, I stopped existing. I haven't seen any papers waiving my adult rights. If they can do this to us, it makes sense that there would be paperwork involved.

What is happening?

Is the floor lava? Why can't we walk around our room? We can't get out. What does it matter if we stand or sit?

"It's been three hours," I say. "How much longer do they need?"

"As long as it takes to get rid of or clean up whatever happened," Bryn says.

Just then, the door locks disengage with a loud click.

Chapter Fifty

The common room is more crowded than I've ever seen it before. What seems like the entire staff stands in the back, and patients fill every available couch and loveseat, with some sitting on the floor. It's as if the room itself is holding its breath. No one's said anything except for instructions to come to the common room and take a seat. My stomach is in knots, and I feel like I could throw up.

Dr. Whittemore walks into the room and stands in the middle.

My ears begin to ring. Sweat moistens my armpits.

"I apologize for the longer-than-average lockdown," Dr. Whittemore says. "Thank you for your patience. It's been a while since we've had to do that. I know it can be unsettling."

Patients start talking among themselves.

"If you could quiet down just for a few more moments, I have an announcement."

Mr. Garrison stands.

"Bruce, could you please sit for just a few more minutes?" Dr. Whittemore pleads.

Dr. Whittemore is visibly agitated tonight. Her thick blonde hair with highlights looks puffy, as if she's run her fingers through it one too many times. She's not wearing her usual blazer over her cream silk blouse, and her knee-length black A-line skirt is creased and wrinkled. She looks tired.

"I thought we were having a going-away party for Derek?" Mr. Garrison asks, his voice warbling with indignation. "I've been sittin' all day. I haven't taken any meds. I wanna party."

Dr. Whittemore clears her throat.

The Black orderly who dragged Derek away a few weeks ago moves to Mr. Garrison's side. Mr. Garrison glances past his shoulder at the orderly, then sits back down.

I guess he didn't want that smoke.

"That's part of the reason I'm here," Dr. Whittemore continues. "There was an incident today." Her eyes water.

A boulder sinks in my stomach. I sit up straighter. Something isn't right.

She clears her throat again. "We lost a patient."

Light brown eyes meet mine, and I understand. I know.

"Derek Boulanger won't be leaving today," Dr. Whittemore says. "He was found unresponsive in the men's quarters restroom late this morning. Unfortunately, we were unable to revive him, and he passed away a few hours ago."

No! No!

NO!

The room spins. I can't see. I feel like I'm suffocating. It's unbearably hot. I slip off the loveseat and collapse to the floor. Tears stream down my face as my heart shatters. An involuntary scream rises from my throat and escapes my mouth. I sob and wail uncontrollably. Then everything goes black.

Days. Weeks. Months. Years. I have no sense of how much time passes. What I do understand is pain. It's a living, breathing thing inside me every moment of every day. I'm trapped in a grief loop. All I see ahead is a vast, empty chasm. No family. No friends. No job. Nothing. No Garrett. No Derek. Nothing.

Why would Derek do that?

When had hopelessness wrapped its venomous tail around him and consumed him? That should have been something he could talk to me about, but he couldn't because of this damn place and its rules. Was the idea of us being happy together so repulsive to everyone here that they'd rather he take his own life? It must have been. I won't believe he wouldn't have come to me if he was struggling. He wanted to be with me. I wanted to be with him. Our lives would have been good together. A new future that I didn't realize I'd allowed to form in my mind's eye evaporates.

No!

"Hey, roomie!" Bryn says. "Want some water or anything?"

I don't look up. I've been lying in the middle of my bed in the fetal position for so long that my limbs no longer tingle. There are no aches or pains. It's as if I've lost the will to live. If I could, I'd will my involuntary functions to cease. Now doesn't seem real either. This place. The lumpy mattress. Nothing feels real anymore. Garrett. Derek. Maybe neither of them was real, and I'm in some kind of purgatory, some hellish place where I'm being taunted with the things I want and then cruelly taken away as punishment. I must have wronged the universe somehow.

"You didn't come to the memorial a few days ago," Bryn says, kneeling into my line of sight. "It was really pretty. There's a small copper-colored placard in front of the largest tree in the garden. Engraved on the placard is, 'In loving memory of Derek Thaddeus Boulanger,' it's beautiful. He would've liked it. Derek was always so understated." Bryn giggles.

It's a joke. All of this is a joke. Derek and Garrett can be accused of many things, but understated isn't one of them. When they entered a room, they drained all the air out. They—Derek and Garrett—were like the same person. I lost that same person twice. Isn't there a limit to how much loss one person should endure in a lifetime? I thought I'd paid my dues. No one in my entire life ever loved me. I wasn't doted on as an infant, child, or teenager. People toss their drama on my doorstep as if I'm the city dump. This time, it's my drama.

Mine.

After years of convincing myself I was fine with living vicariously through movies and TV characters and not minding being alone, I now welcomed three wolves into my hen house. Justin was the first and most villainous. Garrett was the first to infuriate me at first sight. Then there's Derek with all of his psychotic charm. Now, I find myself lying on a borrowed bed in a place I'm not even sure exists in time and space. Serene Meadows is a delusion. Happiness is a delusion.

Bryn crawls closer to my bed. I look past her.

"It's been a few days since you've eaten," Bryn says.

I roll towards her, and I arch a brow.

"Ha. Ha. My job requires me to watch my figure, but I do eat...sometimes," Bryn lies. "They'll force you. If you don't eat for enough days, they will force you, and their methods aren't gentle. Think needles."

I find a spot on the wall to stare at.

"Derek wouldn't want you to starve yourself to death. Neither would your husband," Bryn says, and I can hear the smile in her voice. "C'mon, Amina! Smile. Tell me to get away from you. Roll your eyes at me. Do something, please. Talk."

Through watery eyes, I glance at Bryn. A tear tumbles from my eye. Dr. Whittemore steps through the doorway.

"Bryn, sweetie, it's time for our session," Dr. Whittemore says. "Why don't we let Amina stay here. We'll have our session in the garden."

Light as a feather and flighty as a loon, Bryn hops to her feet and skips out of the room.

"Amina?"

I keep staring ahead. There's no way I'll break my "no talking" streak with this woman, she's the reason Derek decided to end his own life. If she'd have just let us see each other, he'd still be alive. Her hands are stained with his blood.

"Amina, we have another session tomorrow," Dr. Whittemore says. "Maybe this time you could talk."

I don't even bother to acknowledge her words with a nod, and I refuse to look up. She is cruelty incarnate.

Chapter Fifty-One

Patients wander around the common room. Three and a half weeks later, the somber mood still hasn't lifted. I observe the room from my spot on the loveseat. Even those who have animated conversations with themselves, and the walls aren't doing anything but mumbling. Today's the first time I've left my room.

Taking Bryn's warning to heart, I eat small amounts of saltines and graham crackers, but that's all I can handle. Emptiness has consumed me. I've stopped going through the motions of brushing my hair every day. I French braided it down my back and haven't touched it since. If I could, I'd skip showering and brushing my teeth, but I can't stand the greasy feeling that forms on my teeth when I don't brush them. Plus, I may be depressed, but smelling my own BO would make me sick. So, I do the bare minimum. There is no future for me, and I don't care if I never leave this place. I have no desire to be part of the world.

"Hey, roomie! How's it hangin'? Something seem weird to you? 'Cause something seems a *foot* to me," Bryn says from somewhere behind me in a squeaky and scratchy voice.

I glance over my right shoulder and come face-to-face with Derek's sock puppet. Before I can think better of it, I snatch the puppet from Bryn's hand and clutch it to my heart.

"Geez!" Bryn retorts. "I thought I was moody."

I scowl. "What do you want?"

Bryn skips around the loveseat and sits beside me.

"So, I hear that three weeks is the limit for sulking," she says happily carefree.

Taking a ragged breath, I say, "I'm not sulking. I'm grieving, and there is no time limit on grief. But if there were, three weeks wouldn't nearly be long enough."

"*Psst...*" Bryn whispers, leaning in closer. "What if I told you I found a way back to your fantasy land?"

I gape. "It wasn't a fantasy land. It was a delusion. All in my head like you, Derek, and Garrett. Nothing is real."

Bryn's mouth falls open. "What the hell are you talking about? I'm very real, considering I'm sitting next to you, and other people can see me." She pinches the fat under my arm.

"Ow! Why would you do that?"

"See... If I weren't real, you wouldn't have been about to feel that. Now, back to the matter at hand, I've listened to you talk about getting back to your husband and baby for months."

"That was the old me. Derek died, and he took Garrett with him. I have nothing left now."

Bryn balks. "You're kidding? Amina, I won't pretend to understand what happened to you. But the way you described your life, even though there's no mention of cunnilingus, was... I don't know. Idyllic. More than that, it seemed real."

I thought so too.

Biting my lip, I blink back tears.

"You joked about it," I remind her. "Dr. Whittemore is sure my brain was protecting itself, or I dissociated somehow. I'm here, so no matter how believable a storyteller, I'm here. So, I must be delusional."

Bryn's hazel-blue eyes search mine, and her expression morphs into sorrow or pity.

I don't want her pity, anybody's pity. This is my life. This is what's real.

"Don't say that," Bryn says in such a serious tone that I'm shocked. Bryn is peppy to an insane degree, but this is the Bryn I don't think many people see. "I rarely have moments of insight. I shouldn't have made fun of you. I just wanted you to be my friend, and that was the only way you'd talk to me. But, trust me, I have a good idea of how you can go back. I'll tell you my idea, and then you can think it over."

Standing, I shake my head. "I don't care anymore. I have surrendered the fantasy."

The fetal position is my preferred way to rest and sleep. I can no longer support my weight with my spine and neck. Everything hurts. It's an emotional pain that leaves me feeling hollow. My cup is not just empty; it's shattered. I'm shattered. Breathing hurts. Seeing hurts. My skin feels too tight and burdensome. I'm crawling inside my skin to the point I want to shed it like a snake. It takes everything in me not to scratch it off. So, I lie in the fetal position on my bed and pray to disappear.

"Forget I'm your psychiatrist for a minute," Dr. Whittemore says from her seat across from my bed. "Talk to me like a friend. Okay? I'm not Dr. Whittemore, I'm Gretchen."

I give her a droll stare and sigh. "Why do you spend extra time with me? The other patients have individual sessions twice a month, and you see me every other day. Why? I'm not worth sacrificing your personal time."

Dr. Whittemore shifts her chair nearer to my bed.

"Amina, you are worth it. What happened to you was something no one should ever experience. They betrayed your trust and took advantage of you when you were at your weakest. It completely derailed your life."

Who you tellin'?!

This isn't breaking news. If I could time-travel, I'd go back and tell myself not to meet Justin, to run from anyone named Justin.

I shrug and frown. Each move feels as lifeless as I do.

"So," I say in an apathetic tone. "My life got derailed, and being here only makes it worse. But you should be happy. I gave up my fantasy life—my delusion. I don't have anything else, Gretch."

"Be honest with me, Amina," Dr. Whittemore says. "Don't you want to get back to your life?"

With that, I sit up. I'm dizzy from lying down for so long. If all she wanted was for me to say I'd give up, and then she'd help me get back... Wow! For the first time, my heart beats quickly, and hope settles in.

"Yes, I do. A lot. I've tried, but I don't know how. It might be a doppelgänger situation. Or a parallel universe, I'm not sure. Can you help me?"

Dr. Whittemore smiles sincerely and nonjudgmentally. "I sure can. I thought you were placating me, but if you're serious about your delusional life being over... I can help you get back to your life here."

Disappointment is a bucket of ice poured over my head. She doesn't get it. Or maybe I didn't get it. How could I be so stupid to think she'd want me to move on with my real life and not stick to the half-life I was living before?

Strength drains from me just as fast as it arrives, and I slump onto the bed. I curl up in the fetal position.

"I thought you said I could be honest," I mutter. "I was talking about—never mind. Can we be done, please?"

Without argument, Dr. Whittemore stands, black leather-bound journal clutched to her chest, and she puts the chair back under the desk. Making it to the doorway, she stops and turns.

"That delusional life doesn't exist. This is real. Right now. You have to decide which you want more, reality or the delusion?"

Tears spill over the rims of my eyes. Glaring, I clench my teeth and say, "There's nothing here for me but pain. It hurts every day being me. Anything that's ever made me happy has been taken from me. Reality sucks! Get the fuck out of my room."

Chapter Fifty-Two

I'm in my favorite place, the eternal spring garden, sitting on my bench. However, there's nothing here that can really heal me. Before everything fell apart for me, I managed to grab a new book from the bookshelf in the common room. I've bogarted it since then. The spine wasn't broken, so I knew it had just arrived. There weren't any more Gracie Cooper books, but I found one by Leya Layne called *You've Got Bookmail*. I'd planned to show it to Derek, but...

I can't think about that, which is exactly why I came out here to read. My thoughts are tormenting me, all revolving around a life—two different lives—with people I can't be with. Reading will distract me with something else, and I'm desperate for the reprieve.

Picking up the book, I notice something shoved into the crack. A sinking sensation washes over me. I bite my lip in indecision and hesitate.

After taking several breaths, I open the book and retrieve the item. The world around me falls silent, and my breath catches. It's the folded paper Derek gave me. He said to open it after he was gone. Thinking about that moment makes me wonder if he knew he would leave the way he did. His expression had been grave. I chalked it up to the fact that he was going to be taken somewhere he didn't want to go, and we'd be kept apart for the duration of his stay here. But maybe what he was doing was saying goodbye. How did I not realize it? Our passionate moment now takes on a whole new meaning. He was saying goodbye.

Taking a deep breath, I unfold the paper. Tears gather in my eyes, and I wipe them away with a rough hand.

There is a checkered blanket with a vase of red roses in the middle. Two beautiful crystal candle holders each hold a tapered candle. Rose petals are scattered across the blanket. At the edge of the blanket, a note reads: We're Waiting For You.

I study the picture. Once. Twice. Three times. Too many. Something I'd never expect to have again curls my lips.

I grin.

"**M**eds time!" Nurse Dettinger calls out. "Who needs their happy pills?"

A long queue of patients of all ages, sizes, and colors gathers in front of the Dutch door to get their nightly medications. Nurse Dettinger places a tray of Dixie cups and squat Soufflé cups on the door ledge.

I peek out from my hiding spot behind the loveseat.

"Well, hey there, Ms. Bryn. How are ya, suga booga?"

Bryn takes the Soufflé cup of meds and downs it. She doesn't touch the small cup of water.

"Oh, I'm deprived, honey," Bryn says in her overly cheerful voice. "I'm in a bit of a drought."

Bit of a drought, my ass!

This isn't the typical setting most people would think of as a place to find love, but Bryn has several orderlies completely wrapped around her little manicured finger. The woman is never lonely.

"How are you doing?" Bryn asks.

"I'm just peachy, suga. Open up," Nurse Dettinger instructs.

Bryn does as requested.

"I need to work on my gag reflex," Nurse Dettinger says with a playful laugh. "I'm surprised none of those get lodged in your throat."

"Practice makes perfect, darling." Bryn giggles. "Start with a popsicle, that way it melts if you start gagging."

Nurse Dettinger shakes her head. "You are too much! Now, you get to bed. Sleep tight."

Bryn skips over to my hiding spot. I duck down lower so she can't see me. She sits down.

"Hey, roomie!" I say in my best cartoonish voice. "Watcha doin'?"

Bryn's head slowly turns towards the sock puppet on my hand near her shoulder.

"If I wasn't sure before, I'm sure now. You're crazy," she says with a laugh. "Certifiable."

I pop up from behind the loveseat and sit in my usual spot.

"Come to the room in five minutes," I say, then head to the women's quarters.

Chapter Fifty-Three

Sitting on my bed, legs hanging over the side, I swing them back and forth in excited anticipation. I lift my left wrist, and frown. No smartwatch. Old habits die hard. Hours? Minutes? How long has it been? Didn't I say five minutes? Not that I deserve Bryn to jump at my command. It'd be just my luck if she didn't show up at all, especially given how I've treated her since I arrived eight months ago. She greeted me with unconditional friendship from the very first moment, expecting nothing but kindness from me, and I've treated her like a nuisance. She's been a fly buzzing around—no matter how many times I swatted, it wouldn't go away. Even hitting her with a metaphorical newspaper—that is, dismissing her and being ruthless—she's kept coming back, just as eager as ever. To be honest, I envy her energy. Oh, to be young again or full of life.

Speaking of life...

I grab my pillow. Flipping it upside down, I reach inside the case. The flat, government-issue, cotton-stuffed fabric may be worthless, but what it holds is priceless. There it is. My fingers curl around the folded paper. A reminder of a life on pause, but not lost. Nor has it been forgotten by either of us. I'm not big on omens or signs, but I swear the paper warms at my touch. acknowledging me. It's like it's welcoming me home, encouraging me to hold on. It's saying to not give up on my husband. Family. My life. It's obtainable. Where there's a will, there's a way.

"The owner of the inside inn was inside his inside inn with his inside outside his inside inn," I mumble. The tongue twister makes me feel closer to Derek and Garrett than I've felt in weeks.

Voices in the hall grab my attention. I hop off the bed, snatch the door open, and gaze left and right.

"Hey!" Bryn shrieks.

"What took so long?" I ask, gripping her wrist firmly.

She drags her feet as I tug her the last few steps into our room. I slam the door shut behind us. Bryn pushes me towards my bed, then hops onto hers. The springs complain as she gets into position, sitting cross-legged on the worn mattress. Blonde hair flops all over the place with each adjustment she makes.

I sit on the edge of my seat, or rather on the side of my bed facing Bryn, eager to start the conversation. Once again, I wonder if I might be as crazy as everyone thinks I am. I don't even know where to begin to make sense of everything. Actually, it's not me who needs to explain. It's Bryn, if she still wants to. Given my recent behavior, she'd be justified in telling me to go to Hell.

Caressing the piece of paper etched with my past and future, I pray for guidance and hope. Something I've always avoided. Being jaded kept me level-headed, but now, I'm operating on faith and hope. I'll use whatever tools are necessary to return to the life illustrated on this paper—the life Derek drew. Derek, who somehow is Garrett, my husband.

Yep. Definitely crazy.

"That was literally five minutes, maybe six," Bryn informs me.

"Sorry," I say, though it sounds empty even to my own ears. "It seemed longer."

Bryn grips the outside ankle of her crossed legs and rocks back and forth.

"Okay, psycho," she says with a sigh. "What's up with your overly happy mood? It's kinda cringe. It reminds me of the people in that one movie, *No One Will Save You*, where they're all mean at first until they're basically body-snatched at the end, then they're all nice and helpful."

Spoiler alert!

Thank God, I didn't see that one. Something tells me I might take offense to that comparison.

"How about you tell me?"

Confusion scrunches her dark blonde brows. "You lost me."

I remind her, sighing, "You said you knew how I could get back to my other life."

"Other life?" One eyebrow arches. "You mean *Fantasy Island*?"

My eyes roll before I can stop them. Not the best way to endear Bryn to me, but her tone is more judgmental than I expected.

"Please, Bryn. I'm desperate. I need to know what your idea is."

That seems to thaw her a bit. She smiles.

"It's a process," Bryn says in a grim tone. "Have you heard of the Quantum Multiverse Theory?"

"As it pertains to Ant-Man," I nod. "Yes."

Bryn grimaces. "No. What about Hugh Everett?" Off my blank stare, she shakes her head. "He's a physicist." I keep staring. "Neil deGrasse Tyson?"

My eyes lift heavenward, rolling as I search my mind.

"Michio Kaku?"

It's my turn to make a face. My brows scrunch. "How close are you to still speaking English? I've never heard of any of them. Is that last one even a person?"

Her shoulders slump, then they pop right back up, and a grin replaces her frown. "You have to have heard the word multiverse before, right?"

"Only when Doctor Strange traversed it in the *Multiverse of Madness*," I quip. Proud, I understand at least that much of this conversation.

Disappointment mars her features. "Do... You... Do anything but watch movies?"

"Not in a long time. Continue."

"*The Big Bang Theory*?"

I shake my head.

"C'mon! Everyone watched *The Big Bang Theory* at some point. You never streamed it?" She asks incredulously, raising her voice. "*Friends* was way before my time. I've watched a few episodes of that! You had to have watched a couple of episodes. On accident at least!"

Splitting her untidy high ponytail, she pulls on both sides to tighten it. Increased tension pulls at her hazel eyes and features, giving them a brief facelift. Funny, I never noticed until now that Bryn pulls her hair when she's agitated. Being trapped inside my own mind, I hadn't really noticed her. Of course, zoning out while she drones on about TV shows only proves that point.

She might be younger than me, but she's always reached out to me, unbothered by my callous disregard for her feelings. Some might see it as a flaw on both our parts, how she kept returning again and again. Like a wounded puppy kicked countless times by its owner, yet desperate for affection, it comes running back at the first sign of kindness. I was selfish. Everyone here is struggling with some form of distress some are self-inflicted, others stem from trauma or external forces. They're like the kids at Innocent Treasures. Any of them could become Bryn in the future—she's such a gentle soul. She craves love and acceptance, something I should have been able to give her, yet I've treated her as if she were insignificant.

Guilt. I know thee well.

If I had it to do over again, I'd cherish the gift of her friendship.

"Bryn, I'm sorry," I apologize, heavy-hearted. "You don't have to help me. I've treated you like garbage."

"Pish-posh!" She waves away my words as if they're ridiculous. "That's how friendship works. We get on each other's nerves, but we figure it out. '*Best friend, you my motherfuckin' soulmate,*'" Bryn says, breaking into a sing-song, faux hood accent. She must be quoting a song or something. "Our friendship was written in the stars. So, turn that frown upside down, buttercup! There's much to do."

"I still don't have a clue what you're talking about," I say, and I let the subject drop since that's what she wants. Like oil and water, Bryn and serious don't mix. For once, I want to give her something. Plus, I can't change the past, but I will do better by her in the future, starting now.

Bryn growls in frustration. "Those guys I was talking about," she pauses, her bug-eyed stare indicating I'm supposed to remember someone or something.

"Guys?" I mutter more to myself than to her. "Oh! Huey, Dewey, and Louie."

A loud, exaggerated gasp precedes her mouth dropping open. Utter outrage contorts her features. Her expression mirrors the have-you-lost-your-mind stare she gave when I announced Derek was my husband. She slaps a hand over her mouth.

"What am I going to do with you?" she mutters, shaking her head. "Neil deGrasse Tyson is an astrophysicist. Michio Kaku is a theoretical physicist. And like I said, Hugh..." she draws out the name, emphasizing my mistake, "Everett is a physicist. He's, like, one of the first guys to think of the Quantum Multiverse. From what I remember from the show I watched, they called it the many-worlds interpretation of quantum physics."

I nod, not understanding much besides the thes and ands in her explanation. To think, I used to consider myself intelligent until this very moment. Even through the chaos my life descended into, I believed I was smart. It's interesting to be humbled in a mental institution.

"Ugh! You don't get it. Okay." Bryn tightens her ponytail again, and sighs deeply. "So, when I was on the pageant circuit—when my mom wasn't criticizing everything from my posture to my weight—she'd leave on these specials, so I could outshine the other girls with my...knowledge." She shrugs. "Maybe she just wanted me to sit still while she plucked, curled, and made me up to within an inch of my life."

Much of what Bryn said made sense after that glimpse into her past, her flawless social skills. Endless cheerful attitude. Easy smiles. Graceful composure. Even the way she transforms the ordinary Easter-lavender scrubs they give us into an outfit fit for a Victoria's Secret runway. She could turn a messy ponytail into a fashion trend.

"Your mom sounds fun," I joke. "I should've guessed you were a pageant girl."

Bryn snorts. "Pageant girl? Please. Try modeling and some acting, too. I'm a Z-list celebrity, baby. I was getting full sets of acrylics by the time I was four years old. By thirteen, I was the sole breadwinner of a family of five. It wasn't just my mom. She had my dad's full support. When they had me after my sisters, Thing One and Thing Two, they thought,"—she does a sort of fist pump movement— "cha-ching!"

"Really?" Why in the world is she here then? She should be in a fancy Arizona rehab, not slumming it with us common folks in Indiana and our will-they-or-won't-they-pay HMOs. "Why are you here?"

"Girl, this is my vacation," Bryn chuckles. "Those people drive me nuts. Chug a few too many pills, and I get a little break." She beams and wiggles her eyebrows.

Still unable to be cavalier about such deeply concerning mental health issues, I return her smile with a tight-lipped one of my own.

Now isn't the time to go *there* with her, not again. Besides, I'm starting to see that her airheaded, carefree persona is just an act—a carefully constructed mask to hide the intelligence sparkling within her gorgeous hazel-blue eyes, something she revealed with all that quantum physicist talk.

"Your parents used you as their meal ticket and made you watch astronomy documentaries? I don't—I don't understand," I say, confused, shaking my head. "Those seem like conflicting desires."

"It's not exactly astronomy," she sighs. "For the time I participated in pageants, it was a good shtick. Tiny all-American girl with big bouncy blonde curls, rosy cheeks, and wide innocent eyes with a Stephen Hawking brain. One segment, I'm singing 'On the Good Ship Lollipop', then the next, talking about the structure of atoms, the many-worlds interpretation of quantum mechanics, black holes, the universe... It was unexpected and adorable. I cleaned up, swept those other little bitches under the table."

I have no words. After a few moments watching Bryn grin at her memories, I say, "You were saying something about Hugh."

"Oh, yeah!" she exclaims. "Some physicists believe we—this would be a lot easier if you watched *Quantum Leap* instead of movies. Come to think of it, they did a reboot."

"Bryn!" I growl.

"Okay. So, it's believed that for every decision we make, there's a universe where a different version of us made the opposite choice. Let's say you're driving and come to a fork in the road. After some deliberation, you go right. In another universe, an alternate you goes left."

Somehow, I expected this to be more enlightening.

I scrub my face with my hand. Hope is becoming harder to hold on to.

"Bear with me," Bryn implores, seeing my exasperation. "You have to have a really open mind to accept this, and I don't have any edibles. Just try to follow me. Many cosmologists surmise that the universe is infinite. That means if we could figure out space travel without being immortal to get around space in one lifetime and go far enough, we'd run into galaxies that are nearly identical to ours. That means there could be a near-parallel Earth with a nearly identical version of us. The chances of there being parallel universes existing are really good. Humans are ignorant to think we're alone with all that space out there."

"Are you talking about aliens?" I ask, trying to piece together everything she's said.

"No," Bryn groans, head drooping.

She sounds extremely disappointed.

"I swear my mind is open."

"I know. I'm not explaining it right," she grouses. "If I'd known we were gonna have this talk, I would've tongue-in-cheeked my meds today. Anyway, let's say there's a bunch of Earths right next to each other. Like, bam, bam, bam, bam." She pantomimes each bam with a hand gesture. "Some are so similar to our Earth that if we somehow found ourselves on one of them, we wouldn't notice the differences, or at least the differences would be minor. Others would have more noticeable differences. Say you got promoted at work on our Earth and were able to buy a house. On another Earth, an alternate version of you didn't get the promotion and stayed in an apartment with a roommate instead. On a different Earth, you have 2.5 kids, and is a stay-at-home mom, and your husband is a doctor who makes bank. You drive a Tesla. You have a Birkin bag," she finishes in an awed whisper.

There's so much to absorb. I let go of the edge of my mattress. I scoot all the way back on the bed until my spine touches the wall. Sharp pain hits my frontal lobe. Quantum leaps. Many-worlds. Alternate me. Faux-mina. Subject matter beyond my pay grade. And understanding. It sounds plausible in an abstract way, but it's not the connect panel (A) to panel (B) with screw K-8 instructions I thought would take me back to my life.

"So," I start, drawing my legs up to my chest and hugging my knees, "what you're saying is you don't have a clue how to reunite me with my husband and daughter."

Bryn jolts as if shocked. "No! I kind of, sort of, maybe know how to get you back. It's complicated. In movies, there are doorways and shit. There was a mirror these people would, like, step through in one. It was a morgue drawer in another, and a spot in the ocean or something in this weird indie flick I streamed when I was bored once."

"Wait!" Did I hear what I think I just heard? "Morgue drawer? *The Jacket*?! You saw *The Jacket*? That's one of my favorite movies. But that wasn't a parallel universe."

"What?" Bryn recoils as if slapped. "He literally meets Jackie as an adult in a time he doesn't exist in. If that's not a parallel dimension, I don't know what is."

"I think that was a past-present situation like in *Back to the Future*. I can't believe you saw *The Jacket*. Nobody's seen *The Jacket*."

"We're best friends, girl. Duh!" Bryn says, like I'm stupid for not assuming that friendship grants certain movie-seeing powers upon friends before they've even met. "We gotta find your doorway or lake. Something triggered the switch." She shrugs. "Our universes overlapped for a moment, and you and the other Amina—"

"Faux-mina," I grumble, correcting her.

Bryn giggles. "You and Faux-mina swapped places. However, I think an event—a catastrophic one—caused you to switch places. What exactly happened before you quantum leaped?"

Good thing I'm in my favorite position. I don't want to rehash that night, don't want to remember him—Justin. But I need help. Something inside me says it's now or never. So, I take a deep breath and tell her everything, starting with the fateful introduction by Professor McCravy and ending at Petty's parking lot.

"An elderly couple found me," I continue. "This douchebag detective showed up at the worst moment to question me. I didn't even know where I was, and he was throwing information at me, asking questions. Then he tells me that the guy doesn't even exist."

"He was a hallucination?!" Bryn cuts in.

I roll my eyes. "No." *This place!* "He was a real guy who really assumed a fake identity to enroll in college. Apparently, my shitty luck knows no bounds. I managed to be assaulted by a technology genius capable of erasing his entire digital footprint and true identity. What are the odds?" I ask a bit hysterically.

"Good, actually," Bryn asserts in a cheerful conversational tone, as if I did not ask a rhetorical question. "With today's technological advancements, almost anything is possible with a laptop and an Internet connection. In some ways, technology is a blessing and a curse."

"Thanks," I drawl sarcastically. "When the detective said there wasn't any sign of the guy, no paper trail, no CCTV footage, nothing, my mind fractured. He didn't intend to leave me alive. He punctured a lung. If he's tech-savvy enough to leave no trace of himself, he has enough resources to pay for college—even community college tuition—in cash. He'd know that not only did I survive, but I snitched on him. Nothing is stopping him from finishing what he started," I whisper.

Fear lodges in my throat. Maintaining eye contact while recounting what, at the time, was the worst experience of my adulthood was difficult. Every word strengthens my resilience. Even though her intentions are pure, Dr. Whittemore is just doing her job, but she's mistaken. My healing, marriage, and husband are real. My soul knows it. It clings to that truth. It rebelled when my mind tried to forget. Meeting Derek was discouraging at first. Though he looked like Garrett, just a rougher version, they were very different. And yet, the same. Our souls recognized each other. And then there's the picture. A subtle touch over the paper warms my hand, as if reassuring me I'm on the right path, urging me to keep going.

It sounds crazy. The cynical part of me knows how ridiculous all of this is. Since birth, life has forced me to face cold, hard facts. Santa doesn't exist. Tooth fairies don't leave money for teeth. Imaginary friends are exactly that—imaginary. And I've never had the privilege of one. People can be cruel. Those who should love you sometimes don't. People are unreliable. Differences aren't celebrated—they're obliterated. Fantasies are for children, and never for me. Reality isn't a choice. It simply exists.

But this isn't reality. Not mine.

Not anymore.

"Oh! I got it," Bryn says, breaking into my thoughts. "I think. Maybe."

This woman truly knows how to make a girl doubt herself.

"Got what?" I ask. Hesitancy makes my words sound awkward.

Her whole face lights up with renewed vigor. Whatever she's thinking must be spectacular, at least to her...For now. I'm not so quick to get on the excitement train. Curiosity makes me lift my chin off my knees, which is all I plan to do for now.

"Better analogy. One you can understand." Elation makes her bounce in place.

God, help me. Given Bryn's disorganized thinking, this could be anything. I brace myself.

"Long story short. You're Romeo," she states as if that explains it.

"Are you making fun of me again?" Caution raises my voice an octave.

"Nope." That's her flat response.

I exhale loudly, exasperated. "I'm gonna need the long story."

Bryn hops off her bed, startling me. She paces back and forth across the room. Given the size of our room, it's not the most efficient pacing, but I understand what she's doing—releasing nervous energy.

"In *Romeo and Juliet*," she starts, not looking at me, "Romeo thinks he finds a dead Juliet, right?"

I nod.

"But Juliet wasn't really dead, right?" Bryn grins and nods, gazing at me in expectation now.

I keep nodding. "I have no idea what you're getting at."

"Romeo kills himself to be with Juliet. Juliet kills herself to be with Romeo," Bryn explains. She claps, happy with herself.

My gaze stays fixed on her, vacant as the day is long.

Bryn exhales sharply and shakes her head. "You said it yourself, remember? They could only be together in death." She drags out the word and tilts her head towards me.

I'm supposed to be in the know now. I can tell because she's watching me like a parent encouraging a child to use the potty for the first time, and a realization dawns on me.

Who'd have thunk?

"Are you telling me to kill... myself?" Skepticism drips from each halted word. "Kinda the wrong place to encourage me to kill myself, ya think?" I ask, then think better of it. "Or the right place. Depending on how you look at it, I suppose," I say, chuckling.

Bryn grins and nods enthusiastically.

"Not all by yourself. I'll help you," Bryn offers.

How thoughtful.

"Oh, okay, Dr. Kevorkian," I joke, still not entirely convinced she's serious but hoping desperately that she's not serious. There's a lot of hope riding on me today. "I may have come to terms with the fact that I'm a little crazy, but I don't know if I'm quite suicidal yet."

"It's the only way," is Bryn's emphatic reply. "I'm not God, but I'm asking for some blind faith. Just until it's over. Think of it as a temporary health condition."

She's serious, judging by the clear openness in the depths of her hazel eyes.

My mouth opens and closes several times. Many false starts occur before I regain my speech.

"You really think it's the only way?" I lift a brow at her, emphasizing really.

Her answering nod is slow. I have to give it to her; she really thought about the question.

"I believe trauma is the trigger. You thought your life was at risk the first time. Then, presto change-o. If you really want Derek and your family back..."

This is the definition of crazy. What she's asking is insane, ridiculous. For all my flaws, being the end-it-all-over-a-guy type isn't one of them. I don't take the idea of suicide lightly. Someone has to be in a very dark place to make such a decision. Unlike most, I don't see it as selfish; it's deeper than that. The profound sadness someone considering suicide feels is real. Emotional pain doesn't get enough credit. People who have never been in that abyss of desolation don't understand how real that pain is. Despair is as painful as any physical injury.

"I would give anything to have my husband and daughter back." Nothing could be truer, but this is a big request. "If you're wrong about this... I will haunt you. You think you're crazy now? Just wait."

Bryn shrugs as if my threat doesn't matter to her. "Is that a yes?"

What am I doing?

"How are we going to do it? I'm not a masochist."

Bryn skips to the door. Grabbing the handle, she throws it open. I thought she wasn't going to answer as she takes her first step out of the room, but then she turns.

"Patience, darling. All will be revealed in due time."

Chapter Fifty-Four

"Well, this is a welcome change," Dr. Whittemore says, sauntering over and sitting down. "I was shocked you wanted to meet here."

I sit on the bench in the "Healing Garden" with Derek's sock puppet in my lap. She looks surprised, which makes sense since I'm well outside my comfort zone. This will be my last meeting with the "good" doctor, and I want her to remember me, to remember that I'm the woman she told to abandon her delusions. There's a good chance she'll never know what really happened, and that's okay. I'll know, and that's what matters most.

Bryn and I kept talking late into the night. We surmise that whatever parallel universe—and I still can't believe I'm even saying that—I was in time moves differently. I think it moves slower than this one. There isn't a one-to-one time match. I have concerns about sentencing Faux-mina to a life worse than death. Nothing in me wants to hurt her, but I can't give her my life. The situation is complicated.

I smile my brightest smile. "I thought you'd be happy," I say in a cheery voice. "I just woke up this morning ready for a change."

Nodding, Dr. Whittemore smiles. "I do like this. I guess this means you took our last session to heart. I'm so proud of you."

Why does she sound like she's praising a puppy for sitting on command? I don't know how to interpret that, but I won't let her know she bothers the shit out of me.

"Yes, I did," I say, adding friendliness and warmth to my tone, "and you'll be happy to know that I'm following your advice. I'm focusing on myself and my well-being for once."

Dr. Whittemore pats my back.

I want to punch her in the face.

I keep my cool.

"I'm so proud of you," she repeats. "This is such a healthy, important step. I am confident I can help you. I'm so pleased."

I just smile.

Dr. Gretchen Whittemore

Writing in my black leather-bound journal, I rub the back of my neck. It's been a long few weeks. Scratch that, it's been a long few months. The lights are low because my head cannot handle the harshness; being brighter would make the low-level headache I've had since this morning worse. I kick off my heels under my desk. Then I had to be here at the crack of dawn. Putting my pen down, I scan my office while massaging my scalp with my fingertips. The appearance of my office reflects how chaotic life has been lately. Extra books sit on my bookshelf in front of the ones that belong there. Other books are stacked on the corner couch against the far wall. Post-it notes stick to any available surface, and I'm lucky if I can find my laptop under the paper piles on my desk.

The chaos in my office also spills into my personal life. My son kept me awake all night, so I couldn't get any sleep. He's been home more frequently these days, which makes finding time to sleep difficult. I'm burning the candle at both ends. Self-care has taken a backseat for me. Once Ms. Raichand is discharged, my workload will lighten significantly. Losing a patient is never ideal. We do our best to prevent such losses, but they happen. Still, this might be just the motivation Ms. Raichand needs—and the break I deserve.

I stretch my neck to the left, then to the right.

"Hey, Gretchen," Dr. Frankart says as he enters my office. "Burning the candle at both ends, huh?" It's as if he's reading my mind.

"Hardly," I lie with a smile. "I'm just finishing journal work before my vacation."

Dr. Frankart shakes his greying hair. "I still don't understand why you journal. We have those portable tablets to record all our patients' session notes. What you're doing is twice the work."

I wave off his concern. "It helps me keep things straight in my head. Each time I write about a patient, it's like having another session. I can focus on details I might have missed during our session."

Dr. Frankart rests against the door frame. Boy, he's really bad at catching hints. "Mr. Ivy League coming home this weekend?" he asks. "That's usually the only reason you use any of your vacation time."

That's not true. Over the past eight months, I've taken more paid time off than ever before.

"He sure is," I say with a proud smile. "I'm so excited."

As excited as being held hostage.

Dr. Frankart laughs. "You baby him. Dr. Biller and I are going to get dinner. You wanna tag along?"

Hmm... I haven't eaten all day, but I should wait to see if Clinton's had dinner. But...

"Can you give me five minutes?" I ask. "I'm almost done here."

"Sure. I have a few files to review. I'll be back in about ten minutes, just in case."

Rapping his knuckles on the door jamb, he turns and walks away.

Chapter Fifty-Five

Amina Raichand

I sit cross-legged in the middle of my bed. My stomach churns as I think about Bryn's big plan tonight. I'm really unsure how I feel about it. I wasn't lying when I said I'm not a masochist—nothing inside me wants to cause pain to myself. Before leaving the room ten minutes ago, Bryn promised me that what she had in mind wouldn't hurt, but Bryn doesn't always see things logically. She might have a pain kink I'm unaware of, or a higher pain threshold than I do.

My heart races. I'm about to sentence a woman who's probably sitting in her nice apartment, eating cereal, to a life that could be drastically worse. There are no instructions for this situation. If I don't get this right, then I'll inadvertently kill myself, and then nothing will matter. I don't know what she was experiencing while she was here in my place. If I'm to believe Megan and Dr. Whittemore, then she was in a coma and didn't know where she was. What kind of life is that? A pang of guilt slices through my insides. I pray that if trauma does transport her here, she wakes and does something great with her life. I plan to make the most of my life if this switch goes as planned.

Bryn rushes into our bedroom, then presses the door shut with her back. She stands there, with her back to the metal, breathing heavily.

"Before we get started," Bryn says, still breathing hard, "you need to help me."

I smirk. "I thought the dying person was the one who got the last wish."

Bryn narrows her eyes. "Technically, what I'm asking is for you. And you're not dying, you're just going to the brink of it. Now, help me move this dresser, or we're gonna get caught."

Hopping off my bed, I grab one side of the tall dresser. Bryn grabs the other side.

"On the count of three," I say.

"One—"

"Bryn!" I chide. "I was about to count."

"Sorry," Bryn shrugs. "I thought we were doing it together."

"One," I start again. "Lift with your legs, not your arms. Two... Three..."

We strain. Bryn's face turns beet red. It's a fight, but we push the dresser in front of the door. Bending over, I support myself on my knees and try to catch my breath.

"I'm surprised I didn't swap universes just then," I say, panting. "I feel like I'm dying. I don't lift enough."

"Are you scared?" Bryn asks, her hazel-blue eyes deepening with seriousness.

"Absolutely," I say, honestly. "What if this doesn't work?"

Bryn gives a wry smile. "The worst that can happen is you're not in pain anymore. Either way, no harm, no foul...kinda."

"What do you think will happen to Faux-mina? What kind of life am I leaving for her?"

Bryn purses her lips. "I'll help her through things," she finally says.

"How is that possible? You won't even see her?" I ask.

I don't know why I never thought that Faux-mina might end up here. Although, it also doesn't make sense how I ended up here either. From all the stories I've heard, people who come here typically come from money.

"Girl, after what you're about to do..." Bryn scoffs. "She'll be here for sure, and so will I."

"So, we're switching bodies?" I ask. "Like *Invasion of the Body Snatchers?*"

"No!" Bryn exclaims. "Did you have a vaginal birth or a C-section?" *What does that have to do with the price of beans in China?*

"I had an emergency C-section."

"Do you still have a scar?"

Hmm... Why hadn't I thought of that? That would have gone a long way toward proving my story is real and not delusional. I pull my scrub bottoms out, look down, and touch the area.

"Yes," I breathe.

"Then there's your answer, ding-dong!" she says, giving me a wide-eyed look that screams "duh". "You take your body with you."

Opening the top dresser drawer, Bryn pulls out a small Ziploc bag filled with pills of various shapes and colors.

"Where'd you get all of those?"

Bryn dangles the bag in front of my face, swinging it back and forth as if trying to hypnotize me.

"These are the meds I pretend to take most mornings and nights. Hop up on your bed."

This is becoming too real.

I sit on the edge of my bed, my mouth suddenly dry. Am I really about to gamble my life by universe-hopping? "I can't lie down and take pills. How do you know so much about this, anyway?"

"This isn't my first rodeo." Bryn plops onto her bed and bounces. "Now, I've never gone *The Full Monty*, but it's an effective way to win a vacation from my leech family. A year or so here, then suddenly I'm healed."

I frown. How could anyone consider this a vacation spot? Things must be pretty awful for anyone to come here willingly. "Why?" I ask, because I'm curious and I'm biding my time.

Bryn giggles. "You've seen me at my best," she says. "This is a manic phase, but the pendulum takes some pretty low swings every once in a while."

"I'm sorry."

"Don't be. It's the only thing my father ever gave me. You need to focus," Bryn says.

She opens the baggie and holds it out to me. It's a grab bag of prescription drugs—one I definitely don't want to pick from. I reach in and then pull my hand out.

"What is she doing to herself? Is it some version of this, or does my traumatic act yank her out of the bathroom or something?"

Bryn shrugs. "Honestly?" she asks with a raised brow. "I don't know. Maybe. Whatever she was doing the first time you crossed, or now, is something only she'll know. Just like only you knew things were off there. There seem to be just enough similarities and differences to make each of you think you're losing your minds. Neither of you would have known you'd crossed universes. If you couldn't be sure of a bigger reason to explain the changes or irrefutable proof of what you're saying, who'd believe you?" Bryn rattles the pill back in front of me.

With a deep sigh, I grab a handful.

"Wait! Don't do it dry. It won't work. Trust me, I know," Bryn says, handing me a water bottle.

I unscrew the cap, lean my head back, and toss in the random medicine. Then I take a big swig of water. It's like swallowing a rock. It takes several more swigs of water to get everything down.

"You don't have to worry, though," Bryn says, holding the bag open towards me again. "She'll be my best friend too. I'll help her. You're one and the same, but I will miss you."

"How will you know it's not just me being crazy?" I grab another handful of pills and repeat the toss-in-and-chase-with-water routine.

Bryn looks at me with sharp, narrow eyes. "You don't do crazy well. She'll definitely be the real McCoy, the genuine article." She titters.

"If there are multiple worlds or universes, who's to say I'll get back to the right one? What if I swap with a Faux-mina who's in the middle of surgery as a surgeon?"

I take another handful of pills with water.

"Did you ever want to be a doctor?" Bryn asks.

Gulping more pills and water, I wait a minute before I can respond. "No! I'm just saying," I finally answer.

Bryn touches her chin as if she's thinking about what I said. She takes a deep breath.

"Girl," Bryn says after a minute, "you wanna go back or nah?"

I grin, roll my eyes, and take another handful of pills.

"You need to keep these down. Once they're in your system, even if they pump your stomach, it won't matter," Bryn advises.

Feeling woozy, I lie face up on my bed. The ceiling looks dreamy.

"Thanks for helping," I say, infusing as much sincerity into my slurred speech as I can. "I've always had shallow acquaintances, never any friends, and definitely not a best friend." I turn and wink at her.

Bryn's answering smile is so wide it could crack her face. Her jaw should have dislocated.

"I knew it! I'm your best friend."

My hands slip as I try to gain leverage to sit up. Strength drains from my limbs and body. Cotton fills my ears, muffling everything. Without enough strength to turn my head or lift my eyelids, my eyeballs roll to the left just in time to see tears streaming down Bryn's hazy face. I want to say something to comfort her, but my stomach lurches several times. My eyelids drift shut.

Chapter Fifty-Six

*D*r. *Gretchen Whittemore*

For some reason, I couldn't enjoy dinner. My colleagues and I rarely go for drinks or dinner. Most of my time lately is taken up by my son or Serene Meadows. Scanning around my office, I shake my head. This office isn't going to organize itself. Procrastination is a tempting choice, though, and something insidious niggles at the back of my mind.

I reach into the bottom drawer of my desk and grab my black leather-bound journal. It's filled with notes from only one patient, so it doesn't take long to find the page I need. I read the page aloud to myself.

"Patient Amina Raichand appears to be making great progress. She has finally decided to prioritize her mental health, which is a significant step toward her recovery. We met for the first time in the healing garden, and her peaceful smile was really comforting. She sat there holding a—"

I stop reading as a flash of memory strikes my mind. Amina was peaceful, too peaceful. In her lap, she held a sock puppet similar to the one I'd seen in Derek's—

My back goes ramrod straight. I gasp. Picking up my desk phone, I dial the digits to call upstairs.

"Serene Meadows, Nurse Dettinger speaking," she answers on the third ring.

"Pam, it's Gretchen Whittemore."

"Oh, hey Dr. Whittemore, how you doin', suga? I thought you left hours ago."

"No, I needed to finish some paperwork."

"Ah! Okay. Well, I can get you somethin' from the cafeteria—"

Shaking my head as if she can see me, I rush on, "This is an emergency. I need you to send several orderlies to Ms. Raichand and Ms. Schneider's room. I was reviewing notes from our last session and I..." I take a deep breath. "I think she's going to try to take her own life."

"Ya sure? I saw her earlier, and she was—"

"I'm positive, get in there quickly. I'll be there in twenty minutes."

Chapter Fifty-Seven

*B*ryn Schneider

Amina is lying in bed, her head tilted to the side. Her eyes are closed, and she appears so relaxed.

Kneeling beside her bed, I gently smooth her hair away from her forehead. My best friend. I pray I didn't kill my best friend. She's so still. It's been forty-five minutes, so some of the medications should have taken effect, but others might not kick in for several more minutes.

My tears won't stop. She's the only person I've ever met who wasn't paid to compliment me or to be my friend. Most of my relationships with people are transactional, including my relationship with my parents. I starve myself, work unreal hours, and they reap all the benefits. Neither of them works, and neither do my sisters. It's all about what Bryn can do for them. They're basically my pimps. Making half-assed suicide attempts and acting manic are the only ways I find relief. This time, I'm here completely voluntarily. I could decide to leave right now, and no one could stop me. But when Amina came with her sullen attitude and sunken, lonely, golden-honey eyes with green flecks, I knew she needed a friend, and for reasons that don't make sense, I knew she needed me. I traded my single room for a double. Unfortunately, I won't get a refund, but it was worth it. I'm helping her.

The rise and fall of Amina's chest is slow, barely noticeable. I place two fingers on her neck pulse point. She's alive, but she's still here, which means she hasn't shifted to another universe yet. This has to work. Lifting her head with one hand, I pry her mouth open with the other and force a few more pills inside. I fill her mouth with water and then stroke her throat to encourage her to swallow. She does. Keeping her head tilted, I count to one hundred, making sure the pills have gone down her throat, then I lower her head onto a pillow.

Bang. Bang. Bang.

I jump at the sound of the orderlies banging on the door.

"Open the door! Open it, or we'll kick it in!" Stephan yells.

I wipe tears from my cheeks with the back of my hand.

"No one's against the door!" I shout.

Let's see them try to move the dresser with their bodies. They might pull it off, but it'll cost them.

"Bryn?! Suga! Could you please move whatever is blocking the door!" Nurse Dettinger cajoles.

These damn tears! The more I wipe them away, the faster they fall. Looking back at Amina's lifeless body, I sob.

If they get in too soon, I won't know if the pills will have had enough time to do their thing. This is not exactly science.

Banging continues with even more intensity.

My heart races as more sobs are wracked from me.

"We just want to help her, hun! Please move whatever is in front of the door," Nurse Dettinger repeats.

"No!" I shout. "She needs me only!"

The next bang has enough force to shift the dresser by just an inch.

Fear and adrenaline rush through my veins.

"Go away!" I shout again. "She was my only friend! Let me do this."

Several bangs shake the dresser more. Then the door suddenly swings open, and the dresser hits the wall behind it. I shield Amina's supine body with my own.

Nurse Dettinger and two burly orderlies rush in.

"No! She wants this! Don't touch her."

Chapter Fifty-Eight

Dr. Gretchen Whittemore

If getting my hair done weren't so expensive, I'd pull it out. Nothing has turned out the way it was supposed to. My desk is in such disarray that I don't know where to start to make it look halfway decent. Clinton will be home soon, and I should try to get there before him—but this loss is personal and more than I can bear. So much time and energy went into helping Amina. She was going to be the one I could save. I'm of two minds about the entire ordeal. Maybe it's better this way. We have a clean slate now.

I reach into the bottom drawer of my desk and take out my black leather-bound journal from my purse. Flipping through several pages, I try to find a passage that might reveal where I went wrong. This should have worked.

"Knock. Knock."

I look up and see Dr. Frankart standing in my doorway.

"Gretchen, my God! Aren't you supposed to be on vacation?" he asks, chuckling.

He studies me with deep brown eyes. "I'm not gonna lie, Gretch. You don't look good," he says, not holding anything back. "Are you feeling okay?"

Thanks. You don't, either, holding onto your three strands of hair for dear life and your pot belly.

"Thanks for your concern," I say, but I'm sure my stone-faced glare doesn't match the words. "I'm just drained."

He nods. "You really were close to that patient, weren't you? I hear she's on life support. She took enough pills to kill a horse."

Yes, let's smear salt into that open wound. As if I don't feel bad enough.

This matter is personal to me.

"She is," I say, confirming his information. "For three weeks now. They're not optimistic about her chances of survival."

"That's a shame," Dr. Frankart says. "That's one of the hardest parts of our job. We've got to guard our hearts for our own mental health. Getting personally involved is dangerous."

Who does he think he's talking to? Personally involved. This case could never have been anything but personal.

I stuff my journal into my purse, then pull it out from the bottom drawer. There's no way I can sit here and discuss this with such a detached man. He's lucky to have professional distance from his clients. I don't have that luxury.

"Was there anything else you needed?" I ask while locking my desk. "I've gotta get going."

Without so much as an "excuse me," I pass by Dr. Frankart, then close and lock my office door.

As I spin around, my journal falls out of my bag. Dr. Frankart squats to help retrieve my lost item, but then I notice several pages with 3x4 pictures of different young women are dangerously close to flipping open and revealing themselves. Before the wallet-sized picture of Amina slips out, I scramble to pick up my journal and push the picture as far as it will go.

Not wanting to be interrogated, and afraid of what he might have seen, I turn and hurry out.

This is what happens when I delay grocery shopping and wait until the last possible minute. I set the two bags of groceries on the island in my kitchen, then toss my keys into the bowl I keep on the opposite counter to hold all my house and car keys. It has been the longest year of my life. That's if I'm only counting the time I spent at Serene Meadows with Amina. If I go further back, it's been nearly two years of utter stress. When did life get so complicated?

Oh! I remember!

It was about thirty-six years ago. Taking a deep breath, I start to unload the grocery bags.

"Clinton?!" I call out. He has to be here. "Clinton, you home, sweetheart?!"

Chapter Fifty-Nine

D^{r. Eloy}

Not so long ago, I saw this young woman full of life. She had so much to live for, but for reasons unclear to me, she decided to take her own life. Now, her rich brown skin has taken on an ashen hue. Fortunately, we were able to stabilize her enough. I check her intubation tube to ensure it is working properly. Judging by the machine readouts, her vitals are good.

It's been a long eleven hours. One more hour, and I'll be free to... Finish charting for about another hour. The joys of being an ICU doctor are never-ending.

I pull back the curtain and exit the room to check on my next patient.

An alarm blares, followed by a prolonged beep from the room I just left. Ms. Raichand is flatlining.

Nurses rush past me as I head back to the room.

"Nurse," I instruct as I step into the room, "she's in cardiac arrest. Get a crash cart in here now!" Hopping onto the bed, I place my hands over her chest. "Starting chest compressions!"

My focus is on performing timed chest compressions. If I can't detect a heartbeat, there's no need for the crash cart.

Pausing, I glance at the EKG machine during compressions.

"She's in V-fib!" I shout. "Charge the paddles."

Hopping off the bed, I grab the paddles I was asked for, then I rub them together.

"Charge to two fifty..." I shout.

"Two-fifty," a nurse calls.

"Clear!"

I feel, more than see, everyone heed my warning and step back from shocking distance. Then I press the paddles to her chest. Her body jerks under the paddles. Checking the EKG machine shows no change.

Rubbing the paddles together, I shout. "Charge to three hundred... Clear!"

I pray everyone steps back because I don't wait as I press the paddles to Ms. Raichand's chest again.

D*r. Whittemore*

Hand on my hip, I stand at the stove stirring the homemade chili I know Clinton loves so much. I don't know where that kid of mine is. He disappears like he has no responsibilities to this house. I need to figure out that Life 360 app everyone at work talks about. If I had it, I could monitor his location without him necessarily knowing if I set it up on his phone while he's sleeping. I tried the Airtag thing a friend of mine suggested, but Clinton is way too smart for his own good. He found it, crushed it, and threw it away. I knew something wasn't right when it showed him on the side of the house for nine hours.

"Clinton!" I call him more sharply than the last twelve times I called his name. "I'm making dinner!"

Still nothing. Where is that boy? I can't imagine what—

Vivid flashbacks interrupt my thoughts.

Amina lies unconscious in the ICU. Her left arm is in a cast from her knuckles to her biceps. Her face is battered and bruised. There is a cast on one of her legs that extends all the way to her thigh. I watch her from the window of the sliding door that leads into her room.

A nurse opens the sliding door to the room and smiles at me.

"Hi, Nurse Morton, I won't be long today," I tell her before she can ask any questions.

"No problem, Doctor. Take your time. You've been her only visitor," Nurse Morton says with a smile.

I enter the room as the nurse leaves. There's a chair against the wall, and I pull it over to Amina's bedside. They say that patients in comas can hear. I sure hope they can, because I need to unburden my soul.

"I'm so sorry," I whisper. "I'm so, so sorry. This should never have happened."

Ow! A boiling hot pop of chili jabs me from my reverie. I turn the eye on the stove down. If I don't watch this, I'll end up burning this chili, and I'll never hear the end of it. I keep stirring, and another flashback crashes into my mind.

Amina's lying in bed. She has a catheter because, although her eyes are open, she's unresponsive. They say she's catatonic, and I believe them. She hasn't responded to any stimuli. All she does is stare up at the ceiling with vacant unblinking eyes. Her left arm is still in a cast, but the dark black and purple bruises are healing.

I scoot my chair closer to her bed. Some admissions aren't meant for everyone's ears. Taking her right hand in mine, tears spill over and slither down my face.

"I'm so sorry," I whisper. "I could've stopped this years ago—should have stopped it, but, I was never really sure until I found the journal."

I startle when I hear footsteps behind me. Before whoever it is fully enters, I flick tears away with my fingers. I place Amina's hand back by her side, where it was resting.

Dr. Eloy enters, rolling in his computerized charting system. He grabs some gloves from the box hanging on the wall and puts them on. He reviews all the necessary checks of Amina and her monitors.

"How does—" I clear my throat. "How does it look?"

Dr. Eloy shakes his head. "Still no change. By the way, I was meaning to ask you. How did you get assigned to her case? We have social workers on staff who work with patients like this one. We never called for a psych consult."

Shit! I should have thought of that. What should I say?

I give him a professional, polite smile. "It was a personal favor," I offer, and pray that's enough to satisfy his curiosity.

Dr. Eloy nods and exits the room.

I chop some bell peppers to put in the chili. Either I am a good liar, and I don't know how to feel about that, or they were so happy to have someone visit that poor girl that they didn't want to pry too much. Thinking back to another encounter, though, I believe they might not have believed me as much as I thought.

I'm caught off guard as I see through the glass double doors into Amina's ICU patient room. When I called, the nurse said that the doctors had already made rounds. But, gazing inside, I see Dr. Eloy.

He checks her reflexes and uses a small penlight to look into her eyes. His expression is devoid of hope.

As he washes his hands, I stroll into the room.

"I thought you'd already done your rounds," I say with a noncha-lance I don't feel. "You're going to burn yourself out working so much overtime."

I sit in the chair across the room.

Dr. Eloy slips his penlight into his breast pocket. "Ms. Raichand is my last stop. An emergency earlier this afternoon upended my schedule."

"Do you think she'll come out of it soon?" I ask.

He shakes his head. "I believe we missed a TBI, and that could be the cause of her prolonged catatonia. She could wake up today, in three more months, or a year from now. No one knows. Her brain needs to heal. I've ordered a few more tests to confirm my supposition. You wouldn't happen to know how to reach her family, would you? You said this was a personal favor, and I'd like to keep them updated on Ms. Raichand's condition. No one's come to visit besides you."

How do I lie my way out of this?

I nod. "It's a favor to someone she works with. From what I under-stand, she was abandoned at two months old and raised in the foster care system. I don't believe she's in contact with any family members, biological or otherwise. I'll ask around and see if there's an emergency contact I can find."

No, I won't.

"Okay," Dr. Eloy says, "let me or one of the nurses on shift know if I'm not here. Have a good evening."

With that, Dr. Eloy saunters out of the room.

I move my chair to Amina's bedside and take her hand in mine. Hers is clammy against my warm one.

"How are you today, sweetie?" I whisper. "Looks like you had a bath last night."

I run my fingers through her long, wavy hair.

"Like I was saying yesterday, they call it D.I.D., Dissociative Identity Disorder. It's really like meeting a completely different person inside one

body. Once I found your picture...I had to help you. If only I'd done something sooner. Maybe I could've helped the others. I'm so, so sorry."

I wipe my face with a dish towel before tears can spill into my chili. If only I knew then what I know now. I think back to my last meeting with Megan, the real social worker on Amina's case.

I watch through the window as Megan stands by Amina's bedside, combing her hair.

"There," Megan says to a comatose Amina. "Now, you look even prettier. Your hair could get very unruly if we don't get a handle on it now."

I stroll in, letting my presence be known.

"Megan, I didn't expect to see you here at this time," I say, feigning shock.

Megan slips the comb into the purse, hanging off her shoulder. She turns to face me.

"I was just stopping by before heading to my office. I like to do that every day in case there are any new updates on my favorite patient." She smiles. "One of the night nurses reported that they might've seen her blink."

Nodding, I strangle my shock from showing on my face. This isn't good. I need to be here when she wakes.

"And?" I ask, keeping my concerns hidden.

Megan shrugs. "It must've been her imagination or an involuntary tick. I've been here for a good while and haven't seen even a flicker."

I grimace. "That's too bad."

"It is. She was gonna do big things. Did you know she was studying for her B.A. in Social Work? She also worked with children in a shelter setting. On top of that, she was an orphan herself. It's not fair that this happened to her."

Megan shakes her head as tears well up in her eyes. She wipes them away with her blouse sleeve.

"This job never gets easier," Megan says, her voice glum. "I'm going to go. I'll see ya later."

Once Megan's gone, I drag a chair over to Amina's bedside and sit down. I take Amina's limp hand in mine.

"I'm so sorry," I whisper. "You will get your life back. As God is my witness, I will help you. I promise."

Chapter Sixty

Dr. Gretchen Whittemore

I set the table, though I'm not sure why. Clinton knows he's supposed to be home, but I haven't heard neither hide nor hair from him. Considering all of that, I place two bowls, two cups, and two silverware sets across from each other on our small circular dining table. I pour some Moscato wine into my glass and off-brand cherry-flavored carbonated water into the other. Then I ladle the chili into each bowl. A slice of white bread sits on the folded napkin beside each place setting.

The table is perfectly set. I take my seat and sip my wine.

I take a deep breath through my nose and slowly exhale through my mouth.

Where is Clinton?

"Clinton?! I made your favorite chili. There are also Brussels sprouts and ham in the oven. I even got that nasty-flavored stuff you like!"

Finally, I hear sounds of movement from upstairs. I knew he was here. Where else would he go? Unless he got that bracelet off again. Just thinking about the trouble that would cause is enough to give me a headache. I take another sip of wine.

Clinton strolls in as if I haven't been calling him for over an hour. My eyes scan him up and down, giving him a detailed once-over. He reminds me of his father. Both of them are—or were—six feet tall with perfect alabaster skin. With his golden-blonde hair styled into a trendy undercut and light brown eyes, he's quite popular with the young ladies. If only they knew what he hides under those blue jeans and the blue crewneck sweater. But like moths to a flame, they're drawn in by his charming boy-next-door appeal, and it's always too late for me to save them.

I believed I could save Amina. That's why I paid for her stay at Serene Meadows and dedicated so much effort to helping her heal.

Clinton is a good man, but Justin is not. It's hard to believe both qualities reside in one man—my son.

When I found Justin's journal full of pictures of women he'd treated like toys and then broken, I was sickened. He keeps pictures and stats on each of his victims. I stumbled upon it one night three years ago, but it was far too late. All of them had large red X's drawn over the pages. Those were the women he'd killed. There was no way to help them. When I saw the picture of Amina, I knew it was already too late. By sheer luck, while I was visiting an old colleague at the hospital, I caught wind of a story about a girl who'd been beaten, raped, and left to die in a diner parking lot. That's Justin's MO. I visited her every day and vowed to help her if she woke up. Then she did, and although I pulled out all the stops, she ended up right back at death's door.

"I'm truly sorry, Amina. He's my son and my only child. I can't betray him, but I promise I'll become better at finding women like you before he hurts them. Forgive me; that's all I can do. If you had children, you'd understand. A mother would do anything to protect her child—"

"Mom! Wake up!"

I shake my head to clear my thoughts. Clinton's mouth is set in a stern line. His light brown eyes, so to mine, blaze in expectation.

"Sorry, son. I was just thinking about a patient."

"Geez! You gotta leave work at work. I was explaining why I didn't answer earlier when you were calling me," he says before picking up his spoon and digging into his chili.

"Yeah," I say, making my tone light and airy. "I was worried when you didn't answer me, but I knew you were home."

He waggles his eyebrows. "I was on the phone with a special someone."

It's like I'm on a Disneyland roller coaster, and my stomach drops. I take a few bites of chili that I don't taste.

"New girlfriend?" I ask, forcing a smile even though dread washes over me.

"Yep," he says with a grin. "I think she might be the one." Clinton takes a long sip of his drink. "Oh, hey! Did I leave my journal here last time I was home? It's black. Leather?"

Shaking my head, I take another flavorless bite of chili. "Uh... I don't think so. Did you check your room?"

Epilogue

I can't see anything, but I hear voices—distorted, echoing whispers. I don't know where I am. It's too bright to see anything. There's music playing somewhere, but I can't make out what the musician is saying, not that it would matter if I understood. I know nothing about music unless it's in a movie.

Reaching out my hand, there's nothing but empty space in front of me. I swing my hand, checking for anythin—

Ow! That was hard.

I grip a hard...

Knob?

A doorknob.

Warped, upbeat guitars and drums roar loudly. Fill my mind.

♪ *"Imagine me and you, I do..."*

With few options at my disposal, I turn the knob and push.

♪ *"If I should call you up, invest a dime..."*

I blink several times to adjust to the dimmer lights.

♪ *"No matter how they toss the dice..."*

This can't be real. Tears prick my eyes.

Garrett, with his short, dark, copper-colored hair and clean-shaven face, cradles a pink-blanket swaddled bundle. He looks at me, and his turquoise eyes twinkle.

My heart is full to bursting at the sight. Our house.

♪ *"And you for me... So happy together..."*

Garrett grins. "Finally! There's mama. We've been waiting for you," he says in his resonant, deep voice.

"Sorry, I'm late. Traffic was a nightmare."

A buzzing begins in my ears.

A man's distorted voice whispers in my ear, "Stopping chest compressions..."

For the first time, I ignore the whispers. Closing the door behind me, I smile. I'm home.

♪*So happy together...*

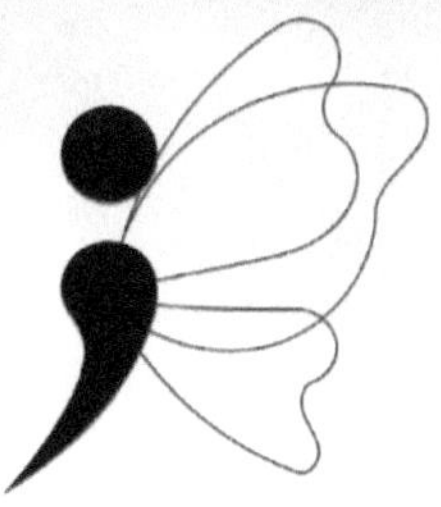

Whispers Soundtrack

1. Beyonce ft. Jay-Z – Crazy In Love {Chapter Forty}
2. Birdy – Skinny Love {Chapter fifty}
3. Buckcherry — Crazy Bitch
4. Cypress Hill – Insane in the Membrane
5. David Cassidy – I Think I Love You {Chapter Thirty-Four & Chapter Forty-Six}
6. Dope D.O.D – Psychosis ft. Sean Price
7. Doja Cat ft. Saweetie - Best Friend {Chapter Fifty-Three}
8. DPR Ian - Don't Go Insane {Chapter Fifty-Seven}
9. Evanescence – Sweet Sacrifice {Chapter Fifty-Four}
10. Gnarls Barkley - Crazy {During the Tattoo Parlor scene}
11. Jimi Hendrix – Foxey Lady
12. Kevin Gates - Me too {Chapter Ten}
13. Lady GaGa – Bad Romance
14. Linkin Park – Crawling {Chapter Forty-Four}
15. Nsync - Thinking Of You (I Drive Myself Crazy)
16. 4Minute - 미쳐 (Crazy)
17. Otis Redding (1966) — Try A Little Tenderness {Chapter Thirty-Six}
18. Pitbull – Krazy
19. Tech N9ne – Am I A Psycho ft. B.O.B., Hopsin {Sneaking out for Tattoos}
20. Smokey Robinson & The Miracles - Tears of a Clown {Chapter Twelve & Chapter Thirty-Two}
21. Skeeter Davis - End of the World {Chapter Thirty-Two & Thirty-Seven}
22. Tom Petty - Last Dance With Maryjane {Theme song}
23. The Turtles - Happy Together {Epilogue}
24. Yael Naim - New Soul {Epilogue}

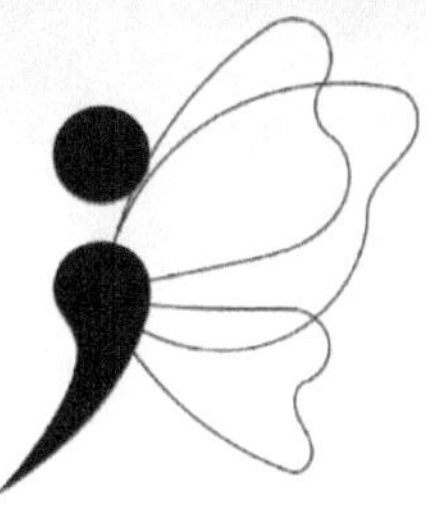

<u>*Acknowledgements*</u>

Thank you to the most amazing editor, Bobbi Isabel, who edited this whopper of a novel. She has been busy writing her own books, but took time to do this for me. Bobbi, you are awesome, and I appreciate you more than you could ever know. Gracie Cooper, you are the most amazing person I've ever met and a wonderful friend to help me with promotions and beta reading. Also, I did like to thank those who know who they are that provided me with a wealth of knowledge to draw from, and I love you all more than life itself. Finally, I'd like to thank my readers for sticking with me while it took time to get this out. I hope you enjoy the read.

Trigger warnings

- **Child Neglect**
- **Loss of Loved One(s)**
- **Sexual Assault (faded to black) on page & Discussed on page (not by the MMC)**
- **Grief**
- **Depression**
- **Visual & Auditory Hallucinations**
- **Varying on page depictions of different mental health conditions**
- **Mental Health discussions on the page**
- **Discussions of Grooming**

<u>*Resources*</u>

If you or someone you know is experiencing suicidal thoughts or ideations, reach out to the national suicide prevention line by:
In America: Dial or text 988
They're available 24/7/365, it's free and confidential. They specialize in helping you, a loved one, or anyone in emotional distress, including struggles with substance abuse.
In the U.K.: dial 0800 689 5652
In India: 8888817666
Ireland: +4408457909090
Mexico: 5255102550
South Korea: (02) 7158600

If you believe you're a victim of intimate partner violence, call 24/7 free and confidential:
United States: (800)656-Hope/Text Hope to 64673
English & Wales: 0808500222

Whether you are a parent, educator, or peer checkout National Eating Disorders Association Helpline:
Call 1-800-931-2237 or Text NEDA to 741741
If you think you are a victim of stalking and need safety planning assistance, call 24/7 to talk. You deserve a life free from abuse and fear, call: 1-800-799-SAFE (7233) or chat at www.thehotline.org

About The Author

Advice writers receive: Write what you know.
I know darkness. I grew up in Scottsdale, Paradise Valley, and Glendale, Arizona. Knowing the uglier sides of life there weren't a lot of options available to me. At least, that's what the world would have me believe. I could've succumbed to the hopelessness and despair that come with having the kind of childhood and adolescence better suited for a Lifetime Channel movie or a cautionary tale. Become a statistic. Or I could allow my past to fuel my creativity.

I devoured anything I could read as an escape. Writing became my calm in the storm. My constant. I published my first book at ten years old. Through college where I studied Social Work, trying to effect change from within the system—I wrote. Modeled a bit. Sang. Became an on-air radio personality. Acted. And still, I wrote. Poetry. Screenplays. Novels. Even placed in the 2010 Beverly Hills Film Festival. All roads lead back to writing. Now, I write dark. Dark paranormal romance. Dark urban fantasy. Psychological and supernatural thrillers. And dark contemporary romance under the pseudonym Wilt Rhys. Because the one thing life's taught me, everything done in the dark comes to the light.

If you're interested in dark contemporary romance check out my other pseudonym Wilt Rhys.

Connect Online
Website: www.piperanderson.org
TikTok: @thepiedwriter
Instagram: @that_chick_piper_tv
Facebook: Author Piper Anderson

www.ingramcontent.com/pod-product-compliance
Lightning Source LLC
Chambersburg PA
CBHW060513160726
47991CB00001B/14